WILLIAM MORROW

An Imprint of HarperCollins*Publishers*

February 2011

Dear Bookseller:

We're so excited to introduce you to an astonishing new talent –
Matthew Dunn. *Spycatcher*, his debut novel, is the freshest
espionage novel to come around in a very long time. Just as le Carré
defined the Cold War espionage thriller so many years ago, Matthew
Dunn brings us a story of counterterrorism as it's practiced today.
With the relentless and urgent pacing of a Lee Child novel, this book
grabs your attention and holds it right through to its bracing and
audacious payoff. It's everything a thriller fan is looking for and
more.

Author Matthew Dunn is a former MI6 field agent, and from the
opening pages— a scene in New York City's Central Park that is
guaranteed to blow your socks off— you will understand how
brazenly authentic this story is. Dunn's main character, Will
Cochrane, is a "hero/antihero" for our times, smart, deft, and deadly
but also convincingly fallible and human. If you are in the mood to
lose yourself in a thriller, this is your book!

I hope you'll love *Spycatcher* as much as we do and agree that it is
the start of an exceptional career for Matthew Dunn.

Best wishes,

Jean Marie Kelly
Senior Marketing Director
William Morrow

In the deadly game of spy vs. spy, one operative stands alone. . . .

He is a man who goes by many names and no name—a master spy who can start wars and end them, and refuses to let rules get in the way of getting the job done. He is Will Cochrane, MI6's—and now also the CIA's—most prized asset and deadliest weapon. Yet few within the intelligence community even know he exists. Meet the ultimate killer of killers who terrifies enemies and allies alike:

Name:
Will Cochrane

Profession:
Intelligence agent

Age:
35

Nationality:
English/American

Expertise:
In-depth knowledge of weaponry, including guns, knives, bombs, and an uncanny ability to read opponents

Experience:
French Foreign Legion (five years), Groupement des Commandos Parachutistes—served as part of an elite, highly trained Special Forces commando unit

Education:
Cambridge University—first class degree

Areas of Study:
Politics, philosophy, and economics

Personal Attributes:
Clever, skilled, loyal, intense, determined, and uncontrollably reckless

Family Status:
Single, no children or family commitments to compromise his work

Cover:
International arms dealer, diplomat— and anything he needs to be to get the job done

Intelligence agent Will Cochrane—working on a joint mission for the CIA and MI6—is out to capture a brilliant and ruthless Iranian spy in this extraordinary international espionage debut by a real-life former field officer

SPYCATCHER

Will Cochrane is a seasoned, battle-scarred officer, but that doesn't mean he enjoys playing by the rules. When a job must be done, he will go all out to finish it—even if it means to hell with convention or loyalty. His controllers from MI6 and the CIA know that Will is a wild card, but his unpredictability may be the perfect weapon to bring down the world's most wanted international terrorist mastermind, an Iranian Revolutionary Guard general whose code name is Megiddo. And Will has his own reasons for catching this madman: He suspects that Megiddo is the man responsible for the horrific death of a special agent in Iran twenty-five years ago—a man Will can barely remember.

When Will finds a connection that might lure Megiddo out—a person from his past—he sets up an elaborate and dangerous trap with potentially lethal consequences. But the wily terrorist is still one step ahead of his hunter, and soon Will finds himself racing across the capitals of Europe and the United States to find his prey and avoid an attack the likes of which the world has never seen.

As an MI6 field operative, MATTHEW DUNN recruited and ran agents, coordinated and participated in special operations, and acted in deep-cover roles throughout the world. He operated in highly hostile environments where, if compromised and captured, he would have been executed. Dunn was trained in all aspects of intelligence collection, deep-cover deployments, small arms, explosives, military unarmed combat, surveillance, and infiltration.

Medals are never awarded to modern MI6 officers, but Dunn was the recipient of a very rare personal commendation from the secretary of state for foreign and commonwealth affairs for work he did on one mission, which was deemed so significant that it directly influenced the successful conclusion of a major international incident.

During his time in MI6, Dunn conducted approximately seventy missions. All of them were successful.

He lives in England.

SPYCATCHER

MATTHEW DUNN

SPYCATCHER

WILLIAM MORROW

An Imprint of HarperCollinsPublishers

HarperCollins books may be purchased for educational, business, or sales promotional use. For information please write: Special Markets Department, Harper-Collins Publishers, 10 East 53rd Street, New York, NY 10022.

FIRST EDITION

Library of Congress Cataloging-in-Publication Data
Dunn, Matthew, 1968–
Spycatcher : a novel / Matthew Dunn.—1st ed.
p. cm.
ISBN 978–0–06–203767–1
1. Intelligence officers—Fiction. 2. International relations—Fiction. I. Title.
PR6104.U54494S69 2011
823'.92—dc22
2010048918

---

11 12 13 14 15 OV/RRD 10 9 8 7 6 5 4 3 2 1

To my children. And to the intelligence officers and secret agents of MI6, the CIA, and their allies.

PART I

ONE

"You're sure that I won't be killed today?" The spy rubbed a hand against his smooth face and looked down at the wet Central Park grass beneath him. It was very early in the morning, and beyond the park the sounds of New York life were distant and mellow. He frowned and shook his head slightly. A fine, windless rain fell. "This whole thing seems odd."

Will Cochrane observed the man for a while before speaking. "Soroush, it *is* odd. That's why you'll have three expert men close by to protect you."

Soroush's frown deepened. He looked up at Will's tall and powerful frame. "Only three? That's all your masters in British Intelligence could give you?"

Will pushed fingers through his cropped dark hair and then reached out to touch the Iranian's arm. "Perfectly adequate for what we need to happen."

The spy chuckled a little. "I thought I was your most valuable asset."

"You are."

Soroush swiveled so that he was fully facing Will. "But good things always come to an end?"

Will removed his hand and quickly glanced left and right. There were few other people in their vicinity, and certainly none close to them. The British Intelligence officer looked back to his companion. "No, it's not like that. The Iranians called the meeting, not us. If we don't do this, then we'll never know what they want."

Soroush jammed his hands into his coat pockets. He lowered his head again.

Will felt a surge of doubt and fear for his agent, but he checked these emotions and spoke calmly. "I found you all those years ago, when you were still working for the Iranian Ministry of Intelligence and Security. I persuaded you to keep working in MOIS and at the same time spy for the British. I got you out of Iran when it looked as if your cover could be compromised. And when it turned out that such a concern was unfounded, I taught you how to continue to spy on your country from the safety of Europe." He forced a smile. "Throughout all our time together, I have always protected you, and I will continue to do so today."

The Iranian said nothing for a moment. He then cleared his throat and shook his head vigorously. "In my eight years in the U.K., I've provided you with intelligence that only a very few current or former members of MOIS would have access to. And I know you have taken action on much of my intelligence, meaning that the Iranians should know they have a breach. A studious officer within the security department of MOIS would be able to narrow down that breach. And then out of the blue a message is passed to me. A message from MOIS saying they want to meet me." He looked intently at Will. "Even if you think I was not compromised in the old days, you have to concede there is a strong possibility that I'm now being set up."

Will did not return his gaze. He had already concluded that the two Iranian intelligence officers who wanted to meet his secret agent today probably had nefarious intentions toward the man. He had also concluded that if this were the case, his agent's cover was blown and Soroush would therefore be of no future use to him. But Will needed the meeting to take place in order to be sure. And regardless, his man was going to be protected.

"Why do you think they chose New York for the meeting?" Soroush's words were hushed and quick.

Will looked around and then back at his agent. The correct answer to this question, he suspected, was that the Iranians knew that Soroush was a Western spy and would not agree to meet in a non-Western city. "You're now an entrepreneur who does a lot of business in the States. They're trying to minimize inconvenience to you."

Soroush's expression seemed to harden. "I'm not so sure."

Will checked his watch and smiled. "Are you prepared to go through with this or not?"

Soroush looked blankly at him for a while but then shrugged. "You know me too well."

"I do."

The two men became silent. The rain hit their faces with increased intensity.

Will drew a deep breath and spoke quietly. "When you're on Gapstow Bridge at the north end of the pond, you won't be able to see me because I'll be hidden. But if you look directly south across the pond, you'll be looking at my approximate location. I will be one hundred and eighty meters from you and will be monitoring you and your meeting through binoculars."

Soroush turned back toward Will. He angled his head. "And your friends?"

"You may see some of them, but they won't look out of place. And if anything happens, they will react with absolute speed, aggression, and precision."

"British Special Forces?"

"Yes, but men who've been given further specific covert-operations training by my service."

The spy nodded. "And straight back to your hotel after the meeting?"

Will also nodded. "Exactly as we discussed. I'll meet you there for your debriefing."

Soroush looked pensive. "But if they want me to go with them?"

"Under no circumstances. You have your meeting and then part company with them." Above all else, Will could not allow his man to fall under the control of the Iranians. He had far too many secrets in his head, secrets which, if exposed, could severely damage the West's ability to counter hostile Iranian activity.

"All right." Soroush seemed happy with Will's response. Soroush then suddenly took one of Will's hands between two of his own. "We've been through so much together."

Will looked down at his hand with surprise. He felt a deep pang of uncertainty but did not show the emotion. Instead he said, "Indeed we have, my friend."

Soroush smiled, and for a moment Will suspected that the man could read his thoughts. Soroush gripped his hand, exhaled, and released his hold. His smile faded. "If anything happens, you'll take care of my wife and my kids, yes?"

"Nothing will happen." Will sighed. "But *if* the need ever arose, of course I'd make sure your family was supported." This above all else was true.

Soroush smiled and nodded. He pointed a finger at Will and then gently touched its tip against Will's chest. "I remember the first time I met you. I remember thinking that I'd never met a man as scary and ruthless as you. But over the years I've come to realize that there is a very different side to you, a side you often try to hide, one that is full of depth and compassion." A look of sadness replaced the smile. "But I also know that you tread a very solitary path."

Will frowned. "Perhaps *you* know *me* too well."

Soroush shook his head. "I would have to live to a very old age to fully understand you. And I'm not convinced that I'll ever reach such an age." Soroush waved slightly, then turned abruptly and walked off in the direction of Central Park's Gapstow Bridge.

Will watched him for a moment, pondering the other man's words. Then he sighed and pushed aside all thoughts besides those he needed to focus on the meeting. He reached into his overcoat pocket and pulled out a cell phone and a Bluetooth earpiece, which he fixed into position. He pressed one number on the phone handset and spoke. "Soroush is on his way. He should be at the location in ten minutes."

Then he took off at a run. He darted into a cluster of trees and brought himself to an abrupt stop before swiveling around and dropping down to a crouch. He brought his binoculars up to his eyes and then reached for his phone again.

"Okay, I've got the bridge. What do you see?"

A second passed before three voices came back at him in rapid sequence.

"Alpha. Nothing."

"Bravo. Nothing."

"Charlie. Have him. Nearly there."

Will dropped even lower to the ground and scanned left and right of the bridge. He saw Soroush walking on the East Drive path and a jogger trotting close behind him. The jogger would be Charlie. The spy turned onto the Gapstow Bridge, but the jogger didn't follow him.

Will pressed the number three on his cell phone. "I see you."

A voice came back immediately. "I know. I'm going three hundred meters north and will then set my position. Our man should now be covered by Bravo."

Will raised a hand and unnecessarily pressed the Bluetooth device harder against his ear. It seemed longer, but in seven seconds Will heard another voice.

"Bravo. Yes, I see him. Walking across the thing. No. Now stationary in the center of the bridge. He's in position and waiting."

Will raised his binoculars and looked. Bravo was right. Will's agent was standing on Gapstow Bridge. He knew that the foot crossing was approximately twenty-five meters long, and Soroush had followed his instructions by stopping in the center of the bridge facing the pond to the south.

"Where are you, Bravo?" Will continued to scan either side of the bridge.

"Where I should be. One hundred meters northwest of the bridge. This is where I stay put."

"Alpha?"

"Sixty meters from our man, by Wollman Rink."

Will looked at his watch and exhaled. Everything was in place. His team had now set a perimeter around his spy by positioning themselves to the north, the northwest, and the northeast of Central Park's Gapstow Bridge. From his own position near the southern tip of the pond, he looked toward Soroush. He could easily see the man's face. Soroush looked calm and still.

Will eased himself up a little and spoke into the Bluetooth as he did so. "Okay, one minute and counting."

Will examined Soroush again. The man was leaning on the bridge, obviously pretending to watch the rain on the water beneath him. There was a slight smile on his face. Will checked the time again and then spoke into his phone.

"All right, men. Any moment now."

He forced himself to breathe and ignored the pain in his eyes from pressing the binoculars too hard against them. He kept scanning the bridge and its surroundings. "Anything?"

A few seconds passed before each of his team members replied with the same word: "Nothing."

Within his peripheral vision, he spotted movement and turned slightly to see an elderly woman walking a dog on an adjacent path. He instinctively moved back into heavier cover, even though he knew that the woman could not see him. The dog walker moved past, and Will continued his surveillance. Soroush was no longer leaning and was now casually looking in either direction along the bridge.

"Charlie. I'm in position three hundred meters to the northeast of the pond. I might have something."

Will immediately swung his binoculars toward Charlie's location. He widened his eyes and focused his mind on the Bluetooth earpiece.

Charlie spoke again, and his words were rapid but controlled. "Yes, something. Two men."

Will waited, not daring to speak. A screech of bird calls suddenly rose from the water before him, and he silently cursed the interruption to his focus. He looked quickly at Soroush, but the man was still alone on the bridge. Will turned back to look in Charlie's direction.

"They're at a stop." Charlie's voice was slower this time. "Fifty meters north of me, meaning three hundred and fifty meters from the bridge."

Will instantly responded. "Your assessment?"

"It's them." Charlie went quiet for a moment. "I'm sure it's them. But they're waiting, and that's bad."

Will lowered his binoculars. He felt his pulse rate increase, but he ignored the natural reaction to the adrenaline release within his body. He put the binoculars up to his eyes again and this time looked to the northwest. "Alpha? Bravo?"

Alpha spoke first. "Four hostiles moving across my vision."

Bravo then came onto the phone line. His voice was hushed. "Another five coming straight at me."

"Damn it." Will thought rapidly. Such a large number of hostiles suggested that they were a snatch squad, which mean that most likely they had a driver and vehicle waiting somewhere nearby.

Alpha spoke. "Mine have stopped."

"So have mine," added Bravo.

Will frowned. "Can they see either of you yet?"

"Don't think so."

"No."

Will was about to speak, but Bravo beat him to it. "Two of mine are peeling off and heading southwest. The remaining three are still static."

Will cursed again. "They must have a vehicle ready for them near Central Park South or Fifth Avenue. The two men heading southwest around the pond are moving into position to secure the team and the target's extraction point." He put his binoculars into a coat pocket and inhaled deeply. "These are my instructions. Alpha and Bravo: Put warning shots down against your hostiles and then move back to the west end of the bridge. Under no circumstances must either of you let them get onto the bridge. Charlie: Eliminate your two men, then move directly to Soroush. Get him off the bridge and head east with him out of the park. I'll take care of the two hostiles heading my way." He checked his watch. "And, gentlemen, we have a maximum of two minutes to get this done before this place is swarming with local law enforcement officers. Time starts now."

Will turned in the direction of his two oncoming targets. His route to them would be under continuous tree cover, and he estimated that they would be nearly three hundred meters away from him. From his right overcoat pocket he withdrew a Heckler & Koch Mark 23 handgun. He walked quickly ahead, scrutinizing each gap between trees while at the same time focusing on anything that might come through his cell phone's earpiece. Within a hundred and forty meters he came to the westernmost point of the pond and then turned to face north. His targets would now be very close.

Will heard four or five rapid bangs from across the pond and then a voice in his ear. "Charlie. Done. I'll be at the bridge in sixty seconds." Charlie had successfully taken out the two Iranian intelligence officers.

More shots then, coming from the north. Alpha and Bravo had also begun their controlled withdrawal to the bridge. Will bent his knees slightly and moved forward with his gun now clasped in both hands. He saw them. Two hostiles were running but seemed oblivious to the fact that they might be heading toward danger. When one of them finally spotted Will, he stopped and shouted. Will shot him in the head and then immediately adjusted his angle and fired twice into the other man's torso. He sprinted up to the prone bodies and fired again into each man's skull.

"Am on the bridge waiting for Bravo." This was Alpha.

Will spoke loudly. "Bravo, get on that bridge." He heard no response. "Bravo?" He ran onward and heard almost continuous gunfire ahead of him.

"Charlie. I'm also on bridge and moving to get—" For a second the line went quiet. Then Charlie came back on the air. He was shouting. "Alpha's down! Multiples ahead! Have to engage!"

"Shit, no! Get Soroush out!" Will yelled, in a full sprint to the fight. Gunfire continued, becoming louder, and within seconds Will saw the bridge. And then he saw Charlie collapse. Four Iranians were about to step unopposed onto the bridge.

Will could easily see Soroush now. And Soroush could plainly see him. The man stared at him for what seemed like minutes but it was probably only a second. He shook his head very slightly.

Save yourself. I am lost to you now.

Will fired at the hostiles. One of them fell to the ground, and the others immediately swung toward Will and returned fire. He sprinted forward, ignoring the bullets that struck the ground on either side of him while continuing to fire. Two more men fell. He reached the bridge and saw the sole remaining Iranian quickly turn away from him. A gunshot rang out, and then the man turned back to face him. The man smiled. Will shot him in the head.

Soroush was now lying on the ground clutching his chest, breathing heavily. Will ran to him, crouched down, and cradled the man's head.

Soroush looked up and smiled through clenched teeth. "Good things do come to an end."

Will looked at Soroush's chest. "Not yet. You're still alive."

Soroush shook his head. "You've got to leave me here. They're all dead, but you're too important to be caught up in this mess."

"Never." As soon as Will spoke the word, he felt a strong blow on his back, followed by immense pain in his stomach. He fell forward onto Soroush and then forced himself up to look at the source of his pain. There was a large exit wound in his abdomen. He looked up and saw eight new Iranian men walking toward the bridge. Glancing over his shoulder, he saw another four men coming toward the other side of the bridge. As he turned forward again, two more bullets struck him in the stomach. He doubled over in pain and placed a hand against his wounds. The men were approximately sixty meters away from Will and Soroush. Will looked at his gun and shook his head. He knew he had only five bullets left in the Mark 23 pistol. And he knew he did not have the time to drag his body over to one of the discarded Iranian weapons. He silently cursed and glanced at Soroush. The man was looking at him and shaking his head while gripping Will's arm. Will breathed deeply and mustered all his remaining strength and focus. He fired four of his bullets at the men before him and watched four of them fall dead. He then ignored everything else and turned fully to his spy.

Soroush smiled again and said softly, "They must not take me alive. We both understand that. You know what has to be done."

What Will knew was that he was losing consciousness, and he blinked hard to try to retain focus. He heard police sirens, but they were too far away. He shook his head. "I can still save you."

Soroush kept his smile. "Not this time, my comrade."

Will exhaled deeply and moved closer to Soroush. His pain was quickly being replaced by numbness, and he knew he had only a few remaining seconds of consciousness. He dragged his body up behind Soroush and pulled the man close to him so that they were both seated. The Iranian men were now only twenty meters away.

Will lifted his gun and placed its nozzle against Soroush's temple. He closed his eyes and whispered, "Good-bye, old friend."

Then he pulled the trigger and shot Soroush dead.

TWO

His eyes had opened, but all about him was pitch black and silent. He felt around his body and realized that he was on his back on some kind of thin bed. He let his left hand fall to the side of the bed, and it felt bare floor. His right hand touched cold wall. He coughed and tried to gauge the effect of the noise. It seemed to him that he was in a very small room. Or a cell.

Will Cochrane sat upright and immediately was hit by a wave of nausea, giddiness, and severe pain. He placed a hand on his stomach and then felt around his torso. Bandages. He breathed slowly to try to control the sickness and focus his mind. He shut and reopened his eyes but could still see nothing.

He rubbed fingers against his temples and decided he must stand. He counted to five and then swung his legs off of the bed. The movement sent searing pain to his lower back and abdomen. He gasped for air and gripped the side of the bed to keep himself from falling. He flexed his bare toes and his calf muscles. His legs felt strong and uninjured. He counted again and pushed upward with his arms, but the action was too much, and as soon as he was standing, he fell forward. Something immediately broke his fall—another wall. Its proximity suggested that he was in an extremely confined place. He concentrated and slowly eased himself backward until he was standing again. He tried to clear his mind and concentrate on the act of remaining upright. After however much time passed, he decided that he would not fall again. He turned ninety degrees and took one pace forward, then another. Within two further paces, he felt what must have been a door, but he could feel no handles. He stepped back two paces and moved his hands over his body again. He was neither cold nor warm, and apart from the bandages around his stomach, he was naked.

Will cleared his throat several times and was surprised to realize that his mouth did not feel dry. Somebody must have been giving him water. He let his arms hang down by his sides and checked his balance again. He inhaled deeply, then spoke.

"I am awake."

His voice sounded normal. He hoped that this indicated there was no damage to his brain. He breathed in through his nose and spoke again.

"I am awake."

Will listened for any other noises. At first there were none, but then he thought he detected the very slightest of sounds, a noise that could have been the scuffing of shoes against floor. Then a more distinct sound could clearly be heard, an electronic humming. Just as it came to him what the noise could be—the humming sound that some lights made a second or two before illuminating—he screwed his eyes shut. From behind his eyelids, he could now see white. He placed a hand to his face to help shield his eyes and then carefully opened them. Even with the shield in place, the brightness was intense, and he had to close his lids and reopen them several times to adjust to the stark contrast. He lowered his hand and looked around him. The room was barely two meters wide and three meters long. The bed was the only item in the room. He turned back to face the door and waited.

Another scuffing noise sounded, this one louder. Then there was a clank of metal. The door opened. Will tensed his arm muscles, even though the action sent new shots of pain down his spine. He took one step forward.

A small, bespectacled man appeared in the doorway. He was wearing a white coat and looked like a doctor. He smiled at Will.

Will did not smile back. "Where am I, and who are you? Answer me in that order, please."

The man looked up at Will's naked body. "Remarkable. You shouldn't be able to stand for at least another week."

He sounded American.

"Do you think you can dress and walk?" The man retained his smile. Will was at least thirty centimeters taller and certainly twice as wide. But this differential did not seem to intimidate the small man.

"If I wish to."

"Trust me, you wish to." The man took a step back, out of the room, and reached for something in the hall. He produced a square, folded white parcel, which he tossed onto the bed beside Will. "Your clothes."

Will looked at the parcel and leaned down to pick it up. He thought he was going to vomit when he made the movement but managed to hide any signs of the feeling. The parcel quickly unraveled in his hand, and he realized he was holding a disposable paper prison jumpsuit. Smiling a little, he climbed into the suit, then turned back toward the small man. "My questions?"

The man frowned. "You feel okay?"

"I feel in excellent health. My questions?"

The man raised his eyebrows. "Well, what do you think I look like?"

"A medical man. Of sorts."

The man nodded once. "Of sorts, correct." He regarded Will's stomach. "Maybe a better medical man than I thought. As to your other question, would you believe my answer?"

"Probably not."

The medical man smiled again. "So why bother asking? You know you must leave this room. And you know that a diminutive fellow like me wouldn't be standing here without having other larger people within an arm's length. So let's take those first steps."

Will ran a hand over his head. His hair felt clean and clearly had been washed. He stared at the man, feeling very calm. "All right. Let's get this over with."

Will stepped out of the room and into a corridor. Three other men, all of them big and carrying nightsticks, were standing there. They said nothing as the small man led Will thirty meters before stopping.

The man pointed at a door to the right of the corridor. "You need to go in there. My job is done." He shook his head. "Three bullets," he said quietly. "You should have stayed in bed."

Will smiled and also spoke quietly. "I'm grateful for anything you've done to assist my recovery. If things go badly here for your people, I will remember that."

The man frowned again. Will turned and opened the door.

THREE

The room before him was large and totally empty. Windowless. A solitary man stood on the far side, leaning against a wall. He wore suit trousers, a white shirt, and no tie. He was tall, slender, and silver-haired, and he looked to be in his fifties.

Will stepped forward. "Hello."

"Hello back at you." This man also had an American accent. He swept a hand in front of him. "Make yourself at home."

Will looked around the room. He walked to the wall opposite the man, turned, and eased himself down to sit on the floor. He partially stretched his legs out before him and clasped his hands over his lap. "Do you have any tea?"

"What?"

"A cup of tea. That would be quite nice."

"I'm sure it would." The man did not move. "Why are you sitting?"

"I can stand if you prefer."

"No, no. Stay where you are." The man chuckled a little. "It's just that most people in your situation would prefer to stand, and generally they choose to do so in the center of a room."

"Because they wish to project strength to hide their fear or any inclination toward subservience."

"Meaning you're doing the opposite?"

"Maybe I'm just tired from the walk here." Will patted a leg. "I get the feeling I haven't exercised for a few days."

The man slightly adjusted his position against the wall. He put his hands into his trouser pockets. He seemed to be observing Will very closely. "No. You know exactly what you're doing."

Will shrugged.

"Who are you?" the man asked.

Will smiled. "Nobody of particular consequence. Just a tourist who found himself in the wrong place at the wrong time."

The man adjusted his position again. "When we found you, you were carrying no form of identity. Ditto your three dead colleagues."

Will nodded slowly, then widened his eyes. "That's great. It means I can be whoever I want to be."

"If you like. Who would you like to be right now?"

Will thought about the question and smiled again. "How about a private military contractor? Possibly South African but of English heritage. Someone engaged by a wealthy Middle Eastern businessman to protect him during a slightly shady transaction. Could that work?"

The man seemed to consider the idea. "Yes, it could work. I presume that the man whose head was nearly taken off with a pistol round would be the Middle Eastern businessman and the other dead Iranians strewn around the park would be the thugs sent by his business nemesis? But as for you, you'd need a lot of documentation to support your identity."

Will shook his head. "Not necessarily. My work is sensitive. My paymasters are dangerous people and are not to be crossed. I'd be totally uncooperative with you."

The man pulled his hands out of his pockets and raised his palms. "Then we'd just torture you to find out what we want."

Will also raised his palms. "You could. But I've got so much non-sense stuffed in my head that you'd come away from the experience more confused than enlightened." He brushed one of his hands against his clean hair. "In any case, you're not going to torture me. Somebody here cares too much about my well-being for that to happen."

"Then it will be a thirty-year prison sentence."

Will pulled back his arms to stretch his back muscles. The pain was excruciating, but he embraced the sensation. "Wonderful. I've often wanted to get away from it all."

The man smiled and to Will's surprise slowly seated himself on the floor. The two men were now at eye level at opposite ends of the large room. "Where do you think you are?"

"I have no thoughts on the subject."

"Well, you must assume that you're still in New York City."

"I could just as easily be in Beijing."

The man sighed. "I know, but you're not. You're actually only a few blocks from where you were shot."

"Prove it."

The man brought his knees up under his chin and rested his elbows on them. "If I need to, I will." He frowned and dropped eye contact for a moment. "The doctors took three nine-millimeter bullets out of your stomach."

"You operated on me here?"

The man shook his head. "No, we took charge of you after you were operated on in a hospital."

"And it's amazing that I'm still alive." Will spoke in a mocking tone.

The man reengaged eye contact. "You have older wounds on your body. From bullets, knives, and shrapnel."

"I've always been a bit clumsy."

"Or reckless."

Will nodded slightly. "How about that cup of tea?"

The man exhaled again. He placed his hands on his on his knees. "The NYPD had to shoot eight Iranians dead before they could get near your body. They took possession of you and brought you to a hospital. But because your actions in Central Park were deemed to be terrorist-related, the incident was given national significance. As a result, I was brought in. I am a senior special agent of the Federal Bureau of Investigation."

"No you're not."

The man narrowed his eyes. "You want me to show you a badge?"

"No thanks."

The man spoke with what sounded like slow exasperation. "Why am I not an FBI agent?"

Will shrugged and rubbed his chin. "It's an issue of agenda. You're not here to solve a crime and close a case." He shook his head. "No, you view me in a different way."

"The FBI is not just about law enforcement."

"I know. But you're just not that type. I can tell from the way you're thinking."

The man chuckled. "You can see what I'm thinking?"

"I can tell that you're thinking on multiple levels and not just about me."

"So what would that make me?"

Will brought his hand down to rest on his lap. "Among many things it would make you an overburdened man." He smiled. "Quite clearly an overburdened intelligence officer."

"How would you know that type?"

Will shrugged again. "As I say, I'm a private military contractor. A man like me would obviously be living in a murky world. Sometimes getting deniable instructions from intelligence services, sometimes being chased by them." He produced a pretend frown and looked away. "Maybe not South African, though. Maybe a white expatriate who grew up in Tanzania." He looked back at the man. "That sounds less of a cliché."

The man started drumming his fingers again. "So you would say that I'm CIA?"

Will crossed one foot over the other. "I didn't say that. You could be an Israeli Mossad agent. Or a Russian SVR officer. Or a number of other things. But"—he looked around the bare room before returning his gaze to the man—"based upon the dangerous assumption that you are American, I will allow myself to conclude that you are CIA."

"So we're now making some progress."

"Your progress. Not mine."

The man nodded, then spoke quickly and quietly. "I'll give you a far better identity if you like."

"I don't mind."

The man leaned forward. "You are thirty-five years old. Single. No children. In fact, you have very few commitments beyond your solitary life."

"That keeps things simple."

"It does." The man eased back a little. "You're English—we can't really disguise that fact—but let's also make you half American."

Will sat motionless. He felt a twinge of pain in his stomach.

"So . . . so let's see." The man tapped a finger several times on his leg. "Yes, I have it. Your American father died when you were a very young boy, leaving your English mother to raise you and your sister in the States. Your mother struggled on alone with you both but was later tragically assaulted and killed." The man frowned. "You were seventeen when that happened, and you and your sister were left alone and with nothing—no other family, friends, money, or home." He nodded. "Nothing. But your sister was four years older than you, and she was about to graduate from law school into an internship with a London law firm. She had prospects. You, on the other hand, decided to do something impulsive and ran off to France to join the French Foreign Legion for five years. You could tell people that it was"—he paused for a moment—"your subconscious need to have a new family of sorts."

"Or maybe I just wanted to kill things?" Will could feel the tension and aggression in his voice.

The man nodded. "Yes, either-or." He smiled. "Okay, now let's think this through." He scratched the side of his head. "My military knowledge isn't great, but I know that within the Legion there's an elite parachute regiment. And I'm pretty sure that within that regiment there's a small, highly trained Special Forces commando unit." He pointed a finger at Will. "But you'd need to check out its name."

"Maybe my military knowledge is better than yours." Will swallowed, and the action felt uncomfortable. "It's called the Groupement des Commandos Parachutistes."

The man clapped slowly. "Excellent. So that would clear up the first five years of your adult life. What next?" He angled his head and smiled. "I have it. You've gotten the boys-with-guns thing out of your system, so you go to England. And now you decide to try to flex your brain. So college beckons—that will get rid of another three or four years—but which one should it be?"

"Nothing too high profile." Will's chest muscles had now tensed.

The man shook his head. "No, unfortunately your grades were just too good. It has to be Cambridge or Oxford, I'm afraid."

Will spoke with an edge. "Make it Cambridge."

"Cambridge it is." The man folded his arms. "I think you would have studied politics, philosophy, and economics, and I think you would have graduated with a star first-class degree."

"As you like."

"As I like indeed." The man looked serious. "And now we can really add some spice to your profile. Let's forget mercenary or military contractor or anything like that. Let's say you were recruited into the British Secret Intelligence Service—MI6, as we sometimes like to call it—and that you've worked there ever since."

Will said nothing. He felt an almost overwhelming sense of anger. He lifted his head and looked at the man. He could feel his pulse rate throbbing in his temples. "You still need to give me a name."

The man waved this away as a mere detail. "Oh, that's easy, because no matter what false names you may give yourself, there is only one true name that can ever be yours and yours alone." He slowly nodded and lowered his voice. "You are the ultimate killer of killers, the man who terrifies his enemies and allies, the man who can start wars and end them, the man who is the West's deadliest and most secret weapon." He raised his hand and pointed. "You are the great Will Cochrane. You are *Spartan*."

Will stared at the man, desperate not to show the shock he felt.

The American lifted himself up from the floor and walked over to Will. He crouched down directly in front of Will and gazed at him. His eyes were as silver as his hair. "How could I even know that you're MI6, let alone the man who has been given its most distinguished and deadly code name?"

Will bunched his hand into a fist.

"After all, you've traveled into my country under a different passport and with no links to your real identity and vocation."

Will narrowed his eyes and slowly exhaled. He thought about the man before him, he pictured the bespectacled doctor and the three large men waiting in the corridor outside, and he mentally rehearsed what he could do.

"So how could I possibly know about you, when your existence is kept secret from most of MI6, let alone other agencies?"

Will smiled and looked away for a moment. When he was no longer smiling, he returned his gaze to the man before him. He decided that, despite his injuries, he could kill this man and everyone outside this room in less than thirty seconds.

The man frowned. He looked quickly down at Will's hands, then back up at his face. He shook his head rapidly and with urgency. "Not that, there's no need," he said softly.

Will watched him for a while.

The man shook his head again. "No need." His eyes had widened.

Will smiled again but kept his fist tightly bunched. "Our games are over. I suggest you speak with candor and speed."

The man glanced once more at Will's large fist and then looked upward. "I know about you because I was called by a friend who asked me to get you. That friend told me that if I did not do so, you would do everything in your power to destroy those who might try to keep you captive."

Will frowned. "You received a call?" His frown slowly faded. "From someone in my organization?"

The man seemed to hesitate for a moment, then spoke quite deliberately. "Not just someone. A man who knows me very well. A man who also happens to be your Controller."

"Alistair?"

He nodded.

"Why did Alistair tell you that I was with British Intelligence? And why did you decide to help me?"

The man exhaled loudly. "The answer to both questions is the same, but it's not my place to give you that answer. Only Alistair can do that."

Will bunched his fist tighter. "How do you know I am Spartan?"

This time the man showed no fear, speaking with steel. "Because your premier authorized Alistair to tell me. I know all about MI6's brutal Spartan Program. I know that it allows only one man to go through the program and, if he is not dead at the end of it, carry the title *Spartan*. No others are allowed to go on the program while the current Spartan lives. That Spartan is you."

Will's heart raced faster. His Controller was one of the most senior operational members of MI6. For Alistair to have any form of bond with the man before him could only mean that this CIA officer held a similar rank within his own organization. And the fact that the British prime minister had authorized the disclosure of Will's code name to the American could only mean that the CIA man was exceptionally powerful and trusted. "What's your name?"

The CIA man looked back at him. His eyes had narrowed to slits and had now become quite cold. "You can call me Patrick."

Will shook his head slightly. "I still deserve to know why you would help me."

Patrick raised an eyebrow. "You deserve nothing of the sort. But I will tell you that Alistair and I share the same debt of gratitude to another man. And that debt brought me to this room today."

"It's fortunate for you that you mentioned Alistair's name." Will looked toward the door and lowered his voice. "What will happen now?"

Patrick also looked toward the door. "You're by no means fit to leave this place, but you can't stay here any longer. Nor can I offer you any more medical support." He glanced back at Will and frowned. "I'm sorry that someone of your status had to be brought here. I couldn't take you to an Agency facility. And the men here were the best I could put together at such short notice. But you have to go now, although I suggest you rest up in a hotel somewhere for another week before attempting the flight back to London. One of my men will get you some clothes and set you up with anything else you need. And I presume you have your passport and credit cards safely hidden somewhere in the city?"

"Yes."

Patrick placed a hand under Will's elbow and guided him to the exit. But before he opened the door, he turned to face Will fully. He spoke quietly and rapidly. "Take a message back to Alistair. Only Alistair. Tell him the following." He nodded once. "The strike against us will be massive, and the great or the little will be the victim."

FOUR

Will checked the map on his screen and noted that he was nearly halfway across the Atlantic Ocean. He was on a Heathrow-bound British Airways night flight and had paid for a first-class seat to ensure space and privacy. Save for occasional reading lights, the area around him was dark and most of the other passengers were sleeping.

Will had not heeded Patrick's advice to recuperate for a few days in New York City and instead had taken the next available flight back to London. He wondered now if he'd been wise to do so. Despite having taken a cocktail of medications before boarding the airplane at JFK, he now felt feverish and in agony. He pulled a thin blanket over his body and tried to sleep again. But the same memory kept coming back.

Soroush, I'm not who you think I am.
I suspected as much.
Good. Then you know, who I really work for?
I do.

So you must also know what I'm about to ask from you.

Of course. You wish me to betray my country.

A new sweat broke out under Will's clothes, and he pulled off the blanket. He opened his eyes, reached for a glass of ice water, and forced half its contents down. His hand shook as he replaced the glass on the table beside him. He now felt very cold again, and he cursed the fever while pulling on the blanket again. He looked once more at the electronic map. The plane barely seemed to be moving.

Will shook his head and spoke out loud. "Why the hell did you not get off that bridge when you had the chance, my friend?"

A flight attendant appeared next to him. "Is everything all right?"

He looked up at her. He tried to smile and lied. "Bloody jet lag. I don't know if I'm coming or going."

The woman nodded and produced a sympathetic smile. "Let me know if you need anything. You're nearly home."

Will closed his eyes again and this time saw Soroush sitting before him. He was eating breakfast on the day of his death. He looked tired. Reflective and sad. He spoke while shaking his head.

How can there be honor in what I do? How can there be any justi-fication for taking others' secrets? How can I expect to keep doing this without one day being punished? Maybe today is that day. And maybe that is a good thing.

FIVE

Will saw the six men as soon as he exited Heathrow's passport control. He knew that under their jackets they would be armed. They looked at him and he looked at them.

One of the men walked up to him. He had the gait and posture of a Special Forces man, and the men behind him looked similar. The man nodded once at Will and said, "We're hoping to avoid any trouble, sir."

Will looked around. To the left and right of the Special Forces men were airport police officers. They held Heckler & Koch submachine guns and were also eyeing Will. He looked back at the man before him and smiled. "If you try to put me into shackles, there'll be plenty of trouble."

The man said nothing, nodded, and gestured toward Will's arm. Will shook his head slightly, and the man quickly withdrew his hand before pointing in the direction of his men.

Will stood for a moment. Then he stepped forward.

• • •

The black car turned into the basement parking garage of the MI6 headquarters in Vauxhall Cross, London. In a moment it was stationary, and four men quickly emerged from the vehicle. One of them looked back into the car and said to Will, "Come on, sir, let's go."

Will was led toward an elevator, shielded by the men. One of his chaperones withdrew a crude-looking burlap hood and said, "We've been given instructions to hide your face from others in this building." He handed Will the hood. "Sorry."

Will exhaled slowly and looked at the men around him. "A hood won't make any difference to me if you try anything silly."

"We know."

Will pulled on the heavy hood and was immediately sightless. He felt the elevator move, then stop and heard doors swishing open. Hands gently gripped his arms, and he allowed them to do so. He was guided forward. All around him was quiet. He knew he was being walked down a special wing of the HQ, a place most intelligence officers were not permitted to enter. They stopped, and Will heard a key being inserted into a lock. He breathed deeply. The walk had been excruciating.

He was moved forward again and then pushed down into a chair. Men spoke, and there was audible movement around him. He heard a door open and shut several times, then silence.

"Take your hood off." The voice came from directly in front of him.

Will did as he was told. He looked around and saw that he was in a windowless room furnished solely with a conference table and surrounding chairs. There was one man in the room, and he sat at the table, opposite Will. Will knew that the man was fifty-seven years old, but he looked ten years younger. His blond hair was pomaded into place. He wore a dark blue suit, a white shirt with French cuffs, and a Royal Navy tie.

The man looked at Will with glistening eyes. "You are an obstinate liability at times."

Will smiled. "Hello, Alistair."

Alistair did not smile. Instead Will's MI6 Controller pointed a finger at him and asked, "Do you realize what you've done?"

"I was coming straight here. It was unnecessary to get me at the airport."

"Do you realize what you have done?" Alistair repeated.

Will nodded, tenting his fingertips. "Obviously, I have killed a man."

Alistair frowned, observing him for a moment, then exhaled slowly and shook his head. "You have done much more than that. You killed MI6's best-placed Iranian agent, a man who took us into the very heart of Tehran's decision making and intentions toward the West. You of all people"—Alistair raised his voice—"know that Soroush's intelligence gave us invaluable insight into the Iranian nuclear program, into Iran's export and support of terrorist activities, into its conventional military strategy in the Middle East, and into the leadership power struggles within its political machine. And you also know that the intelligence you gleaned from your agent has enabled us, on more than one occasion, to take essential timely, preemptive actions. Actions that have almost certainly stopped Iran from blundering into war with its neighbors." The man opened his eyes wide. "You did not just kill a man. You killed a major component of our collective defenses against a hostile and unpredictable regime."

Will spoke quietly. "You are correct to say that Soroush had unique access to Iranian secrets. But you've forgotten that his years of servitude to the British intelligence community gave him significant information about us—information that could not fall into the hands of the Iranians." Will pointed at Alistair. "Killing Soroush was the only solution. If we had allowed him to be taken away by the Iranians, they would have extracted everything from him via torture before murdering him. I killed Soroush to protect the integrity of what we do and to protect a man from unimaginable torment."

Alistair shook his head. "You are a rule breaker, and I've always tolerated that because of your effectiveness. But even by your standards, engaging in a gunfight in the middle of New York City was the height of recklessness."

Will reached into a pocket and pulled out three little blister packs of medication. He withdrew pills and threw them into his mouth, wondering how long the painkillers and antifever tablets would take to work. A fresh sweat had broken out under his clothes. "I don't give a damn about rules. All I care about is getting the job done."

"What you care about is prosecuting and punishing bad people. Thankfully, it just so happens that those bad people are also enemies of the West." Alistair caught Will's eyes and held them. "I know why you have an absolute sense of right and wrong; I know where all that unflinching sense of morality started for you. But you have to understand that I am your boss and that there are rules to be followed."

"Your rules, not mine." Will looked away for a moment. "My decision to kill Soroush was the correct one."

"Your decision," Alistair snapped, "very nearly compromised your role. You should have left Soroush to his fate. You know how hard I work to protect your identity and your missions for MI6. You are our most clandestine officer, and only the chief of MI6 and I know about your existence."

"Not anymore. Apparently you told a CIA man called Patrick who I was."

Alistair tapped a finger on the table. "What did Patrick say to you?"

Will swallowed to try to dislodge a pill stuck in his throat. "He said the strike against us will be massive and the great or the little will be the victim."

Alistair spoke sharply. "Victim or victims?"

"Victim." Will frowned. "What does it mean?"

His Controller glanced away for a moment. "As far as certain inflammatory Iranian commentators are concerned, America is the Great Satan and Britain is the Little Satan. Iran clearly intends to do battle with evil." Alistair smiled briefly, then looked serious. "Soroush's death has come at the worst possible time." He spoke the words quietly, and they did not necessarily seem directed at Will. Louder, he said, "Tell me what you know about Iran's Islamic Revolutionary Guard Corps and specifically its IRGC Qods Force."

Will chuckled. "As head of the Middle East and Africa Controllerate, you should have whole teams of analysts who could produce reports on the IRGC for you, I'd have thought."

"I do." Alistair looked back at Will. "But given your time spent with Soroush, you should have a bit of knowledge on the subject. And I don't have time right now to wade through reports."

"All right." Will adjusted his position in his chair and felt fresh pain sear across his stomach. "The Islamic Revolutionary Guard Corps is the component of the Iranian military used to enforce and protect the principles of the Iranian Revolution of 1979. Its exact size is unknown, but it's estimated that the IRGC is approximately one hundred and twenty thousand strong and with its own army, air force, and navy. It is almost certainly structured along the same lines as Iran's conventional military forces. The IRGC Qods Force, translated as "Jerusalem Force," is a small unit of the IRGC. It is tasked with special operations, including assassinations, export of terrorism, and intelligence gathering."

"And why have we never been able to recruit a Qods Force officer?"

"Three reasons. First, merely identifying someone as a potential target is very difficult, given that Qods Force personnel aren't exactly visible. Second, individuals within the unit are totally dedicated to their task and are handpicked on the basis of their loyalty to the revolution. It is highly improbable that a Qods Force officer would have any chinks in his armor to make him malleable to an approach by MI6. Lastly"—Will shrugged—"you've never tasked officers like me to recruit such an individual. Our efforts against Iran have so far focused on the Ministry of Intelligence and Security and on senior politicians."

Alistair nodded slowly. "I see. Well, things have now changed." He paused for a moment before speaking with intensity. "It has become essential that we identify and capture a high-ranking Qods Force officer. Actually, I want us to find a very specific officer: the Qods Force Head of Western Directorate. The man responsible for all covert Iranian or Iranian-backed terrorist actions against the U.S., the U.K., and Europe."

Will showed no expression. "We do not know if such a man actually exists. And even if he does, finding him would be like hunting for the proverbial needle in a haystack. In all probability he'd be ensconced in Iran, inaccessible to men like us."

Alistair shook his head. "Patrick thinks otherwise. He's seen National Security Agency reports suggesting that the Qods Force Western Directorate is being run out of Central or Eastern Europe." He smiled. "Which brings me back to you. Our Sarajevo station head has been contacted by a former agent, code-named Lace, who thinks he might be able to help us get alongside a senior Iranian military officer, given that the Iranians have been very active in Bosnia during and after the wars in what used to be Yugoslavia. I want you to meet Lace and find out what he has to say."

Will observed Alistair silently. "You'll have regular intelligence officers for a task like that," he said at last. "Are you trying to punish me? If you are, you know you'll fail."

Alistair sighed and looked down at his cuff links. "I'm not angry with you because you took Soroush's life. I know you well enough to know that that must have been a terrible decision for you to take and no doubt one that was made with Soroush's own consent. But as vital to us as he was, you should have left him to his fate rather than trying to protect the man when all was lost. Soroush *was* vital." He looked back up. "But you are *Spartan* and therefore invaluable. That is why I am angry."

"I never leave anyone to his fate." Will spoke with anger, and then he sighed, too. He looked around at nothing for a moment before returning his attention to Alistair. "Will our service take care of Soroush's family? His wife and children have been totally reliant on his income and will struggle without financial support."

Alistair did not meet his eyes. "I have spoken to our Benevolence Department. They are adamant that they cannot help Soroush's family, because in their eyes Soroush was not killed by our enemies. He was killed by you."

Will banged his fist on the table. "Idiots."

"They follow rules. You do not." Alistair steeled his voice. "You should have left Soroush to his fate. You should have got out of that park. You should have realized how invaluable you are to MI6."

"If I'm invaluable, then why task me on a regular intelligence mission?"

Alistair shook his head. "There is nothing regular about this mission." He tapped fingers again on the table. "But to start with, I do want you to pose as a regular intelligence officer. Our MI6 Sarajevo head knows nothing about you, so I will give you a new identity for your meeting with him. Meet him, meet his agent Lace, and see if this lead of theirs can take you to the Qods Force commander. If it can, then I give you total authority to use your . . . own methods to track the man down."

Alistair paused before speaking again. "It is vital that we identify and recruit this high-ranking Qods Force man, and I need to you to be fully fit for the task." He checked his watch. "Patrick's men did their very best for you, but under normal circumstances you should still be in hospital. Goodness knows how you're still conscious. After we've finished here, you are being taken to see the best London doctor I could find who specializes in gunshot wounds and resultant trauma. I've told her to finish your treatment. And I've told her that she has her work cut out for her, as I need you on an airplane to Sarajevo tomorrow afternoon."

Will frowned. "Patrick's message. Is it in any way connected to your requirement to capture the Qods Force commander?"

"Yes, it most certainly is related, William." He pointed at Will. "I need you to identify and hunt down this man. I need you to interrogate him and find out what he plans to do to us. I need you to do what you do best and what no one else is capable of." Alistair's face looked somber. "This will be your toughest and most critical mission. You must succeed despite the odds against your doing so." Alistair nodded once. "Do whatever you have to do. But you *must* succeed. You must stop him."

"Stop him from doing what?"

Alistair nodded slowly. "The Qods Force Head of Western Directorate has planned to inflict upon us a huge massacre the likes of which the world has never seen before. You must stop him from committing genocide."

SIX

Will opened the door, returned the keys to his pocket, and looked down at the pile of letters on the floor by his feet. He stepped over them and allowed the door to slam shut behind him.

He had not been to his apartment for more than two years, and despite its being clean and tidy, a musty odor hung heavy in the air. He walked along the corridor and entered the minimalist open-plan dining, lounge, and kitchen area. Light from the Thames-facing windows illuminated floating dust, and Will opened one of them to allow a fresh breeze to course through. He looked out at London. From his position on the building's top floor, he could see much of the great city and be reminded of all the memories it held for him. He turned, walked to his kitchen, and placed a grocery bag on one of the counters.

Will breathed deeply for a while and wondered why he had come here. He wondered why he so rarely used the place. He wondered why it had never really felt like a true home for him. He shook his head, frowned, looked around the kitchen for a moment before opening a cupboard. He withdrew a small saucepan and a china teapot, rinsed both in the sink, and placed the pan on a burner. From within the grocery bag, he pulled out a bottle of Gleneagles Natural Spring Water, unscrewed the cap, and poured half its contents into the pan. Then he turned on the burner, walked to his bathroom, and stripped off his clothes. The mirror before him showed his muscular but battered physique and the thick bandages that had been expertly applied over his most recent wounds by the London doctor. He stood for a while and wondered how much more abuse his body could take after the years of violence inflicted on it. Considerably more, he decided, and dressed as he heard the water reach the boiling point.

He reentered the kitchen, picked up the pan, and poured a little of the water inside and over the teapot. From the grocery bag, he withdrew a packet of loose-leaf Scottish breakfast tea. He gently opened the packet and smiled as he held it to his nose. The smell instantly reminded him of good times, of times before now, of times he often could not remember in detail. He drizzled some of the tea into the pot, shook the pot a little to spread the tea evenly in its base, and poured boiling water over it. From an adjacent drawer, he withdrew a long spoon and a tea cozy. He stirred the tea three times with the spoon and placed the cozy over the pot.

He moved to his Garrard 501 turntable and crouched beside it to look at his record collection. He knew what he wanted to listen to, and when he found the record, he carefully extracted it from its jacket and set it on the turntable. He switched on the machine and watched its stylus move over the vinyl before setting itself down to play. Speakers beside the Garrard hissed and crackled before emitting the sounds of the Spanish classical guitarist Andrés Segovia playing Isaac Albéniz's "Sevilla." Will closed his eyes for a moment and recalled the time he had traveled from America to London as a teenager and attended what was to be the old maestro's last British concert. He remembered Segovia's final words as Will and others in the audience repeatedly called for more encores.

The old man is tired now and most go.

He remembered hearing shortly afterward that the old man had passed away.

Will opened his eyes and walked back into the kitchen. He searched through cupboards before finding a china cup and saucer, examining both to ensure that they were clean. He carefully poured tea into the cup, walked back into the lounge area, sat at his bare dining table, and looked around. On one wall he saw a framed photograph of a younger Will and three other men standing on a mountain runway wearing high-altitude Foreign Legion parachute equipment and carrying assault rifles. Inscribed at the bottom of the photograph were the words "We gave them hell." He smiled at the machismo of the sentiment, and his smile faded as he recalled the deaths of two of the men in the picture. Next to the photograph was a family portrait showing a very much younger Will, his sister, and their mother and father. He knew that he could have only been four or five years old when the painting was made. He knew that his father had been taken from him soon afterward.

Will cursed his memories of death and loss and drank a sip of the breakfast tea. The warmth of the drink and the sounds of Segovia calmed him and briefly took his mind to a place of tranquillity. He let himself enjoy the moment before reality intruded as a twinge of pain from one of the bullet holes in his stomach.

He stood and walked into the apartment's master bedroom. The bed that was usually dressed in crisp, white, fragrant linen was now bare. He vaguely remembered the many women who'd been to this room. They seemed anonymous now. Or maybe it he who seemed anonymous, not they. He walked out of the bedroom and looked around the apartment one more time. He knew now that he hated the place. It was too cold and bare. He knew that it could have been something very different had there been a lover in his life to share it with him.

Pulling out his phone, he called his bank. He gave instructions to the man at the other end of the line, listened to the banker argue with him and tell Will that he would be mad to do as he was suggesting. Will told the man to shut up and just do what he was told. He checked his watch. Seven hours before he was due to board a plane to Bosnia. Rain was now falling heavily over the city. He decided that he had just enough time to visit two other places in London. Being in the rain was preferable to being here.

Will walked quickly at first, the collar of his overcoat turned up, his head low to shield himself from the weather. When he was satisfied that there were no other people nearby, he slowed and looked around. He was in Highgate Cemetery, North London's prestigious and eerie old place for the dead, and at first he was unsure where to go. He looked at gravestones, at statues of angels, at Gothic architecture covered with vines and moss, at dark and tangled trees and the narrow twisting footpaths. Everywhere around him seemed designed by nature and the place's sleeping occupants to keep the grounds secret from outsiders. He rubbed his hands and walked some more until he found a pathway that felt familiar. Rain lashed harder against his face, and he increased his pace, dodging sporadic stones and exposed roots and darting through side alleys, short tunnels, and occasional open ground. He passed tombs and soon knew that he was heading in the right direction. He checked the bunch of flowers in his hand, and even though their paper wrapping was now sodden and falling apart, the blend of golden chrysanthemums and ivory poppies still looked fresh and pretty. He moved around two bends on his trail.

Then he stopped in surprise.

His destination was directly in front of him and approximately thirty meters from where he was now standing. But a man and a woman were standing right where he wanted to be. Umbrellas shielded their heads, and their arms were interlinked. They stood motionless and silent, looking downward, their backs to him. They were well dressed and looked like visiting executives. Will rubbed a hand over his face to wipe away water, took two steps forward, then stopped again. He felt unsure what to do. He knew that the couple could be random tourists, as the cemetery was filled with dead celebrities, academics, politicians, and famous writers and therefore had become a ghoulish attraction of sorts. But he wondered what kind of tourists would come out on a day like today and stand in a part of the cemetery that held dead people of no particular notoriety or interest.

He walked toward them slowly and silently. They did not move, and Will was sure that they were unaware of his presence. He stopped again, breathed in deeply, and sighed. He now knew exactly who they were.

He looked left and right, wondering whether he should turn around and quietly remove himself from this place. He almost did exactly that. But then he silently cursed and looked back at the couple. He felt his stomach tighten and cramp over his wounds, felt a wave of sickness. He breathed deeply again to try to calm himself while rain pelted his exposed face. He shook his head, made a decision, and spoke loudly enough to be sure he could be heard by the people before him.

"Sarah. Sarah. It's Will."

He watched the couple turn quickly toward him, saw their umbrellas rise to expose their faces and give them a sight of him, saw the man's face shift from surprise to anger and the woman's mouth open slightly before closing. The man took one step away from Will, stumbled, then tried to pull the woman after him. The woman stood still and seemed to resist her companion's efforts to get her to move.

Will raised his flowers and an open palm. "I didn't know you would be here. How could I?"

The man pointed at Will and shouted, "Go away! You shouldn't be here." He turned quickly to the woman and said in a quieter voice, "Come on, Sarah, let's go."

Will stood still. So did the woman.

She glanced at her companion, uttered something inaudible to him, and broke free from his grip. The man replied and strode off, stopping out of earshot of the woman but not out of sight.

The woman glanced at the ground, causing her long blond hair to fall straight downward and hide her face briefly. She smiled and then did not do so, looked back up at something before turning her attention directly to Will. Her expression was sharp, her features stunning.

She beckoned to Will and said, "Come closer so that I can see you properly."

Will hesitated for a moment. He looked at the man and saw that he was watching them both, that he looked even angrier, that he looked possibly scared. Will turned back to Sarah. He hadn't seen her for eight years. She was his sister.

"Come closer." Sarah's voice was both delicate and strong.

Will glanced again at the man and nodded at him, even though he knew that the action would do nothing to placate him. He gripped the flowers tightly and walked to Sarah. Once he stood before her, he wondered if he should try to kiss her on the cheek. But he just stood there and allowed the rain to stream down his face and neck.

Sarah looked barely older than when he'd last seen her. She was tall for a woman, only a few inches shorter than Will, and slim and beautiful. But her clothes looked very different from the attire Will had last seen her wearing. Back then she had been dressed in jeans and a T-shirt; now she was wearing an expensive suit underneath an open raincoat. He briefly wondered if the nearby man, who Will knew was called James and was her husband and was a senior partner in one of the top London law firms, had bought her the clothes. But he knew that Sarah would never allow anyone to spend money on her. She had always been fiercely independent. She had always believed that she must succeed in life without asking anything of anyone but herself.

Will tried to smile but felt nervous and uneasy, even though he was glad to be with his sister. He coughed and repeated, "I had no idea you would be here."

Sarah raised her umbrella higher over her head. Her eyes flickered.

"As you say, how could you? I've not been here for a while, and when I do come, it's on a whim."

Will nodded slowly and asked, "How have you been?"

She smiled slightly. "Is that what you really want to ask me?"

Will shrugged. "It's a normal question."

Sarah shook her head quickly. "It's a question that you should know would take me much too long to answer. Therefore it's either stupid or thoughtless, or you're asking it simply because you don't know what else to say."

So Will said nothing. Rain hit him harder. Sarah held her umbrella quite still.

She seemed to be examining him and narrowed her eyes before asking, "Why are you here?"

Will glanced down before looking up. "You know why."

"What I know, my brother, is that this may be the first time you've ever come here." Sarah's words sounded hard, but her eyes glistened and they didn't seem as cold as her voice. "At least the first time since it happened."

Will nodded and looked around. Trees were bare of leaves and shoots, stone headstones and monuments were dimpled with age, and everywhere the place smelled of winter. But despite their purpose, the grounds around him seemed oddly alive and felt as though they were closing in on him. He looked once more at Sarah. "I've been away. Now I'm back, and in a few hours' time I'll be away again. I came here because I needed to come."

Sarah huffed. "That's just like you."

Will frowned.

She, too, looked around, then back at Will. "Just like you to avoid spending time with the living in London but instead choose to come and spend it with the dead."

Will felt anger surge through him. "Sarah, that's not fair—"

"But not incorrect."

He breathed slowly and tried to control his anger while

simultaneously wondering why he was angry. He knew that he could never really be angry with Sarah. He smiled gently and nodded once. "Without wishing to sound stupid again, may I ask whether you are okay?"

As he saw Sarah's eyes flicker again, he suspected that her fierce intellect would be tempted to produce another riposte, but instead she spoke softly. "I'm doing very well in my job and will make partner in the law firm next year. I make a good living, have a lovely house, may have children soon, and am married to a man"—she glanced over at James—"who is kind and clumsy and funny and forgetful and boring and loyal." She looked back at Will. "I am happy with my life, happy with everything, happy that I survived the worst of it all and found the strength to do normal things with normal people." Her eyes softened and fixed directly on Will's. "You of all people must see that and understand what I've just said."

"I do." Will understood exactly what she'd said, plus the hidden meaning within her words. "I also know you're very lucky to have those things."

Sarah shook her head. "No. I got them through effort and application, not luck."

Will smiled. "Don't make the mistake of thinking you have happiness and I don't."

"How could I make that mistake? I don't know you anymore." Sarah frowned and took a step closer to him. She lowered her voice. "But I still understand how you think."

"You always were the clever one."

"But not as dangerously clever as you."

Will held her gaze even though he knew that Sarah would not look away. He knew that she had far too much strength to feel intimidated by him. He had always loved her for that.

Sarah moved her umbrella so that it was now covering them both. To Will's surprise, she placed a hand against his cheek and ran her fingers gently down his face. "You think you're a loner, Will. Maybe you are. Maybe that's who you want to be. Maybe"—she paused—"maybe that's what you have to be."

Will chuckled. "I can be whatever I want to be."

"Not in your line of work you can't."

He stopped chuckling. "You don't know what I do for a living."

Sarah brushed her fingers down across Will's face before resting her hand on his arm. "Not exactly, no. But I can see enough to tell me that you do unusual things, hard things. And remember, I was there when it all started for you. When you had to make that terrible decision to end your boyhood and become not just a man but a man with the blood of the dead on his hands."

"Sarah, you know why—"

She raised a finger to Will's lips and spoke in a near whisper. "Of course I know why. I wouldn't be alive now if you hadn't made that decision . . . if you hadn't rescued me from them."

The two of them were silent for a moment, and this time both broke the other's gaze.

Will looked at the ground. "Regardless, we're both here today for a reason. I couldn't stop that from happening. We're here because I failed in the past."

Sarah cradled her fingers gently under Will's chin and raised his head so that he was looking at her. "I look at you now and know that whatever it is you do with your life, you wouldn't allow anything like that to happen again. I see the strength in you, the focus and the determination. And I also still see the things I saw in you when you were a boy. I still see your huge heart, your compassion, your love, your sorrow, your humor and intelligence. But I also see a man who has become not just a loner but very lonely."

Will smiled, touching his sister's fingers. The rain banged against their umbrella, but he ignored the sound and focused only on the moment. It was a moment he wanted to hold on to forever. It was a moment that he feared would be stolen from him, just like the few other good memories. He gripped her hand harder. His voice felt thick in his throat as he asked, "You will be okay, won't you, Sarah?"

Sarah nodded and returned his grip. A tear ran down her cheek. "Of course I'll be okay. I have finally come to believe that there are more good people in this world than bad. I no longer believe I need protection from imaginary ills. Even though"—she frowned—"even though I still sometimes wonder if that belief is right." She glanced at James and said quietly, "I've told him everything about what happened. He fears you, but he's not angry with you. He's angry with himself." She looked back at Will, and her voice sounded stronger. "He knows he could never do what you did. He knows that in the face of terrible danger, like what you faced and defeated all those years ago, he would cower and watch me die rather than risk his life to save me." She smiled. "And as odd as this may sound to you, I love him for that, because it mean he's normal. That normality separates you and me now."

She leaned forward, kissed him on the cheek, held him for a while, turned, and walked toward her husband. Will watched them both move away into the wilderness of the cemetery. He watched his sister until she was out of sight, then kept watching in case she returned. He desperately hoped she would. He knew she would not.

Then he looked down at the grave beside his feet. He knelt, placed the flowers on the grave, leaned forward, and kissed the headstone. He stayed still for a while and spoke quiet words of love and reverence. When he rose, he regarded his mother's grave for what he knew would be the last time.

For all her insight into Will, Sarah had been wrong about one thing. As he approached the terraced house in London's Paddington district, he knew that his final meeting in this city today would be with the living. Even though it was about the dead.

He knocked on the door. When it opened, a girl stood before him. Will knew she was ten years old. Will looked over her shoulder, then back at the girl. "Is your mother in?"

The girl stared at him for a moment. Her black hair hung in two braids, black ribbons woven into them. She wore a black blouse and a black skirt. She had black circles under her eyes, circles that Will knew came from crying.

The girl nodded and disappeared into the house. Will stood still and allowed the rain to hammer at his bare head.

The mother walked toward him and stopped by the open door. Like her daughter, she was dressed completely in black. Like her daughter's, her face looked exhausted and drained by emotion. She frowned at Will.

"Mrs. Abtahi, I am a representative of the British government. I knew Soroush. He was my friend."

He saw Soroush's wife open her eyes wide. He saw tears wet her cheeks. He felt sick. He felt giddy with his own emotion.

He cleared his throat, glanced up at the FOR SALE sign on the house's exterior, and looked back at the woman. "I am here to tell you that your husband helped us on certain matters. I am here to tell you that we are indebted to him. I am here to tell you that nothing we can do can in any way compensate you for your loss. But I am also here to tell you that we have taken the liberty of making arrangements to help you with your future." He felt a surge of increased sickness rise within him, and he breathed deeply to try to calm his voice. "You do not need to sell your property. We have contacted your bank and paid off your mortgage in full. We know that this will do nothing to ease your grief. But I hope that it will unburden you of any current financial worries."

Will looked down. The rain struck him with increased force. He wondered if he should say anything else. But then he turned and walked away.

He walked until he was out of sight of the house. When his legs became weak, he stopped and leaned against a wall. He felt as if he was going to vomit. He swallowed hard.

He knew that his decision to transfer his life savings to Mrs.

Abtahi's bank was the correct thing to do, savings that had been carefully accrued over seventeen years and amounted to more than a hundred thousand pounds. He knew that he had made the transfer with no care or desire to ease his conscience. He knew that he wished he had more money to give to Soroush's family.

He pushed himself away from the wall, cursing the way events had unfolded in New York. He cursed the things he had to do in his job. But more than anything else, he cursed himself.

SEVEN

I'm surprised that our paths have never crossed before." The MI6 Head of Sarajevo Station lit himself a cigarette and was clearly studying Will. "Which controllerate are you working in?"

The two men were seated at a corner table of the Inat Kuća restaurant on Veliki Alifakovac in Sarajevo. It was early evening, and there were only a handful of other diners in the place.

"For the time being, the Middle East and Africa Controllerate." Will glanced at a menu. "But that's only temporary. They've got me hopping between different desks at the moment. Apparently I'm to be posted overseas somewhere soon, so I'm currently just filling in time doing whatever's asked of me." He sighed and looked up.

The station chief continued to analyze Will. The man was in his late forties and had the air of leadership but also looked as though he had become tired over time.

Will put down his menu. "What about you, Ewan?"

The man inhaled smoke from his cigarette. "I'm only three grades below the chief, but this is as far as I go. I'm now in the stratum where politics and patronage matter more than experience and insight." He took a sip of beer. "During my career I've worked in three control-lerates, seven operational teams, and four overseas stations. Also, I've undertaken secondments to MI5, GCHQ, and the cabinet office. You may think all of that would have set me up nicely for a position on our Service's board of directors. But"—he chuckled softly—"our Service generally remembers only the last thing one did, and in my case that was to dare to suggest that we should be devoting more energies to Bosnian and Herzegovinian issues. Not my wisest move, given that an MI6 senior-management reshuffle has now produced a pro-Serb European Controllerate." Ewan shrugged. "It means that the only war going on out here now is between me, the Head of Belgrade Station, and the Head of Zagreb Station. I'm going to lose. My colleague in Belgrade will soon make Europe Controller, my colleague in Zagreb will get Central Europe Team Head, and I will be retired."

Will adjusted his position in his chair. "Tell me about your man."

Ewan nodded slowly. "He's a bit of a mongrel in every sense. His ethnicity is difficult to define, although we know that he's part Alba-nian and part Norwegian. He's had schooling in Winchester College and as a result has impeccable English." Ewan looked serious. "We recruited him during the wars and siege out here in the early 1990s and gave him the code name Lace and an alias identity. At that time he was working as what the locals called a fixer, getting armaments primarily to the Bosnian Muslim paramilitary units but ultimately delivering arms to whoever would pay him the most."

"How on earth did he pass our scrutiny to be recruited as an agent?"

Ewan spoke slowly. "You have to remember that at that time all around us was chaotic conflict. We knew that Lace had no real alle-giances and therefore no ideological motivation to help our service. But he did have two facets we thought were interesting. First, while motivated solely by money, he did take great risks to access parts of the country and groups of people who in turn gave him excellent intelligence that would have been otherwise out of our reach. Also, he was and continues to be conceited, and we believed that his vanity alone would warm him to working with our service. Both factors would not be sufficient for his recruitment in peacetime, but they were enough during *those* desperate times."

"He produced, then?"

"Yes, he produced very good intelligence for us." Ewan extinguished his cigarette and leaned forward a little. "So good that our service saved his neck from appearing before the Hague as a suspected war criminal." The man smiled. "In February 1994 he and thirty soldiers took five trucks containing guns and ammunition to a Bosnian Serb village. He was supposed to receive payment upon delivery from the head of the village, a man who was also the leader of a Serb paramilitary unit, but for whatever reason a dispute over costs broke out and the Serb refused to honor the deal. A standoff resulted between Lace's soldiers and the Serb's men. Lace knew that he was not going to get his money, and he also knew that the situation was in danger of going out of control, so ordered his men to cover his back while he exited the place. He told them that when he was safely away they were to carefully retreat from the village. To the Serb he said that business was more important than bloodshed and that he would call him in a day or two to see if terms could be peacefully agreed." Ewan sighed. "Unfortunately, when Lace was safely away from the village, his men took matters into their own hands. They gunned down the Serb's men, kept their leader alive so that he could tell others what had happened, picked out six women and six children from their homes, and forced them onto their knees. They then cut their heads off with long knives." Ewan turned up his palms in a gesture of futility. "When Lace found out what happened, he was appalled. But Lace is first and foremost a businessman, and he quickly realized that he could use the atrocity to his advantage. He allowed rumors to spread that he had ordered the massacre so that fear and respect would surround him."

Will shook his head slowly. "And as a result he would receive prompt and uncontested payments for every arms deal thereafter."

"Correct. Trouble was, word got to the UN as well. Our Service had to blow smoke all over the village affair and say he was elsewhere at the time. And as insurance, we changed his identity again, giving him the alias name Harry Solberg. That's the name we still call him, although I suspect he's got other identities we don't know about." Ewan leaned back and rubbed a hand over the nape of his neck. "They were different times then. Mind you, ever since Al Qaeda's attack on the States we seem to be back in the business of turning a blind eye to some of our agents' predispositions in order to further the greater good." He sighed again. "But I know Lace well enough to know that underneath his charm and sometimes ruthless business persona, he still unfairly blames himself for what happened in that village. It still haunts him."

"Why has he reapproached you after all these years?"

Ewan looked away and then back toward Will. "He's getting old, and age begets vanity. It happens to many of us. We want at least one last chance to prove our capabilities to others. Lace thinks he has a swan song in him."

Will was about to speak, but before he could do so, Ewan looked over his shoulder.

"And here he is now."

Lace was small, maybe in his early sixties, and was dressed in cream slacks and a blue sport jacket, with wiry but well-lacquered hair. He looked like a wealthy man who cared about his appearance. Ewan introduced Will to Lace as Charles Reed and in turn introduced Lace to Will as Harry. A waiter came to their table.

"Get me a Red Label," said Harry, shaking Will's hand. To assimilate, Ewan and Will ordered the same drink and then sat. "So you've come to meet me, Charles. Have you been to Bosnia before?" Harry produced a gleaming white smile and brushed something from one of his shoes.

"This is the first time for Charles." Ewan lit a cigarette, inhaled, and passed it to his agent. He then took out a small notepad and pencil.

Harry put away his smile and appeared to be studying Will for several seconds. He bared his teeth again. "Let's eat fish and get three more of these." He tapped his whiskey glass.

"Do you live permanently in the city?" Will asked, and then he took a sip of his Red Label. He wondered if the drink would have an adverse effect on his body, given all the medication in his system.

Harry looked at Ewan, who nodded at him and signaled to their waiter. He looked back at Will. "I've got a house on the outskirts of town, but I'm on the road a lot. My business interests require me to spend more time in hotels than at home."

Ewan laughed. "I think we all know how that feels."

Will did not laugh or even smile. "Do you like it here?"

Harry blew smoke across the table and seemed to consider the question. "It suits me as a base. And I like the fact that it's a quiet city these days."

Will narrowed his eyes. "Not too quiet, I hope. Otherwise I've just taken a wasted trip."

Ewan looked quickly between the two men. "Not a wasted trip at all, eh, Harry?" He placed both his hands flat on the table. "We think there are some things about this city that might interest you a lot."

The three of them were silent for a moment, and then Harry flashed his white teeth again. "You're not a man for small talk, are you, Charles?"

Will pointed a finger at the Head of Sarajevo Station while looking at Lace. "He is your case officer. That means he has to go through the pain of idle chat with you, of making sure you're okay, laughing at your jokes or whatever." Out of the corner of his eye, he could see Ewan frowning slightly. "I, on the other hand, am simply here to see if you have anything worthwhile for me to take back to London."

Harry smiled wider. "So you are a messenger boy, then?" He

turned to Ewan. "I would have thought your head office would have sent me someone better than that."

Ewan raised a hand. "It's irrelevant who they send, Harry. You work for me and me alone. Whatever comes out of this arrangement, it will be business as usual as far as you and I are concerned. Nobody meets you without my permission and without me being present. That is how it works."

Will leaned back in his chair and watched Harry. "I understand that you may be able to help us identify and recruit a senior Iranian military intelligence officer. But have you been told that we're looking for somebody quite specific?"

Harry tilted his face toward Ewan. "Yes, I've been told about the type of man you seek." Then he looked up again. "And to reach such a person will be a layered and complex task."

Will sighed audibly. "Do you know him?"

Harry shook his head. "As I said, a layered task. I do not know this person, but I can be useful to you because of my knowledge and connections in this region. And"—he examined one of his manicured fingernails—"such knowledge and connections can bring you a significant step closer to finding this man."

Will drummed fingers on the table between them. "I am listening to you, but for all our benefits please be brief and to the point."

For a moment Harry's smile faded. He then seemed to compose himself. "The Iranians are all over this city. It started during the war, and they've been here in different guises ever since—Iranian charities, businesses, military advisers, religious institutions, to name but some. Much of their presence is organized by Iran's IRGC and MOIS organizations."

"I'm not interested in MOIS, only IRGC."

"I know, I know." Harry swirled the remnants of whiskey in his glass. "But you must understand, it will be complicated. IRGC people can't be bought. And the man you are hunting will be the most incorruptible of them all."

"So." Will sighed again. "How can your knowledge and contacts help me?"

Harry smiled fully. "You need to take a subtle yet surgical approach to your task. Your biggest challenge will be identifying your prey, but I believe that I may have the solution to that problem."

"Go on."

Harry paused and looked at Ewan. "Everything must go through you?"

The Head of Sarajevo Station placed a hand on his agent's forearm. "Rest assured, Harry, everything goes through me."

Will caught a look on Harry's face and wondered if Ewan's words were as reassuring as they were intended to be.

Harry gulped the last of his whiskey. "I can see that you don't want to eat, Charles. That is a shame, because the trout here is excellent." He placed the glass down on the dining table. "There is an Arab woman who used to work out of Sarajevo during the war all those years ago. She was then a very young journalist, but my business interests brought me close to her because she was also working for the Iranians. They used her to discreetly deliver Tehran cash to Bosnian Muslim paramilitary units across the country, money that was often"—Harry smiled—"then used to buy my goods. I heard that she was controlled by one man who was in charge of all Iranian activity in Bosnia during the Balkan wars. I also heard that the man was an IRGC Qods Force officer."

"That was a very long time ago, and we've no way of knowing whether that man is of interest to us now."

Harry raised his hands in the air. "I know, but it could be a good starting point."

Will recalled Alistair's words during their meeting on the preceding day:

To start with, I want you to pose as a regular intelligence officer.

He felt anger surge within him, and he breathed slowly to calm the emotion. "This is all you have?" He directed the question to Harry and then glanced at Ewan, who in turn lowered his gaze.

Harry seemed unfazed. "You will see, it is as good a starting point as any."

"All right, Harry. As you say, we will see. Who is the woman, and where is she?"

Harry rubbed his hands together. "I knew you'd be interested. Her name is Lana Beseisu, and for years she's been living in Paris working as a freelance journalist. I've seen some of her articles in the French and British press and specialist journals. She should be easy to track down." Harry's hands stilled, and he now clasped them as if in prayer. "There's also one other thing I should mention. As well as working for the Qods Force officer during the wars here, there was a strong rumor that Lana was his lover."

"What do you think?" Ewan lightly stamped his feet on the ground. He and Will were outside now, having watched Harry depart ten minutes earlier. It was close to 11:00 P.M., and despite being on one of the city's main tourist streets, the men were alone. Snow was falling.

Will looked down at the snow under his feet and then back up at Ewan. "You know what I think."

Ewan sighed and nodded. "I realize Harry's idea is a long shot. Does head office have any other targeting leads?"

"None that I'm privy to."

"Then a lot rests on this woman Lana." Ewan exhaled and turned fully to face Will. He frowned. "Given my seniority and length of service within MI6, it *is* incredible that we've never met before."

Will shrugged.

Ewan steeled his gaze. "The service may now be blocking any chances of further promotion for me, but one thing it can't take away from my twenty-three years of work for MI6 is a highly tuned ability to read people."

"It comes with the territory."

"It does." Ewan stood very still and kept his gaze locked on Will. "You don't look like a messenger boy or indeed a man who does what others tell him to do."

"Looks can be deceptive." Will smiled. "Maybe you're losing your touch."

"Maybe." Ewan held his gaze for a moment longer and then looked away. Snow fell fast over his face. "Two years ago I heard a rumor within MI6 about an event in Algeria. A female MI6 agent and her daughter had been kidnapped by Al Qaeda, which made it clear that they were going to execute them both for no reason other than publicity. MI6 quickly learned where the kidnappers were most likely holed up with their captives and notified the SAS in Hereford. An eight-man SAS team was scrambled to rescue the agent and her daughter, but during their flight across to Africa it was learned that the kidnappers had decided to speed up the time of the execution. The SAS team had no chance of reaching their destination before the mother and daughter would have their heads cut off."

Will yawned in an attempt to look tired and bored. Snowfall around him became heavier.

"But—and this is where the rumor gets interesting—an MI6 officer was nearer to the Al Qaeda hideout. A man who did not operate out of an MI6 station, an embassy, or indeed anywhere official. A man whose existence was so carefully concealed that even current and former British prime ministers are sworn to uphold lifelong secrecy about his existence. A man who is a lone wolf and lethal."

Will tried to smile. "Rumors."

"But this was a well-founded rumor." Ewan did not smile. "Anyway, despite having no authority to do so, this mysterious MI6 man goes into the Al Qaeda house on his own, kills all thirteen terrorists, frees the woman and her daughter, and walks them to Algeria's border with Morocco, where he hands them over to the now-arrived SAS team. With his job done, he then disappears."

Will checked the time on his watch and stretched.

Ewan looked back at him and said nothing for a while. Then, "I often wonder if that man really exists. It would be wonderful to know he does."

Will stopped his attempts to show fatigue and turned fully to face Ewan. "If he did exist and you met him, what would you say to him?"

Ewan nodded slowly, and the faintest of smiles appeared on his face. "I would say to him that I do not envy the huge burden of responsibility he must carry, nor the isolated life he must surely lead."

As he stopped speaking, Ewan spun around and collapsed to the ground. The movement was too quick to be self-induced. Will immediately stepped back two paces and looked up and down the street and at windows and rooftops. The streetlights around him produced only a dim glow, which, coupled with the snowfall, meant he could barely see beyond thirty meters. He kept still for a moment and crouched down beside Ewan's body. He placed a thumb and forefinger around the man's nose and pulled Ewan's head sideways. The man had been shot through the brain with a silenced weapon. Will checked the man's breathing. Ewan was dead.

He patted his hands against Ewan's legs and stomach, reached into one of the dead man's pockets, and drew out his cell phone. He placed it into his own jacket and rose to a standing position, surveying his surroundings and listening carefully. He could not see or hear anything that suggested a nearby attacker. Besides, even if the killer was still nearby, Will decided that he would have been shot already if he were also a target. He thrust his hands into his overcoat pockets and walked rapidly away from Ewan's body toward the city's side streets and alleys.

EIGHT

Will looked out of the adjacent window and could see the first indications of sunrise. He was sat in an Air France carrier, and the early-morning light gave glimpses of the snow-clad Swiss Alps beneath him. He took a sip of his tea and rubbed his temples. He shook his head as he pictured Ewan twist and fall down dead, then sighed as he recalled the man's words:

I often wonder if that man really exists.

He looked away from the Alps and closed his eyes. He rarely dwelt on past missions, but Ewan's words forced snippets of what had happened in Algeria into his mind.

He remembered Alistair's message:

The team can't get there in time. The woman and her child are going to be slaughtered.

He recalled his own response:

I'm going to stop that from happening.

And he recalled Alistair's command:

No you aren't. It's too dangerous.

He remembered observing the house, seeing men arrive, seeing lights go on and off in rooms, checking the time on his watch, seeing dusk turn to night, pulling out his handgun and knife, breathing carefully, focusing on the gun-carrying sentry by the front door, sprinting at him, thrusting his knife into the man's stomach. He remembered running into the house, shooting as he moved along corridors and through rooms and seeing men fall as his bullets struck them in the head. He remembered jumping down a set of stairs into a large basement. He remembered his heart beating fast as he saw the camera and other equipment. He remembered thinking the room looked like a film studio. He remembered seeing two men rush toward him with guns raised. He remembered kicking one of them away as he shot the other, then shooting the prone man. He remembered training his gun on the four men who stood behind the kneeling mother and her seven-year-old daughter. He remembered how the men smiled as they held their swords firmly against their captives' throats. He remembered hesitating for the tiniest of moments as he calculated the distance between each man. He remembered shooting four bullets in less than a second. He remembered seeing all four men fall down, each with a bullet in his brain.

He could see the prisoners before him now. He could see himself cutting through their ropes. He could see the mother shaking with fear and shock. He could see the girl look at him, grab him with both arms, and pull him to her. He could see him holding her gently and telling her she was safe now. He recalled thinking that nothing else mattered to him besides saving these two innocent lives. He could see him lifting the girl in his arms. And he remembered her words:

Did God send you?

NINE

Will had arrived in Paris.

It was the morning after Ewan's assassination, and the city was covered with frost rather than snow. Will pulled out a pad and checked his handwritten notes again. Via telephone, Alistair had provided him with an address and a concise biography of the person he wanted to meet. Will closed the pad and placed it back in his coat pocket. He stepped out of the Charles de Gaulle International Airport terminal and hailed a taxi.

Within thirty-five minutes, he was in the Marais district of the city. He paid the taxi driver and walked northwest along rue Sainte-Croix-de-la-Bretonnerie before turning right on to a narrow side street. Moments later the small terraced house was before him. Will checked the time on his watch. It was nearly 8:00 A.M., and he hoped that the occupant had not yet left for work or other duties. He knocked.

The woman who opened the door was tall, with silky teak hair that she had gathered and rested over one shoulder and breast. She was beautiful, and it was obvious to Will that beneath her thigh-length sweater and jeans she had an excellent figure. However, it was her face that interested him. She was stunning, but she also looked as though her nerves had been visibly fraying over several years, and as a result she had a hunted look.

"Miss Lana Beseisu?" Will smiled as unthreateningly as he could.

"Yes." The woman frowned and looked cautious.

"No need to worry. My name is Nicholas Cree. I'm with the British embassy here in Paris, and I need to update our records of your residency in this country. May I come in?"

The woman retained her frown. "I filled in some new forms only a few months ago. You should have everything you need."

Will rubbed his hands together to make it look as though he were look cold. "We should, but unfortunately our database has crashed, and as a result our records are a mess. It's caused chaos, and the only way we can try to get out of this muddle is to update our records manually. If we don't get it done, there will be all sorts of bureaucratic problems for British residents living here in France." Will folded his arms and squeezed them tight against his chest. "I could come back later, but it would be great if we could do this now. I've got another eleven people to see today who are in exactly the same position as you."

Lana stood still for a moment and then nodded. "My mother's at the health clinic. I need to be around for her when she gets back, so it's better for me if we deal with it now." She glanced quickly up the street and then back at Will. "All right, come in."

Will followed her through a small hallway into a cluttered living area. The place was strewn with books and newspapers. Lana grabbed an armful of journals and papers from a chair and dumped them next to an open laptop on a small table. "Please, sit."

Will removed his overcoat to reveal his suit and sat down. He took out a pen and his small notepad as Lana pulled out and perched on a dining chair.

Lana smiled. "I did not know that the British embassy had such handsome men working there. What do you want to know?"

Will sighed. "I do apologize in advance. We're in a thorough mess, so I'm afraid I'm going to have to confirm with you some of the basics." He looked down at his notepad and spoke quickly. "Half Jordanian, half Saudi. But you've had a British passport for nearly twenty years."

"That's correct." Lana lit a cigarette. "My mother managed to get me one when she was living in London." She looked worried. "We only moved to France a few years ago because of her health and so that she could be close to a particular specialist. She has chronic anemia, and they have to keep running tests. We intend to return to the U.K. as soon as she's better."

Will held up a hand. "Rest assured we have no problem with you and your mother having British passports. The only problem the embassy has is with an IT database system that was supposed to make our lives easier but instead has made them hellish." He looked down at his supposed notes again. "Now, it says here that your father is deceased, and your mother is obviously living with you. You're single. Your vocation is journalism."

Lana grimaced. "When I can get the work."

Will tried to look sympathetic as he wrote nothing in particular on his notepad. "And besides your mother you have no other dependents with you in France?"

"None."

Will nodded and scanned the tip of his pen across notes. "I can see that you've regularly checked in with our embassy—that's good, as it *normally* makes our lives a lot easier."

Lana tapped ash. "Anything else?"

"It's just a formality, but can I see your passport?" He checked his watch as if he were in a hurry, then smiled. "I always have to confirm the identity of people I interview."

"Sure." Lana stood and looked around the untidy room, frowning. She walked to a spilling-over wall bookshelf on the opposite wall, rummaged among some loose papers, and returned with the passport. She handed it to Will and sat down.

He quickly glanced at the passport's last pages. He nodded, handed it back to Lana, and made a small scrawl on his notebook. He was satisfied that the woman before him was Lana Beseisu rather than a protective housemate or friend. He decided to change the nature of the meeting.

"Let me just check if there's anything else." Will spent a few moments reading his notes again. He opened his eyes a little wider and tried to look impressed. "You were in Bosnia during the wars in the early nineties?"

Lana laughed. "That was another lifetime ago. I was barely out of school."

He went on reading, even though he had memorized the notes before coming here. "You initially worked for a German media outlet in Sarajevo before they closed down their representative office there, but you then got approached to work with an Iranian-backed newspaper based in the city." Will nodded. "Must have been terrifying times, working in a war zone?"

Lana shrugged. "I was young then. I was blasé to the danger."

Will slowly closed his notepad and put it away. "The naïveté of youth." He flashed a smile that cut off as quickly as it had appeared. "Still, you would not have been so naïve as to not know that the newspaper you worked for was in reality a front for the Iranian military intelligence services."

"What?" Lana looked shocked.

"Maybe they got their hooks into you slowly and subtly, but pretty soon you would have known exactly whom you were working for and what you were doing for them. After all, journalists don't secretly take Iranian money to Bosnian paramilitary units spread across the country. That's a job for a spy."

Lana's shock seemed to turn into anger. Her eyes narrowed, and she spoke slowly. "Who are you?"

"Mind you"—Will ignored her question and grinned—"it would have been a logistical nightmare to work on your own in a besieged city without guidance and time-sensitive instructions. Which can only mean that you had someone with you in Sarajevo. Maybe even an Iranian intelligence officer." He frowned. "More specifically, an IRGC Qods Force officer." He smiled again. "But you would have been lonely as well. I'd say that it was probable your Qods Force man gave you comfort as well as orders."

"Whoever you are, get out of my house!" Lana was standing.

Will did not move. His speech was sharp. "Whoever I am or am not, I am most certainly someone who can change your life for the worse. So I suggest you sit back down."

Lana seemed to hesitate. She then reseated herself and picked up her cigarette with a shaking hand. "What do you want?"

Will leaned closer to her. "I need to know if you are still in contact with the Iranians. I need to know if you are still in contact with the Qods Force man."

Lana stubbed out her cigarette, and a tear slid down her cheek. "Who are you?" she repeated.

Will leaned farther forward. "I work for MI6. And I will not leave this house until you tell me what I need to know."

Lana shook her head, and tears were now freely spilling from both eyes. "Please don't do this."

Will made his voice stern. "Lana, look at me."

She wiped the back of a hand against her face.

"I am a British intelligence officer. I have no desire to hurt you or get you in trouble. That's not why I'm here. But you will clearly understand the implications of being a past or present Iranian spy who has a British passport. We call people like that traitors, so unless you help me, the alternative is prison. And the French authorities will not stand in our way to obtain such justice." Will's voice was now loud. "Are you still in contact with the Qods Force man or any of his friends?"

Lana shook her head vigorously. "No. No."

"Anyone from Iran?"

"Nobody." She was sobbing now.

"We can check. If we ask the French security services to analyze your phone calls over the last year or so and they find just one number dialed to Iran, you realize that all will be lost for you?"

"Then check!" Lana spat the words.

"Prison is not my objective—it does not serve my purpose in any way. I have another reason for needing to know if you are in contact with the Qods Force man." Will leaned even closer. "Let me put this bluntly. If you are still in contact with the man or his colleagues, I can save you from prison. If not, then you are of no use to me and I will throw you to the British judicial system."

"I've done nothing wrong. I've never spied on Britain. All I did was to try to help stop some Bosnian Serb fanatics from being given carte blanche to commit genocide."

"Very touching. But you were still a covert employee of an enemy of the West. And who knows what else would come out at a trial? What actions your Qods Force man may have taken based upon the secrets you fed him? Maybe you helped stop genocide, but maybe you wittingly or unwittingly helped fuel it. A British trial will be supported by United Nations evidence. They will no doubt be able, fairly or otherwise, to pin any number of atrocities on you."

Lana dropped her head into her hands and pulled at her hair. "I understand, I understand, but I've not had any contact with him since 1995. And I've never had contact with his colleagues or anyone else from Iran."

"Prove it to me."

"Oh, come on!" Lana sounded exasperated. "How?"

Will leaned back in his chair and considered. He decided that for the moment he had been hard enough on her. Quietly, he said, "Tell me more about your time in Bosnia."

Lana stared at him for a while and then pulled out another cigarette, lighting it with deliberation. She inhaled deeply and then spoke in a thin voice. "After I graduated from university, I took a job as a freelance journalist with the Düsseldorf-based media outlet you mentioned. They sent me to Sarajevo in 1991 to cover Bosnia and Herzegovina's impending referendum for independence from Yugoslavia. Shortly after my arrival, all hell broke out in the Balkans, and one of my colleagues in Sarajevo was killed. Düsseldorf then lost its nerve and decided to cover the conflict from Germany." Lana shrugged. "And I was therefore without work."

"That's when you were approached?"

"Not immediately." She took another draw on her cigarette. "It was another two months before that happened. After I lost my job, I kept myself occupied helping in any way that I could: getting food parcels to the city from the airport, working in shelters, doing basic first aid—anything, really. They were terrible times. And then"—she studied the burning embers of her cigarette before returning her gaze to Will—"then he introduced himself to me."

"His name?"

Lana shook her head slowly. "I never found out his name."

"Age?"

"He was then in his late twenties."

"Why did you agree to work with him?"

Lana's smile faded, and she looked down at her feet. "The first time I met him, I was working in a makeshift hospital trying to care for victims of bombs and sniper bullets. He came up to me and told me that he worked for a special unit in the Iranian army. He told me that Bosnian Muslims were being slaughtered throughout the country and beyond. He told me that he'd been sent to Bosnia to try to help stop that from happening. He said he needed my help."

"Why you?"

Lana slowly turned her gaze back up toward Will. "Maybe because I am a Muslim. Maybe because I looked young and impressionable. Maybe because he had few other options available to him."

"Or maybe because you still had a media identity pass, which in theory offered you a bit of protection when traveling?"

Lana said nothing.

"What did you do for him?"

She coughed. "Initially it was mapmaking. Establishing secret routes in and out of the city, finding small ways to breach the siege. Then, after a few months and when the maps were ready, he started using me to take cash to the Muslim paramilitary groups beyond Sarajevo so that they could buy armaments, food, clothing, and medicine. I would make the journeys, then come back and report anything he needed to know, and then he would send me on new journeys. I did that for nearly four years."

Will was silent for a moment and then said quietly, "Extremely dangerous work. If you had been caught on one of those trips, you could have been raped, tortured, and executed."

"I know." Lana's face had grown stoical. Her tears had ceased.

Will tapped his fingers on a knee before bringing them to a stop. "Tell me about the man."

Lana extinguished her cigarette and then immediately lit another. "I worked out recently that over the four-year period I saw him on fourteen occasions, and then only for a few hours or less at a time. It was only during the last three meetings that we became"—she shifted slightly in her chair—"better acquainted."

"That's still fourteen meetings. What can you tell me about them?"

Lana frowned. "To start with, he seemed inexperienced and headstrong, but nevertheless very clever. Toward the end of the war, though, he seemed totally in control of his work. In some ways he had also grown cold and extremely calculating. And it became clear to me that this unit he worked for, the Qods Force, was in some way testing him, encouraging him to prove himself to them."

Will's eyes narrowed. "What do you mean?"

"He said to me once that he was the only Qods Force officer in the Balkans, that there were others from his unit but they were merely foot soldiers, that Bosnia was just an overseas school for him. He said that if he could demonstrate sufficient promise in the former

Yugoslavia, his masters had significant plans for him beyond the war."

"What plans?"

Lana raised her palms. "I'll never know. Because NATO joined the war in 1995 and fighting ended almost overnight. He disappeared, and I've not heard from or seen him ever since."

Will exhaled deeply. He glanced away toward the far side of the room and began tapping his fingers again. He looked back at Lana. "It benefits me to believe you."

Lana breathed heavily. "I'm glad. I have told you the truth."

Will held up a palm. "I told you that it *benefited* me to believe you, not that I *do* believe you—or certainly not that I believe you have told me the entire truth." Will patted his hand against the breast pocket holding his notebook. "For example, when the war ended, why would you then fly to Rome and present yourself to the British embassy there? Why would you plead to them that you had information about the Iranians' intentions to use their experience from the wars in Yugoslavia to strike Western targets and Arabian Gulf targets? Why would a noble heroine, who was concerned only about saving Muslim lives during the war, ask the embassy to pay her money in exchange for the information she claimed she had, information that was inconsistent and clearly fabricated?"

Lana sighed. "I was desperate."

"That is certainly possible. There are also a number of other possibilities. One such is that you felt rejected by your former agent handler, the Qods Force officer who was also your lover. You wanted revenge against him and therefore concocted some rubbish about Iranian terrorist plans. You did so purely out of spite."

"I was fucking desperate and alone." Lana stood suddenly, and her chair fell backward. "Even though he would never deign to give me his name, I still shared my bed with the man. And then one day he was gone and I was penniless. Yes, I asked your embassy for money, and when they turned me away with a sneer, I did not stop there." Lana's voice had grown loud and frenzied. "I got on the next available flight to Abu Dhabi. I told the Emiratis a similar story. You know what they did?"

Will said nothing. As he was listening to her words, he was also rapidly processing and calculating the implications of what she was saying. He was starting to feel a sense of optimism about Harry's lead.

"They put me in a prison in their desert for forty days and beat me because they, too, said I was lying." Lana kicked the prone chair away and then took a step closer to Will. "I'll show you, Nicholas Cree."

She swung her arms up to remove her sweater. She wore nothing beneath it. Her upper body showed multiple old scars, each at least six inches long. She turned, and he could see that her back was covered with more of the same.

Will sprang up and grabbed her sweater, which he held out to her. He said softly, "Here, get dressed. There was no need to show me your wounds."

Lana frowned at him, and fresh tears emerged. She pulled on her sweater with shaking hands and said, "Bamboo canes. And they did worse than that. My back teeth and toenails were removed with pliers. I was drowned and then revived at least five times."

For the briefest of moments, Will wanted to hold her, to comfort her and tell her she would never suffer like that again. But he knew he had to continue to appear threatening. It was a part of his job he detested. He nodded and sat back down. "And I bet that during that horrible forty-day period your anger against your former lover must have intensified significantly."

Lana sat and lit herself yet another cigarette. She seemed to be calming down. "I tried to tell myself that my anger was futile. I tried to tell myself that he must have been killed by the Serbs or maybe captured by the UN or NATO."

"Either is a strong possibility."

She shook her head and smiled. "I was merely fooling myself. He took my maps. He got out of the country alive. I'm certain."

Will sat quiet for a moment. Then he said, "How do you feel about this man now?"

Lana waved a hand dismissively. "I was a young girl then, full of energy and purpose. But since the end of the war and my experience in Abu Dhabi, I've spent the rest of my life feeling hollow and frightened. I'm approaching middle age now, and all I have to show for my life is four years of doing the right thing in Sarajevo. But even that"— she raised a finger toward Will—"was discarded by him. He used me for what he needed, cast me aside, and sullied the only good memory I have." She looked around her and then directly at Will. "How do I feel? I feel that he has stolen my life."

Will nodded slowly. He kept his eyes locked on Lana. When he next spoke, it was with a firm and deliberate voice. "I can give you your life back."

She frowned. "How?"

He rose from his chair and picked up his overcoat, then turned and looked down at Lana. "I'm going to try to lure him out into the open. And when he's there, you can watch me steal *his* life."

TEN

Sixty minutes later Will was in a taxi heading back to Charles de Gaulle International Airport. He took out his medication and popped pills into his mouth. He then realized that today was the first day he'd been without pain; his body was starting to feel strong and confident again. He reached into another pocket and pulled out Ewan's cell phone. He knew that MI6's European Controllerate would conduct a full analysis of all data within the phone, but right now he needed only one number. He found it and dialed.

On the fourth ring, a man answered. "Ewan, I was just thinking about you. Let's meet soon. But nothing serious this time—just a few drinks."

The man's voice belonged to Harry, and he sounded jocular.

"Harry, this is Charles Reed. I'm with Ewan right now, and he's lent me his phone to speak to you."

"Ah, Charles. The messenger boy who does not like small talk. What can I do for you?"

Will smiled a little. "Ewan thought we had a good meeting last night. So did I. Listen, there have been some positive developments since we met, and I wondered if we could get together again . . . just so I can run some ideas by you?"

There was a pause before Harry spoke. "Sure. Is Ewan going to join us?"

"Normally he would, but on this occasion it will just be me, I'm afraid."

"Okay." Harry sounded unfazed. "There's one thing, though. After our meeting I had to dash straight off and catch a flight to Munich. I had some business problems to attend to in Germany. I thought I'd be back in Bosnia tonight, but it looks like I might be stuck here for a couple of days. Can our meeting wait?"

Will thought for a moment and then said, "It's probably best that we meet sooner rather than later. I can be with you by early evening."

"Great." Harry sounded very upbeat. "It means that this old man will have some company tonight. Meet me at my hotel room in the Königshof—it will be a bit more private. Say seven P.M.?"

"Done." Will closed the cell phone and looked out the taxi window beside him. His car was pulling up at the airport. He checked his watch. He had just enough time to get his luggage out of storage and buy a business-class Lufthansa ticket for the early-afternoon flight.

Will walked through the grand lobby area of Munich's finest five-star hotel and approached the concierge. He gave the name Charles Reed and said that he was expected by Harry Solberg, a guest of the hotel. The concierge checked a computer screen, nodded, and gave Will a room number and directions to see Harry.

Within two minutes Will was standing outside Harry's room. He pulled out the purchase he'd made at a small shop on Rosenheimer Strasse during his journey from Munich's airport to this hotel. He cupped the purchase in his left hand so that it was held flush against the back of his forearm, out of sight. He pressed the door's buzzer.

"Charles, good to see you." Harry was dressed in cream slacks and a pale pink shirt. He looked energized and extended a hand, which Will shook. He grinned, baring his white teeth. "Come and have a look at my room. It's incredible."

Will followed Harry into the room graded superior by the hotel. It was clear that Harry was a man of means who sought luxury. The place was as big as a reasonably large apartment.

"What do you think?" Harry stood with his back to Will, his arms outstretched.

Will stepped forward rapidly. He punched a knee into the small of Harry's back and swept a leg around the man's ankles, throwing his right arm around his throat. Harry fell to his knees. Will brought his left hand up before Harry's face. He placed the tip of the German hunting knife against Harry's right eye. He said nothing, holding the man in his frozen grip.

Harry remained absolutely still. "What in God's name are you doing?"

Will did not reply.

"What have I done wrong?" Harry wheezed the words.

Will did not answer.

"What have I done wrong?" Harry repeated.

Will brought his mouth close to Harry's ear. "Who else knew about our meeting last night?"

"If you mean did I tell anyone else that I was meeting you and Ewan, then the answer is no, I did not."

"A lover? A business associate? Anyone?"

"Nobody."

"Somebody knew." Will tightened his grip. "Because after you left, a professional shot my colleague dead."

"Ewan's dead?"

"Yes."

Harry wheezed again. "Mr. Reed. I've had to live my entire life being suspicious of people, and that includes people who might think they are friends or colleagues of mine. I would never have let slip to anyone that I was going to the Inat Kuća restaurant, let alone that I was meeting members of British Intelligence there. I have far too much to lose by being careless."

"Someone could have followed you."

"Could have, yes, but to what end? In any case, someone could have followed Ewan. Or you, for that matter."

"We're trained to spot surveillance. You're not."

"I thought you said Ewan was killed by a professional."

Will moved his mouth away from Harry's ear. He thought for a moment and leaned in again. "You were officially retired from service to MI6 over fifteen years ago. Why did you reapproach us after all of that time?"

Harry said nothing, and Will heard him breathe in deeply before exhaling.

"It is not a difficult question." Will slightly adjusted his hold on the hunting knife while keeping its tip exactly in place against Harry's eye.

Harry breathed again. "I know. But now that you have posed the question, I realize that my response will sound foolish."

"Under the circumstances, sounding foolish should be of little concern to you."

Harry groaned before speaking. "Lovers? Friends? I have none. For every million dollars that I have made, I have also made a hundred enemies. And that has suited me just fine. But enemies don't give you adulation."

"But you decided that MI6 could," Will whispered into Harry's ear. "Because we spend time with our agents, listen to them, tell them how vital their work is, and make them feel special."

Harry seemed offended. "Certainly that's what Ewan did for me. You're obviously different."

"Adulation?"

"I said it would sound foolish."

Will moved the blade to Harry's other eye. "Well, here I am, spending quality time with you and hanging on your every word."

He could feel Harry's heart pumping faster through his carotid artery.

Harry sighed. "Charles, you have to understand. I need this. I did nothing to compromise Ewan's safety. I would never do anything to jeopardize my work for you guys."

"And what exactly is that work?"

"I gave you a name. The woman Lana. You can use her to identify your target."

"That means you are now redundant."

"Only if you fail to realize my potential. You can use me in other ways: my knowledge, my contacts—God, you can even use my money if you need to."

Will tightened his hand around the knife's hilt. He knew that he would have to move the blade only a few millimeters to permanently blind Harry. He frowned as an idea came to him. "I have no need for your money. But I am prepared to test you and your contacts." He smiled. "I want you to find out if there are any other IRGC officers working in Central Europe. I require only one name. And it is crucial that the person is working in an official capacity rather than covertly, maybe someone attached to an Iranian embassy or working as a military observer. Can you do that for me?"

"There are no other IRGC Qods Force officers working in Europe. The lead I've given you remains the best."

"I'm not asking you to find me another Qods Force officer. Just a regular IRGC person. Can you do that?"

"If it's what MI6 wants, then yes."

"Forget MI6. You work only for me now." Will's lips were touching Harry's ear. "Only me."

"Yes, yes!" Harry's voice was urgent.

"Good. Now I believe that you and I have a much better understanding of each other. Would you agree?"

"Of course. Under the circumstances, why would I say anything different?"

Will smiled. "Very good, Harry. Very good indeed. But there is still one other thing I need from you."

"Tell me." Sweat from Harry's forehead had begun to course down his face.

"The Qods Force commander. You must know who he is."

"I don't! Nobody did!" Harry shouted the words.

Will slowly moved the hunting knife away from Harry's eye and brought it down against his throat.

"Please, no!" Harry gasped. "Please, no!"

Will's words were now barely audible. "Unlike you, I have no need for company, acceptance, or adulation. All I need is a name. And I'm absolutely convinced that a man like you, a man who by his own admission is so well connected in the Balkans, would not have been able to go about his business during the war without knowing the name of this Iranian."

Will brushed the edge of the blade up and down against Harry's skin.

"We all gave him names." Harry's body was shuddering. "But they were our names, not his."

"You are a businessman. Your brain deals in trades." Will stopped moving the knife. "The trade I am offering you is beyond obvious."

Harry's legs began to shake. "A rumor! Just a rumor!"

Will sighed and moved the knife a hairsbreadth from Harry's throat. "A rumor?"

"That's all, Charles. That's all. That's all."

Will brought the knife up to Harry's eyes. "What do you think I am?"

"God only knows."

"Maybe I know, too. Or maybe I don't." He could see Harry's eyes in the reflection on the blade, and they were wide with fear. He wondered if his actions were too much. He decided they were not, because he knew that a man like Harry had to be tamed first before telling the truth. "But for now I'm prepared to play the good intelligence officer and listen to your conjecture and rumors. What did he call himself?"

A fresh sweat emerged across Harry's whole face. He emitted a noise that sounded like a moan. His left arm began to twitch, and then his whole body convulsed. He took several deep breaths before speaking. "Megiddo. We believed that he called himself Megiddo."

ELEVEN

"It's been only seventy-two hours since I gave you my instruction." Alistair took a sip of his Château Margaux. "And within that time you have been to three countries, terrified two people into working for us, and witnessed the murder of a senior MI6 man."

"I did advise you to send a regular intelligence officer." Will smiled and pushed his own wine to one side.

"And maybe your advice was correct."

Will narrowed his eyes. "But that officer would have met Lace, taken notes, and then returned to London to give you a well-written but ultimately useless report. I, on the other hand, have given you our target."

The two men were sitting at an oak booth in Simpson's on London's Strand. The restaurant was an elderly eatery, popular with government mandarins and senior business executives. It was also a place to eat meat, and among many other things Will's Controller was certainly a consumer of flesh.

Alistair peered at him. "Do you trust Harry and Lana?"

Will shook his head. "No. Harry thinks he's reached a state of grace where business no longer matters to him, but he will always be someone who sees enemies around him. If it came to it, the only side he can choose is his own. Lana is motivated by abandonment-fueled anger and a desire for meaning, but those are dangerous and unstable emotions. Trust will never come into play, but I believe I can channel and control both Harry and Lana's mind-sets to my advantage."

Alistair looked out over the rest of the restaurant and its lunchtime diners. "What will you eat?"

"Nothing."

"As you like." Alistair took another sip of his drink. "You'll need to be careful with Lace."

"I know." Will spoke the words slowly. He thought for a moment before saying "I'm certain that Harry did nothing careless to lead a killer to Ewan. But somebody knew that our man was going to be at that restaurant. Do you have a view on Ewan's death?"

Alistair shook his head. "I suspect that Ewan was running up to fifty agents and as many operations out of his Sarajevo Station. There are a number of people of whom he could have fallen foul."

Will nodded. "Harry's given me the Iranian man's code name," he said quietly.

Alistair cursed. "A code name? That's hardly going to help identify the man." He shook his head. "What is it?"

"Megiddo."

Alistair's eyes immediately narrowed. "Megiddo? You're sure?"

Will frowned. "Of course."

Alistair said nothing for nearly a minute while continuing to hold his gaze on Will. He then nodded slowly, and Will could see that a slight smile had emerged on his face.

"Is the name relevant?"

Alistair broke his gaze with Will and seemed lost in thought. He muttered something, but whatever the words were, they seemed more for his own benefit. "I have moments where I wonder if I have overcapitalized upon your terrifying desire for retribution against the world's ills."

Will leaned forward and spoke firmly. "Do not wonder anything about me, Alistair. I make my own decisions."

Alistair regarded him and smiled, but the look seemed bitter. "I know you do," he said quietly. "You always do. But I sometimes wonder what sort of man you might now be had those men not murdered your mother when you were barely out of boyhood."

Will leaned even closer. "It's a pointless thought. When she died, my childhood died."

"Memories don't die, William."

"I have too few to know."

"There may be more to be discovered."

"What do you mean?"

Alistair looked down and seemed to ignore the question. "My interest is anything but pointless." When he looked up again, he said, "I wonder how long I can continue to exploit your incredible mental and physical strength before I can tell myself that I have failed in my duty. I wonder what sort of man I am continuing to allow you to be. I wonder if I am about to make things even worse for you."

"What do you mean?" Will repeated.

Alistair nodded. "Your tiny number of childhood memories has produced a man who takes absolute measures to kill those you deem worthy of such punishment and who saves those you deem helpless. You have left very little if anything for yourself. But"—he pointed at Will—"there is still a chance for you to address that."

Will rested back into his chair and exhaled loudly. "I do my work. That's all that matters to me."

"I don't believe you." Alistair spoke sharply and quickly. He glanced around the restaurant and then back at Will. Sighing, he lowered his voice. "You're a good man, William. I of all people know that. But I also know that you have exceptional skills, which I have shamelessly utilized for the sake of our work. That is what I do; it is my job.

But"—he shook his head—"there is a part of me that hopes you will one day find peace and happiness. And I know that is what you really want, too."

Will frowned. Alistair's eyes were locked onto him and seemed to be burrowing though his mind and soul. He felt a moment of total discomfort and had to look away. He wanted Alistair to say something, but the man just sat in silence. He wanted any distraction to stop him from reflecting on his Controller's words. However, a surge of thoughts entered his mind and culminated in one unspoken sentence, *You're right, Alistair. So please release me now from your control and let me try to find that happiness and peace.*

The Controller was still staring at him.

Will breathed in deeply. He felt anger rise within him, anger that Alistair was perhaps the only man who could, with words alone, strip off his armor and lay bare his compassion and his heart and his fantasies about a life different from that which he had. He wondered, though, whether Alistair knew everything. He wondered if the man knew that what terrified Will the most was the idea of taking those first few steps toward a different life. He decided that Alistair did know everything. He decided that Alistair was testing him.

Will smiled. "I'm sure that right now we have more pressing matters to discuss."

Alistair remained very still for a moment, exhaled loudly, and then smiled. "Indeed we do." He lowered his voice. "Have you ever been told about Operation Hourglass?"

Will shook his head.

Alistair inhaled deeply. "In 1979 we had advance indications that the shah's corrupt regime was going to be imminently overthrown and replaced with an Islamic republic, and we needed to understand what that meant for a reborn Iran. Specifically, we needed to understand what decisions were being made by the revolutionaries about Iran's future military strength and its intentions toward its Arab and Israeli neighbors. But we knew that our existing Iranian agents and allies, some of whom were SAVAK officers loyal to the shah, would be redundant or killed as soon as Iran's old regime collapsed. As a result, we were worried that we would be left with an almighty intelligence blind spot."

Alistair quickly surveyed the room before settling his gaze back on their oak booth. "We shared these concerns with our CIA friends, and it was decided that we would construct a joint operation, code name Hourglass, to try to drain every available MI6 and CIA Iranian asset of relevant intelligence before we lost them to the revolution."

Alistair placed his hands on the knot of his tie and pushed upward, even though Will could see no indication that it had slipped even a fraction of an inch. "The logistics in putting together Hourglass were huge. The operation involved approximately four hundred intelligence officers and analysts from Langley and London as well as signals-intelligence support from the National Security Agency and Government Communications Headquarters. But worse than that, there was a tortuous political resistance to declaring MI6 assets to the CIA and CIA assets to MI6. However, in the end we overcame that resistance and as a result constructed a joint-operation task force that was probably unprecedented in its level of collaboration."

He went on quietly. "Once the green light was given, Hourglass immediately commenced approaching and debriefing some two thousand agents. It was an enormous task, and for three months Hourglass intelligence officers barely had time to sleep. The analysts had an even harder task, as they were charged with evaluating and collating all of the intelligence that was coming back from the agent debriefings. They achieved their task, but"—Alistair smiled ruefully—"the result was an unwieldy mess." He narrowed his eyes and spoke more quickly. "The agents had produced conflicting intelligence, conjecture, rumors, and blatantly self-serving lies. It was a disaster."

"Surely we should have predicted such an outcome? When agents are put under that amount of pressure, they often tell us what they think we want to hear."

Alistair shook his head. "We had no choice, because time was our enemy." He placed his hands flat on the table. "The operation was about to be closed down when, by chance, the Hourglass task force struck gold. Or at least we thought that was the case."

For the briefest of moments, Will spotted what he believed looked like regret on his Controller's face.

Alistair exhaled and brought his hands together. "A junior CIA officer, working in the American embassy in Iran with one other more senior CIA officer, was approached by a young Iranian man who claimed to be a revolutionary. The man said that he had been coerced into joining the revolutionary movement, that he had comprehensive intelligence relating to postrevolutionary Iran's proposed domestic and foreign policies, and that he would give us this information if he could defect to the West. The CIA officer interviewed the man and established that if he was telling the truth, he was capable of supplying us with superb intelligence. But," Alistair added, rubbing his hands together, "we had a problem."

"The officer had to find a way to get the defector out of Iran?"

"Exactly." Alistair frowned. "There were uprisings and hostilities across the country, and Iran had therefore become a very dangerous and unpredictable operating environment for the few remaining Western intelligence officers based there. The CIA had exfiltration plans in place, but these had not been properly tested. However, MI6 had a route out which they believed would work. So the Hourglass task force instructed the CIA officer and his senior colleague to work with one Tehran-based MI6 officer to get the revolutionary out of the American embassy and to take him to the Iranian port of Bandar-e 'Abbâs in the south. The three intelligence officers packed the man into the boot of a car and then drove across the country to their destination." Alistair looked away again. "It was clearly a frightening journey, as the men must have known that they would have been executed had they been caught." He looked back at Will. "Several years earlier the British had recruited an Iranian captain of a trawler vessel. The plan was for the three officers to take their prize onto that vessel and then sail across the Persian Gulf to the United Arab Emirates."

"What happened?"

Alistair sighed. "They were driving along a straight country road about seven miles outside of Bandar-e 'Abbâs when the men spotted a roadblock of revolutionary militia four hundred meters ahead of them. Even though they knew they could be seen by the roadblock soldiers, they immediately stopped the car and spoke to each other. They made some very rapid deductions about their situation." The Controller nodded slowly. "All of which turned out to be true. They decided that the roadblock was unusual. They decided that somebody knew about them and their revolutionary man. They decided that such a security breach could not have come from their own services. And they decided that their revolutionary was most certainly not a defector."

"They were being set up?"

"Yes, a trap." Alistair shrugged. "We still don't know what purpose the trap served. It could have been to flush out the mechanics of the exfiltration route, or maybe it was to catch three Western intelligence officers with their pants down. But whatever the reason, the men realized that their situation was dire. For thirty seconds they argued and debated as to what they should do. And then the senior CIA officer made a decision all on his own. He picked up his handgun, got out of the car, and walked to the back of the vehicle. The officers knew that his actions were being watched by the roadblock guards, as those soldiers had now swung weapons in the direction of the vehicle. Nevertheless the CIA man removed the revolutionary from the vehicle's boot and placed the gun against his head. The CIA officer told his colleague and the MI6 man to run while he held his captive." Alistair exhaled loudly. "The two men were reluctant to do so at first, but they also knew that it was their only option. There were approximately fifteen soldiers ahead of them, so to stand and fight would have resulted in the capture or death of all three intelligence officers rather than one. They therefore left the CIA man to his fate."

"Did the two men escape?"

"Yes, they did. They got into Bandar-e 'Abbâs and used the trawler captain to take them to the emirate of Ras al-Khaimah."

"And the CIA man they left behind?"

Alistair leaned forward. "We later found out from some of our Iranian agents who survived the revolution that the CIA officer was captured and subjected to terrible torture. We know that he revealed nothing to the Iranians. We also know that he was finally executed and that his body was dumped somewhere in the Persian Gulf."

Will was silent for a moment before asking, "What is the point to your story?"

Alistair did not reply immediately. Instead he stared at Will, as if analyzing him. He tapped a finger once on the table. "The story is another memory for you. But I fear that it will drive you even harder. I fear that it will snap any remaining possibility for you to one day gain peace with yourself and others around you."

"As you said, so far that has suited you just fine."

Alistair nodded. "It has, and it continues to suit me. After all, it was I who spotted you when you joined MI6. It was I who identified your extreme and peculiar potential. It was I who took you away from the normal corridors of MI6 and put you on the highly classified Spartan Program. No man of your generation had ever done the year-long program and lived. However, you not only survived but excelled in the program, and as a result you became our most deadly and effective operative. There is never allowed to be more than one of you, so while you live you are the only man who has our most distinguished code name: Spartan."

A memory came to Will. It was the first day of the Spartan Program. He was standing barefooted in the Scottish Highlands wearing blue overalls. It was winter, snowing heavily and well below freezing. An instructor walked up to him, pointed north, and quietly gave him his first task:

You've got two days to cover one hundred miles on foot across the mountains. Armed men with dogs will be trying to hunt you down. If they succeed, you fail. If you don't get to the objective within the time allocated, you fail. If you try to get help from anyone you might meet on the route, you fail. And know this, if you succeed we're going to take you away and put you in a prison cell for two weeks. There you're going to receive your first taste of intense torture and total sleep deprivation. We will make you wish that you were dead. With every frozen step you take over these mountains, remember that.

Will pushed the memory away.

Alistair's eyes narrowed. "As Spartan you have provided exceptional results in the field. But one day I am going to have to look in the mirror and ask myself some hard questions."

"One day, but not yet?"

Alistair leaned farther forward. His words were hushed and rapid. "Right now the Qods Force Head of Western Directorate is the West's most dangerous opponent. He is not a fanatic or an ideologist or a martyr. Instead, and from the little we know of the person, he is an exceptional strategist and an intellectual who also happens to be a killer. He plans to massacre thousands of people in one of our cities in Europe or the States. And I need you to stop him. But I cannot allow your desire for vengeance against the world's evil to cloud your judgment." Alistair reached across the table and gripped a hand over Will's muscular forearm. Despite his age and thin frame, Alistair's grip was surprisingly strong. "Whatever happens, whatever you subsequently hear, can you assure me of that?"

Will looked down at Alistair's hand and then back up at the Controller's face. "My judgment has always been absolute and unclouded."

Alistair nodded once and released his grip as he leaned back. He took a sip of his Margaux and then replaced the glass on the table. "Tomorrow you will fly to CIA headquarters in Virginia. There you will meet Patrick, who will brief you on our Qods Force commander. He will also be on hand to help you throughout the mission."

"This is to be a joint operation between the CIA and MI6?"

Alistair smiled crookedly. "Technically, yes. But you would do better to view this as a joint operation between Patrick and me."

"I see."

"No, you don't, but Patrick will ensure that you do."

Will considered this. He looked away, frowning in thought before turning back to face Alistair. "I presume you must have been the MI6 officer in that car outside of Bandar-e 'Abbâs. Would I be right in saying that the CIA man who escaped with you was Patrick?"

"You would." Alistair was motionless while watching Will.

Will frowned as he recalled Patrick's words to him in the New York room:

Alistair and I share the same debt of gratitude to another man. And that debt brought me to this room today.

Will's frown increased. "Who was the other CIA officer?"

Alistair nodded slowly. His eyes glistened. "He was a private man who kept his work completely secret. Even his small family believed that he was an American diplomat whose death was a tragic accident." Alistair was very still now. "I think about him every day. I think about how calm he looked when he took the decision to save me and Patrick. I think about how defiant he looked when he held the revolutionary man against his body and shoved the handgun's muzzle to the man's head. I think about how resolute he looked as the soldiers rushed toward him while we escaped." Alistair placed fingers again over Will's forearm, but this time the grip felt tender. "Every day . . . every day I never fail to think about your father."

PART II

TWELVE

S o Alistair's given me the great hunter." Patrick was standing in the corner of the room beside a small table. He lifted a jug of hot water and poured liquid into a bone china cup. He stirred the cup's contents before bringing the drink over to the room's main table. He looked at Will. "There is no doubt in my mind that you're the right officer for this job. But there's also no doubt in my mind that you're an extremely dangerous and unpredictable individual." He pointed a finger at Will. "How can I be assured that you will do what you're told?"

Will inspected the cup and saucer before him. "How can I be assured that what you tell me to do will be the correct course of action?" He smiled and changed his tone. "Thank you for the tea. It's been worth the wait."

Patrick stared at him for a moment and seated himself at the opposite side of the table. The two men were alone in an anonymous room within the headquarters of the Central Intelligence Agency in Langley, Virginia.

Between them were several loose papers and some files. Patrick brushed a hand over some of the papers and picked up a single sheet. He glanced at it and then tossed it across the table to Will. "It all started with this."

Will read the report before him. It was dated two weeks earlier and had been produced by the United States National Security Agency.

OVERVIEW

1. Iran intends to attack a location within the United States or the United Kingdom.
2. The location and timing of this attack is unknown, but it is assessed that the attack is imminent.
3. The scale of the attack is unknown, but it is assessed that the attack may produce significant casualties.

DETAIL

1. The Islamic Revolutionary Guards Corps' Qods Force has been given authority by the Supreme Leadership of Iran to plan a terrorist strike against a location within one of the cities of the United States of America or the United Kingdom of Great Britain and Northern Ireland. The reason for the attack is unknown.
2. The Qods Force Head of Western Directorate has overall responsibility for the planning and execution of this attack. He has completed the planning phase of his operation, and it is therefore anticipated that he intends to execute his attack within an imminent time frame.
3. The Qods Force Head of Western Directorate has been given authority to choose the location and victims of the attack. He has ensured that no information relating to his plans is released to any other individuals within the IRGC. It is therefore assessed that only the Qods Force Head of Western Directorate has details of the location and timing of the attack.

COMMENT

1. The Qods Force Head of Western Directorate is Iran's most active intelligence-operations officer. He holds the rank of general. While he nominally reports to the Head of Qods Force, it is known that in practice the Head of Western Directorate receives his orders directly from the Supreme Leader of Iran.

2. The Head of Western Directorate's name is kept secret from all other members of the Qods Force and IRGC. While separate NSA reporting provides some details on the man, his identity remains unknown [NSA/SIGINT/8861/09 refers].

3. It is assessed that, due to the Head of Western Directorate's command of this operation, the planned attack must have significant strategic importance to Iran. It is therefore further assessed that the attack will be on a very large scale.

SOURCE

1. The source of this report is HUBBLE. This report is therefore assessed to be highly reliable.

2. Any enquiries relating to HUBBLE must be directed to this report's distributing department.

Will placed the report on the table. "I presume that Hubble is a technical attack against certain Iranian communications systems?"

Patrick held up a hand. "I've just broken a thousand NSA security protocols by showing you this unsanitized report, and NSA could try to put me in prison for doing just that. Heaven only knows what would happen if I told you about Hubble itself."

Will tapped a finger on the document. "I understand, but I need to hear what you think about this report. Do you assess Hubble reporting to be accurate?"

Patrick leaned forward, took the report away from Will, and placed it within a file. "Hubble reporting is pure gold. There is no doubt that this report is accurate." He looked down at the paper and frowned slightly.

"But?"

Patrick picked up another paper. "We'll come back to the 'but.'" He went quiet for a moment, reading the contents of the new paper. "We know next to nothing about our man. The little that we do know about him has come from a variety of our Iranian sources, although by those agents' own admission much of that is hearsay, because it seems that the Head of Western Directorate is deliberately shrouded in secrecy. However, for what it's worth, the hearsay is consistent with the following: He's been groomed for great things within Iran's regime since young adulthood, he has a brilliant mind, he excels at intelligence work, he is revered within not only the IRGC but also the Ministry of Intelligence and Security, and he's a loner who has no family or friends."

"Because he has no need for them. He lives to please his masters."

Patrick angled his head a little. "Well, that's the odd thing. The rumors are also consistent in saying that the man has no religious beliefs, no loyalty to the Iranian regime, no personal political agendas or persuasions." Patrick set the new paper down on the table. "He's tolerated by the Iranian leadership because he's so good at what he does. And he tolerates them because they allow him to do what he does best. But he serves no one."

Will nodded. "He sounds like my kind of person."

Patrick looked stern. "For all his brilliance, he's a murderer." He flicked a finger against the report. "We rarely ever see his hand—he's too astute for that to happen—but I can confidently say that he's had involvement in every major terrorist action against the West during the last five years, as well as numerous actions against Arab and South Asian countries."

"Impossible."

"If I were in your position, I'd probably draw the same conclusion. But I'm not in your position, I'm in my position. And I know that not one major terror act against Western or Western-allied targets can take place without his implicit or explicit authorization. Even groups that are the sworn enemy of the regime of Iran find themselves working for him, usually without knowing they're doing so. We can't name him Public Enemy Number One, as to do so would declare our intentions toward him, but privately we all agree that there's no other man on this planet we would rather see dead or behind bars." Patrick nodded. "He's the mastermind. My position allows me to know this."

Will observed Patrick for a while before speaking slowly. "What *is* your position within the CIA?"

Patrick stared out over Will's head. "I have no rank, title, or designation. I work for no definable office or department. I have no specific remit or function." He smiled a little. "Even my budget is vague." He looked back at Will. "Alistair told you about Bandar-e 'Abbâs?"

Will felt an immediate sense of unease. Since his departure from Simpson's the previous day, he'd thought about little else. "He did."

"How does that make you feel?"

Will rubbed a hand against his face and said quietly, "I have very few memories of my father, because I was just a young boy when he was taken from me. But I have many memories of what happened afterward." He shook his head slowly and cast his eyes down. "My mother struggling alone with me and my sister, trying her best and giving us more than she had until she was—" He looked up and spoke with stronger and more deliberate words. "Everything changed after my father died. And to know that his death was not a tragic accident but rather intentional and premeditated makes everything that happened even more abhorrent and unnecessary."

Patrick said sharply, "It was completely unnecessary. After we escaped and subsequently learned that your father had been brutally killed, Alistair and I felt enormous guilt. We told ourselves that your father was right to tell us to run. We told ourselves that if we, too, had been captured, then the impending revolutionary regime would have achieved a potentially catastrophic victory against Western intelligence capabilities in their region." He frowned. "We told ourselves lots of things. But none of those things could negate the guilt we both lived with. So we decided that from within our respective organizations we would do everything we could to track down and ruin the lives of anyone involved in that trap on the Bandar-e 'Abbâs road.

"Our task had become a vendetta, and over seven years Alistair and I abused our positions within the CIA and MI6 to seek our revenge. It worked, and by the end of our vendetta we had punished nearly everyone involved in your father's death, punishments meted out by my hand and by Alistair's."

"*Nearly* everyone?"

Patrick narrowed his eyes. "The person we wanted the most was the young man who had clearly planned the whole thing, the man who had approached us at the embassy. We never got him. But we did not fail with his associates.

"And even though our successes were driven by vengeance, both Alistair and I produced significant results, which came to the attention of our bosses in Langley and London." Patrick nodded once. "We were promoted rapidly, although in slightly different ways. Alistair was fast-tracked to the Controller position he now holds, and no doubt he will soon be Chief of MI6. I on the other hand was promoted toward the position I now hold, a position that is in equal measure powerful and invisible. The former is good. The latter means I will never be able to take the post as head of the Agency."

Patrick shrugged. "What's my position in the CIA? I can't give you a clear answer. But I can say I'm used on extreme matters." He gestured in a way that seemed to take in more than just the single room they occupied. "And I can also say that I answer to nobody in this building."

Will's fingers did their habitual drumming on the table. "So why do you need me?" He stopped drumming. "And please say that it's not to do with some debt of honor to my father."

"I'll say that it is nothing of the sort." Patrick's voice was quick, loud, and stern. "I'll say that the man you know as Megiddo is the Head of Western Directorate, because I know that the director was given his first major overseas challenge during the wars in the former Yugoslavia. I'll say that you therefore have the start of something with this man Harry and this woman Lana. I'll say that the man you have in your sights is the man I want."

Will frowned. "Why do you think he calls himself Megiddo?"

"I don't know if he chose that name or if the name was chosen *for* him. But I do know that the name refers to the ancient Palestinian site of terrible battles, battles that came to symbolize the wars of Armageddon." Patrick's gaze intensified. "He is called Megiddo because he is a man who exacts ultimate judgment and destruction." He paused. "Just like you."

Will breathed deeply. "Who else has seen the Hubble report?"

"NSA has shown it to everyone they think may care about its contents."

Will looked surprised. "Everyone?"

"Oh, yes." Patrick's eyes flashed red. "The self-important fools have thrown a sanitized version of the report to all our European allies."

"But that will create a feeding frenzy," Will protested. "Even though the report only references Britain and America, every European country will assume that it could be the target for the attack. They'll all deploy their intelligence and security services to try to counter the assault."

Patrick nodded. "They have."

"In that case there can be no operation against Megiddo. To try to conduct a precise mission against him while in competition with multiple other agencies will produce nothing but chaos."

Patrick shook his head quickly. "The United States and its allies are completely within their rights to deploy every tool they have to stop this attack. And maybe some of these other operations will succeed. But no one else knows about Megiddo."

"How on earth have you managed to keep that"—Will paused—"shall I say private?"

"Private? That's a delicate word." Patrick gathered up most of his files and papers. He stilled his hands and looked directly at Will. "We have the Hubble report, and you have the Megiddo lead. Therefore this has to be a joint operation. But Alistair and I have made certain that nobody else in the CIA or MI6 or any other organization can muddy our waters. And we've done that by very privately obtaining an Imperative Status for this operation."

Will narrowed his eyes. "All normal chains of command," he said slowly, "are circumvented?"

Patrick nodded. "As soon as the Imperative Status was granted, I was instructed that there was only one Western intelligence officer sufficiently experienced and capable to conduct an operation with such status." He pointed at Will. "I understand that you are the ultimate resort for extreme operations such as this. And as much as your presence in this room gives me significant unease, I have accepted that there is no alternative to your deployment." He huffed. "I cannot afford for our mission to be distracted or damaged by others. I need it to be completely autonomous. The Imperative Status means that only five officials currently know about your lead to Megiddo: me, Alistair, you, the prime minister of the United Kingdom, and the president of the United States."

Will clasped his hands. "We don't yet know if we even have a starting point to this mission. Harry and Lana have given us our target, but we still have no means to get to him."

"You know we do."

Will stared at Patrick. "I cannot do that."

"You can and you will do so."

Will shook his head as anger surged through him. "On whose orders?"

Patrick leaned close. "Alistair and I are in complete agreement on this, as are our respective premiers. It is our only option. You must use Lana to lure out Megiddo. You must use her as bait."

Will banged his fist on the table in frustration. "Every instinct I have tells me that she should not be deployed in the field. It's far too dangerous."

Patrick smiled, but his eyes remained cold and penetrating. "No doubt you've deployed female agents in the past. What's different about this woman?"

Will glanced away for a moment, recalling Lana's haunted and hunted look and his urge to tell her that she would never suffer again. When he faced Patrick again, he spoke with no effort to hide his anger. "Of course I've used female agents before, and they did courageous things in dangerous situations. But this mission will be in a different league. Dangling a woman like Lana in front of a ruthless mastermind like Megiddo is a risk too far. There must be another way."

"If there is, then tell me."

Will sat in silence.

Patrick nodded. "The stakes are the very highest. Believe me, none of us wants to put Lana at risk. It is"—he paused—"not a part of our work that either Alistair or I take pleasure in. But thousands of lives are at risk, and the imperative to stop their deaths must be paramount."

Will cursed inwardly, shaking his head. "I cannot ask her to do this."

Patrick sat still for a while. He then spoke quietly. "You are quite a contradiction. On one side, I can see that you are impeccably ruthless and will take inordinate risks with your own life, but on the other, it surprises me that you're unwilling to sacrifice others for the sake of the greater good. Why is that?"

Will shook his head harder. "I'm willing to do what it takes and work with people who know the risks. A man like Harry, for example, knows exactly what he's doing and I'm sure is no stranger to making hard decisions. But Lana . . . Lana has seen enough. She's done only good things in her life, and even for that she was brutally punished.

She's an innocent. I don't put innocents at risk. I save them." He repeated, "I cannot ask her to do this."

Patrick observed him for a while, then nodded. "I understand. But *you* should understand that I have no choice other than to seize any opportunity to stop Megiddo." He frowned. "Maybe you underestimate Lana."

"What do you mean?"

"Maybe she would be willing to take this risk."

Will shook his head again. "She wants revenge against Megiddo, and that emotion may blind her to potential dangers. But *I'm* not blind to those dangers. I can't ask her to do something that would place her in jeopardy."

"Maybe not, but you could ask her what she wants."

Will frowned.

"Why not?" Patrick widened his eyes. "Be honest with her about the dangers. Then ask her whether she's prepared to take the risk or whether she would rather remain safe but embittered for the rest of her life."

"That's just manipulation."

"No, it's a straightforward question and one that a woman like Lana should be able to respond to with her own mind and conviction. She has a right to define her own path in life. That's her right, not yours."

Will sighed. "She should not be given the choice."

"Nor should you, but here we are confronting terrible decisions in the face of unimaginable dangers. So I'm making that choice for you. Ask her what she wants. I give you my word that if she refuses to help, I'll honor that decision. And I give you my word that if she chooses to cooperate, I'll afford you resources to protect her throughout the mission."

Will thrust out his chin. "I don't need any other shooters. I work alone. I *am* the shooter."

"You had other men with you in Central Park."

"Against my wishes. They died and let me down. I should have been there alone. My agent would still be alive if I hadn't put my faith in others to help him."

"And yet it was ultimately you who ended his life."

Will was silent.

Patrick inhaled deeply. "However you intend to construct this operation, Alistair and I are in complete agreement that you must have support. And your priority must be to capture Megiddo, not protect Lana. You certainly can't do both."

"I can damn well try."

"You talk of risk." Patrick smiled a little, but his look remained cold. "Is that a risk you're willing to take?"

Will said nothing.

Patrick nodded. "We've calculated that you need at least eight men for all surveillance, protection, and attack requirements. But I can only get you four specialists, and Alistair has advised me that he can't get any shooters from MI6."

"I thought this operation had been countenanced from on high? Surely the premiers would give us all the resources we needed?"

Patrick glanced down at an inch-high pile of loose papers. "You bring me back to that 'but.'" He placed a thumb against the pile and strummed the papers' edges. "The Hubble report I showed you is without doubt genuine. However, since its release, something else has happened. Hubble has been inundated with further signals intelligence about other intended attacks across Europe and the U.S. It's caused a state of high anxiety, to say the least, and it has stretched resources beyond reason. I was lucky to secure you four CIA paramilitary officers."

Will frowned. "Are you getting results from actions taken on the content of these other NSA reports?"

Patrick shook his head and looked frustrated. "That's the thing. The reports are informative enough to be taken seriously but not specific enough to guarantee results."

"What does NSA say?"

Patrick rose from his chair and walked to a window. He placed his hands in his pockets and stared out. "You have to understand that we live in a world of bureaucracies and conflicting agendas." He turned to face Will. "NSA is so damn protective of their precious Hubble operation that they've decided it cannot be challenged. I've asked them about the new reports, and they've told me to mind my own business. I can't even get the president to order them to cooperate with me, since for him to do so would prompt too many intrusive questions from Congress."

Will shrugged. "Well, providing you're convinced of the validity of the initial Hubble report, these other reports should be of no concern to us. Aside from the fact that according to you it means my operation does not have enough resources."

Patrick folded his arms across his chest. "I think these other reports could be of every concern to our operation."

"What do you mean?"

"I can't prove anything to you yet. What I can say is that these other reports look too similar to the original Hubble report of two weeks ago. But unlike the original report, I think the subsequent reports have been manufactured. The trouble is, only NSA can substantiate that view."

"Good luck."

Patrick smiled. "I should be wishing *you* good luck."

He turned back to look out the window. "I told you that I'm used on extreme matters. I told you I needed you because you had a head start with the operation against Megiddo. What I didn't tell you is that you also have another use to me." Patrick turned again to look at Will. "You're deniable."

"What do you have in mind?"

"At seven-thirty tomorrow morning the children and wife of the NSA's Head of the Middle East Counterterrorism Desk will leave for school and work. At eight-thirty the NSA officer himself leaves for work. I need you to be in Baltimore tomorrow to have a little chat with him before he heads off for his morning duties."

Will frowned. "You want me to interrogate a senior NSA officer?"

"Do you have a problem with that?"

Will thought about the question. "I'm willing to frighten him, even hurt him a little, but I refuse to torture a man who's on our side."

Patrick held up a hand. "I *do* have to make tough decisions, but thankfully making a decision to torture a Western intelligence analyst isn't one of them right now." Patrick walked back to the table. He said nothing for a while, just stood looking at Will. He then spoke quietly. "Alistair has warned me that you view your work as a means to take revenge against the tragedies of your early life. He's warned me that you never stop, that you make immense personal sacrifices, that you care nothing for rules or protocols, and that your compassion for the weak and innocent is balanced with an unflinching desire to slaughter evil." He raised his voice. "But he's also warned me that there are aspects of your character that neither he nor you yet fully understand." His voice hardened. "The operation to capture Megiddo requires us to play with the very highest stakes. For reasons that will become clear to you in a moment, I need to know that you can be controlled."

Will narrowed his eyes. "I control myself."

"How? How can you do that?" Patrick demanded harshly. "How can you do the things you do without professional and personal guidance? How can you continue to exist without those things?"

Will was silent before saying, "When my war ends, I may be forced to face those questions. But by then it won't matter, because I'll most likely be dead."

Patrick waved a hand in what looked like frustration. "You are your father's son, but through circumstance you've also become a distillation and a corruption of the man I last saw in Bandar-e 'Abbâs."

Will stood quickly and kicked his chair to the floor. He took two paces toward Patrick and glared at the man.

Patrick stepped back and raised a hand. "Please sit down."

Will didn't move.

"Please sit down."

Will held his gaze on Patrick. "Be very careful with your words." He sat and watched Patrick do the same.

Patrick seemed to be composing himself. "There's another reason Alistair and I know that you're the best officer for this mission. And that reason will change everything for you." He nodded slowly and lowered his voice. "Everything."

"What do you mean?"

For the longest time, Patrick studied Will. "What's your last memory of your father?"

Will narrowed his eyes. "I was five years old. I remember seeing him walk across a stretch of tarmac to an airplane. I was waving to him with one hand while holding my mother's hand with the other. I saw him get onto the plane. And I never saw him again." The anger within Will receded as he pictured the memory. "I later learned that the plane was bound for Iran."

Patrick nodded. "That would have been his first and last trip into Iran and three weeks before his capture." He broke eye contact for a moment, and when he looked back at Will, there was sadness in his eyes. "For the first year of his captivity, we knew from our agents that your father was moved around Iran by the revolutionaries and kept in cellars and other secret locations. But after the revolution of 1979, the revolutionaries became officials and your father's incarceration was formalized. He was transferred to Evin Prison in Tehran and kept in solitary confinement between the frequent bouts of torture inflicted on him. In the seventh year of his imprisonment, your father was taken into the room that was normally used for his torture, but instead of seeing one of the many usual torturers, he was confronted with the revolutionary man who had set us all up. That man had now become an important person, and the prison guards stood back as he set about his task."

Patrick closed his eyes and then slowly opened them again. "I later spoke to one of those guards, before I killed him, and found out everything that had happened in that room. I found out that the revolutionary man cut pieces off your father. I found out that the man attached a saline drip to your father's body so that he could be kept alive longer while undergoing this brutal savagery. I found out that at the very end the revolutionary plunged his knife into your father's broken body and extinguished his life.

"Since the murder of your father and later your mother, you've spent your adult life righting other people's wrongs. This mission will be different for you, but Alistair and I fear what effect it will have on your already ruthless psyche. This mission will be different because the man who tore your father apart gave him his name before killing him.

"That name was Megiddo."

THIRTEEN

Will stopped his rental car and checked his watch. He exited the vehicle and stood on Sycamore Road in Baltimore's desirable Cedarcroft residential district. He wore a British-purchased Gieves & Hawkes suit and a raglan overcoat, and he carried in one pocket an American-lent Beretta M9A1 pistol. He pulled up the collar of his coat to help shield against the icy early-morning rain and then thrust his hands into the pockets. He could see fourteen spacious houses on this two-hundred-meter-long road, and the house he needed was toward the end of the route. He lowered his head and walked quickly forward. Within a minute he was standing before a Dutch Colonial–style building. He rang the bell. A man opened the door, and Will instantly kicked him in the stomach, then stepped over the man's shuddering body. He closed the door behind him and listened. There were no other noises coming from inside the large family home.

Will returned to where the man lay and crouched. He placed a hand around the man's jaw and said commandingly, "Breathe." Then he stood, ignoring the man's moans, and walked through the front foyer and into a large kitchen. He turned and walked back to the man. He gently cradled a hand under the man's head, pulled him though to the kitchen area, and placed him on the floor but in a seated position. The man wheezed, clutching his hands against his chest.

Will sat on the floor next to him. He prodded the man's forehead and asked, "Has Hubble been compromised?"

The man inhaled deeply several times and then shook his head. "Whoever you are, go to hell."

Will crossed his legs and interlocked his fingers. "A silly response."

The man held a hand up to his mouth as if he were going to vomit. He screwed his eyes shut, and his breathing began to slow. Then he removed his hand and looked at Will. "If I don't report in to work, armed men will come looking for me."

"Because you're a senior NSA officer?" Will smiled. "I doubt that anyone will come, but if someone does, then I'll kill him just after I've killed you."

The NSA officer shook his head again. "Who sent you?"

Will leaned back against the breakfast table. "Well, you can probably tell from my accent that it's unlikely I work for one of your agencies."

"Then how do you know about Hubble?" The man's breathing seemed to be recovering from Will's blow.

"Because you stupidly send Hubble reporting to everyone you deem to be an ally."

The man took his hands away from his chest. "I doubt you're my ally."

Will grinned. "Maybe not. But I represent an affiliation of intelligence interests who are allies of Hubble's insight. And we think you have a problem."

The officer's eyes narrowed. "You'd be crazy to think I'd tell you anything about how we get Hubble intelligence."

"I'm not here to learn about Hubble itself. I'm simply here to ascertain whether you believe that Hubble reporting has been corrupted during the last fourteen days." Will glanced around the kitchen and saw two used adult-size and two child-size cereal bowls beside the sink. He then looked back to the man. He hated the lie he was about to speak. Yet he knew that it was vital. "And I'm prepared to stay here with you all day to get my answer. But I swear to you that I will shoot dead the first person who interrupts our little chat."

The man said nothing.

Will nodded. "I know how important the Hubble operation is to you personally. After all, the inspiration and the technology behind the Hubble technical attack was yours. As a result, Hubble has quite rightly given you praise and promotion within the National Security Agency. So"—he opened his hands and drummed fingers on his leg— "it must be difficult for you to accept that your greatest achievement has been identified by hostiles and manipulated to their advantage."

The officer sat in silence for nearly one minute. Then he, too, glanced over at the sink area before looking back at Will. He closed his eyes a little, rubbing a hand over his belly. He shook his head. "Two weeks ago we did start receiving a new stream of reporting from the Hubble source. Over the course of a few days, it became clear to me that the style of these new reports was nearly identical to the old stuff, but with content that was forcing us to chase after bomb plots across the West without results. I formed the opinion that someone had breached Hubble and was feeding us false information."

"How could that happen?"

The man peered at him before repeating, "I won't tell you how we get Hubble intelligence. Whatever you think you can do, my masters will be able to do worse to me if I betray Hubble."

"I understand, but hear me out. What would you say if I told you that a person or persons unknown had discovered a technical attack against Iranian military communications and other data systems, that the person then realized that his operation to strike a massive blow against the West had been discovered, that the man then decided that instead of shutting down the breach he would manipulate it in order to try to cast doubt over his operation, that the man then manipulated Hubble by sending certain e-mails, making certain telephone calls, and sending certain text messages? You don't have to tell me about Hubble, but what would you say in response to my little hypothesis?"

The man lowered his head and said nothing.

Will smiled and pushed himself up from the floor. "Then that's all I need to know."

The NSA officer looked up at him. His eyes had watered. "You're wrong about one thing. When I decided we had a breach, I immediately brought it to the attention of my superiors. But it was them, not me, who decided to ignore it."

"Why would they do that?"

The man sighed. "My Hubble operation is as comprehensive as it gets. The breach accounts for less than one percent of the Hubble attack. The rest remains intact and undiscovered. The NSA decided that to do anything about the breach would compromise the whole setup. So they chose to ignore it in order to save the wider operation."

"But why then distribute the reports from the breach when you know them to be false?"

The man shrugged. "Our intelligence customers believe wholeheartedly in the Hubble project because we tell them it's completely accurate. For us to withhold any of its reporting could prompt them to question the entirety of it." He smiled a little, but the look on his face seemed bitter. "Hubble alone has secured an extra two hundred million dollars of funding for the NSA this year."

Will nodded. "I see." He observed the man for a moment before speaking again. "You will go to work now and make sure that the breach continues to go unchallenged. You will also ensure that NSA never learns about our conversation this morning." He glanced one last time around the kitchen before looking back at the NSA officer. He thought the man seemed honest and honorable, like a decent father and husband who didn't deserve to be threatened in the way that Will had been forced to do to him on this day. He hated the actions he often had to take and the lies he often had to speak. He pointed at the man. "Do this, and you and your loved ones get to live. Fail, and everything you love will die."

FOURTEEN

Will turned off the reading light above his seat in the Delta Air Lines 777 and closed his eyes. He knew he wouldn't be able to sleep, but he desperately hoped that his mind would give him some rest on this flight. He tried to relax, tried to detach himself from the man he was, tried to imagine being one of the normal people he was surrounded by in first class.

But the thoughts and memories coursed through him with ferocity and intensity before settling on the one memory he least wanted to confront.

He saw the large teenage boy smile and sniff the spring air as he strolled through the midafternoon day toward the house. He saw the boy kick at loose stones for no other reason than they were there. He saw the boy smile wider as he patted the school bag containing his report card. He saw the boy increase his pace so that he was almost running toward the nearing house.

The boy stopped and frowned but was not perturbed. The cars around the house were unusual, given that few people ever visited, and certainly not during a weekday. But the boy was still really a child, and he loved changes to his routine, and so he embraced the notion that something exciting and different lay ahead. He walked onward and combed fingers through his tousled hair to try to make himself look at least a little bit presentable. He examined the cars more closely and memorized the models so he could tell his friends about them the following day. He had no interest in cars, but he knew that some of his friends did.

The boy rubbed his shoes against the back of his trousers and then approached the rear door of the house. It was open, and he decided that was normal for such an airy and fresh day. He walked into the house, set down his book bag, and wondered if he could have some lemonade.

He called out, "Mother."

He walked into the living room.

His life changed forever.

FIFTEEN

At eight-thirty the following morning, Will was again standing on rue Sainte-Croix-de-la-Bretonnerie in Paris. The muscles in his back ached, and he stretched his arms to try to relieve the discomfort. The road around him was busy with pedestrians forcing their way through an overnight snowfall, and Will scrutinized them all.

He saw Lana emerge from her side street and then followed her. She was dressed in a heavy winter coat and boots but nevertheless looked elegant and sexy as she strode on, turning on to rue du Bourg-Tibourg. She walked into a café and sat at a window table. Will stood for a moment on the street, watching her. He saw her remove her scarf, and he saw her hair fall down across her back. He saw her order something from a waiter, and he saw her take out a folded newspaper. He walked into the café.

"Hello, Lana." Will sat down opposite the woman and pulled her newspaper away from her face so that she could see him.

Lana's eyes widened. She glanced quickly around the café before looking back at Will. She produced a slight smile. "Hello, Nicholas. You came back for me."

"I told you I would." The waiter immediately attended their table, and Will muttered to the man, *"Un café allongé, s'il vous plaît."* The man left them, and Will turned back to Lana. "I do hope nobody is planning to join you here."

Lana put her newspaper down and gathered her hair in one hand to place it over a shoulder. "Nobody."

Will nodded, studying her face. She still retained the beautiful and hunted visage, but she seemed now to be projecting some strength, or hope. "How did you feel after our meeting?"

Lana frowned a little. She gave a slight shrug. "More than anything else, I was surprised that I showed you my scars." She leaned forward. "Why would I have done that with someone like you?"

Will smiled. "Someone like me? Who do you think that type of person is?"

She waved a hand. "You are someone who captures secrets and souls. That is what you do, is it not?"

"I suppose it is."

Lana looked down at Will's ringless fingers and then back up at his face. "Are you a kind man, Nicholas?"

He frowned and then laughed. "That's a strange question."

"Not really." Lana placed one of her own manicured hands flat down on the table between them. "I've met so many unkind men in my life. It would be nice to know that you are not one of them."

"I can be unkind when I need to be."

"But not when you don't have to be." She smiled a little, and her eyes twinkled.

Will was about to respond when the waiter delivered two coffees to their table. He sat in silence for a moment and saw Lana move her fingers slightly closer to his. He looked out the window and watched fresh snow begin to fall on Paris, then turned back to Lana. "He is called Megiddo."

Lana looked down and spoke quietly. "I know. It is the only name he ever gave me."

"Then why did you not tell me that was his name during our first meeting?" Will felt the anger in his voice.

Lana shook her head. "It is not his real name, so it has no relevance."

He gripped his coffee cup so hard it was a wonder the thing did not shatter. "Only I can decide what is relevant or otherwise."

"Why is he so important to you?"

Will took a deep breath and relaxed the grip on his cup. He looked at Lana's lips and then her eyes and nodded once. "He is important to me because he wishes to kill others. It is my job to stop men like him."

"That must be a lonely and thankless task."

Will immediately recalled his meeting with his sister in Highgate Cemetery. He pushed the memory aside and smiled. "Why is it that people like you always think people like me are lonely?"

"People?" Lana's voice hardened. "You said that if I'd been caught on my journeys in Bosnia, I could have been raped and tortured and then executed. How do you know I was never caught? How do you know some that of those things never happened?" She reached for her coffee but then withdrew her hand. "Do you think I am just like everyone else? That I'm just another person?"

"No, I don't." Will gazed out at the snowfall again and smiled as an unexpected memory came, the memory of five-year-old Will Cochrane throwing snowballs with his father. He wondered why the memory had come to him at this moment, then sighed as he understood that it was about innocence—his innocence, before the bad things came into his life, just like Lana's innocence and purity before the bad men had beaten her and maybe worse. He looked at her. "I am sorry. I didn't mean to disparage you."

Lana frowned before gently smiling. "Why did you come back to me?"

Will breathed deeply while watching Lana. He looked at her beautiful olive skin, her teak-colored hair, her large brown eyes, and her lips. He said nothing for a while, just looked at her. He wondered what her response would be to his next question, then suspected he knew. He toyed with the idea of not asking her at all, of reporting back to Alistair and Patrick with a lie. But Alistair and Patrick were men who lived and prospered in a world of lies and could never be deceived, not even by him.

He opened his mouth and said, "Lana, I—" His throat instantly felt dry. "Lana, I have something I must ask you."

"I think I know what it is."

Will frowned.

She looked away from him and spoke quietly, almost as if to herself. "There have been many times in my life when I have been reckless, knowingly foolish, maybe even naïve." When she looked back at Will, her voice became stronger. "But I am not a stupid person." She nodded. "You think I might be a means to lure out Megiddo. You want to know if I am willing to help you trap him."

Will studied her eyes, tried to detect her emotions. He looked for signs of fear, hesitation, uncertainty, anger—anything. But he could not see any clear indications of the way she was thinking. He nodded slowly. "That is precisely what I want to know."

Lana reached for her coffee cup again, and this time she placed her fingers around its base. She raised the cup and took a sip, then carefully set it back down. "I know why I stripped out of my clothes to show you my wounds. I did so because I wanted you to really understand what I've been through and what I'm still going through. I wanted you to look at me and decide that I was someone who could be exploited; someone who could be used to help you get Megiddo." She frowned. "But I was surprised. You came to me and did not want me to stand before you seminaked in such a vulnerable situation. Other men in your situation may have been different. But at that moment I saw a gentle man who wanted nothing more than to protect me. I saw a man who was horrified by what he saw." She smiled a little. "I think in that brief moment I saw a very kind man."

Will felt confused and angry with himself, and before he could stop himself, he blurted out, "Would a kind and gentle man ask you to do something that was anything but kind or gentle?"

Lana frowned and shook her head. "I wanted you to know the truth about me. I wanted you to understand how much I've hated the man you now seek." She leaned forward. "I want you now to know that the man you want is the man I want. I need you to understand that I want to help you in whatever way you see fit. Please, this may be my only opportunity to change my life for the better."

Will wondered what to say. He then decided he knew precisely what to say. "Lana, the only way you can help is by being dangled as bait for Megiddo. I would protect you as much as I could, but nevertheless you would still be in severe danger. Regardless, I'm supposed to be here to counsel you that your desire to help me is the correct one. But I'm not going to lie to you. I want you to tell me that you will not help us catch Megiddo."

Lana didn't understand. "Surely you want to catch him?"

Will looked away for a moment. He thought about what Alistair had told him about his father. He thought about what Patrick had told him about the Evin Prison room. He thought about Megiddo.

He looked back at Lana and tried to hide the aggression he felt. "I desperately want to get my hands on him." He sighed. "But there must be another way for me to get him."

Lana smiled and reached out to cup Will's large hands in her own. Her embrace felt tender. "Then I know what you think. Now I know that my instincts about you were correct. Now I know that you truly are a gentle man." She squeezed her hands around his. "But nor am *I* going to lie to *you*. You would not be here if you or others in your organization had alternative means to lure Megiddo from the shadows. So I have to take this opportunity. I have to help you, and if that means letting you use me to bring him out of hiding, then I am willing for that to happen." She withdrew her hands and smiled.

Will kept still for a moment. He looked out the window again, at the table, at the lipstick traces on her coffee cup. Anywhere but at Lana. "You could be killed."

"I feel as if I'm half dead already. What have I got to lose?"

He sighed and finally met her eyes, and this time he could clearly see strength and defiance in them. "I suspect that you have more reasons to live than you think."

"Then let me find out. Let me do this and feel alive again."

He nodded. He knew that there was nothing he could say to dissuade her from her decision. He also knew that she could have no real comprehension of the dangers she would face. An idea came to him.

He drummed his fingers on the table and said quietly, "So be it." He thought some more for a moment before saying, "I want you to send a letter to him. I want you to seek his audience."

Lana chuckled. "Do you have an address for him? Because I certainly do not."

Will shook his head. "Not yet, but I'm working on that. The letter will be our mechanism to draw him out, for you to meet him and identify him and for me to capture him."

"Why would he want to meet me?"

"You can say in the letter that you love him."

Lana's eyes flashed anger. "You *are* asking a lot of me. And in any case, he won't meet me unless I have something considerably more valuable to him"—she frowned—"than love."

"I agree." Will took another sip of his coffee. When he put his cup down, he reached across and placed his hand over Lana's fingers. He hoped the act would soften her anger.

Lana smiled. "You say he plans to kill people. They must be important people if he is involved and if you are tasked to stop him. He will not be distracted from his task."

"Then, as you say, we must bring him something better than your love."

For a brief moment, the anger returned to Lana's face. She then laughed quietly.

Will smiled and drained the remainder of his coffee. His face was close to hers, and he stopped smiling. "You need to give Megiddo something irresistible, and I know what that can be." He pulled her closer to him. "I can't stop you from agreeing to help me, but maybe I can stop you from being the true bait. So this is what we'll do. I want you to write to Megiddo saying that Western intelligence services have approached you. I want you to tell him that they know he plans to strike a massive blow against one of their countries. Tell him that an intelligence officer called Nicholas Cree has asked you questions about Megiddo. Tell him I want to capture him. Tell him that you need to meet Megiddo urgently to pass along what you know. Tell him that you can help deliver the intelligence officer to him so that Cree can be tortured to ascertain whether Megiddo's operation is completely compromised." Will smiled. "Tell him that you will do this only if in return you can be with him again."

Lana had been studying Will's lips as he spoke. When she looked back up, her eyes held tears. She gently withdrew one of her hands from Will's hold and ran fingers over the side of his face, shaking her head slightly. "Do you understand the risks you are taking with such a man? You are telling Megiddo to kill you."

Will imagined the pain his father must have felt in the Evin Prison torture room. "I want Megiddo to come after *me*. I want him to view *me* as tethered bait. I want him to realize too late that it is *he* who is the prey and *I* who am the predator.

"And then, like all true predators, I will rip my prey apart."

SIXTEEN

I forgive you for holding a knife to my throat. But it's going to take me some time to forgive you for thinking that I might have done something careless to lead a killer to your colleague." Harry took a gulp of his Red Label whiskey. He was dressed in immaculate casual business attire and had one leg loosely resting over the other. He replaced the whiskey glass on the table beside him and wagged a finger at Will. "Mistrusting a man is one thing. Believing him to be stupid is another thing altogether."

It was the evening now, and Will had been in London for three hours. He was sitting with Harry in the bar at Park Lane's Dorchester Hotel.

"How long are you in town?" Will took a small sip of his own whiskey.

"Just one night and one day." Harry brushed a hand over his trousers. "I have a very large shipment deal, and the paperwork can only be arranged here." He grinned. "*Discreetly* arranged here."

Will nodded. "Would the shipment be armaments and their destination somewhere dubious?"

Harry rubbed his hands together rapidly and smiled mischievous-ly. "You're not a secret policeman, are you, Charles?"

"No, I don't think I'd make a very good policeman, secret or otherwise."

Harry uncrossed his legs and leaned in close. His voice was a near whisper. "True. And they wouldn't have someone like you in their ranks, would they? Not someone who has your kind of problems." He pulled back quickly while chuckling and then clapped his hands together. "Now, I think I have something for you," he boomed.

"Am I going to be impressed?"

Harry's eyes narrowed. "I hope so. You asked me to find a man, and I have done so. The defense attaché at the Iranian embassy in Zagreb. He's an IRGC officer."

Will nodded in appreciation. "How long has he been posted there?"

"Sixteen months. It's his first posting in Europe." Harry widened his eyes, and the look in them seemed expectant. "He's only regular IRGC, mind you—a major in their army, nothing unusual. I believe that is what you wanted?"

"It is. What's his function?"

Harry reached for his drink. "He's doing what a regular DA in his position should be doing: schmoozing with the Croatian military, trying to persuade them to sell military equipment to the Iranians or maybe buy from them, and most likely drinking with them until the wee hours."

"Age?"

"Thirty-one."

Will resisted the urge to smile. The man's profile was perfect for what he needed. His age was an additional bonus, as it could mean that the man was still eager to prove his worth to his superiors in Teh-ran. "That is very good, Harry. Very good indeed."

Harry grinned widely again. "See, I knew I could be a valuable asset to you." He pointed a finger at Will. "Hey, the woman Lana—have you spoken to her yet?"

Will lifted his drink. "If I use her, she will be oblivious to the fact that she is working for British intelligence."

Harry nodded and chuckled again. "I like the way you work." He finished his whiskey and checked his watch. "Well, unless there's anything else we need to cover, an old man requires his bed. I've got a big day tomorrow."

"There's nothing else right now." Will reached out and placed a hand over Harry's watch. "But I need you to stay in touch with me. I need you and your contacts to keep eyes and ears open for any sign of Qods Force activity in Central Europe. Anything at all, even if it's just rumor."

"Of course." Harry placed his own hand on top of Will's fingers, the mischievous look on his face having returned. "Of course." He grinned even wider and laughed harshly as he broke Will's grip and stood. "I do forgive you for holding a knife to me. But you should know that I never make threats. If I ever have cause to put a knife against *your* throat, the next thing you will feel is unimaginable pain as my blade slices through your life."

"I don't think so Harry." He smiled and regarded Lace. He saw the man's humor, his deviousness, his business-sharp intellect, and his wisdom. He also saw hope and sorrow in the man's eyes. He saw a man he could not help but like. He nodded. "I, too, never give threats, but I do give warnings to those I feel are capable of redemption. Remember that, Harry. Because I have just warned you."

SEVENTEEN

We all arrived late last night." Patrick poured coffee into a mug. Will rubbed a hand against his chin and felt morning stubble on his face. He took a gulp of his own coffee and looked out a window toward Zurich's Limmat River. They were in a CIA residential house on Rössligasse near the Swiss city's old town quarter. He turned, walked to the dining table, and picked up a piece of paper. "So these are the others?"

"Indeed."

Will read the paper.

Roger Koenig. Age thirty-eight. Married, three children. Seven years CIA Special Operations Group. Two years as team leader. Deployments include China, North Korea, Borneo, Russia, and Uzbekistan. Five SOG commendations at "outstanding" grade. Previously eight years SEALs, five of which DEVGRU. Global operations. Specialist in business cover, surveillance, all arms, disruptions, hostage rescue, HAHO and HALO parachute insertions, transportation (specifically maritime). Fluent in Mandarin, Russian, and German.

Laith Dia. Age thirty-four. Divorced, two children. Five years SOG. Deployments include Syria, Zimbabwe, Afghanistan, Pakistan, and Iraq. Previously five years Delta. Global operations. Twice recommended for Congressional Medal of Honor. Previously NCO in Rangers. Specialist in all arms, protection, hostage rescue, mountaineering, surveillance, disruptions, communications. Qualified sniper. Fluent in Arabic and operational Farsi.

Ben Reed. Age thirty-three. Single. Four years SOG. Deployments include Colombia, Mexico, Afghanistan, India, and Somalia. Previously nine years Green Berets. Global operations. Specialist in medicine, explosives, communications, HAHO and HALO insertions, hostage rescue, protection, surveillance, offensive and defensive driving, all arms, and unarmed combat. Operational Arabic, Urdu, Pashto, and Spanish.

Julian Garces. Age thirty-one. Single. Three years SOG. Deployments include Sudan, Russia, North Korea, Pakistan, Iran, and China. Previously seven years Air Force Combat Control Team. Global operations. Specialist in communications, HAHO and HALO, combat scuba diving, demolitions, all arms and unarmed combat, offensive and defensive driving. Fluent Spanish and operational Russian and Farsi.

Will placed the paper back down on the table. "Their experience looks perfect. I presume Roger will act as their team leader on this operation?"

Patrick poured more coffee into his mug. "He will."

"I want to meet the team."

"Of course. I'll get them here now."

Will shook his head. "Not all of them together. Get Laith, Ben, and Julian here first. We'll meet their team leader separately."

•   •   •

Will looked at the three men before him. He knew that to most people they would appear, from a distance, to be average men, and that was as it should be, for these men spent most of their time hiding among the ranks of normal people. But Will could immediately tell that the three specialists sitting in the Rössligasse house were anything but average men. He could see that they were highly professional. He could see that they were killers.

Patrick was leaning against a wall, also studying the men. "Introduce yourselves."

"Laith Dia." This came from the man on the left and was spoken in a deep, rich voice. The American looked tall, sinewy, and very strong. He had striking straight black hair and jet-black eyes. His physique, features, and name suggested that he was of both Moorish African and Levantine Arab heritage.

"Why did you join the CIA, Laith?" Patrick folded his arms.

Laith pulled out a cigarette and lit it. "To help senior officers like you get out of the shit." He blew smoke. "Plus, in Delta we got to travel a lot, but it was always a quick in and out of places." He smiled. "In this job we get to mix much more with the locals. It gives me the chance to take in the sights and shop for presents for my kids."

Patrick nodded at the man in the center.

"Ben Reed." The man was not large and looked like a lawyer or a doctor rather than a Special Forces–turned–CIA paramilitary man. He had immaculate blond hair and a fixed grin showing perfect teeth. "And before you ask"—he also sounded Harvard-educated—"I joined our service to impress women. But nobody told me back then that I had to keep my job a secret from them."

The three men laughed, but Patrick did not. He pointed at Ben. "I wasn't going to ask you that. My question is, what's the hardest thing you've ever had to do, in either Special Forces or the CIA SOG?"

Ben seemed to consider the question and then smiled wider. "Filling in my last tax returns."

Patrick said nothing for a moment before slowly turning his attention toward the third man and nodding at him.

"Julian Garces, ex–U.S. Air Force special operative. Currently deployed in the CIA with a guy who likes shopping and a guy who can't get laid."

The three SOG men laughed again, and this time Will saw a slight smile emerge on Patrick's face.

Julian was evidently Hispanic and was as tall and sinewy as Laith. He had dark, cropped curly hair and a scar down one whole side of his face. He reminded Will of the ancient and lethal Iberian warriors he'd seen depicted in paintings.

Julian's laugh slowly receded until his face grew serious. He looked straight at Patrick. "I've killed ninety-seven men, which is only three less than Laith and only seven less than Ben. Add all of those deaths together, and you've got the number of men Roger's killed." His eyes looked cold. "Like my friends, I've been in almost every overt and covert American war that's happened during my adult life. If you want to ask me, the hardest thing I've ever done is spend three months in a village in northern Afghanistan teaching medicine and other survival skills to the women and children and elders, protecting them day and night, and then having to walk away from that village when my job was done, only to see the place destroyed by Taliban guerrillas a few days later."

Ben nodded.

So did Laith.

The three men looked at Patrick and then Will with icy gazes.

Will held their gaze before turning to address Patrick. "They'll do."

"Will is the intelligence officer who is running the operation." Patrick was sitting on the dinner table. The man he was speaking to was sitting on a chair in the center of the room. "Do you understand?"

It's not a difficult thing to comprehend," Roger replied.

"Good." Patrick nodded. "Will's British. Could that be a problem for you?"

"Only if he has a problem with the fact that I'm of German descent."

Will laughed.

"I'm sure that he doesn't have a problem with that." Patrick's words were rapid and not jocular. "Are Laith, Ben, and Julian now bedded down?"

"Why would you feel the need to ask about my men, Patrick?"

"I don't have such need. I simply have a need to hear how you respond to me."

"Then you should now know that despite your profile I have no desire to be unduly deferential to you."

"Which in turn would mean you wish to project independence and control." Patrick slapped hands. "I need that."

"What a man like you needs is rarely shared with people like me."

Will turned from the window and looked at Roger. He walked toward the middle of the room, grabbed a dining chair, and spun it around to sit opposite Roger. Despite being seated, the man before him was obviously quite tall, but Will was pleased to note that Roger betrayed no obvious signs of being a special operations officer. Will could tell that Roger was visibly older than his men, and even though he was clearly a handsome man, with short, straw-colored hair, there was nothing in his face that spoke of a lifetime of living with extremes.

Will nodded once. "I can tell you exactly what I want."

Roger regarded Will for quite some time, then frowned. "You've been in the military. Special Forces, I would say."

"How do you know that?"

Roger waved a hand. "You've got dead eyes."

Will had been told by others that his eyes had died long before he joined the army. "French Foreign Legion. I was a GCP operator."

Roger said, "When I was in DEVGRU, we did some cross-training with you guys. We taught you underwater insertion techniques. You taught us how to kill people while diving through the sky in a HALO insertion."

Will sighed. "Is it of any particular relevance what units we previously worked in?"

Roger shook his head, smiled before going serious again. "I come from a family of fighters who all served different organizations and flags. I've served the country of the United States as a DEVGRU SEAL and now as a team leader in the CIA SOG. My father and my uncles served deep behind enemy lines in Vietnam with the Australian SAS and on secondment with the secret MACV-SOG. And my grandfather served as a paratrooper in Germany's elite First Fallschirmjäger Division in most of the European and Russian hellholes that existed for Wehrmacht soldiers in World War Two." He smiled. "They're all dead now, and all I have to remember them by is a bunch of medals and photos and citations." He looked at Will. "But I know that none of us—my forefathers, their brothers, or me—has fought for our organization or our country. We've all fought for the man by our side."

Will glanced at Patrick, then turned back to Roger. His first impressions of Roger were very positive. "I'm going to give you every single detail about this operation, and I have a very specific reason for doing so. There is a strong possibility that I will be eliminated by the man we seek. If that happens, the operation must continue, and you will be in charge in the field."

Roger shrugged. "That's fine by me. I just need to know my objectives."

Will smiled briefly without taking his eyes off the paramilitary officer. "You have two primary objectives: monitor a woman while she tries to make contact with our target and then help me seize the target when he reveals himself. You may have secondary objectives, but they will be determined subject to on-the-ground developments."

Roger nodded almost imperceptibly.

Patrick spoke. "Unless something catastrophic happens, you take your orders from Will rather than me."

Will snapped his fingers. "Forget that." He looked at the man's face. "Forget orders. All I need to know is this: Can you and I work together?"

Roger placed his hands neatly together and then nodded. "I made up my mind about you the moment you sat down before me. You look like you know what you're doing. The only thing that concerns me"—his words slowed—"is that you do not appear to fear your own death."

EIGHTEEN

The following morning Will and Roger entered Croatia. They took a taxi from the country's main airport in outer Zagreb, and within twenty minutes they had arrived at the five-star Regent Esplanade, on the city's Antuna Mihanovićeva. Roger got out of the car first and walked quickly into the imposing hotel. Will stayed in the vehicle, fiddling with bills to pay for the drive. When he was satisfied that Roger was in position, he handed the cash across to the driver, grabbed a bag, and made his own way into the Regent.

Will looked around the elegant, spacious reception area and spotted Lana in a corner sofa area. He walked casually up to her and kissed her on both cheeks. He had a smile fixed on his face and hoped that to anyone else in the hotel he looked like Lana's husband or lover.

When they were seated, Will said quietly, "You've checked in?"

"Yes." Lana gestured to take in their surroundings. "I've never stayed in a place like this. My room is lovely."

"Don't get too comfortable. You won't be here long."

She was dressed in a suit with a short, boxy jacket, a slim skirt, and leather pumps, with a gold silk scarf carefully wrapped around her throat. Her hair was pinned up high to reveal her stunning Arabic features. He felt instantly attracted to her and for a moment wondered how it would feel to genuinely be Lana's lover. He decided it would feel good.

"Do I have your approval?" Lana raised an eyebrow, crossed her legs, and placed her hands on her lap.

"You fit right in here." He reached down to his side, picked up his small bag, and swung it across to the floor by Lana's feet. "I bought you some gifts."

Lana looked at the bag and then smiled at Will.

He wagged a finger and smiled. "There's nothing in that bag to get too excited about. While you're here, you need money and communications equipment, so I've treated you to a laptop, a cell phone, a credit card in your name, and three thousand dollars. I've also enclosed my contact details." He smiled wider. "I did, however, throw in a gold necklace for no reason other than to make you feel positive thoughts towards me."

"Positive thoughts?" Lana smoothed a hand over her hair and frowned. "Why am I here?"

Will checked his watch, even though he knew exactly what time it was. "It's nearly nine A.M., meaning the place you need to go to is open." He withdrew from an inner jacket pocket a folded sheet of plain paper, an envelope with a printed name and address on its cover, a fountain pen, and another sheet containing the words Lana needed to copy. He carefully placed all of it on the coffee table between the two of them.

Lana picked up the sheet containing the words and silently read its contents. Then she sighed and picked up the pen. Her hand shook as she did so.

I would like the contents of this letter to be communicated to a dear old friend.

My friend is a Persian man who knew me during troubled times in Central Europe. I helped him with his dangerous tasks, and then one day he suddenly disappeared. I believed he must have been killed, and for years I have mourned his absence from my life.

Something has happened, though, which has given me hope that my friend may not be dead. A British man who works with secrets approached me nine days ago at my home in Paris. The man told me that my friend was still alive and now held a very senior and powerful position within the Iranian military. The man said that he wanted to capture my friend in order to prevent something bad from happening in the United States or Great Britain. The man asked me questions about my friend. The British man gave me his own name and contact details and said he would return to speak to me again soon.

I am scared. I have fled my Paris home, even though in doing so I have left an ill mother alone. I have traveled eastward to put distance between me and the secret British man, although I am sure he will find me if he wishes to do so.

But I hope that my old friend can find me first. It is my hope that my name is still on your records and can be linked to my old friend so that this communiqué can be passed to him with urgency. It is my hope that he replies to this letter. For the time being, I can be found at the Regent Esplanade hotel in Zagreb.

If my friend is alive, I cannot bear the thought that he may be captured and incarcerated or murdered. I am willing to help prevent that from happening. I am willing to tell him all that I have learned from the British man. I am willing to give him details about the British man so that he may be seized. I will do so if my friend will do something for me in return. Please tell my old friend that I wish to be with him again.

Yours,
Miss Lana Beseisu

• • •

Will pressed his cell phone against his ear and listened to Roger's words.

"I watched her go into the building. She's now back at her hotel."

Will nodded. "Good. When are your men joining you?"

"They'll be with me in one hour."

"All right. Then your first primary objective has commenced. Even though she'll be unaware of it, your team needs to stay around her day and night."

Will closed down the phone and tapped fingers against the inner door of his airport-bound taxi. Lana had hand-delivered the letter to the Iranian embassy in Zagreb. It was addressed to the attention of the defense attaché of the embassy, the IRGC man whom Harry had identified. Will hoped the man would realize the importance of the letter and immediately communicate its contents to the IRGC headquarters in Iran. If he did so, it should take the IRGC minutes to link Lana Beseisu to Megiddo. In turn, Will hoped that Megiddo would feel he had no alternative other than to respond to the letter in order to ascertain whether his operation against the West was completely compromised. He hoped that Megiddo was not based in faraway Iran but instead was close by in Central or Eastern Europe. However, Will knew that so much now rested on hope itself. He breathed deeply and for the first time in days felt that he was no longer in total control of events.

Will sat in the Zurich safe house, opened the laptop, and read Lana's e-mail.

Dear Nicholas,

I have received a reply. What should I do?

Love, Lana

Patrick emerged with a mug of coffee and a serious expression on his face. "There are no more flights back to Zagreb for at least eight hours."

Will checked his watch. "It's not ideal, but find out which member of Roger's team is on rest and get him to bring the letter to me."

He typed on the laptop before Patrick could respond.

Dear Lana,

At seven-thirty this morning, please go to your hotel's 1925 Lounge. The place should be empty, but please choose a corner seating area with a table. Place the letter response on the table and leave the bar no later than seven forty-five.

Yours, Nicholas

Will sent the e-mail and took two big gulps of his steaming coffee. He looked up at Patrick. "It will be tight, but there's a nine twenty A.M. Croatia Airlines flight out of Zagreb. One of Roger's team should be able to get the letter to me here by midday." He glanced back down at his laptop as it bleeped. Lana had responded and would follow her instructions.

Laith Dia pulled off his Helly Hansen arctic parka and tossed it over the back of a chair. He tousled his straight black hair with his fingers and then rubbed a large hand over his neck. He pulled out an envelope, which he gave to Will before sitting in one of the armchairs.

Will studied the envelope, gently feeling its weight in the palm of one hand.

"If it's got explosive in it, then that should have been detected as I went through security at the airports this morning." Laith lit a cigarette and jabbed it in the direction of the envelope. "But its contents could be coated in poison."

Will nodded slowly while examining the edges of the envelope's seal. He then carefully opened the letter. Within was a single sheet of paper, which he withdrew and examined. He saw that it had been cut along the top. He held it up to the light coming through the room's window and then placed it on his lap. He scrutinized the envelope before smiling and discarding it to one side. He picked up the letter again and spoke to no one in particular.

"It was written in a hurry. The nearest stationery available was used, and in this case it was stationery belonging to the Iranian embassy in Zagreb. The author of the letter cut off the paper's header to try to disguise its origin, and there is no watermark on the sheet. But the author forgot to check the inside of the envelope. If he had done so, he would have spotted a tiny giveaway inscription underneath one of the glued folds."

Will read the letter.

Dear Miss Beseisu,

I am delighted to receive your letter, and it seems a lifetime ago since we last saw each other. I regret that I had to leave Sarajevo without saying good-bye. I would have liked to thank you for your work, but alas I was needed urgently in my own country and therefore had to leave more promptly than I anticipated.

It is an appealing thought to become reacquainted with you. It is important, however, that you understand that since we knew each other I have grown to become a cautious and suspicious man. The information you say you carry may prove invaluable to me. It may also be a means to expose and capture me. I do hope that is not the case.

But I do wish to trust you, and I have an idea how that can be achieved. Call your secret British friend and tell him to meet you somewhere. That place must not be in Croatia, as, if you are telling me the truth, it is important that you do not actually draw him close to you. When the meeting has been arranged, you must give me the man's name and tell me where he will be. It will be me, rather than you, who will then meet the British man.

For now we can continue to communicate via the embassy in Zagreb.

Your friend

Will handed the letter to Patrick, who read it and smiled.

Will rested his head on interlocked hands. "I thought he might go straight for a meeting with Lana."

"Then you've underestimated your quarry. I believe he's too cautious to take the bait on the first pass." Patrick folded his arms. "But there are seven positive points to this letter."

Will pushed himself up from his chair and walked to a window. He thought for a while before nodding and turning. "We've successfully tested a line of communication to the man; he's responded; the response has been very quick; the man writes as if he is the man who knew Lana during the war in Bosnia; he's interested in me; he's given Lana an instruction; and he wants to hear from her again."

"Exactly." Patrick handed the letter to Laith and said quietly, "Memorize this letter and relay its contents to Roger."

Will stuffed his hands in his pockets. "We can't agree to his terms—not yet, in any case."

"I agree." Patrick walked and stood close to Will. "If she were genuine, it would be illogical for Lana to follow his instructions."

"So Megiddo is testing her?"

"I think so."

Laith spoke. "How do we know that the man who wrote this letter is Megiddo? It could have been written by anyone from within the Qods Force. Megiddo may still be a dead and distant memory."

Will and Patrick turned to look at the CIA paramilitary man. It was Patrick who spoke to Laith.

"The letter was handwritten by the defense attaché of the Iranian embassy in Zagreb. The man appears to have immature tradecraft skills due his carelessness with the letter's stationery. Such lack of tradecraft means the man has no special credentials, so he would have reported Lana's communication to those who do have such credentials. He would have been scared to have done anything otherwise. In turn we can be confident that the response letter was dictated to him by someone else, and that person clearly feels that for the time being he has to rely on the DA to maintain contact with Lana."

"You're right, though, Laith." Will nodded at the ex–Delta operative. "We don't know that the letter was dictated by Megiddo. At the moment it's convenient for us to think that way because of the speed of his response, but it could well be a response from others within the IRGC."

A cell phone rang, and it was Laith who reached into a pocket to answer the call. He listened and then nodded as he said, "All right, I'll be on the next available flight." He ended the call and looked at Patrick and Will. "I should not have been brought here. One hour ago Lana took a walk through Zagreb's old town. As you would expect, Roger and Ben followed her. As you may not have expected, so did an Iranian surveillance team of six men and one woman."

Patrick shook his head and muttered, "He doesn't trust her."

"And why should he?" Will shouted the words. "I told you and Alistair that she shouldn't have been deployed! I told you it was too dangerous!" He pointed a finger at Patrick. "Lana's safety is now in serious jeopardy."

NINETEEN

At 7:00 P.M., Will watched Roger walk up to his table in the Piano Bar of the Sheraton Zagreb Hotel. As he seated himself opposite Will, a waiter approached them, but Roger waved the man away.

"Where's Lana?" Will pushed his cup of tea to one side.

"She's back in her room, meaning that the Iranian surveillance team has scaled back its coverage of her, meaning I'm able to be here with you right now." He checked his watch. "So far she's dined in her hotel, but if this evening she decides to do otherwise, I'll have to head straight off."

Will sighed. "Is she okay? Safe?"

Roger smiled a little. "You care about her, don't you? In my experience it's unusual for intelligence officers to care about the people they deploy."

Will nodded. "Tell me about the Iranian team."

Roger's smile brightened. "They're good. They move around Lana with experienced drills, and they've obviously analyzed this city, because they use its routes with confidence."

"Are there any indications they might have spotted your team?"

All vestiges of a smile vanished. "Impossible. But you made a very good call not to tell Lana about me and my men. If she knew we were around her, there's a strong likelihood that her body language would betray her awareness of us to the Iranians."

"What are their intentions?"

"It's too early to be certain at this stage, but so far they're just watchers."

Will breathed in deeply. "I need to see her this evening to help her write another letter. How can I get to her room without being spotted?"

Roger said nothing for a moment and seemed to be deep in thought. He then said, "Send her an SMS saying that you're in town and would love to meet her for a drink at the Khala bar on Nova Ves at nine-thirty tonight. Tell her that if you're not there by ten P.M., it's imperative she return straight to her bedroom and stay there for the rest of the night." Roger reached into one of his pants pockets. "Here's a spare copy of her room's swipe key. You of course don't meet her at the bar but let yourself into her room while she's out."

"Drawing the Iranians away from her hotel." Will frowned as he took possession of the key. "That was quick work getting a copy of this."

Roger shrugged "Even though their intentions toward her currently appear passive, I need to know what we should do if Lana is attacked by the team."

Will looked around before returning his gaze to Roger. "If you ask Patrick that question, he will rightly tell you that the priority is Megiddo. That if you step in to prevent Lana from being snatched or assassinated, our operation has failed. That all you can do in that situation is watch it happen and then follow the team with the hope they'll lead us to their master." He paused and leaned in close to Roger. "But you work with me. And *we* do not sacrifice innocent women."

Roger responded with a nod. "You really are unlike other intelligence officers I've worked with." He smiled. "I'm glad."

Will tapped a finger on the table, lost in thought. He said, "When she gets back to the hotel around ten P.M., the Iranians will be with her, so I'll be trapped in her room. How can I leave?"

Roger exhaled. "You can't until she leaves and draws them well away from her hotel again. For her to do that in the middle of the night would look suspicious. Plus, I presume you don't want to tell her that she has seven Iranian intelligence operatives now following her. You'll have to stay with her until she leaves the hotel after breakfast."

Will shook his head. "She'll misinterpret my intentions."

"I'm sure you'll cope." Roger then pointed at Will. "Just make sure that she follows her normal routine in the morning."

Will read the text message from Roger.

She's on her way out, and her friends are with her. Best you head over now. By the way, she has a big smile on her face.

Upon arrival at the Regent, Will walked confidently through the lobby area of the large hotel and took himself to Room 85.

The room was lavish but had signs of Lana everywhere—clothes flung on her bed and draped over the backs of armchairs, four sets of shoes tossed on the floor, towels hung in odd places, her open laptop resting on a bed pillow, hair dryers, half-spilled vanity bags, magazines and books, and a stuffed laundry bag awaiting next-day collection. Will spent the ensuing forty-five minutes exploring the room and all its contents, including Lana's computer and e-mails. He was pleased to find nothing out of the ordinary. Helping himself to a glass of Prosecco, he sat and waited.

He received another text message saying Lana was back at the hotel and without a smile on her face. The Iranians were with her as well.

• • •

Will heard the door lock open and movement in the room's entryway. Within a moment Lana turned into the room and stood before him. She was clearly astonished to see him and glanced back at the closed entrance before looking at him again. "Nicholas."

"It's okay, Lana." Will smiled and did not stand. "I thought this would be a little less public."

Her evident nerves were joined by an angry tone. "You have a key?" She placed her handbag on her bed and removed a neck scarf.

"Yes, I do."

"You could have told me." She took out a cigarette, which she proceeded to ignite. "It would have saved me the shame of being stood up."

"I'm here now. And I made the effort to come to see you. Would you like a drink?"

She looked at Will's glass of sparkling wine. "Yes, one of those."

He nodded. "Sit down and relax, Lana. I am sorry I shocked you. I was delayed and thought that it was easier for us to meet here." He rose from his armchair and removed a small bottle from the minibar. He poured her the drink, which he took to her before sitting back down.

Lana rested in one of the large room's many chairs, but not too close to Will. She wore a thigh-length black sleeveless dress, evening heels, and a gold belt. Her long hair was down, partly braided and pinned. On the top of one arm, Will could see a hint of one of those old bamboo scars. "When did you arrive?"

"Just before you." Will glanced around the room. "It's okay, I've not touched your things."

Lana sat and regarded at him without much of an expression. "It would have been nice to have a drink with you outside." She drank some wine and then smiled slightly. "You are an odd and edgy sort of person, Mr. Cree."

"I probably am."

The woman seemed unsure what to say next. "Do you have a family?"

"I have everything I need."

"I mean a lover? Children?"

"I knew what you meant."

Lana ran a finger and thumb around the neckline of her dress. Slitting her eyes against the smoke, she took another drag of her cigarette before extinguishing it in an ashtray. "Why are you here?"

"You need to reply to the letter." Will had another sip of his wine before pointing at the table between them. "Everything you require is on there."

Lana read Will's script and then wrote. When she had finished, she lit another cigarette and was silent for a while, looking angry again. Will picked up her letter.

To my dear old friend,

I am overjoyed to hear from you. It seems to me that you are back from the dead and that I now have a chance to fill the void of a life that has been hollow since you disappeared.

I understand your reticence. Why would you blindly trust words on a piece of paper? Only when you look into my eyes will you be able to tell that my emotions are pure and without any agenda other than to be under your wing again. But I, too, have reticence. How can I do as you instruct until I am fully in your protection? I am certain that the British man and his colleagues can find me if they want to do so. If something happens to the British man and I am still here, his friends will come after me and will no doubt severely punish me. And the British man is all I have to bring me close to you again. If I give him to you now, then what use am I to you thereafter?

Please, can we meet? Please, can we look in each other's eyes so that we can both know that our feelings for each other are honorable and trustworthy?

But I know that I must give you something in this letter, so I will give you the British man's identity. His name is Nicholas Cree.

Yours,

Will nodded and said, "Good. You'll need to deliver it to the embassy first thing in the morning."

Lana was looking away while smoking ferociously. "It is very hard for me to write to Megiddo as if I love him." She glanced down at her letter and then back at Will. "You've achieved what you needed to do this evening. You may go now, if you wish."

Will sighed again and took a gulp of his wine. He placed his glass down on the table and spoke gently. "I'm not in a rush. Do you have other plans?"

Lana frowned and brushed a finger against her face.

Will slowly stood and walked over to the curtained window. He knew that he could not open the blinds for fear of being seen by hotel-gazing Iranians, but he stood there anyway and closed his eyes.

He smelled Lana's perfume before he felt her fingers interlock with his hand. He felt her body press against his back and her lips gently kiss his neck. He felt her long hair brush against his face. He squeezed her hand a little and turned to face her. She was truly beautiful, and as he beheld her proud and complex face, he wondered why she had chosen to be alone for so long. He decided that it was because her hatred for Megiddo had not allowed her to love another. He decided that the wish she had expressed in Paris might now be coming true.

Let me do this and feel alive again.

He said, "I will stay in your room with you tonight, but we cannot be together in that way." He saw the look of disappointment and confusion on her face. He saw a tear creep from one of her eyes. He saw her looking at him as if she knew that he had made a mistake. He gently ran a finger over her tears and whispered, "I am not the man for you, Lana."

She stepped closer to him. "Maybe I am the woman who can change that."

Will shook his head. "I don't know."

Lana placed a hand against his cheek. "I know you care for me. I know you worry about my safety. But"—she frowned—"I need to know. . . . I need to know whether you've ever thought what it would be like . . . for us to be together?"

Will placed his arms around her waist. He wondered what he should say. He told her the truth. "I have imagined what it would be like. I have wondered about the future—when this is all over." He pulled her closer and kissed her on her cheek. "I have thought about us." He smiled even though inside he felt turmoil and confusion. He knew that he had spent years developing a shield against love and normality, that his shield was there to help him do the things he had to do. He knew that right now and for the moment that shield was lowered because of the woman he now held. He kissed her cheek again and said quietly, "Maybe when this is over, you can be the woman who changes things for me." He shook his head and felt bitter and hollow. "But nothing must change right now."

Will watched Lana sleeping on her bed while he sat in an armchair on the far side of her hotel room. Her duvet only partially covered her body, and a naked leg lay exposed over sheets. Will walked up to her and quietly arranged the duvet so that it was fully covering her. He looked at her and wondered whether she was dreaming. He looked at her and wondered what it would have been like to share her bed with her, to feel her naked warmth against him, to smell her hair and perfume, to wrap her in his arms.

He smiled and looked away from Lana toward the windows and saw that early-morning sunshine was just visible behind curtains. He knew that beyond the room were men who wanted to capture and kill him. And he knew that they did not scare him. He looked back down at Lana, and his smile faded. He now knew that she could be the woman to change everything for him. And that knowledge terrified him.

TWENTY

I t's delivered. She's on her way back to the hotel."

Will ended the call from Roger and drank his coffee. He was back at the Sheraton, alone, surrounded by businessmen and -women, tourist couples and families. Normal people. He rubbed a hand over his face, and as he did so his cell phone bleeped with a message from Patrick.

Stay where you are. I'm coming to you with something urgent.

Patrick's face looked tired, but he still moved with a vigor and purpose that defied his age. He was pacing back and forth in Will's hotel room. "Since you left yesterday morning, I've traveled to Langley and back to get hold of the paper you're now holding."

Will read the document. It was a telegram from the National Security Agency to the Bundesnachrichtendienst, Germany's foreign intelligence service, known as the BND.

SUBJECT

Berlin-based terrorist cell plans to attack Reichstag Building of German Bundestag while the United States secretary of state makes his address to the parliament.

OVERVIEW

Details have been obtained of five active terrorists. Details have been obtained of their location in Berlin. Details have been obtained of their intention to destroy the Reichstag Building while parliament is in session and receiving an address from the United States secretary of state. Details have been obtained of their intention to carry out this attack using devices that combine thermite cutting agents and explosives.

MAIN TEXT

1. The following five individuals are known to have terrorist-related backgrounds:
   a. Sonmaz Faturachi, male, age twenty-seven, Azerbaijani.
   b. Raheem Abdul Abdullah, male, age twenty-four, Canadian of Iraqi origin.
   c. Abel Zaidi, male, age twenty-six, Yemeni.
   d. Imad Nabulsi, male, age twenty-seven, Lebanese.
   e. Soraya Nashat, female, age twenty-two, British of Lebanese origin.
2. The five individuals are located in house 7, Onlauer Street, Treptow, Berlin. The five individuals have been in this location for nine days.
3. Twenty-five portable canisters containing combined thermite cutting agent and explosive materials are believed to be located at house 7, Onlauer Street, Treptow, Berlin.
4. The individuals intend to deploy and detonate the portable canisters around the structure of the Reichstag Building of the German Bundestag.

COMMENT

1. Separate reporting gives full details of the above five named individuals and their affiliations to Shia Islamic terrorist organizations. The five individuals are known to have received funding and training from Iran [NSA10/11832/L refers].

2. The type of canisters referenced suggest devices intended to destroy building structures and materials by explosion-propelled burning methods [NSA09/19985/L refers].

SOURCE

1. The source of this report is assessed as highly reliable. Multiple means are available to check the accuracy of the source and its reporting.

Will glanced up from the report. "Looking at the source, I presume this is Hubble reporting?"

Patrick nodded. "A valued friend within the BND called me to tell me they had received the telegram from NSA. He wanted to know what I thought, and I told him that I'd check it out. It's from Hubble."

Will set the report on a desk. "The American secretary of state and the entire German parliament? That's a huge target."

"It would be the worst attack on German soil since British and American aircraft bombed the place in 1945."

"Do you think this could be the one we've been looking for? Megiddo's operation to strike his blow against the West?"

Patrick shrugged. "I don't know." He stopped pacing and pointed at the document. "We have a puzzle. This does not look like the corrupted Hubble reporting, because it is far too specific. But if it is uncorrupted Hubble reporting, then why would Megiddo be careless enough to expose his operation to NSA when he knows that they've already penetrated his communication systems?"

"Maybe the mastermind behind this German operation isn't

Megiddo. Despite receiving previous funding from them, the terrorists may not be acting on Iranian instructions."

Patrick shook his head. "An attack of this magnitude wouldn't be allowed to proceed without Megiddo's authorization." He began pacing again. "Even if the planners were outside his control—and I can't believe that to be the case—he would still find out about the attack and quash it for fear of compromising anything he's planning."

"You're saying this has to be Megiddo's operation but you can't believe he would now have been caught out by NSA?"

"I'm saying I do not know." Patrick brought himself to a halt. "The BND has handed the report to their Bundesamt für Verfassungsschutz, who in turn are no doubt working with Grenzschutzgruppe 9 to stop the attack."

"Then Germany's Security Service will use its police antiterrorist unit GSG 9 to capture the terrorists and learn the truth behind the attack."

Patrick exhaled loudly. "Therein lies the problem. An intended attack of this scale will be met with extreme countermeasures. My friend in the BND has told me that Germany cannot allow the terrorists to live, and so we will never know who was behind the plot. My friend also told me that GSG 9 is striking the house tonight."

Will slammed a fist on the desk. "But we have to know whether this is Megiddo's plot. If this is Megiddo's operation, then Lana's information becomes irrelevant as soon as the attack is thwarted. Megiddo will therefore disappear from our grasp. That means the only chance we have of tracking him down for retribution is via an interrogation of the terrorists."

Patrick sighed. "I did warn you that ours would not be the only operation against the attack. If other Western intelligence services have prevented Megiddo from conducting his assault, we should just accept that and walk away."

"Just as you walked away from my father's killer once you had decided that your conscience was clear?"

The fury on Patrick's face was vivid. He walked up to Will and stood very close. "I spent seven years trying to get that man, and with no care for my own safety or career. Along the way I personally killed twelve men, destroyed the lives of numerous others, had a death sentence imposed upon me by the Iranians, and lost two marriages. I did not give up. Megiddo simply disappeared."

Will looked back into Patrick's silver eyes. He smiled. "I understand. And you will therefore understand why it is simply unacceptable for us to now consent to a situation where Megiddo disappears again from our grasp." Will's smile vanished, and he looked away from Patrick. "We can't allow the Germans to send their GSG 9 execution squad into that house. Our trail to Megiddo would vanish if that happens."

Patrick held his gaze for a moment and then nodded slowly. "Then it's just as well that I'm one step ahead of you." He backed away from Will and checked his watch. "My trip to the CIA in Langley was to secure a copy of the NSA report, but I also made a quick stop in Washington." Patrick looked back at Will. "Because the U.S. secretary of state is among the intended victims, that should allow the United States to have some degree of involvement in actions to prevent the attack. I have a letter written by my president that authorizes me, and any colleagues with me, to consult with the BfV and relevant German police services. You and I are booked on a two fifty P.M. Lufthansa flight to Germany today to see if we can persuade our German friends to keep at least one of the terrorists alive."

The BfV woman studied the piece of paper and then a man who was leaning in the corner of the room within the headquarters of the Bundesamt für Verfassungsschutz. She turned to face Will and Patrick. "We recognize your letter of introduction, but you do realize that you have no authority within this matter?"

"We do." Patrick clasped his hands in subtle supplication. "All we're asking for is for you to hear what we have to say."

The BfV woman smiled a little. "We're grateful your NSA gave us advance warning of the attack on our parliament and your secretary of state. But the terrorist attack will now not take place, and in any case your Secret Service has canceled your politician's visit. All American interests in this operation are now dead."

"They are, but even with the destruction of this terrorist cell, German interests should most certainly remain alive."

"Why?"

"We have new intelligence that this cell is but one of many who wish to attack your country."

Will resisted the urge to smile with Patrick's lie.

"What do you mean?" The BfV woman again glanced at the other German man and then looked back at Patrick.

"I mean that if you kill all the terrorists tonight, you will have no chance of linking them to other cells in Germany. I'm counseling you to at least spare the life of one terrorist so that he or she may be interrogated by you."

"Our federal law forbids us to interrogate in a meaningful way. If a terrorist is spared, that person will immediately be afforded full legal protection. For that reason alone, we have decided that all the terrorists must be killed tonight." The woman sighed while looking away and nervously rubbing her fingers against her palm. "If your new intelligence is correct, I would dearly like to get my hands on one of the terrorists to find out about the other cells. But I simply cannot authorize that."

"Then let us do the interrogation." Patrick's voice was hushed.

The woman laughed shortly. "No."

Patrick was silent, and Will knew that he would be feeling the same degree of disappointment Will himself now felt. He wondered what Patrick would say next, but just then the man in the corner of the room spoke rapidly in German to the BfV woman. She responded with equally rapid but harsher-sounding words. The engagement between the two people lasted for almost two minutes before the woman shrugged and chuckled.

She addressed Patrick. "My friend here is the GSG 9 officer in charge of the assault on the Onlauer Street house tonight. He has an idea he wishes to share with you. I have permitted him to speak freely."

The GSG 9 man leaned upright from the wall and folded his arms across his chest. He regarded both Patrick and Will. "We are striking the house at two A.M., and nothing you say will stop that from happening. I have a team of eight men who will be conducting the assault, and we have reconstructed the house to practice the assault fourteen times since we received our instructions. We therefore know every square inch of the Onlauer Street house, and the terrorist cell will not be able to repel our assault." The man glanced at the BfV woman and then back at Patrick and Will. His look was serious.

"Nevertheless, tonight I am risking the lives of eight extremely experienced and skilled operatives. I can accept that risk if the likely outcome is total success. I cannot accept that risk if the death of this cell merely fuels greater outrage from its friends." He nodded at Patrick. "Maybe those friends intend to strike our country." He smiled briefly. "Or maybe they intend to strike interests closer to your hearts. But either way I want my assault to have strategic value rather than just being a minor reactive defense." He stared straight at Will and seemed to be analyzing him. He said, "The assault plan can be modified slightly. We will go into the house and kill four of the terrorists. We will then exit the building for a maximum of one minute. We will then reenter the building and execute the final terrorist if he or she is still alive. After our initial assault, the building will feel like hell, because it will be saturated with smoke and fire from our guns and grenades. But if one of you two gentlemen is prepared to do so, then I will allow you that one-minute interval to enter the house and interrogate the living terrorist."

TWENTY-ONE

Will pulled on a black one-piece Nomex 3 flame-retardant suit and donned Adidas tactical boots and Oakley assault gloves. He placed his SF–10 respirator on his lap next to a flashlight and checked his Glock 17 handgun one last time. He looked around the rear of the truck in which he was seated. There were nine other men with him, and eight of them were dressed like Will but also wore knee and elbow pads, bulletproof vests, assault vests containing stun grenades and tear-gas canisters, radio harnesses, and armored helmets. All of them had Glocks strapped to their thighs, but their other weapons varied. Five of them had Heckler & Koch MP5 submachine guns slung across their chests; one carried a G3 sniper rifle with nightscope attached; the remaining two carried Remington shotguns, which Will knew would be loaded with Hatton rounds to remove door hinges. The latter two men also had EDX frame charges attached to their assault vests and door-breaching hammers resting over their legs. Will watched the eight men fit their SF–10 respirators to their faces and check the fittings to ensure that they were positioned correctly.

The vehicle slowed and then stopped. The man who wasn't wearing any assault gear but instead was dressed in jeans, jacket, civilian hiking boots, and a radio with earpiece was the GSG 9 officer. He looked at his watch and said nothing, but after nearly thirty seconds he nodded once and pointed at the man with the sniper rifle. That man quietly opened the rear door of the truck and disappeared into the black night. They waited for what seemed like two minutes before the officer placed a hand against his radio earpiece and held up two fingers. One of the shotgun-carrying men and two who carried submachine guns rapidly and quietly exited the vehicle and similarly vanished from view. Within a further ten seconds, the officer raised three fingers, and the remainder of the team got out to move to their positions. Only the officer and Will stayed in the rear container area of the truck.

The officer bent and spoke to Will, keeping his hand against his earpiece. "It will begin in two minutes." He straightened and looked toward the open truck doors.

Will glanced at his own watch and attached his respirator to his face. He picked up his Glock handgun and held it tightly in his gloved right hand. His left hand clasped a flashlight. He sat motionless and waited.

He heard two explosions occur almost simultaneously, followed by the low boom of shotguns. He knew that the front and rear doors of the Onlauer Street house were now breached and that the assault team would be entering the building to kill four members of the terror cell. More explosive sounds indicated that the team had deployed stun grenades, and these sounds were followed by rapid but controlled bursts of submachine-gun fire.

These noises continued for nearly thirty seconds before the GSG 9 officer held up his hand and nodded at Will. "Top floor. Second bedroom on the right. Go now."

Will thrust himself upward, jumped out of the truck, and ran. The house was nearly two hundred meters away, but despite the distance and the darkness Will could see smoke billowing out of the building's broken windows and its front door. The residential street was obviously awakening from the noises of the attack, and within his peripheral vision Will saw lights in other houses flicker on. He focused on the target house's front door and ignored the two GSG 9 men who stood on either side of the entrance. He ran straight into the building. Everywhere was dark, and Will switched on his flashlight and swung its beam in an arc before him. The place was thick with smoke. Ahead of him Will saw flames licking up the stairway he needed to climb. He also saw a man sprawled in an awkward position over the stairs. The man's face had been removed by bullets, and a line of entry holes marched across his chest. A semiautomatic rifle was close to one of the dead man's hands. Will inhaled deeply, the sound of it exaggerated by his respirator. He raised his handgun and walked quickly up the stairs, ignoring the fire around him.

The smoke in the hallway of the top floor was less dense but still swirled around his legs. He moved his gun left and right and saw that the rooms to either side of him were on fire, sending sporadic flashes of light into the corridor he was in. He stepped forward, and as he did so, he felt his leg brush against a large inanimate object. He angled his flashlight downward and saw the dead body of another man. He walked on and crouched low before sidestepping into the last bedroom with his gun directly in front of him. The smoke in this room was thicker, and curtains were on fire. On the floor in the center of the room Will saw a body lying on its side. It was rocking back and forth, a hand clutched to one leg. Will checked the surroundings but could see no weapon. He moved closer and put the muzzle of his Glock against the body's neck before slowly pulling it onto its back. A woman looked up at him. Will glanced down at her leg and saw that she had been shot in the thigh. Her trousers were torn and covered in blood. The bullet had clearly done severe damage.

Will bent to the woman's face and said loudly, "Who sent you?"

The woman's eyes blinked rapidly. She looked terrified. Tears were streaming across her face, and they were clearly caused by pain, fear, tear gas, or all of those. She looked very young.

"Who sent you?" he asked her.

The woman began coughing, and the sound instantly told Will that she had gas in her throat and lungs. He knew that he could not allow her to suffer like this. He ripped off his respirator and fixed it over the woman's head. He said to her, "It's okay. I'm going to get you out of this place."

He swept his arms under her body and lifted her, retaining hold of his gun and flashlight. He swiveled to face the room's exit and quickly walked the woman into the hallway and down the stairs. She moaned as he carried her through flames and more smoke. Will pulled her closer to his body to try to shield her from the fire. The heat on his own exposed face was intense. At the bottom of the stairs, he turned and made his way toward the building's rear door. He stepped over two more dead bodies and scattered guns as he did so. He walked out of the house and onto a small grassed area of garden. Four GSG 9 men were standing waiting there, and when they spotted Will, they immediately swung their weapons toward him and the woman, shouting in German. Will ignored them, placed the woman down on the wet grass, and removed the respirator from her face. She stared at him with a look that remained one of terror and pain.

Will again leaned in close to her and spoke quietly and gently. "I'll make sure you get medical help. This is not your fault. None of this is your fault. But I need to know who gave you instructions to attack the Reichstag Building."

The woman clamped her hand again over her leg wound, and Will saw that more blood was pulsing from under her palm. He knew that it was likely the bullet had torn through a vein, and he also knew that the woman would probably soon be in hypovolemic shock.

"Who sent you?" Will's voice remained hushed but urgent.

The woman's eyes widened. She said something inaudible. Will leaned closer so that his ear was against her lips. He heard her moan again, and then he heard her words.

"The Iranian." The woman's voice was accented and raspy. "He sent us to die. But it was all a game."

"What do you mean?" Will remained motionless.

The woman exhaled raggedly, and as she did so, she said seven words before pushing Will away and clutching her chest. Will watched her, knowing that the bullet had done more than just damage her leg. It had also induced a fatal heart attack.

He stood as the GSG 9 men took charge of her dead body and carried it back into the burning house. He pulled off one glove, ran fingers through his hair, and remained still for a moment, breathing heavily. He cursed and shook his head as he wondered what kind of life the young woman could have had if she hadn't chosen the path that had brought her to this house. He frowned as he repeated the woman's words in his head:

It was a game—to trick you.

TWENTY-TWO

Agame?" Patrick was hunched over a cup of instant coffee in his room at the Ritz-Carlton in Berlin. It was four hours after the attack on house 7 of Onlauer Street in Treptow.

Will shook his head. "The German police found the twenty-five canisters containing the explosive and the thermite cutting charges in the attic of the house. They also found detailed plans of attack. The attack was going to happen."

"But Megiddo told us all about it via Hubble because he wanted us to believe that it was his main target."

Will rubbed the back of his neck. "We failed to anticipate the possibility that the Hubble Berlin report was both genuine and manufactured. It's incredible that Megiddo constructed an operation of this magnitude and then sold it out."

Patrick clasped two hands around his coffee mug. "It means he's hiding something far worse than the destruction of the German parliament."

Will stared at Patrick for a moment and then frowned in thought. "We've got to take things up a level."

Patrick's silver eyes flickered. "I agree. But are you ready for that?"

Lana showed no surprise when she saw Will waiting in her Zagreb hotel room. She set her two shopping bags on the floor, walked up to him, and kissed him on the cheek. Then she removed her coat and sat on the end of her bed, pulling a cigarette from the pack in her handbag. She was dressed in jodhpur-style cord slacks and a thick rollneck sweater. As ever, her look was one of casual elegance.

"You have hesitation in your eyes, Nicholas." Lana lit her cigarette and smiled slightly. Her cheeks had color in them, and she exuded confidence and energy. "Are you wary of my intentions toward you now?"

Will thought about her question and shook his head. "No, because I can control any such intentions."

Lana inhaled smoke, placed her elbows on her thighs, and rested her chin on her hands. She watched him for a while before saying, "I'm sure you can. But something is making you uneasy."

Will frowned.

Lana retained her smile. "Maybe you are wary of yourself."

"You could be right." Will *knew* she was right. He wanted more than anything to sit next to her and hold her.

Lana studied him for a while longer before reaching back into her handbag. "The concierge just gave this to me." She withdrew an envelope and held it out at arm's length.

Will moved closer, took the envelope, and unsealed it to remove a letter. He turned it over a few times and decided that it was not written on Iranian embassy stationery. The words were handwritten in a blue ink.

Dear Lana,
    Of course you would not deliver to me the British man without being under my protection. I am reassured that you have taken such

a stance. I am also grateful that you have sufficient confidence in my intentions to give me the man's name. But hiding from him no longer serves any purpose. You must bring him near to you so that after you and I are reacquainted, I can make swift plans.

Contact him and tell him that you are scared. Tell him that you are sorry you left Paris without telling him you had done so. Tell him where you are staying in case he needs you.

I am closer to you than you may think. We will meet very soon.

Your dear friend,
Megiddo

Will read the letter three times before handing it to Lana. He watched her read and then look up. Her expression had changed, and she now seemed agitated.

"It's him. It's really him." Lana extinguished her cigarette and immediately lit another one.

"You're sure?"

She rocked back and forth a little. "I'm sure." When she rubbed a hand over her mouth, the action smudged lipstick onto her chin. "What happens next?"

Will walked over and took the letter from her hand. "We'll give him what he wants as well as something unexpected."

He then gave her a new sheet of stationery and dictated her response to Megiddo. When she had placed the completed letter in the envelope, Will pointed a finger so that it was touching the document. "You need to take that to the Iranian embassy now."

Lana nodded and placed her hand over his. She squeezed tight and said, "It's funny. I've lived with years and years of hatred and a desire for revenge against Megiddo. That's all that mattered to me. But now"—her smile faded, and she looked longingly at Will—"I wonder if that's all that matters."

To my dear Megiddo,

I did what you asked, but when I spoke to him, he sounded angry. He told me that he was in Berlin and had prevented you from doing something dreadful. He told me that you were playing games and that you were trying to mislead his people.

He wants to see me again, and he will be traveling to Croatia within the next day or so. He told me that I had now become important to him. He told me that he needs to know what you look like.

Please tell me what I should do. Please hurry and take me away from here.

Yours,
Lana

"Okay, so what's this idea of yours, Harry?" Will had traveled to Oslo Airport merely so that he could spend a few moments with Lace in the transit lounge where he was now seated. He had come straight here after receiving an SMS from Harry as he was leaving Lana's hotel. Harry was flying on to Helsinki, and Will intended to leave the Norwegian airport on the next available flight to Zurich.

Harry took a large gulp of his complimentary whiskey. "Human Benevolence Foundation. Have you heard of it?"

The name sounded familiar to Will. "A nongovernmental organization?"

"Yes. It's Iranian and quite small. Not like some of the other Iranian NGOs and less obvious than the likes of Red Crescent, which we all know is a front for their intelligence services. HBF's been in Bosnia for about three years and has been mostly building and rebuilding religious places. They seem"—Harry angled his head a little—"quite legitimate."

"You think this is where Megiddo is working from?"

"I think it *could be* where he's working from. I would not like to put it stronger than that."

"Why do you believe he could be there?"

Harry smiled and swirled ice within his glass. "One of my other business interests is construction. We use a lot of subcontractor companies, and there's a Bosnian guy who works for one of them who I've known for a long time. We go way back—before, during, and after the war. His own company has recently been awarded the contract to build a mosque in Sarajevo, with HBF money and according to their designs." Harry waved one of his manicured hands in the air. "So my guy is working with HBF people. And there's a man there. He's mid-fifties in age, quiet, does nothing. My guy recognizes him."

"Qods Force?"

"Yes." Harry set his glass down. "At least he was when he was last in Bosnia during the war."

"A name?"

"Nothing. My guy's asked around to try to find out more." He held a finger up. "Carefully, mind. He made it look as though he was just checking up on HBF to make sure they're good for their money." Harry dipped his little finger into his whiskey and then sucked the spirit off it. "Nobody knows anything about this Iranian man. It seems he keeps an extremely low profile, which is quite a difficult thing to do in a goldfish bowl like Sarajevo. And he seems to have no involvement or interest in HBF projects."

Will thought through a few issues. "Why would your guy do this? Why would he try to check up on this man?"

Harry shrugged. "Because I asked him to." He laughed. "Don't worry, none of my people know about our arrangement."

"Do you trust him?"

"Trust?" Harry sniggered. "You know my views on that word. But I can say that he and I have been through too much together for us to distrust each other."

Will nodded his approval. "That's excellent, Harry. I think your guy may have stumbled onto the Qods Force Western Directorate's location. Maybe even Megiddo himself."

Harry finished his whiskey, and for once the man looked quite fatigued. He checked his watch and then said, "Business beckons. My flight will now be boarding." He managed a tired smile. "On price I've just lost a deal with the Russians, but I'm hoping to offload the same deal to the Finns."

"Weapons?"

"Warships."

Will leaned forward so that he was closer to Harry. "I have a request, but given the level you operate at, you may think it somewhat beneath you."

Harry waited.

"If, and I only say if, I were to need guns for an operation in Bosnia," Will asked, "would you be able to get them for me?"

"How many users?"

"Five men."

"Special operations gear?"

"Yes."

Harry smiled in earnest this time. "I can arrange such a thing in seconds, but surely a man of your standing would not have need for under-the-counter equipment?"

Will mimicked Harry's shrug. "What you and I are doing has to be completely off the radar. Nothing can be official. You understand?"

Harry flashed his white teeth. "Absolutely." He forced himself upright and grabbed his leather overnight bag. "When you need the stuff, just call me and I'll arrange everything."

Will stood and shook hands with his agent. As he did so, Harry pulled him closer to his body. All traces of his smile had vanished.

"My associate's name is Dzevat Kljujic." Harry's words were clipped and quiet. "He lives on Bulevar Branioca Dobrinje in the west of Sarajevo."

Will frowned. "You don't need to tell me this. Your guy's information is enough for me."

"No, it's not because there's more." Harry gripped Will's hand tighter. "Yesterday morning Kljujic called me with an update. He said that he was still drawing a blank on getting information about this

Qods Force man. But he also said that he managed to discreetly take a photograph of him."

Will felt a rush of adrenaline course through his body. "When can you get hold of the shot?"

Harry looked around quickly and then returned his gaze to Will's eyes. "That's the problem. I was supposed to meet Kljujic this morning before I traveled here. But he never showed up, and since then his cell phone's been switched off. He's disappeared."

It was 4:00 A.M. and very cold and dark as Will trudged over fresh Bosnian snow toward the urban house on Bulevar Branioca Dobrinje in Sarajevo. As he neared the property, he stopped and took shelter within the doorway of another house on the same street but across the road. He stood hidden in the unlit entrance and carefully examined his surroundings. Widely spaced lamps lined one side of the street, casting a dim yellow light over patches of the route. Some cars were parked near the properties, and judging by the snow cover on them, none had been driven for several hours. Will scanned the area of snow around the front door of Kljujic's house but could see no sign of footprints or indeed any disturbances over the snow. He listened carefully but could hear nothing out of the ordinary. He looked directly at Kljujic's property. It was part of a terraced complex and appeared quite modest from the outside. There were six windows on the façade, and all were dark, with wooden shutters closed behind glass. Will placed his hands inside his overcoat and waited for thirty minutes while analyzing every house that could overlook the target property. It seemed to him that the street was asleep.

Finally he walked quickly across the street to Kljujic's front door. He pressed the buzzer a total of five times, waiting fifteen seconds between attempts. He glanced up to look for lights being switched on, but there were none. He repeated the ritual, waited another twenty seconds, and strode back up the street, counting the number of houses on his left as he went. When he reached a small alleyway, he cut through the place so that he was facing the rear gardens of the properties on Bulevar Branioca Dobrinje. He counted again as he walked alongside the backs of the houses until he knew he was standing directly behind Kljujic's house.

The garden before him had wooden fencing that Will estimated was ten feet high. He leaped up and swung his body over the top of the fence before dropping down into a crouch within the garden. He'd been hoping that the place around him would contain at least one feature or item that could help him with his task, but instead the garden was bare. He looked at the six windows on the rear of the house and saw that those on the ground and first floors had external bars to protect the property from forced intrusion. But the windows on the top floor had no such bars, although the wooden shutters behind the glass were clearly shut. Will made some quick mental calculations, breathed in deeply, and sprinted forward. As he neared the house, he jumped to place one foot on the sill of the ground-floor window, thrust upward so that he could grab the bars of the second window, and then pulled up so that his other foot was on that window's sill. When both his feet were on the first-floor sill, he released his grip from the bars and allowed himself to fall backward a few inches before again thrusting both legs to jump up and grab a metal overhang above the top-floor window. The overhang moved a little with his weight, but he quickly fixed his feet into position on the top-floor sill so that his weight was now accommodated. He stayed in this position for a moment while listening. He heard nothing and quickly punched his fist into the glass. The sound from the strike carried down the windless street, and Will held his breath as he again listened, glancing left and right. He placed his gloved hand into the hole and started gradually and quietly breaking away pieces of glass. Within a minute he had stripped the window of all its glass. He placed both hands back onto the overhang and kicked hard into the center of the closed shutters. It took two attempts before they gave way and swung inward. He climbed into the house and total darkness.

Will turned and pushed the broken shutters back so that they were as closed as they could be. Then he pulled out his flashlight, cupped a hand over the top of it to minimize its glare, and switched it on. He was in a bedroom, and the place was a mess. Sheets were half pulled off an empty mattress, and a table lamp lay smashed on the floor by its side. Two chests had all their drawers pulled out, and clothes were strewn everywhere. He spent a minute looking around the room before moving into the floor's adjacent bathroom. A frameless mirror had been wrenched off its wall, and shards from it had fallen into a sink and toilet. He moved slowly back into the intervening corridor and took careful steps down to the first floor. To his right was a room that appeared to be a guest bedroom. A mattress had been lifted off the bed, upended, and sliced vigorously with a sharp object so that stuffing and springs were exposed. He moved to the other room. It was clearly a study of sorts. It contained a desk and office chair, metal filing cabinets, and bookshelves filled with books and file boxes. This room was much neater, although upon inspection Will noted that all of the file boxes were empty and that there were a corresponding number of piles of loose papers stacked on the floor. He moved his light over the desk and spotted nothing except a small cradle and a connecting cable. He lifted the cradle and saw that it was an electronic battery charger for a digital camera. Next he swung his light up to look at the books. Most of them were architectural or construction manuals, and upon opening some of them Will saw that they had been well thumbed. Below the bookshelves the beam of his flashlight flickered over an array of framed photographs that had obviously once been positioned upright on the side table they occupied but were now lying scattered there with the backs of the frames torn away. Will looked at the photographs; they seemed to be mostly business-related, and it was clear that Dzevat Kljujic had no family—or if he did, their images were apparently not deemed worthy of being framed in this study. Will's flashlight stopped over one photograph that looked older than the others. It showed two young men dressed in jeans and quasi-military jackets. They were standing in wooded hills and smiling. Will picked up the photograph and brought it closer to his eyes. He did not recognize the man on the left, but the one on the right was certainly the Harry he knew, although the picture showed him to be around two decades younger. He pulled the photograph out from its frame and stuffed it into one of his pockets. He then set to work and spent the next ten minutes rapidly going through the stacks of paper to find and remove any reference to his agent Lace.

With more papers secreted on his person and his task complete, Will moved downstairs. Once there, he could smell what seemed like sour milk, and the odor was strong everywhere. He walked into the room on his left and saw that it was a kitchen. Cupboards were flung open, and some broken crockery lay fragmented across surfaces and on the stone floor. A fridge door hung ajar, and the light from the fridge was cast over a dining table and a half-full bottle of vodka. He left the kitchen so that he could see the last room in the house.

It was a lounge area, and as Will moved his flashlight around, it produced snapshot images of the place. He saw three dining chairs that were positioned to face the middle of the room; he saw a side table containing three plates with remnants of bread and meat on them; he saw three tumblers; he saw pictures that had been pulled off the walls and now lay broken over the floor; he saw a small television that looked as though it had been kicked onto its back; he saw a man hanging from the ceiling in the center of the room.

The smell of sour milk grew stronger as Will moved closer to the suspended body. He ignored the dead-flesh odor and looked at the rope around the man's throat. It had been tied professionally and was threaded through a metal loop in the ceiling that was out of place in this room and next to a lampshade; the fixture had obviously been screwed into one of the room's beams. The rope then traveled diagonally downward to a corner of the room where a similar metal loop had been inserted by the baseboards. Will looked around the three positioned chairs and saw cigarette and cigar butts on the floor by their sides, as well as ash. He picked up one of the tumblers from the side table and placed its lip against his nose. He went back to the body and looked at the face. Judging by its expression, the man had been hanged in such a way as not to snap the neck but instead exhaust his body of air while his three executioners had sat in the chairs and eaten meat, drunk vodka, smoked, and watched him slowly die.

Will checked the man's pockets but found nothing in them. He pulled from his own pocket the picture of Harry and the other man. He shone his flashlight between the image of the unknown man in the picture and the face of the dead man before him. Despite the age difference and the strangulated contortions of the hanged body, it was clear that the men were one and the same. The man had to be Dzevat Kljujic.

Will decided he had to leave and shone his flashlight one last time from the top of the body to its feet. As he did so, he noticed a dark streak on one of the man's trouser legs. He followed the streak upward, taking a step closer. The streak moved into the man's shirt, and Will touched the garment to find that it was cold and wet. He knew that the shirt was not, as he had previously thought, dark in color but instead was saturated with blood. He held the back end of his flashlight in his mouth and tore the shirt open.

One word had been carved with large letters into the dead man's chest. The word was in Farsi, but Will knew what it meant.

The word meant "spy."

TWENTY-THREE

Dear Lana,

*Stay where you are and meet the British man when he arrives.
Give him a false description of me, but do not be vague with details
or he will view you as uncooperative. Ask him about Berlin and
what bad thing he prevented me from doing there. If he is willing
to give you details—and I believe he will in order to gain your full
allegiance—then be horrified with his response. Tell him that you
will help him in any way that you can.*

Yours,

Megiddo

Will placed the letter into his jacket and looked at Roger. The CIA
man had collected the letter from Lana's room after Will had instructed her to leave it there and take a walk in Zagreb.

The two men were silent for a moment, and Will knew that, like
him, Roger would be thinking through logistical issues.

Will spoke first. "Kljujic was obviously spotted taking the

photograph of the Iranian man working from the Human Benevolence Foundation's building. Kljujic's house was torn apart, and I'm certain the Iranians recovered his camera and the photo. But while I removed all reference to Harry from the house in order to hide his name from the police, I can't be certain that Kljujic's killers haven't already linked his action to an instruction from Harry."

"But if they grab Harry, they'll torture him. He'll reveal all details about Lana, and the operation will be dead. Harry's safety has become as important to us as Lana's deployment." Roger rested his chin on his fingertips and seemed to be absorbed in thought. "Harry's the sort of man who could naturally have some degree of security around him, given his line of work. He's going to find out about Kljujic's murder, so I suggest that he hear it from you, and I suggest you advise him to surround himself with a team of men as soon as he's back in Bosnia in the morning."

Will called Patrick. "I'm doing it today."

Patrick was silent for a moment before saying, "You're still sure this needs to be done?"

"I'm sure. We've got to make him grow frustrated and desperate. My escape from a snatch effort will increase Lana's value to him. If he can't get me today, he may feel that he has to rely totally on Lana to set me up, and he knows she won't do that until she's met him."

"They might not go for you today, though."

"They will. When I'm seen with Lana, our man won't be able to resist deploying members of his team to capture me. He won't take the chance of seeing me disappear from his grasp in the hope that I reappear some other time."

Will could hear Patrick breathing heavily. "All right," the other man said at last, "but whatever they try, do not engage with them. Just get out of the situation and allow them to report back to their master that their attempt has failed."

•   •   •

As Will sat with Lana in the Diana Bar of the Westin Zagreb hotel, he knew that she would be oblivious to what was really happening. She had no knowledge that Megiddo's men had been watching her for days; she had no knowledge that Will's highly specialized team had been around her for slightly longer; and she certainly could not have known that in meeting Nicholas Cree out in the open she had brought the Iranians directly to their prey.

Will smiled at her as he pushed her glass of Graševina wine toward her across their small table. He took a sip of his own mineral water while observing the woman. For the occasion of being seen out with Will, Lana had chosen to wear a sleeveless sapphire blue evening dress. Her long hair was draped over one shoulder and breast, and her already prominent facial features were accentuated with Egyptian-style makeup. She looked stunning. Will, on the other hand, was dressed in the most robust attire he felt he could get away with in a five-star establishment.

"You look tired, Nicholas." Lana spoke gently and with care in her voice.

Will ignored the comment and casually looked around the bar. The place was quite full, with an eclectic range of late-afternoon guests. He quickly brought his glance back to the beautiful woman who sat opposite him.

"How is your mother?" As soon as he asked the question, Will wondered why he'd done so.

Lana frowned slightly, then reached across to place her fingers over Will's hand. "Thank you for asking. She is still undergoing tests in the Paris clinic."

Will nodded thoughtfully. "It must be expensive for you both."

Lana sighed. "It is, but I would rather live humbly and have her get better than anything else I can think of."

Will said in a barely audible voice, "I have temporary access to money. It may help with your living conditions and with your mother's medical costs."

Lana inhaled deeply.

Will held up a hand. "Don't misinterpret what I've just said. I would help you simply by way of reward for what you're doing for me. And such help would be given only when all this is finished."

Lana shook her head in amazement. "I'm not doing this for reward." Her voice trembled a little. "But I would gladly accept such a gift."

Will looked downward and felt momentarily uncomfortable. He wondered if the emotion was visible to the Iranian surveillance operative who was reading a menu while sitting in the far corner of the bar or to Laith Dia, who was bent over a large glass of untouched beer in the center of the room. Will breathed deeply and looked up at Lana. The woman was watching him.

"I'm sorry."

Will frowned. "What for?"

Lana sighed. "I'm sorry for the other night . . . forcing you to tell me what you thought of me." She twisted the stem of her wineglass back and forth and looked nervous. "I know you are a professional, and I should have realized that you would not have taken advantage of that moment. I also know that you have a big enough burden to carry in your task without having to worry about me confusing matters or adding to that burden."

Will smiled and shook his head. The discomfort he'd felt a moment earlier was replaced by a feeling of complete comfort, and he knew with utter clarity that it was because he was with Lana. He marveled at the sensation. "I carry many burdens, but you're not one of them."

Lana looked surprised and then smiled. She took a sip of her wine, and as she did so her smile faded. "What will you do to Megiddo if you capture him?"

"I will force him to tell me about his plans. I will do whatever is necessary to the man."

She nodded. "I hope so." She looked away and for the briefest of moments seemed sad. "For a time I did love Megiddo, probably as much as I've subsequently hated the man." She met Will's eyes. "When I knew him in the besieged city of Sarajevo, we were in one of the most chaotic and hellish places on Earth. Food, water, and sanitation were minimal. The place was constantly bombed from the artillery placements in the hills. Serb snipers shot men, women, and children every day, and we had very little knowledge of what was happening beyond our city. It was hell. The predominantly Muslim people of Sarajevo were brave and resolute despite everything that was happening, but even the bravest of them could not tolerate the uncertainty, the chaos itself. Megiddo was different. I watched him stand still as shells blew buildings apart right next to him and as bullets flew over him. I watched him look toward the hills containing those mad dogs and smile. I watched him and knew he had no fear, because for him there was no chaos. He understood exactly what was happening and what he was doing." Lana looked into her wine and shook her head a little. "But there were the briefest of moments when I saw wonder and confusion within him." She looked back at Will. "Before I ever shared my bed with Megiddo, there was an occasion when I was sent by him to deliver cash to a Bosnian Muslim paramilitary unit in the north. The unit had just completed a daring and successful assault against the Serbs in Mount Vlašić, but as a result their supplies were diminished. So, on Megiddo's instruction, I used one of my maps to exit Sarajevo and walk a one-hundred-kilometer route to the mountain. It was my most difficult task during the war, and along the way I traversed minefields, hid from Serbs and other armies, and suffered mild hypothermia from the cold. It took me ten days to reach the mount, but I found the unit and gave them their funds to buy more weapons, medical supplies, and food. I then used a different route to return to Sarajevo." Lana's voice was hard. "I nearly made the return journey untouched, but fifteen kilometers outside of the city I was caught by men while sleeping in woods. It was a group of five Bosnian Serbs who belonged to a notorious paramilitary unit called the Panthers. Thankfully, they believed I was a displaced peasant. But they knew I was a Muslim, and they took turns raping me." She stared down at her hands, and Will knew that she was trying to control her emotions. "I remember writhing on the ground, I remember the bitter cold, feeling dreadful and seeing them standing there laughing at me. I remember looking at one of the men, the man who was clearly their leader and had tabs on his jacket to show that he was their captain, and I remember him staring at me with a look of hatred and disgust. I remember one of the other men asking him, 'Captain Princip, can we kill her now?' I remember the man they called Princip smiling, lighting a cigarette, and saying, 'Let's give her the worst death. Let's take her coat and leave her to freeze to death.'"

Will tried to picture the young, wretched Lana in such circumstances and somehow relate her to the glamorous woman sitting before him. He could not do so. He felt revolted by what she was telling him. More than anything else, he wished he could move to her side and hold her.

"But I refused to die. I refused to be a victim. So I waited for what seemed an age, until I was sure the men were far away, and I picked myself up and walked." Lana brushed fingers though her silky hair. "I don't remember the journey—I was in a daze and no doubt was suffering all sorts of mental and physical distress. But I made it back to the city and fell onto its streets. Some men and women found me and took me straight to Megiddo. He told the people to leave and carried me into his shelter. I was half conscious, but I remember him lighting a wood fire to heat a bucket of water. I remember him stripping me of my clothes and standing me naked before that fire while he washed my body. I remember him giving me the only set of spare clothes he had while he used the bathwater to hand-wash my own soiled garments. I remember him looking at me with both strength and confusion in his eyes." Her voice was very quiet now. "I loved him at that moment. I loved him because he seemed to me to be my savior." She shook her head. "So when he later abandoned me, I felt as if nothing made sense anymore. I felt as if something in me had died. I felt as if all I had left was hatred toward the man who I had thought was better than all the others I had known." She looked back at Will. "And ever since, I've felt that hating someone was safer than trying to love another man and have that love taken away again." She smiled and looked a little embarrassed. "Maybe that's not true anymore. Maybe it never made sense."

Will shook his head. It made perfect sense to him, because he knew all about the fear of love and loss. He knew all about the ways to hide behind other emotions or put up barriers to stop love. He stopped shaking his head and wondered whether, like Lana, that was true for him anymore.

Will breathed deeply as he stood by the entrance to the Westin hotel. It was still light, although he knew that darkness would begin to fall in an hour or so. And judging by the color of the clouds above him, it looked likely that fresh snow would soon drop to add to the stuff that already lay thick over Zagreb. He walked up to a hotel attendant and handed the man his parking valet ticket. Within two minutes his car was delivered to him. The Audi A8 was the most powerful sedan available from the rental dealership he'd visited earlier in the day. Will gave the attendant some money and asked him to stay with the vehicle for a moment. He walked back into the hotel and spoke to the front-desk concierge. He told the woman he'd heard that the views of the city sunset were magnificent from the vantage point on Medvednica Mountain, and he wondered whether the road to it was passable today. The woman advised him that the solitary road to the mountain's summit was clear but icy and that he would be better advised to wait a few days until conditions improved. Will thanked her and explained that he would at least try to make the drive now, given that he was leaving Croatia in the morning. He walked back out of the hotel and entered his vehicle. He hoped that what he'd just done had been sufficient to allow members of the Iranian surveillance team enough time to prepare a vehicle to follow him. If they were savvy enough to overhear or subsequently get the information from the concierge, he had also given them his destination and reason for going there. His cell phone beeped, and he saw he had a message from Roger.

Four men in two vehicles are onto you. The rest of them are staying with our lady. Good luck.

Will closed his phone and drove.

For fifteen kilometers he traveled west across the traffic-laden city. He drove within the speed limit and occasionally looked in his rearview mirror to search for anything out of the ordinary. But he was not yet worried about spotting the Iranian vehicles, which would have been difficult anyway, thanks to the density and movement of other cars around him. It was only when he turned northeast onto the hilly Route 2220 that traffic evaporated and just two sets of headlights remained behind, but at a moderate distance from, his vehicle.

It was dusk now, and snow began to hit the Audi's windshield as Will drove steadily up the hilly route. He took the bends in the road slowly, hoping to appear to be a cautious driver looking for signs of ice. There were houses bordering the road for fourteen kilometers as he continued his gradual ascent. The houses then vanished, and Will's observation of the two distant vehicles behind him significantly increased. Around him now were no residential or road lights, only forest. The road veered eastward just as the snowfall became heavier and more rapid. Will squinted to focus his eyes through the blizzard that was now striking his car. When he looked in his rearview mirror and saw one of the set of headlights become larger, he had to resist the urge to speed away and instead kept glancing ahead and behind.

The first set of lights moved rapidly toward Will's car until they were directly behind him. He braced himself for an impact, but to his surprise the car passed him at speed and traveled rapidly up the hill before him. Will flashed his lights so as to appear annoyed with the careless maneuver of the other driver, then glanced back to see that the other vehicle had moved a little closer to him. As he looked ahead again, the first car disappeared up the road and into the rapid white dots of falling snow.

Will drove another three kilometers, and the whole time the vehicle behind remained at a distance of approximately two hundred yards. He knew that within ten minutes he would reach the vantage point he was supposedly aiming for, and he also knew that the isolated stretch of road he was now on was as good a place as any for the Iranians to hide an assault.

The forest on either side of the road had grown thick, and its trees acted as barriers to prevent vehicles from moving off their route. In warmer times, Will imagined, the place around him would contain idyllic walks for hikers and families, but right now it looked dark, lonely, and hostile.

He eased around yet another bend and saw that the road stretched straight ahead for several hundred yards. At that very instant a set of headlights turned up to full beam came driving toward him at high speed. He glanced in his mirror and saw that the rear vehicle was also now approaching him, but at a slower speed. He knew that the vehicles were being driven to trap Will's car between them. He slowed his Audi to thirty miles per hour, downshifted, and placed his left hand on the right-hand side of the steering wheel. He moved the car into the center of the road, poised his right hand over the handbrake, eased off the accelerator while depressing the clutch fully, and then yanked the wheel hard to the left. A split second later, he pulled up the handbrake and felt his car spin around. As it did so, he moved the steering wheel in the opposite direction. He was now facing back down the hill and had come to a total halt. But the car that was now ahead of him had clearly increased its speed. Will knew he had no more than three seconds to get out of the Audi or be crushed.

He opened his door and dived out of the vehicle at the same time he heard the noise of impact behind him. He didn't look back. Instead he ran straight into the forest ahead of him. He sprinted between trees while counting to ten in his head and then turned ninety degrees to continue sprinting to another count of ten. He spun around and crouched. Breathing rapidly but silently, he looked at everything near him. The forest was obviously wild, as trees grew naturally here— they were unevenly spaced, and some areas around him were dense while other areas were more open. Everywhere was covered in ankle-deep snow, although Will knew that the combination of blizzard and twilight would make it difficult for anyone to use the snow to track him. Nevertheless, there were four men after him, and he knew that if he stayed still for too long, he would be caught.

Will saw flashlights. They belonged to two of the Iranians, who were approximately seventy meters away from his position. The men stopped for a moment and then split up. One of them headed in Will's direction, and the other moved off on a different route. Will inched very slowly backward into undergrowth and lowered himself so that he was prone on the ground; he heard the man's footsteps crunching in the snow, and he saw the beam from his flashlight cover the ground just next to Will's position. The Iranian walked past him at a fast pace and turned into a channel of open ground. Will was about to attack the man when he saw that at the head of the channel the other man was emerging with his flashlight. The men were obviously covering ground using search drills wherein they would separate and then rejoin before either of them was isolated for too long. Will cursed silently. This team knew what it was doing.

He watched the two men stay together for seconds and then split up again, with one man going to the right and the other directly onward. The light was fading fast now, and Will was grateful for the additional cover. He lifted himself up to follow the man who had traveled directly forward. Will moved into the trees using long, quick, but delicate strides while in a semicrouch stance. He placed himself prone on the snowy ground again and watched. As he had predicted, the man soon came to another stop and was rejoined by his colleague, who joined him from the right. Will was much closer to both men on this occasion, and he could see that in addition to flashlights, the men carried nightsticks. He presumed they also had concealed handguns, but the exposed batons were clearly an indication that they wanted to incapacitate and capture Will rather than kill him. The two men whispered, pointed in several directions, and separated again.

Will decided that he had a maximum of thirty seconds to get it done. He pushed himself up and moved silently toward the man who was nearest to him. He expected to have to sprint the last few meters, but the blizzard had grown even stronger and the sound of his movements. He came directly up behind the man and placed his right hand on the man's chin while jamming his left hand hard against the back of the man's skull. He deliberately fell backward with the man while twisting his head. The man's arms and legs flailed wildly, but Will held him firmly while screwing the man's head around until he was satisfied that his neck was broken. He pushed the dead body off him and quickly dragged it away from the track it was on. For a brief moment, Will looked at the body. The man's build and light-colored clothing were similar to Will's own frame and attire. An idea came to him, and he grabbed the dead man's flashlight and nightstick. He continued on the route the man had been taking while moving the beam of his flashlight ahead of him. After walking for fifty meters, he stopped and looked around. He saw the other man coming toward him from his left. Will swept his beam over the ground and stayed still. He wondered how close he could let the man get to him before the man realized that he was not moving toward his colleague.

When the man came to within a few meters of Will's position, Will swung his flashlight into the man's face to momentarily blind him. The man uttered something harsh-sounding in Farsi and held the fist that was clutching his nightstick up to his face to shield it from the light. Will ran at him, dropped low, and swept his nightstick against the shinbone of one of the man's legs. The man fell forward onto his knees, and Will seized the moment to jab the end of his weapon into the man's gullet. He then struck the side of the man's head and watched him slump to the ground. Will looked at the man, hesitated, wished that he had a better weapon to do his job cleanly, and then struck him another four times on the head until he was satisfied the Iranian was dead.

Will patted his hands against the corpse's pockets and waistband. When he found what he was looking, for he dropped the nightstick and flashlight and then proceeded ahead with his newly acquired CZ 75 pistol. It was nearly nighttime now, and Will had to move slowly while navigating his way through the trees. He headed toward the area to the left of his entrance into the forest, as it seemed to him to be the logical place for the other two team members to be searching. He moved several paces forward, stopped, crouched, listened, then moved a few paces more. He continued this routine until he had covered nearly three hundred meters. He had no particular plan, apart from keeping one of the men alive so that he could deliver a message of failure back to Megiddo.

Will was taking another step forward when a bullet struck him in the shoulder and sent searing pain down his arm and over his chest, bringing him to his knees. He saw a flashlight flicker on his left side, and he awkwardly pushed himself back up onto his feet to swing his gun toward the light. But as soon as he did so, the light was turned off and Will was back in blackness. He cursed and moved several steps away from the position where he'd been shot. He heard movement and rotated 360 degrees to try to identify its location. His left arm was now limp by his side, and he grabbed its wrist with his right hand and shoved the limb's useless hand partway into a pocket to hold his arm still. He knew that the only reason he hadn't been shot in the head was that the man who fired at him wanted him alive. But he also knew that the man would take no chances: if he had to shoot at Will again, he would shoot to kill.

Will thought rapidly. There was no more element of surprise, and the gunshot wound had significantly reduced his physical ability to hunt down his assailants. His hope lay in the fact that the men wanted to capture him. He decided that his only option was to bring them to him. He chose a random direction in the woods and ran.

Ahead of him the ground sloped down into a dip, and Will followed the route while tucking his gun into his belt. On the other side of the dip, the ground rose sharply, and he used his only capable hand to grab onto anything that would help him get up the slope and continue forward. He stumbled several times as his feet caught snow-hidden roots and bracken, but he managed to stay upright despite how hard his useless arm was making it to keep his balance. Occasional flashes hit the ground before him, and Will knew they came from the lights of the men behind him. He also knew that he needed sufficient distance from those lights as well as open space to do what he had to do.

He reached flat ground and pushed harder, even though he risked injury from running near-blindly toward trees. He broke left and right to make his route odd and unpredictable and then carried on fast, desperately hoping to reach some treeless ground that would give him a little more visibility than he currently had. He ran for what felt like thirty minutes while trying to ignore the pain of his wound and the pain in his lungs from constantly sucking in icy air. He ran even after he no longer saw the telltale signs of flashlights flickering behind him. He ran even as he finally emerged from woods into a tree-ringed meadow of snow. He crossed the meadow toward the tree line on the other side, and only then did he stop and turn to face the direction from which he'd had just come. He pulled out his pistol, breathed deeply, and tried to calm his oxygen-starved and agonized body. Almost instantly the two men ran onto the meadow, looking around. They had discarded their batons in favor of their sidearms.

What little light there was from the night sky was casting a blue hue over the area before Will. He waited until the two men were nearly in the center of the meadow before he stepped away from the trees so that he stood exposed. The men stopped and could clearly see him. They were approximately 125 meters away, and as Will raised his pistol, he guessed that they had little to fear from his gun, given the effect his current condition would have on making a meaningful shot, not to mention the distance between them. It was a near-impossible shot, but nevertheless he inhaled three times and then half exhaled before holding his breath. He focused his mind and pulled the trigger. One of the men flipped backward and fell awkwardly as Will's bullet hit him in the head.

The sole remaining member of the Iranian special operations team fired back at Will three times, but the bullets flew wide of their mark. Will ran toward him and saw the man turn and quickly race back across the snow-covered meadow in the direction of the trees. With all the energy he could muster, Will moved his legs as fast as he was able in order to close down the distance between him and his prey and to stop the man from escaping back into the darkness of the forest.

The Iranian was very fast, but Will still managed to get to within forty meters of him before firing two shots near the man's feet and shouting, "Stop or I'll kill you!"

The Iranian slowed and then stopped altogether. Will also slowed to a fast walk while pointing his gun at the man's head. The Iranian held his arms outward and dropped his weapon to his side. Will moved cautiously up behind him, flicked the discarded gun away with his foot, and thrust the heel of his boot into the small of the man's back. The Iranian immediately buckled under the impact and fell sideways, then onto his back. Will walked around the man, continuing to direct the muzzle of his pistol at the man's head. He looked at the man's face and saw no expression save that his eyes were blinking rapidly. The man had the look of a professional.

Will stomped on the man's stomach and then dropped his knee onto the same spot, putting his full weight behind the position. He said, "I'm not going to kill you unless I have to. But I need to know why you attacked me."

The man moaned softly, and Will knew that he was probably exaggerating his discomfort in order to minimize communication.

Will pressed harder with his knee. "Why?"

The man shook his head and spoke in a heavy accent. "I don't know."

Will smiled a little after he heard the lie. "You don't know?" He said it slowly and deliberately. He punched the muzzle of his pistol into the man's mouth and leaned in closer. The man writhed in agony, and Will knew he was no longer exaggerating his pain. "I want you to live so that you can take a message back to the man who most certainly does know. Tell him he underestimated me and will have to do much better than this if he wants me captured or dead." Blood from the man's broken teeth seeped onto Will's gun. "One day I'll meet him on my terms." Will leaned in closer. "And when we do meet, I'll kill him and everyone around him."

TWENTY-FOUR

Y ou were damn reckless!" Patrick was yelling. "I gave you an instruction not to engage them!"

"And I told you on our second meeting that your instructions may not always be correct." Will looked at the medical dressing that had been expertly applied to his naked shoulder. Patrick was on the far side of Will's hotel room in the Sheraton, and the man nearest to him was Ben Reed. Roger had sent over the former Green Beret and specialist in medicine as soon as he'd heard that Will was injured and back in his room. Will looked up at Ben. "Prognosis?"

Ben rose from his seat and started gathering up his battlefield medical kit. The blond Ivy League–looking paramilitary man smiled, exposing his immaculate teeth. "You were quite fortunate. The bullet glanced off the top of your humerus and then exited your body through flesh. There's no muscle damage and only a minor fracture to your bone. You'll have yet another scar on your body, but I can see from the rest of your torso that scars don't bother you. Still, it was a nine-millimeter bullet that hit you, and it must have hurt like hell."

Will smiled as he pulled on a T-shirt to cover his upper body. "What's the latest?"

Ben shrugged. "It's three A.M. Lana's in her room and is no doubt asleep. I most certainly should be asleep. And Roger, Laith, and Julian are on duty around Lana's hotel."

"The Iranians?"

"One man and one woman are on watch at the Regent. The other is not around and so is either on rest or more likely is trying to work out what on earth happened to his colleagues six hours ago."

Will nodded. "Thanks, Ben. You'd better go get what sleep you can before you're back on surveillance."

Retaining his perpetual smile, Ben left. Will knew that Patrick was going to use his departure to launch into a full tirade, so he decided to get his in first. "I told you that we had to make Megiddo desperate and frustrated. I'm confident I have achieved that. And in killing three of his men and sending a taunting message back to him with the fourth, I'm fairly certain that I've also now pissed him off."

Patrick walked across the room and pointed a finger at Will. "Well, you can be dead certain that you've pissed *me* off."

Will narrowed his eyes. "You know that my course of action was right. You know that we have to get Megiddo's thinking off kilter. And you know that to achieve such an objective requires me to take extraordinary risks."

"You always have to take extraordinary risks. God, Alistair and I knew you were like that when you were a kid." He grunted in frustration. "Even the Foreign Legion wasn't dangerous enough for you, so you had to volunteer for their special operations unit so that you could be thrown into even more hazardous missions. If Alistair and I hadn't stepped in when we did, you'd no doubt now be long dead." Patrick grimaced as soon as he'd uttered that last sentence.

"What do you mean, you and Alistair stepped in?" Will said the words slowly.

Patrick's face was a mask of regret.

"What do you mean?"

The CIA man rubbed a hand over his chin and inhaled deeply. He then fixed his eyes firmly on Will, with a gaze that once again held steel. "What happened after you finished your five-year career with the Legion?"

Will looked at the man for a moment and then said, "I was approached by a woman representing MI6. She told me that I had to flex my brain and go to university. She told me that after I completed my degree, MI6 would give me a home."

"How did that make you feel?"

"It made me annoyed, because the woman was the best thing I'd seen in a long time. I wanted to have sex with her."

"But once she politely explained that that was not going to happen, you went along with what she offered." Patrick shook his head a little. "Did you not wonder where the financial sponsorship came from to get you through Cambridge?"

Will frowned. "I did, but I assumed it came from MI6." His voice grew quieter. "There were, however, times when I did ask myself whether it came from some fund my dead father had left for me."

Patrick stepped forward quickly. "See, this is where Alistair and I disagree." He brought his face close to Will's. "We both do share the same amount of guilt about your father's death, but unlike Alistair I also have an equal ration of anger."

"Why anger?"

"Because his death led to a wife having to fend for herself and die and a son growing into something even more efficient than his father—but also something far more ruthless."

Will closed his eyes for a long moment. When he opened them, he looked at Patrick. "Why should that matter to you?"

"You don't get it, do you?" Patrick shook his head. "Alistair and I secretly paid out of our own pockets to put you through college and discreetly introduced you to MI6 in order to direct your talents away from what would inevitably have developed into criminality. We did this because, whether we liked it or not, we had a responsibility for your father's son. My concern about you goes well beyond what you do as an intelligence officer. If you die, Alistair and I have failed in our pledge to stop more death in your family. This operation is yours because we know you thrive on what it delivers to you. But we also know that the things you thrive on both keep you alive and bring you closer to death. Among many reasons, I'm here to make sure that the one does not become the other."

Will stepped back and pointed at Patrick. "You have no responsibility for me. You're here because, while you know that I'm the one man who'll stop at nothing to capture Megiddo, you also know that I'm the one man who'll stop at nothing to kill him. And you can't allow that to happen, because your priority is to keep him alive so that you can discover the details of his plot. You're here to stop me from seeking my revenge." He felt the anger raging through him. "You will fail in that task, and I will succeed in my task. When the time is right, I will do to him what he did to my father. I will make Megiddo beg me to kill him. I will ensure that there's nothing left of the man who destroyed my father and ripped my family apart."

TWENTY-FIVE

Kljujic was executed by three men. The way he was killed by them clearly shows that they believed he was not working alone. They left a message intended to frighten off Kljujic 's associate or tell him that they were coming for him. Either way, you've got to take precautions to protect yourself." Will looked at Harry to watch for the effect of his words.

"Can't your organization protect me?" the agent asked.

Will shook his head. "I have people who could do, that but they are invisible." He looked around the hill-situated tourist restaurant, Kibe. It overlooked Sarajevo and had good views of the city, although Will had chosen to meet Harry here because the route to it enabled excellent antisurveillance capabilities. "I need you to have visible security around you."

"A deterrent?"

"Precisely."

Harry nodded slowly but displayed none of his usual jocular or mischievous character. "I can arrange that, but it's a big inconvenience. My business requires me to travel a lot."

"Then keep traveling. Just make sure that you always take your men with you."

"Sure. I'll do it, but for how long?"

"Until I know that you're no longer under any potential threat."

Harry exhaled loudly. "My associate's death must mean that the man in the HBF building is significant. Why don't you just attack the place and finish this?"

"We can't because we'd be attacking blind. If we had the photograph that Kljujic took, things might be different, but even then we can't be certain that the man Kljujic spotted was Megiddo."

The agent rubbed his face with two hands. He looked very weary.

"Is anything else troubling you, Harry?"

"Things could have gone much better for me in Finland."

"A man like you always bounces back."

Harry managed a weak smile. "Hey, does Megiddo have a price on his head?"

Will laughed a little. "If he does, *I* will never see any of the bounty." He looked around the restaurant again. The place was beginning to fill with the breakfast crowd.

"Yeah, I heard you guys were underpaid and always in need of cash."

Will shrugged and reached into his pocket. "I went to Kljujic's house to find his photograph. It wasn't there, but I came away with something else altogether. This belongs to you now." He handed Harry the photograph of him and Kljujic.

Harry looked at the image and quickly secreted the photo into one of his own pockets. "Thank you for getting this. But when I'm home, I'll burn it."

He exhaled loudly. "Kljujic used to work with me in the war. He was my right-hand man, and he and his crew would do most of the . . . heavy work I needed done."

Will waited silently.

"The photograph needs burning because it was taken just before we went to that village, taken before Kljujic ignored my orders to get his men out of there and instead did something truly unimaginable. . . . But to my shame I've stayed in contact with him ever since." He shrugged. "Men like him are always useful to men like me."

Will kept his eyes fixed on his agent. "Harry, you did not kill those women and children."

Harry looked at him sharply. "No, but I damn well profited out of people thinking I did."

The two men shared a long silence.

"Only you know how long is your road to redemption, Harry, but I have a task for you which might shorten that journey."

Harry frowned.

Will bent close. "During the wars in Bosnia, a woman was raped by five Bosnian Serbs fifteen kilometers outside Sarajevo. I want you to find out who those men were."

Harry looked incredulous. "You are asking the impossible. Rape was commonplace then. How can you expect me to pinpoint this specific act?"

"The event would have happened a few days after a Bosnian Muslim unit fought and captured strongholds from the Serbs in Mount Vlašić. Find out when that happened, and you will have a fairly precise idea of the date of the rape. The five men who raped the woman belonged to a terror unit called the Panthers. The leader of the five men was a man called Captain Princip. Do you think you can trace that name and the men who were with him?"

Harry nodded. "Without the name it would have been impossible. But you know I have my connections, and that includes connections to"—he sighed—"former members of units like the Panthers. After the war many surviving members changed their names to avoid punishment for war crimes. But that does not matter, because some of my other contacts"—now he smiled—"were the people who arranged new identities for those kinds of men." He shrugged. "But it is probable that some or all of those five men were killed in the war."

"I know. But can you at least find out for me?"

Harry nodded again. "Leave it with me. If at least one of them is alive, I'll track him down."

"Discreetly, Harry. Just a name and location. Do nothing else."

"Of course. Who was the girl?"

Will held up his hand. "We have enough secrets binding us already. Just focus on finding these men for me. Who knows, if you succeed, you might get a good night's sleep for once."

By lunchtime Will was back in Zagreb. He looked at Roger and frowned. "Thirteen men?"

Roger nodded. "They came into town this morning. Three of them have immediately taken up duties in the Iranian surveillance team to replace the men you killed. But the other ten don't look like they're here to monitor Lana."

"No. They're here to capture, interrogate, and kill me." He swore softly and checked his watch. "I'm seeing Lana after this meeting. She'll be sending a letter that we hope will heighten her value to Megiddo and stop him from trying to get to me without using Lana. But that letter may not reach Megiddo until tomorrow. Where are the men staying?"

"They've taken a rental home on the outskirts of the city."

Will narrowed his eyes in thought.

"I'm not on surveillance for another fourteen hours," Roger told him. "If you need my help, tonight might be the best time to resolve this problem."

Will sat before Lana reading her words once again.

Dear Megiddo,

I met him yesterday, and he told me about Berlin. I did as you asked and said that I would do whatever I could to help him get to you. He told me that he had new information about your intentions. But what have you done? He came to me again some hours ago

and slapped me several times. He said that I had set him up and
that he had been attacked by Iranian men. I was very frightened,
but I told him the truth, that I had done no such thing. He seemed
to believe me after a while, but he then told me that I must have
been followed to my meeting with him. He asked me if I had done
anything to cause Iranian specialists to be interested in me. I told
him that I had done nothing.

I trusted you to leave Nicholas Cree alone until I was under
your protection. I cannot allow you to use me like this again. I am
confused and feel betrayed.

Lana

"Excellent." Will handed the letter back to Lana. "You need to get this to the embassy straightaway."

"You were really attacked?"

He smiled. "Sort of." He rose from his chair and nodded toward the door. "I'll go first. You leave in fifteen minutes."

"His people are watching me, aren't they?"

"Not as far as I know."

"Don't take me for a fool." Lana's words were forceful, but the anger didn't show on her face. She walked up to Will and touched his arm. The action caused him to wince in pain. She spoke in a hushed but urgent voice. "Nicholas, you are hurt."

"It's an old injury that's just been acting up lately. I'm fine."

She shook her head, then kissed him gently. "Why don't you wait for me here so that when I return from delivering the letter I can attend to your wound?"

Will sighed. "Lana, you know I can't."

Lana walked toward the door, then turned to look back at him. "One day you'll be here for me. I know you will."

As Will exited Lana's hotel, his cell phone rang. He listened to Roger's voice.

"The surveillance team has immediately changed formation and has certainly spotted you. One of them has made a call. They must have put the hit team onto you."

Will nodded. "Let's hope they bring their passports with them. I'll wait here for an hour so that I can be certain the hit team has me in its sights. Then I'll move and meet you there."

"Understood. Hold on." Roger was silent for nearly thirty seconds before speaking again. "I've just heard from Laith. He's been watching the hit team's house. Six of them have just left, but the remaining four are sitting tight."

"Damn it. I was hoping they would put the whole team onto me."

"It looks like they're too professional to take that kind of risk. They've kept some men behind as backup should things go wrong."

Will thought for a minute. "Can one of your team get me a weapon for when I return to Zagreb? Preferably something better than a handgun."

"I'll see what can be done."

Will closed his phone and sighed. He knew that whatever happened, there would be a lot of death this night.

TWENTY-SIX

It was evening now, and Will dined alone at a rear corner table in the prizewinning Steirereck restaurant in Vienna. He had decided to dress appropriately for the venue and wore a Manning & Manning suit, a Dunhill French-cuff shirt, and a silk tie that he had bound into a Windsor knot. He ate smoked catfish on a hot artichoke salad, paprika beef goulash with toasted bread wrapped around leek and pumpkin, and a warm damson tart. He drank a glass of Grüner Veltliner with his food and ordered a glass of Hine cognac when he had finished.

As his digestive was delivered, some new diners arrived at the empty table nearest to him. Judging by their attire, they'd just come from the opera. They were a middle-aged couple and a boy, probably their son, of twelve or thirteen. The boy seemed bored and tired. Will asked the waiter for his bill and found himself observing the trio. The mother was animated, and though Will's German-language skills were limited, he was able to ascertain that she was explaining the opera's story to her son, laughing and waving her arms in the air while reenacting the dramatic climax. The father sat quiet, smiling gently at them. Will watched the man reach a hand across their table and squeeze his boy's shoulder. The boy looked at his father's hand and then grinned. He suddenly seemed reinvigorated and happy.

Will took a sip of his cognac and then exhaled slowly. He wondered what the future held for the young Austrian boy at the next table. He hoped it was a good future and that the boy would never have to say a routine good-bye to his father only to hear days later that he'd been killed in an accident, would never have to feel ashamed that his youth prevented him from looking after his mother, and would never grow into a man who would do things like what Will had to do this evening.

Will's feet crunched over snow as he walked across the Stadtpark before exiting into Gartenbaupromenade. He walked quickly in a northwesterly direction across the city center. Despite its being near midnight, there were too many pedestrians on the streets, and Will knew he had to find a place where he could be alone and unobserved. But the place also needed to be public, so as not to arouse suspicion. He went past hotels, shops, restaurants, and bars, and then, as freezing weather seemed to be finally driving people off the streets and back to their homes, he spotted a small café. He entered and ordered an espresso, which he drank while perched on a window-facing stool. He made the coffee last fifteen minutes before he stepped back out onto the city streets. All around him was now nearly deserted, and he continued his journey northwest before arriving at the place where he hoped things would happen.

Before traveling to Austria, Will had carefully studied the route he'd just taken and the grounds of the building now before him. The church was called Votivkirche, built in 1879 at the request of Archduke Ferdinand Maximilian Joseph after his brother, Emperor Franz Joseph I, was stabbed in the throat on the site by a Hungarian nationalist. Votivkirche was tall, with two illuminated towers, but its base and the expanse of snow-covered woodland before it were dark. Will could see no one around him.

He stood facing the church and listened, but aside from occasional distant traffic noises he could hear nothing. Although his legs began to ache from the cold and lack of movement, he ignored the discomfort and tried to remain as still as he could. He counted seconds and minutes in his head, then finally gave up when he realized he'd been in this position for close to half an hour.

Doubt overwhelmed him. He wondered if he had overestimated the Iranian hit squad's ability to follow him to Vienna. He wondered if he should have waited longer at Lana's Zagreb hotel to allow them to pick up his trail. Either way he began to wonder if his trip to Austria had been in vain. He waited, still listening, for what seemed like another ten minutes. He took his cold hands out of his pockets and stretched his arm to expose his watch, flicking on a lighter to illuminate the watch's surface. It was nearly midnight. He sighed and placed both hands back in his pockets. That's when he was struck from behind with terrific force.

For a split second, Will was aware only of the sound of rapid breathing, the weight on him, and the sensation of snow against one side of his face. He tried to move his limbs but could not do so, and the pain from the impact shot up his spine. He shook his head and struggled desperately to think. More noises. They sounded like rapid footsteps, and then he heard two distant snapping sounds, followed by two louder thuds. He summoned all his strength and forced himself to focus. He managed to twist slightly, catching sight of the man who was pinning him down with a viselike body hold. The blurred image of a second man's face appeared and seemed to be saying something, then disappeared. The man holding him adjusted his position slightly and jammed an elbow against Will's throat and pressed down. Will knew that his attacker was trying to render him unconscious.

The man raised himself a little to improve his leverage. But the action and the increased distance between the two men gave Will the chance he needed. Pulling one arm loose, he punched the palm of his hand repeatedly upward into the base of the man's nose. It took seven strikes before his assailant fell limply over him. Will pushed the dead man aside and immediately rolled before standing. One other man was standing twenty meters away, with his back to Will. Two men lay dead on the ground at his side, and Will knew they'd been shot by Roger. He also knew that the man standing over them was most certainly not Roger and was probably scanning the area to find his colleagues' killer. And the fact that Will could account for only four rather than six of the unit meant that in all probability the other two were now engaging with Roger near his out-of-sight position by the church.

Will sprinted toward the person before him, but before he could reach him, the man spun to face him. As Will crashed into him, the man spun back in the other direction, grabbing one of Will's arms. The maneuver sent Will straight down to the ground, where he was immediately kicked in the solar plexus by a hard boot. His lungs seized up. The man grabbed Will's hand and wrenched his arm sideways, at the same time pulling back his leg to kick Will again. Will knew that he would not be able to survive another such blow. Although the movement caused almost intolerable pain on his arm, he swung a leg hard against the man's only planted foot, causing him to lose balance and crash to the ground. Will pushed himself up and moved toward his assailant, but as he got closer, the man punched a heel against his shin, stopping him in his tracks. The attacker sprang upright, reaching into his jacket. He pulled out a knife and stood motionless for a moment, looking at Will.

Both men were breathing deeply, their breath steaming in the icy air. Will looked at the knife, then at the man, then back at the knife. He knew he had to wait for the attack so that he could avoid the angle of the knife thrust in order to strike back. He also knew that he had only one chance of repelling such a strike.

The attacker kept the knife quite still, but instead of going for the kill, he started moving slowly backward. Will looked away from the knife and toward its holder's visage. The man was smiling. Then he turned and sprinted away from Will and the church.

Will glanced toward Votivkirche and for the briefest of moments wondered whether he should pursue the man or go to help Roger. But he knew that he could not allow even one unit member to get out of the country alive, particularly now that they must have known they'd been set up. The death of this six-man unit would buy him the few hours he needed, but an escapee carrying a message back to his team members in Zagreb would scuttle Will's plans for those men. He looked away from the church and decided that Roger would have to deal with his opponents on his own.

Will sprinted. His quarry had left the church grounds and was running fast down Rooseveltplatz before heading east on Türken-strasse toward the direction of the river Danube. He was now at least thirty meters ahead of Will and showed no signs of slowing. The man crossed the road and continued onward before disappearing down a side street. Will ran straight into the street and saw the man ahead of him again. He knew that at the end of this street was the busier Maria Theresien Strasse. He decided to try to take the man down before he reached that road. While still at full sprint, he eased his body out of his weighty overcoat and allowed it to fall to the ground. He instantly felt faster, and within moments he had reduced the distance between himself and his prey to just ten meters, although the intersection was now very close. But the man he was pursuing did not continue onward. Instead he slowed, stopped, and turned to walk right at Will. Like Will, he had clearly decided that matters would now be resolved in this dark, empty street.

Will forced himself to a halt and saw that the man's knife was out again, held low in his right hand. The man was walking rapidly and this time had no hint of a smile on his face. He moved to within a yard of Will's body, thrusting the knife upward at his belly. Will jerked sideways and placed his right hand over the man's wrist, simultaneously stepping closer and punching his left elbow into the man's throat, forcing him to the ground. With his right hand, he twisted the man's knife arm and bent his wrist backward, causing the knife to fall from his grip. He kicked the knife away, applying even greater pressure on his assailant's wrist. The man writhed in pain and moaned loudly. Will held him in the lock for a moment before yanking harder on the wrist and dropping his body weight onto the man's back. He wrapped his free left arm around the man's neck and squeezed.

"I truly regret that this has to happen," he said as he did so.

In two minutes the man's legs stopped twitching and he was dead.

TWENTY-SEVEN

Will was back in Zagreb. It was now 4:00 A.M. and very dark. It had been only four hours since he and Roger had killed six members of the Iranian hit team in Austria. His objective now was to kill the remaining members in Croatia.

From his position under the illuminated streetlight Will watched the black BMW pull up to a stop alongside him.

Laith exited the vehicle and walked up to him. "Roger's not back in the country yet. I've got to change objectives and get on surveillance of Lana. You're on your own with this one." He handed Will the car's keys, thrust hands into his coat pockets, and walked off.

Will entered the vehicle, checking the map on the passenger seat beside him. He was on Vlahe Bukovca in the district of Zaprešić to the northwest of Zagreb, and he knew that he would need to move only a few hundred meters to spot his target on Pavia Lončara. He breathed deeply and swiveled to look at the vehicle's backseat. In its center rested a Diemaco C8 Special Forces Weapon and two spare thirty-round magazine clips. He picked up the assault rifle and quickly checked over its mechanics before jamming the carbine between the passenger seat and the handbrake. He placed the spare clips into his outer coat pockets, switched off the interior light, and turned on the vehicle's ignition and headlights. He drove casually forward.

Within a few minutes, Will brought the car to a halt. He was on Pavia Lončara, and approximately one hundred meters ahead of him he could just see the house containing the Iranian hit team. Turning off his lights, he waited, drumming his fingers on the steering wheel. All around him this residential street was still, dark, and quiet. The BMW's performance engine idled silently.

He stayed like this for thirty minutes, observing the house. He placed a hand on the assault rifle and decided that now was the time to walk into the house and kill its contents. He was about to open the car door when he suddenly froze.

Two upstairs lights came on almost simultaneously in the house. Will frowned. He reached down to the car's automatic gearshift and waited. Within twenty seconds the front door opened and a man ran out to a vehicle parked directly by the building. The man opened the driver's-side door and then all other doors. Will knew that their car's engine would now be running. Something must have unsettled them at this early hour. He concluded that the team had contingency plans in place in case they did not hear from the six men who'd followed him into Austria. He decided that the men leaving the house were extremely professional and extremely dangerous.

After five seconds another man ran out and took position by the front passenger door. He looked around the street and held one hand close to his body, then nodded toward the entrance of the house, whereupon two other men emerged from its door. One of them walked around the back of the car to the other passenger door. Once the other man had entered the car, it moved forward quickly.

Will shifted into drive option and followed them without headlights and at an even distance of 150 meters. As their car turned right onto Maršala Tita and out of sight, Will switched on his headlights.

He paused at the Maršala Tita junction and allowed another random vehicle to cross in front of him, then turned onto the road and followed his target from behind the secondary vehicle. Within moments the secondary vehicle turned left onto Pere Devčića and disappeared to wherever it was going. Will looked ahead, frowning. His target vehicle's taillights were rapidly moving away from him. The car sped onward to the Sava River and its parallel-running road, Aleja Bologne.

"Fuck." Will pressed his foot hard on the accelerator. He knew that his target was aware that something was wrong. They could have spotted him, but Will thought it was unlikely, as a pair of headlights behind a car in Zagreb suggested nothing. More likely, he decided, the occupants of the car had concluded that they were in severe potential threat from anything around them. He took the turn onto Aleja Bologne at high speed and knew that he would now be seen as a visible threat to the car ahead of him. He cursed again.

His quarry was dashing along the Aleja Bologne toward the epicenter of Croatia and one of the most heavily armed police districts in Central Europe. His target was drawing him toward a place where an attack would be futile. But Will knew that he was still eight kilometers away from that place, and therefore he had time to make a decision to abort his quest or to continue and commit to the attack before it was too late. He made his decision.

Judging by the speed of his own vehicle, Will believed that his target was now traveling at nearly 190 kilometers an hour. He dearly hoped that the vehicle he was driving was faster than the car ahead of him. He pressed the BMW's accelerator down to the floor and watched the road-straddling lamps beside him blur into one continuous line of light. He changed lanes so that he was driving on the right-hand side of the road, heading straight toward oncoming traffic. He careered up to his target and yanked his steering wheel down to the left, causing his car to collide with the Iranians' vehicle. Both cars immediately veered away from the road toward buildings. Will swung his wheel right and accelerated again before braking hard. He looked in his rearview mirror and saw his target perform what must have been a handbrake turn in order to face the opposite direction. Will swore. Whoever the men were, they were clearly well trained and most likely Qods Force.

He stopped his car, grabbed his rifle, and got out. A loud screech accompanied the spinning tires of the target car as it sped away. He raised the C8 and shot twice at both rear wheels. The car slumped and spun slightly left and right before stopping. It was about a hundred meters away from him. Will lifted his carbine's sight toward the rear window of the vehicle. A door immediately opened, and one of the men shot in his direction six times. Will ignored the bullets and stepped forward to send three rapid rounds toward the shooter. They hit the man in the chest and face and dropped him to the ground. The other men jumped out of the vehicle and moved back to shelter behind their car. Will sent further controlled bursts of fire toward them. He heard them shouting, but in a measured and disciplined manner. Then they became silent. Will stopped in the road, moving his gun's sight to the left and right of the vehicle ahead of him. Another car drove toward the stationary target car and slowed suddenly. It was clearly not hostile, but Will couldn't afford his targets to have any more shields to use as cover when firing back at him. He sent a long burst of bullets into the second car's engine block, which immediately stopped the vehicle a sufficient distance from his opponents. The men remained static behind their vehicle.

Will took another step forward and fired again at nothing to the left and right of the vehicle, then quickly replaced the gun's magazine clip. The action must have been anticipated or heard by his opponents, since one of the men momentarily showed himself just as Will jammed tight his new clip of bullets. Will instantly fired his fresh rounds at the man, causing him to fall away from the vehicle. The man was not dead, and he lifted his own handgun toward his assailant. Will hesitated for the tiniest of moments, then shot him in the head.

One of the remaining two men aimed his handgun in Will's

direction without exposing any of his body. He fired once. The bullet was easily wide of its mark, but Will fired back. Cars were braking to a standstill behind him, and he hoped they were innocent bystanders rather than armed police-response vehicles. He could not dare to look, though, as the men before him would use even a split second to kill him. He decided he had a maximum of one minute left to resolve the standoff. He heard sirens in the distance and from different locations. He decided he now had seconds.

He took measured side steps to the left while holding the rear of the vehicle in his sight. The new angle exposed one of the men, who was looking straight at Will with his handgun leveled directly at Will's body. Will moved slightly as he and the man simultaneously fired at each other. Will felt a bullet brush over his shoulder and saw the man who had fired it slump down dead. He sprinted forward and reached the target vehicle just as the last man rolled out before him, ready to engage in combat. It was an extremely brave act, since the man would have known that he could be exposing himself to a hail of automatic gunfire. But Will was now right by him and instead swung the butt of his rifle upward into the man's face. He immediately jabbed the rifle's muzzle into the man's ribs. The man was incapacitated but conscious. Will looked at him and raised his gun. For the briefest of moments, he wanted to leave the brave man alive, just turn and walk away. But he knew he could not allow the man to live.

He shot him.

TWENTY-EIGHT

Will stood on the hillside looking down at Zagreb. It was nearly midday, and a bright blue sky shone over the snow-clad city.

Roger walked up to him and stood by his side. "I got in this morning."

Will nodded but did not look at the man. "You've received an update from Laith?"

"I have. He told me what you did to the remaining members of the hit squad."

Will rubbed a hand over facial stubble. "Has Laith disposed of the vehicle and weapon?"

"Don't worry about that. None of us can be linked to what happened. But we've got to tread very carefully now. The Croatian police will be on high alert, and in all probability they'll soon link what happened here with what happened in Austria."

Will exhaled slowly. "Megiddo should have Lana's letter now. It should give him a new perspective on her. It should stop him from making extreme attempts against me." He studied Roger. The man looked exhausted. "But that does not mean we can slow down. I need one of your men to go to Sarajevo and watch the Human Benevolence Foundation building and the movements of its occupants."

"Sure. I'll send Julian Garces. The man can be a ghost when it comes to surveillance."

"Good. Julian's got twenty-four hours to understand everything about the exterior of that building, because tomorrow night he's going to watch my back while I burgle the HBF place."

At 1:00 A.M. Will was on rue Sainte-Croix-de-la-Bretonnerie in Paris. He turned into the side street containing Lana's house and pulled out an envelope while standing at her front door. He knew that he could have mailed the envelope or sent it by courier, but he'd wanted to deliver it in person. He took out a pen and addressed the envelope to Lana's mother, then pushed the package containing thirty thousand CIA dollars and nothing else through the mail slot.

He stepped back and looked at the house door. All around him was silent.

He thought about Lana's mother. He wondered if she was sleeping. Or maybe she was lying awake, hoping for her daughter's return.

He closed his eyes and allowed his worst recollection to come searing into his mind.

The teenage Will Cochrane threw his school bag onto the kitchen table, smiled nervously, and called to his mother. No response. He heard nothing.

He kept going as he wondered if his mother would hug him when she read his school report and saw that his exam grades would take him to England and Cambridge University. He wondered if she would cook him his favorite meal of roast chicken. He wondered if she would even allow him a small glass of wine as she sometimes did these days.

He entered the living room.

The four men looked at Will but did not move much when they

saw him. Instead they remained standing and glanced at his bound and gagged mother before looking back at him. One of them smiled and spoke.

"Where is the money?"

Will felt sick, giddy, and overwhelmingly confused. He looked at his mother. Tape had been wrapped around her head and body. She was sitting on a chair, her eyes rolling in their sockets. He had never seen a human being look so ill and so odd.

"Where is the money, boy?"

He looked at his sister. She was curled into a ball on the floor, sobbing. One of the men had a large-booted foot planted on her head.

Will looked at the man who spoke and answered him with a voice that did not seem his own.

"What money?"

The men laughed loudly and then went silent. Their spokesman pointed a finger at Will.

"Big houses like this mean big money."

Will shook his head and felt as if he'd done something wrong. He tried to make his voice strong and measured, but instead he just blurted the truth.

"We have no money. This house belongs to the government. My daddy used to work for them before he died. All the rich people around here know that we have nothing."

Two of the men laughed again, but two of them did not. The spokesman was one of the those who remained impassive and suddenly looked very scary. He took a step toward Will.

"Find us money, or we'll kill your mother and your sister."

Will looked at his mother. Her eyes were now closed, and her head had slumped down. He called to her.

"Mother?"

The scary man's eyes widened.

"She can't breathe. The clock is ticking, boy."

Will felt a burning sensation in his brain and eyes and knew that it was the sensation that preceded tears. He looked at all the men. Even though Will was easily as tall as they were, they looked so big and strong and like nothing else he had seen.

He slowed his breathing. He saw his mother starting to twitch. He wanted to run to her. Words came from him without any evident thought behind them.

"I've told you the truth. But we have some cash in a drawer. If I get it for you, will you help my mother?"

The men glanced at one another. Three of them shrugged and nodded at their spokesman. That man then stepped closer to Will. His breath smelled bad.

"Get it. But if you run, we'll kill her. Then we'll do worse to your sister."

Will's mother was now no longer twitching or even moving at all. Will imagined that she was pretending to sleep. But he knew she was not. He turned and walked out of the living room. He walked into the kitchen and looked around. He walked to a drawer. He opened it and instantly thought about lemonade, as this was the drawer that contained the bottle opener to the glass-bottled brand of lemonade his mother bought for him. He brushed fingers over the bottle opener and then moved them toward the carving knife that his mother used when slicing his favorite roast chicken.

He had always been scared of this knife, but now that he held it for the first time it felt so light and innocent in his hand. He convinced himself that it would not be scary enough for the big men in the other room. He decided it wasn't the knife that mattered but the hand carrying it.

He walked back into the room. He felt energized but no longer himself. He felt as if everywhere around him was on fire but only he could feel no heat or pain. He felt a blackness descend upon his mind.

He looked at the men and smiled.

And then he destroyed them.

·   ·   ·

Will looked up at the star-filled sky and exhaled. He shook his head and closed his eyes. He gripped his fist tight and felt his heart pounding strong and fast. He breathed rapidly before holding his breath and then exhaling again. He felt his heartbeat slow. He felt his body and mind calm. He opened his eyes, glanced at the stars again, and looked down at Lana's mother's door. He nodded toward it and whispered, "I'll bring your daughter home soon. I swear."

He turned back toward Central Europe and the perils it held.

TWENTY-NINE

Twenty-one hours later Julian Garces handed Will a backpack and said, "Everything you need is inside the bag."

Will took it and nodded at the former air force special operative. "You're satisfied you've obtained an accurate layout of the place?"

The big Hispanic man angled his head in assent. "I'm satisfied. And I'm also satisfied that this is going to be tough."

The man turned and jogged off into the darkness. Will attached a radio earpiece to himself, and within a few minutes he heard Julian's quiet voice. "One man is exiting the building. He enters parking lot. He halts at vehicle. He enters vehicle. He drives." Julian said nothing for a moment before recommencing the commentary. "Vehicle moves on to Nedima Filipovića. It drives onward. It's now out of my sight. That should be the last of them, but continue to hold position."

Will looked around the snow-covered business area of western Sarajevo. There were three rectangular office buildings here that shared two parking lots. Based on Julian's reconnaissance of the place, Will knew that the Human Benevolence Foundation rented five rooms within the central building of the three. He also knew that a further twenty-two companies used the same building. But right now there was no evidence of business activity around the place. The lots were empty, and now that the last of their occupants had left work, the buildings were in darkness save for the glow from their sporadic external security lights. Nevertheless, Will remained alone in the shadows and awaited Julian's instruction to proceed.

"Okay. My three-sixty sweep of the building is complete. Go."

Will lifted the small knapsack and walked quickly around the perimeter of the three-building area. As he reached the westernmost point, he slowed his pace while focusing on his earpiece. Then he heard what he was waiting for.

"Stop. You're at the camera's blind spot."

Will turned and looked at the building nearest him. Julian had told him that he needed to tread a very careful path across the fifty meters between where he now stood and the first building. He fixed his eyes on one specific part of the building and walked forward.

"You're straying. Take one pace to the left and then continue."

Will did as he was told and then moved forth. Within thirty seconds he was flush against the wall of the building. He stayed still for almost a full minute until Julian spoke again.

"Right. This is the tricky part. Do exactly what I say."

Will knew that he would have to follow Julian's instructions with split-second precision in order to avoid alerting the guard.

"Move to the southwest corner in three, two, one, go."

Will sprinted twenty meters alongside the wall and then stopped.

"Hold. Hold." Julian's voice was calm. In twelve seconds he said, "Move."

When Will had reached the next corner, he could see that the central building was approximately seventy meters away from him. He tightened the straps of his knapsack and waited.

"Okay. Turn to face the northwest corner of the target building. Take thirty of your paces. Ready in three, two, one, go."

Will moved into position within this parking lot. He felt quite exposed in the open ground, although he knew that Julian's instructions would give him perfect protection from the cameras.

"Adjust position to face the center of the building."

Will did so.

"Good. This next part needs to be very fast. Nine meters per second. On my command. Three, two, one, go."

Will sprinted as fast as he was able over the forty-meter distance and did not slow as he reached the building. He crashed into its wall and ignored the pain in his hands and shoulder wound from doing so.

"Now walk slowly toward the northwest corner until I tell you otherwise."

Will moved while allowing the wall to graze his jacket.

"Stop."

Will stopped. It was thirty seconds before he heard Julian's voice again.

"Ready your equipment. When I say go, you've got twenty seconds to get inside."

Will removed the knapsack from his back and took out one of the implements from within the bag. The object weighed exactly twenty pounds and had been made by Julian. Though crude-looking, the two-handed ram would be extremely effective against all but the most sophisticated door locks. Will put his pack back on and held his ram in one hand.

"Make it quick. Three, two, one, go."

Will ran fast, turned the corner of the building while keeping its wall directly by his side, and kept running as he approached the side door. He barely slowed his pace as he reached the door and swung the ram with both hands against the lock. He then stepped back and forth as he struck the ram against the upper and lower hidden hinges on the other side of the entrance. He swung the ram into the middle of the door and pulled at its handle. The door fell to one side, and Will stepped into the building. He put the ram back in his bag and pulled out a flashlight.

"Good. The alarm will now be sounding in the security office. I'll let you know when trouble comes, but I'd say you've got a maximum of ninety seconds."

Will followed the route he'd been given earlier by Julian. He ran through a corridor and up two flights of stairs before heading along the top-floor corridor. He counted eight doors on his right before turning left and coming to a halt opposite the door he needed. He crouched down and pulled out a five-piece lock-pick set. Despite being crude, the tools were more than a match for the door's basic Yale lock, and within five seconds he opened the door and entered the suite of offices rented by the Human Benevolence Foundation.

He walked though two offices and then another and another. They all looked messy and bore no sign of being sanitized to protect secrets. He reached the last office and realized that this was the place he need-ed to search. It was immaculate. There were two desks and chairs in the room, and aside from pens and other stationery items, each desk was empty. He examined drawers, cupboards, telephone message sys-tems, and wastebaskets, but all contained nothing. He was swearing silently in frustration, but then a thought came to him, and he walked out of the room. He moved back and forth between the four genuine and cluttered HBF offices until he found a filing cabinet. He pulled it open, and as he did so, he heard Julian's voice.

"The guard's just left his building. He's walking, but he'll still be with you in thirty seconds."

The cabinet contained labeled drop-down files, and Will scanned his eyes over them all. Most seemed to relate to HBF construction con-tracts or financial matters, but one did not. Will smiled as he read the title "Fire Roster" on the file's label. He looked inside and saw one sheet of paper. He pulled it out and shone his flashlight over the con-tents. It listed the names of eleven people as well as other information about them. He withdrew a digital camera and photographed the paper.

"Come on. Time's up."

Will replaced the paper in the file, shut the cabinet, and walked through the office suite to the exit. He closed the door behind him and knelt in the corridor with his lock-pick set.

"Guard's by the building. He's seen the broken door. He's speaking on his radio. He's entering your building."

Will maneuvered three of the pick levers until the door to the HBF suite was locked again. He pulled out his ram and walked along the corridor. The fourth door to his left bore a plaque stating that it belonged to a company called Adriatic Travels. Will smashed his ram against the door, stepped into the office, and grabbed two desktop telephones, which he placed in his pack. Then he moved out into the corridor and struck another random door belonging to a different company. He stepped into the room, stole a laptop computer, and stepped back out into the corridor. He walked quickly to the top of the stairs and looked down. He saw a flashlight bean and heard radio chatter. The light became stronger, and Will knew that the guard was moving up the stairs. He turned off his own flashlight just as Julian spoke.

"Two private security vehicles pull up outside your location. Three men exit. They walk to your building. They enter."

Will turned and silently jogged back down the corridor. He wanted to avoid any contact with the guards, because to engage with them would produce adverse effects. An act of burglary, he had reasoned to himself before this evening's venture, would probably be kept quiet by the building's landlord from all but the victims, for fear of scaring off other tenants. But an assault on security guards would bring an intrusive police investigation that would inevitably come to the attention of all office tenants, including the HBF men and the two Qods Force officers who were hidden within their ranks. In turn those two men could very easily become suspicious of the event and disappear from the premises for good.

Will reached the end of the corridor and looked into the rear stairway. It was still dark, and he moved carefully down its steps until he was positioned on the first floor. He moved along the corridor until he reached a corner. A cone of light immediately hit the floor close to him, and he knew that it came from a guard who was now traveling along the corridor to his position. If the man turned the corner, Will would be seen and would therefore have to assault the guard. He turned to face the direction he'd just come from but then saw more light emerging from the previously dark stairwell. One of the guards was coming up from the ground floor, and if he stopped to examine the first floor, Will would be trapped between two guards.

He heard more radio chatter, and the flashlights stopped still. Will knew that the guard around the corner must have turned away, since his light was disappearing. The light from the man in the stairwell then increased and just as quickly decreased, and it was clear that he was now moving up the stairs and away from Will toward the top floor. It was also obvious to Will that both guards had been summoned by a third guard who had now discovered his forced entry into the two companies above him. Will ran to the rear stairwell, glanced down, and moved slowly to the ground floor. The place before him was in semidarkness, and he walked swiftly along its corridor before coming to an area where he could either turn left toward the broken side entrance that he'd used to enter the building or continue onward to the building's sealed main entrance. He waited and then saw more beams coming from the side entrance's corridor. It meant that the fourth security guard was standing in position at this portal and was blocking Will's exit. The position of the flashlight meant that the man was facing forward and would see Will as soon he continued ahead toward the main front door. He thought fast. Julian must have been anticipating Will's predicament, because his words echoed Will's decision.

"Put your hood on. Keep your head low. Don't stop for anything."

Will covered his face as much as he could with his Gore-Tex winter jacket and pulled out his ram one last time. He looked at the main door. It was twenty meters ahead of him. He breathed in deeply and began to sprint, knowing that he had instantly exposed himself to the guard in the corridor to his left. He heard more radio noises and then shouting, but he ignored the sounds as he raced to the door, swung his ram at its thick glass panels, and smashed his way through the exit. His coat protected his head and upper body, but shards of glass lacerated his legs. He resumed sprinting as soon as he was clear of the door and the building. He ran in a northeasterly direction with no care for avoiding cameras and after four hundred meters he reached the business area's perimeter. He momentarily slowed to look behind him before moving into streets and alleys and more streets. Only then did he ease up into a walk. He looked down at his legs and saw glass splinters the size of knives protruding from his thighs and calf muscles. When he stopped to pull out some of the splinters, his legs nearly buckled beneath him.

Will pressed his throat pressel switch and spoke to Julian in a rushed and breathless voice. "I've got them. I've got the bastards' names."

CHAPTER THIRTY

W e're dealing with professionals." Will pulled out his digital camera. "At the end of each day, the Qods Force men leave their room with no telltale evidence of their activities. But they made one mistake." He brought up the image of the paper he'd photographed. "Or rather I suspect a mistake was made without their knowledge."

He handed the camera to Patrick. The two men were in the CIA safe house in Switzerland.

Patrick looked at the camera for almost a minute before speaking. "That was quick thinking to check the fire roster. And I suspect you're right: I'd bet that somebody in the HBF complied with the building's fire-drill safety protocols and supplied all this information to their administrative department without even first clearing it with the Qods Force men." He smiled as he looked at the photographic image showing the sheet containing the names of three females and eight males as well as all their passport numbers and dates and places of birth.

Will pointed at the camera. "Judging by the layout of the HBF office suite, I'm certain two of those people on the list are Qods Force."

Patrick nodded and pulled out his cell phone. He made a call and relayed all the information contained in Will's photograph to somebody who would most certainly be based in Langley. "I should have an answer in ten minutes."

Will poured himself some coffee and gulped down the brew despite its heat. He rubbed his eyes and walked to a window just as the sun exposed a fraction of itself to the snow-drenched Zurich morning. He felt detached from time and the mechanics of normal day-and-night routines, and the sunrise had no meaning to him other than to clarify that he had one less day to capture Megiddo. It could have been five or ten minutes before he heard Patrick's phone ring quietly. He turned and watched the CIA man stand motionless as he listened to whoever was speaking on the other end. When the call was over, Patrick picked up Will's camera. "We can't identify which of them the Qods Force men, and that comes as no surprise. But we can identify which ones are, without doubt, *not* members of the Human Benevolence Foundation." He nodded at the digital image. "Jamshed Alavi. Male. Born thirteenth of June, 1979, in Bandar-e 'Abbâs." He smiled. "Gulistan Nozari. Male. Born twenty-ninth of April, 1956, in Esfahan."

Will exhaled and smiled. Due to his age, Gulistan Nozari was the one man on the eleven-person list who was senior enough to be Megiddo.

"We should put him under immediate surveillance, get a photograph of him, and show that shot to Lana." Patrick's voice was strident. "If she says it's Megiddo, we don't have to wait for her to meet him. Instead we grab him and interrogate the man."

Will spoke quietly, deep in thought. "That's not the correct course of action."

Patrick looked sharply at him. "Why the hell not? Harry's given you a damn good lead that has potentially enabled us to bring a quick end to Megiddo's mission. Give me one reason"—he paused for a moment—"that my instruction is not correct?"

"I can give you three reasons. One: Lana knew Megiddo when he was a much younger man. Even if we get a good photo, she still may be uncertain that it's him. Two: We know from the Kljujic experience that Megiddo is savvy to the threat of potential observers."

"Roger, Laith, Ben, or Julian would not be spotted. They're in a different league from someone like Kljujic."

Will held his hand up in protest. "But the risk is still there, and if there *is* some compromise while trying to photograph him, we may lose Megiddo for good." He cleared his throat. "Three: We've got no need to make such a reckless move when we have Lana in direct communication with Megiddo. I remain convinced that this is the only true route to guaranteeing his capture."

"How long, though?" The anger in Patrick's voice seemed coupled with frustration.

Will studied Patrick briefly before saying, "Are you under pressure now to get this finished?"

Patrick laughed, but the sound was false and sarcastic, and he stopped abruptly. "Alistair and I have always been under pressure to get this finished. Megiddo is holding a mighty sword over the United States or the United Kingdom, and both my president and your prime minister know that he could strike at any time. Our premiers are both leaders of men, and they trust Alistair and me to do our job. But they're waiting day and night by their phones to get the call from one of us saying it's done." Patrick pointed a finger at Will. "A call telling them that Will Cochrane has done his job."

Will nodded understanding and checked his watch. "Then let me *do* my job. My breach of the HBF offices has given us insurance. If all else fails, we can always blow open this operation, track Gulistan Nozari via his passport, and then lift him with the help of Central European forces. But all else has not yet failed."

"Do you expect the premiers to share your confidence?"

"I don't care what they think. But I demand that *you* share my confidence."

●   ●   ●

Will opened his cell phone and listened to Harry's information. The agent spoke for nearly two minutes. Will closed his phone and smiled.

In her hotel room, Lana lit a cigarette and brushed her hand over the letter. She inhaled deeply on the glowing tobacco and looked apprehensive. Then she pushed the letter across the table toward Will.

He read it and immediately felt a jolt of nausea and panic. It was all he could do to try to control the overwhelming fear he now had, fear for Lana's safety. He looked at her and asked, "How do you feel about this?"

She tapped ash from her cigarette, and Will noticed that her hand trembled a little. "How do *you* feel about this?" She smiled. "Of course, I know how you feel."

Will said nothing. He felt helpless.

Lana said, "You knew that it would come to this. You knew that I had to meet him. You know that it's what I want. And I know you did everything you could to stop me from doing this."

Will shook his head. "None of which changes anything. I don't want to lose you."

Lana sighed. She crushed her cigarette and immediately lit another. "It will seem odd to meet him in that city."

Will tore himself away from his thoughts and fears. "It makes sense. After all, it's where this whole thing started for you."

Lana huffed. "He chose the location because for some reason it will be convenient to him. He's not the type of man to place stock in symbolism or symmetry."

Will observed her for a moment. "You don't have to do this. You still have the chance to walk away."

Lana took another drag and looked intently at Will. "But if I did that, I would be walking away from the one chance I have to take my revenge on Megiddo." Then she smiled. "And I would also be walking away from you." She shook her head. "I'm not going to walk away. I need to do this." She drew a deep breath. "I received a call from my mother this morning. She sounded like she was in a state of exultant shock. She said an anonymous donor had sent her thirty thousand dollars." Lana smiled. "You told me that you would help us only when this was finished. But it must have been you who gave her the money."

Will felt uncomfortable. He wondered what he should say. He looked at his hands. "The money is simply to help her while you are away. But what I really want to give her . . . what I really want to return to her safe and well . . . is you."

Dear Lana,

You are right to feel anger and frustration. My imperative to speak to the British man drove me to impetuosity and momentary lack of care for our arrangement. That will not happen again.

I will give you the protection and counsel you need. I will give you the chance to know me again.

Time, however, has become a crucial issue. The embassy can no longer be used to reach me, but that is of no concern, because we must now progress matters beyond written communication. We must meet in three days' time at ten A.M. in the Black Swan café on Ferhadija Street in Sarajevo. I will expect to see you there.

Yours,

Megiddo

THIRTY-ONE

Will drove for four hours on hill and mountain roads before he arrived at the place. It was nearly dark now, but the church before him had exterior lights illuminated, and they cast a dim glow over the area around the building. Beyond the place there was nothing but mountains and forest.

He turned off the ignition and stepped out into an icy Bosnian wind. Everywhere was thick with snow, and the wind blew snow dust into his face. He looked around. There was only one other vehicle near the church, and it was caked in ice. He wondered if it had been abandoned due to the weather. He could not imagine even the most devout person making the journey up to this isolated mountain church on this night. It seemed to him that God had momentarily abandoned the religious site and everything around it.

Will trudged through the snow with his head tilted low to try to protect his face from the needles of ice that were now shooting horizontally at him and to force his way through the power of the wind until he reached the church and the shelter its walls provided. He brushed off ice and water, then looked around again. The place did feel as if it were beyond life and normality.

He turned the handle of the church door and welcomed the warmth and silence that greeted him from within. He stepped forward, stamped his shoes to release them from clinging snow, and the noise of his doing so reverberated around the church's inner walls. The place was small, and Will estimated that at full capacity it would be able to hold no more than fifty people in prayer. He shut the door and chafed his icy bare hands to restore some circulation. The space was quite dark, but there were some corner lamps that gave sufficient light for him to see the empty wooden pews, the altar, the religious icons, and little else. He removed his overcoat and walked a ways up the center aisle before stopping. Everything within the thick walls was quiet. He laid his coat over the back of one of the pews and stood still in his immaculate bespoke suit. He had dressed to show respect for this place and his presence here.

He breathed deeply and moved along a pew before sitting to face the icons. A statue of Mary Magdalene seemed to be staring at him. Her face looked sorrowful and scared.

A noise came from Will's right, and he half turned to a light and a man. The light belonged to an oil lamp, and the man holding it was clearly this church's priest. He approached Will and said something in Serbian. Will shrugged in a way that he hoped looked apologetic and said, "I am sorry, I don't speak your language."

The priest came nearer and frowned. He looked middle-aged and had a smooth face and lacquered hair. He smiled. "I have some English—enough English to advise you that you must be mad to have made this trip here tonight."

Will also smiled. He wondered why this church had been built in such a harsh part of this country. He wondered if it had been done in order to test people's commitment to their faith. He returned his gaze toward the figure of Mary.

The priest sat on the pew next to him, placed the lamp between them, and followed Will's gaze. "She is in need of some new paint." The priest's voice echoed a little. "She carries a heavy burden and has grown tired. But her eyes still see and understand everything."

Will nodded and looked back at the man. "Am I intruding here?"

The priest shook his head. "The doors to my church are open to everyone." He smiled crookedly. "Even though most people choose not to come here anymore."

"I cannot remember the last time I visited a church," Will admitted.

"That matters not. What matters is that you are here now." The priest touched Will's shoulder. "Would you like me to make you a hot drink?"

Will rubbed his hands again and felt their coldness being replaced by pain as his circulation coursed through them. He nodded. "That would be very kind, provided that it's not inappropriate?"

The priest chuckled. "You have made a journey that others could not or would not make. The very least you deserve is something to warm you through." Then he walked away toward a dark recess.

Will wondered why he *had* made this journey. He tried to understand his thoughts. He tried to understand why being in this lonely, sacred place was so important to him. He recalled his own words:

I do my work. That's all that matters to me.

And he recalled Alastair's riposte:

I don't believe you.

He closed his eyes and felt the vastness of the silence around him. It held him for a moment, and it seemed to Will that it did not want to let go. He opened his eyes and breathed loudly.

The priest came to him again and sat by the oil lamp. He gave Will a mug of hot tea, which Will gratefully gulped down.

Will gripped the mug between his freezing hands and said, "Sometimes it seems impossible to get rid of the coldness."

The priest nodded slowly while keeping his gaze on Will. "I can see that this is not normally a place you would come to. I can see that you are trying to find something which has been lost, perhaps something inside you." He gently placed a hand on Will's forearm. "If you would like me to, I can help you with that quest."

Will looked down and shook his head slightly. "I don't know."

The priest squeezed Will's forearm. "You are safe here. You have nothing to fear."

Will looked at the man's hand and then his face. "I fear myself," he said quietly.

"And yet you have come here, on tonight of all nights." The priest exuded a kindness that Will had not seen for a very long time.

"I came here to face one of my demons."

"Then you have conquered some of your inner fear." The priest removed his hand from Will's arm. "But perhaps you would prefer that I left you alone."

Will glanced around the church. "I did not know if this place would be open." He looked at the priest. "And I certainly did not expect to find someone else here."

The priest nodded sympathetically. "You need to be alone."

Will shook his head. "It's okay. It would be nice if you have time to stay with me a little longer." He frowned. "But this must be a lonely place to do your work. Do you have help?"

"I like the solitude," the priest replied. "I have no need for support. But I have every need to give support."

Will looked again at the figure of Mary. "Maybe I was hoping that you would be here."

"Maybe."

Will turned slowly back to face the priest. He felt no surprise when he saw that the man was now holding a CZ 99 pistol, which was pointed directly at Will's head. He'd known that the man had retrieved his weapon when he went to make the mug of tea. He'd known that the cleric had simply been waiting for the right moment to withdraw the pistol. He'd known that no amount of self-projected humility or anguish could disguise the fact that a man like Will would never be in a place like this unless bad things were within it.

Will smiled a little. "I came here to face a demon."

The priest nodded and narrowed his eyes. "Who sent you?"

Will glanced at the altar and muttered, "I answer to no one." He looked back at the priest.

A bead of sweat was trickling down one side of the man's face. "What do you want?"

Will smiled fully. "Your life."

Anger flashed in the priest's eyes before he grinned. "I'm sorry that I am going to have to disappoint you."

Will's face grew cold. "Did you expect to go unpunished? Did you expect that your crimes of two decades ago would be forgotten?"

The man sneered. "You know nothing about me."

Will stared at him. "I know that you were once a captain in a Bosnian Serb paramilitary unit called the Panthers and that you led your men on killing sprees that involved rape and mutilation of your victims before you murdered them. You personally slaughtered hundreds of women and children and threw them into unmarked mass graves. You cut unborn babies out of living wombs and then strangled them with your bare hands. You degraded their good in favor of your evil." He gestured at the church. "Hiding in a place like this was meaningless. Its fortified walls and sacred grounds could never protect a man like you from a man like me. But for all your abhorrent crimes, I am here to prosecute you for one crime and one crime alone."

The priest sniggered. "Too bad, because I am the one holding the gun."

Will nodded. "True."

The man pressed the barrel against Will's head. "Which crime?"

"You and four of your men raped an honorable woman a few kilo-meters outside Sarajevo while it was besieged by your compatriots."

"A single rape?" The man sniggered again. "There are too many to remember."

"A Muslim woman. You took her coat because you knew that in doing so she would likely freeze to death. The four men with you later died in the war, but that does not matter to me, because it was you who gave them their instructions."

The priest frowned thoughtfully, then brightened. "Yes, now I remember. A peasant, a woman asleep in the woods. We woke her and brutalized her." He laughed loudly, and the noise filled the church. "You represent that woman?"

"I represent the need for justice."

The man leaned close to Will and pressed the gun harder against him. "Then it is a shame that justice could not find a better representative."

"So it seems."

In a movement that was quicker than any man's trigger finger, Will grabbed the priest's gun hand and twisted his arm to lock the muscles. With his other hand, he seized the back of the priest's head and punched it down at the oil lamp. Glass from the lamp's flame shield shattered and splintered into the man's face and exposed the lamp's flame to his head. Will stood and yanked the head with tremendous force, so that the priest flew from the pew to the church's central aisle. Then Will walked up to his writhing body and punched him very hard on the side of the face.

He looked down at the man. "I know why I came here. While demons still exist, I have to take a stand against their evil. And I have been given the ultimate power to stop creatures like you."

He withdrew his handgun and pointed it at the man's head. "I did not lie to you. I came here for your life."

He pulled the trigger.

PART III

THIRTY-TWO

There they are." Roger grabbed Will's forearm, looking down from their vantage point high in an upper balcony inside Zagreb Cathedral. "One's walking down the central aisle, and the other two are taking positions in the rear of the cathedral."

Will looked at the large floor area beneath him. There were seated men and women in prayer, groups of tourists, as well as Lana, two members of the Iranian surveillance team, and the three new men whom Roger had identified.

"The fourth member of their team is outside." Roger's voice was so hushed that Will could barely hear him.

Saying nothing, Will focused his gaze on Lana. She'd done as he had previously instructed her and positioned herself toward the center of the cathedral floor. While he could't see it from his perch, Will knew that she would be carrying a tourist guide and occasionally referring to it between her observations of the cathedral surroundings. He looked back at the three men, the two Iranians, and then again at Lana. He saw her turn and walk toward the exit. She would now be heading for the Preradovićeva flower market.

"Let's see what happens," Roger was saying. "One of the Iranians moves in behind Lana, the other stays where he is, but what are our new friends going to do?"

Will watched the three men and saw one remain motionless while the other two moved deeper into the cathedral, in the opposite direction from where Lana was going.

"Okay," the CIA paramilitary man continued his narration of the scene unfolding below. "They're allowing the fourth member of their team to get onto Lana when she's outside. Their new position also suggests they're fully aware of the Iranian team around her."

"But can we tell if the Iranians are aware of these other men?" Will kept his own voice very quiet.

"It depends. If the Iranian and the other three men stay here for more than ten minutes, we can be confident that both teams know about the other and that the Iranian is sending them a message to stay put. But if the Iranian leaves in under that time, it tells us nothing. He could be oblivious to the other men, or he could want the other men to think that the Iranians haven't spotted them."

Will and Roger just watched, saying nothing for the next five minutes. Finally Will saw the last Iranian surveillance man walk slowly toward the exit and leave the cathedral. A minute later one of the three men also left, and after a further three minutes the remaining two men followed him.

Roger turned to face him. "We have a very serious situation."

Will ran his fingers through his hair and thought for a moment. Roger had summoned him to this place after the CIA team leader had spotted not only the fact that the Iranian surveillance team had acquired new members to bolster its head count back up to seven but, more important, that another team of four unknown persons had positioned themselves around Lana this morning. Will knew that his operational use of Lana was now in dire jeopardy.

Roger pulled out his cell phone to read a new message. "I sent Ben to check up on them. They're French."

Will frowned. "DGSE?"

Roger nodded once and said, "They must be."

The Direction Générale de la Sécurité Extérieure was France's equivalent of the CIA and MI6, and it was the only French covert organization authorized by its government to conduct overseas surveillance and other intelligence activities.

"But how the hell did they get onto Lana?" Will's mind was working rapidly.

"We don't have the time to be certain," Roger replied, "but I'd say it started with the discovery of the Iranian surveillance team. We know they're staying at the Hotel Dubrovnik, so maybe the local DGSE representative in Zagreb has recruited one of the hotel's reception staff. That person alerts the DGSE man that seven Iranians have just checked into the hotel. The DGSE person wants to find out more about them, so he has his hotel spy look in their rooms. Maybe the hotel gets lucky and finds covert photographs of Lana, but assuming that the Iranian team is better than that, certainly the spy should be able to find bus or train tickets, store or restaurant receipts. That data would show patterns, and those patterns would tell where the Iranian group goes. So our DGSE person looks for the most frequented location and then just waits there. He or she will also choose the location because of visibility and because it is a bottleneck, meaning high levels of exposure for the group. It may not happen on the first day or the second, but odds are the Iranians will come through that place eventually. The DGSE person observes their formation and behavior. He or she establishes with certainty that they're a surveillance team. If I were in that situation, I'd be able to positively identify which person was the team's target, so let's assume that's what happened."

"But how would the DGSE person then be able to put a name to the Iranian's target without following her and thereby risking being compromised to the Iranians?"

"Again, receipts. The Iranian team is holed up in the Hotel Dubrovnik. So how come they've got so many of their receipts for mineral water purchased from the Regent Esplanade's 1925 Lounge? The DGSE person can't shortcut this process and just go straight there rather than spotting team and target on the street, because a single person in such a small bar, unlike a rotating team, would risk compromise." Roger seemed certain. "But with a face for the target and without the Iranians around, there are then any number of options. Maybe there's an on-site Regent concierge to talk to or a loose-lipped after-hours bartender. The DGSE person shows the a photograph taken covertly from a bag camera during his street surveillance. Or if not, he just asks about an Arab-looking woman—there'll be very few in Zagreb compared to Sarajevo, and certainly very few in the Regent. Then it's not that difficult to put a name to a room, no matter how strict the hotel is about its security procedures."

"And then they discover that woman in question is a resident of France."

Roger folded his arms. "And the French intelligence officer therefore decides to put a four-man DGSE surveillance team onto both her and the Iranians to find out what's going on."

Will looked around the cathedral and then back at Roger. He felt his heart rate increase. "We've got to pray that the DGSE team is still hidden from the Iranians, but we have to stop them before they're spotted, or else the Iranians may panic and attack Lana. If that happens, everything will be ruined." He felt his stomach tighten into knots. "Everything."

"What do you have in mind?"

Will checked his watch. "She doesn't know it yet, but in three hours' time Lana needs to be boarding a plane to take her out of here."

"Where do you want her to go?"

"Anywhere . . . Anywhere outside the Balkans, but not too far. I need her to be in Sarajevo tomorrow evening, because the day after that she's meeting Megiddo."

Roger checked his own watch and said, "There's a five forty P.M. Croatia Airlines flight to Prague. Will that do?"

Will nodded. "She'll be on that flight. So will Laith, Ben, Julian, and no doubt certain members of the Iranian and French teams."

Roger said, "If I'm correct in my assessment of what you plan to do, then Laith, Ben, and Julian won't be enough for the job."

"I know. I can't be on the same flight as your men, because the Iranians will recognize me. And I can't have you with them either, because it would be foolhardy to put all four of you on the same flight. You and I will get the next available flight out after your men's flight, and then we'll join them when we arrive in the Czech Republic."

Roger reached for his cell phone. Will, too, pulled out his phone to call Lana and tell her to pack her bags.

The Iranians could spot the DGSE team at any moment. And he was going to do something very drastic to stop that from happening.

THIRTY-THREE

It was the first time that Will had seen the four-man CIA team together. They sat with him in a room within the small Savic Hotel in Prague's Old Town. Smoke from Laith's cigarette lingered over them and mingled with the steam from the mugs of coffee each man held. It was nearly 1:00 A.M., but all the Americans looked edgy and energetic.

"Why are we not on Lana?" Laith's voice sounded hostile.

"Will and I are taking a risk leaving her alone right now, but we have vital reasons for doing so." Roger spoke slowly, glancing at Will before returning his gaze to his men. "Which hotel is she in?"

"She's in the Clarion." Ben took a swig of his coffee and then wiped his mouth with the back of his hand. "It's about one kilometer away from here on the other side of the Old Town."

"And the DGSE team?" Roger again.

"All four of them have arrived." Laith blew smoke while speaking. "Like us, they've taken one room to use as their base. They're staying in the Hotel Josef."

"What's their drill?"

Laith smiled a little. "Last time we looked, all four of them were watching Lana's hotel. But that was before you called us here, so right now I've no idea."

"Do they have weapons?"

Julian shook his head. "Very unlikely. No time to get any, plus why would they feel the need to arm themselves?"

Roger nodded. "All right. How do they look?"

"Highly professional." Laith extinguished his cigarette. "Their movements are slick, they barely talk to each other, meaning they don't have to, and they're using creative surveillance maneuvers."

"Do they look like they could handle themselves in a confrontation?"

Ben frowned. "They look and move like Special Forces. They'll be able to take care of themselves if the Iranians do spot and assault them."

Roger wordlessly ceded the floor to Will.

Will breathed in and spoke. "In one hour's time, Lana will leave her hotel to take a walk through the Old Town. This will come as a surprise to her Iranian and French watchers, but I doubt they'll view it as suspicious, as Prague is at its most beautiful at night, when its streets and alleys are empty. I think all four of the DGSE men will be on her, because this is their first night of observing her. Unlike the Iranian team, they've not yet had the chance to define a pattern of her behavior that could allow them to decide whether they can scale back coverage of her at particular points of the day. But the Iranians will most likely have only one or two people on her, as they're far more familiar with Lana's movements and they know that she's never before left her hotel after midnight. Nevertheless, when they see her taking her walk, they'll alert at least two of their colleagues to join them, and within thirty minutes of that alert they'll number three or four men." Will looked at each of the men in turn as he spoke. "That thirty-minute gap is crucial, because during that time we're going to kill the DGSE team."

The CIA men were silent for a while, and Will wondered who would speak first.

Roger looked at his men. "Do any of you have a problem with this task?"

Julian looked directly at Will. "As long as we're authorized to do this, I've got no problem. But how are we going to do it without being seen by the one or two Iranian specialists?"

Will nodded at Roger, who then spoke. "The Old Town is a labyrinth. A team of two Iranians won't be able to do much more follow Lana wherever she goes and stay pretty close to her for fear of losing her position. But the DGSE team of four will be able to box her position from a greater distance, given their higher numbers. That means we can attack their perimeter without being seen by the Iranians."

"What about the bodies?" Laith took out another cigarette and held it unlit.

"We don't have the time or the resources to get rid of them," Will replied. "But it is essential that the Iranians know nothing about the assault. When it's done, Lana will take a route back to her hotel that will draw her Iranian watchers and any of their colleagues away from the scene. She'll then check out of her hotel, head to the airport, and travel on to Sarajevo."

"Does she know anything about our plans?"

"She suspects that Megiddo has put someone, or even several people, around her, but she doesn't know about our team or the DGSE team, and she certainly doesn't know anything about what we're going to do. She has of course asked me why she needed to come to Prague and why she needs to make this specific walk, and I've told her she'll have her answers when I next see her." He shook his head. "I will, however, give her no such answers."

He arose from his seat. "Gentlemen, I suggest you spend the next fifteen minutes mentally preparing yourselves, because after that we need to move into position." He walked to the far corner of the room and replenished his mug with more coffee. As he did so, Roger moved next to him.

The CIA man spoke very quietly. "*Are* we authorized to do this?"

Will looked at Laith, Ben, and Julian and saw that they were in discussion and out of earshot. He looked at Roger. "You have *my* authority."

Roger's eyes narrowed. "What about Patrick's authority?"

"He's back in Washington right now, so that he can calm some waters. He doesn't need to be bothered with this."

Roger stared at Will for a long moment. "We're going to be attacking a Western ally. If something goes wrong and we're caught, the repercussions on us will be terrible."

Will nodded. "I know."

Will was on Týnská, and he could see no one else on the street. The place was partially lit with streetlamps, and he sat on a bench beneath one of them so that he was easily visible. He rubbed his gloved hands together and reached into his jacket pocket to pull out a bottle of Becherovka. He then unscrewed the bottle's cap and poured some of the alcoholic liquid over his jeans and coat and exposed face. Taking a swig from the bottle, he felt its contents burn course down his throat. He placed the now half-full bottle by his side, pressed a number on his secreted cell phone, and said, "I'm here."

Within seconds Will heard Roger's voice in his earpiece. "Good. We're all in position. In five minutes our lady should be at the place."

Will stretched his legs out before him and crossed his feet. The temperature was well below freezing, although the streets were free of ice and snow. He breathed slowly and watched his breath turn to steam in the shadowy air. He began to gently hum a tune, caressing the base of the bottle of bitters.

"One minute until she's there. Radio silence from now on, so earpieces stowed away." Roger's voice was quiet and calm.

Will kept humming as he casually removed his Bluetooth device and dropped it into his pocket. He visualized Lana's route from her hotel, taking her to where she would now be and then to where she had to be in less than sixty seconds. That place had been carefully chosen by Roger to be the intersection of V Kolkovně and Dlouhá. Roger had reasoned that if she was there, then he could accurately pinpoint to the nearest twenty meters where each member of the DGSE team should be positioned and by extension where his own team should be waiting. Will knew that right now Ben was five hundred meters away from him on Vězeňská to the north, that Laith was on Haštalská to the northeast, that Roger was somewhere on Kostečná to the west, and that Julian was following Lana. Will also knew that Roger had chosen to position Lana in the intersection because it had five exits; the Iranians would have to move in very close to her in order not to lose her to one of these routes. Will again lifted the bottle to his lips and tilted it back, but this time he prevented any of the liquid from entering his mouth. He hummed his tune a little louder so that its sound echoed off the nearby building walls, and as he did so, he moved his head slightly left and right to observe the street.

He saw the man. At first he was merely an almost shapeless variation of the darkness at the end of the street, but as Will moved his vision in a figure-eight motion around the shape, his eyes adjusted and he knew that it was him. The man was walking slowly along the street and toward Will's location. He was alone, had hands thrust into coat pockets and his head bowed low. Will tightened his grip around the bottle and took another pretend swig of its contents. He closed his eyes for a while and stretched the muscles in his legs and back.

When he opened his eyes again, the man was nearer. Will held the bottle in his lap. He hummed some more, laughed a little, and took a genuine swig of the Czech liquor. The man kept walking at the same pace. Then, as he came to within twenty meters of Will, he started crossing the street toward the opposite pavement. Will breathed in deeply and laughed again.

"You want a drink?" Will said the words loudly and with slur.

The man said nothing and went on walking until he was directly across from Will.

"Hey, you want a drink?"

The man walked on.

Will stood up, grabbed the neck of his bottle, and lurched across the road toward the man. "Just trying to be polite. No need to fucking ignore me."

The man kept walking. He was of medium build, but Will could tell from his posture that he would be very strong. Will staggered after him until he was within two meters of the man's back.

"I said there's no need to ignore me. Just want to share my goodwill."

The man turned, took one step forward, and punched the flat of his hand against Will's chest. The force of the impact was so powerful and precise that it lifted Will's two-hundred-pound-body into the air and backward. As he crashed to the pavement, his bottle smashed around him, and he lay for a moment, trying to breathe. The man turned to continue his journey with the same steady pace. Will brushed glass off his coat, pushed himself up onto his feet, and cursed loudly.

The man continued onward, and Will smiled. This was the moment he'd been waiting for. He sprinted forward, thrust his left hand into the small of the man's back to grab a bunch of his coat and the belt underneath it, smashed his right elbow upward into the man's jawbone, and thrust up and backward so that both of them were in the air. As they fell back, Will twisted the man's body so that it was beneath him and falling headfirst toward the sidewalk. He held his elbow in position, and as they landed on the ground, the man's neck snapped instantly from the impact. He was dead.

Will rummaged through the man's pockets and took his wallet, passport, cell phone, and all other materials that might show his identity. He knew that police would still be able to trace the dead body, but the things he'd removed would, he hoped, delay identification by a few hours. The light around him was bad, so he switched on a small flashlight to examine the man's passport. He frowned, swung the light at the dead man's face, then back at the details in the passport.

"Oh, dear God, no."

THIRTY-FOUR

Will turned away from his view of the snow-carpeted Sarajevo and looked at Roger. The two men were standing in the lounge area of a superior suite at the Radon Plaza Hotel.

"I was a kid when I joined the French Foreign Legion," Will said. "It was very tough at the beginning, but there was a slightly older guy who had joined up with me and took me under his wing to help me get through training. That man became a friend and later served with me in the GCP. Last night I killed him."

Roger took a step forward toward him, then stopped. "You had no way of knowing it was your friend. You barely saw his face."

Will walked to a chair, sat down, and dropped his head into his hands.

"Will?"

Will looked up at Roger. He tried to put memories of his dead friend out of his mind. But he still remembered how, seventeen years earlier, the man had smiled as he showed the eighteen-year-old Legionnaire Cochrane how to shine the buttons on his uniform, polish his parade boots, and avoid getting ruthless punishment from the NCOs in their barracks. Will tried to focus. He had to—for the sake of Roger and his men, for the sake of Lana, for the sake of his mission to capture his father's murderer, for the sake of the mission to stop an atrocity, for the sake of everything. He breathed in deeply and asked, "How do you intend to deploy us tomorrow?"

Roger looked at him for a moment before nodding once. "Ben's our best driver, so he'll be in the vehicle. The rest of us will be on foot. What about our weapons?"

"I'm collecting them from Harry today. The exfiltration plan?"

"All set."

"Good."

Given Roger's expertise in these matters, Will had asked him to construct a plan to extract Megiddo from Sarajevo once he'd been captured. Roger had considered a number of different options, including going over Bosnia's land borders, escaping via air, and the option of the sea. But Will had made it clear that they did not have the use of American or British facilities, and that therefore ruled out some of Roger's ideas that included the use of military vehicles such as helicopters, freight aircraft, and submarines. The only thing they did have was American and British money.

Roger had therefore decided on the most viable option. Megiddo would be captured and taken to a vacation rental home approximately thirteen kilometers outside the town of Konjic, which itself was almost fifty kilometers southeast of Sarajevo. The house was secluded on the edge of Jablaničko Lake in a wooded, mountainous area and could hold six people if required to. Will, Roger, and Julian would take Megiddo onward from Konjic to Bosnia's only seaside town, Neum on the Adriatic coast. Laith and Ben would not travel with them on this leg but instead would take conventional transport out of the country and travel to the United Kingdom. The remaining team, however, would leave the country on a chartered yacht. Megiddo would be stowed away in the yacht's hull. The captain of the vessel, who ran a popular tourist charter business, was well known to Roger. As a sideline he was also a smuggler of heroin, among other things. Illegal human cargo would not bother him at all.

Will and Roger had analyzed the risks they would face at every stage of the extraction. They had decided that the point of highest vulnerability would be between exiting from Neum and reaching Italian waters. Their destination was the English Channel, but Will had decided that if they were seized anywhere outside the Bosnian and Herzegovinian jurisdiction, he would have no other option than to escalate matters by involving their premiers to plead their release on the basis of a mutual Western intelligence imperative. He hoped, however, to avoid such a requirement. He liked the idea of quietly sailing into one of England's ports with his prize.

"What about the meeting itself?" he asked Roger now.

"Lana needs to give us a visible thumbs-up or thumbs-down. I suggest that we have her place her handbag on the coffee table if the man is Megiddo and on the floor if it's not him. Can you confirm to me now that that will be the signal?"

"I can confirm. Handbag on the table if it's him."

"Good. Now, what happens when the meeting is over? If it's him, she needs to get the hell out of Dodge. She must go straight to the airport and get on the next flight to Paris. She must not go back to her hotel. She'll be safe on the route from the meeting to the airport because it's all built up, and once she's at the airport, there are too many armed cops for the Iranians to do anything silly. If it's not him, then where will she go?"

"Back to her room in the Holiday Inn for a debrief by me."

"All right. We know that all seven Iranians are now in Sarajevo. They're still rotating their numbers on Lana, but obviously the full team will be out to play tomorrow. And I'm betting they'll be armed."

Will shook his head. "It should never have had to come to this." He looked straight at Roger. "What kind of men would place an innocent woman into the epicenter of a circle of danger and potential death?"

Roger grabbed Will's arm with unexpected force. "*We* are not that kind of men. *We* did not want this. *You* did not want this. But here we both are doing what we have to, even if we hate our job. Stay focused, Will. We all need you more than ever right now."

Will sighed and nodded. "What are the next steps?"

"Depends on what the man does. If he goes on foot, we follow him on foot. If in a vehicle, then Ben will be on him. It depends which route, but if we're lucky—and I stress lucky—Ben may be able to pick one of us up while he's on the tail. Objective: pin Megiddo down to one location. Then we improvise."

Will frowned at Roger. "You improvise? You have no prior plans?"

"How can we? All is good if he goes to the HBF building. If it's there, we have an attack plan. But will it be? It could be a hotel, could be a house or an apartment building, could be inner city, outer city, or just about anywhere." Roger had been ticking off the possibilities on his fingers. "We get him in one location and then we improvise. But we improvise with speed and accuracy."

What he said made sense to Will. The team would have to react to whatever circumstances they faced. "Okay, Roger. Where do I fit in?"

Roger considered the question. "You can't be too close to Lana, because you may be recognized by the Iranians. But you've got to be on the ground with us, because Megiddo's exit from café to fixed location to our assault and extraction could take place within thirty minutes, start to finish. Then it will be directly on to the house in Konjic. You need to be with us, but you can't take an active role in surveillance of the meeting."

Will wasn't happy, but he knew that Roger's assessment was correct. Nevertheless, he would dearly like to have seen the moment when Lana placed her handbag on the table to indicate that his quest was near its end.

Roger rubbed the stubble on his chin. "Well, there's nothing more that can be said right now. I need to get back to watch Lana. Are you seeing her before the meeting?"

"I need to see her tonight."

"Okay." He looked at Will with an expression that was both stern and understanding. "When this is over, we can examine our consciences. But right now I've got to stop a woman from being attacked or worse, and you've got to capture a mass murderer. For the moment let's just focus on that."

Two stationary vehicles were parked on the side of the otherwise deserted hilltop road. Will drove up behind them and pulled to a stop. He flashed his lights and exited the car. The vehicle in front of him was an S-Class Mercedes that contained one man. The other was a Jeep Grand Cherokee, and Will could see four men inside the SUV. He walked through deep snow to get to the first vehicle and banged his fist on its trunk.

Harry got out of the car and grinned. "You're always creeping up on me from behind, Charles. You don't have a knife on you this time, though, do you?"

Will smiled and shook the man's hand.

Harry nodded at him. "So things must be coming to a head if you need my equipment now."

"I hope so."

Harry looked away to the direction of Sarajevo city beneath them. His smile slowly receded, and he remained still for a while before turning back to Will. "I guess that means I have no further value to you?"

"I doubt that. Our paths will cross again."

Harry smiled again, although the look was doubtful. He walked to the rear of his car, opened the trunk, and pulled out a duffel bag that he swung toward Will. "This is what you asked for. SIG Sauer handguns with silencers, ammunition, Motorola walkie-talkies, and an HK417 sniper rifle."

Will took the bag. "How much do I owe you for this?"

Harry rubbed a hand against his chin thoughtfully. He said, "I tell you what: just stay in touch. That will be compensation enough."

Will nodded toward the Jeep and its four passengers. "I'll let you know when you no longer need protection."

"Good, because I've never been the type of man to hide behind others."

Will swung the bag onto his back. "I can see that. But I can also see that you've reached a stage in your life where you feel you may need others around you."

Harry seemed to be considering this. "You could be right. But I've carved out a life for myself that cannot readily embrace the possibility of friendships."

Will smiled. "You carved out a life for yourself that's too close to the shadows of your past. Why not move on?"

Harry shrugged. "To where?"

Will started to answer, then stopped. He thought for a moment. He decided that Harry needed his help to face a better future. He decided that Harry needed help to take the final steps on his road to redemption. He looked at the old man. "You already have wealth, so therefore I can't reward you with money for what you've done to help me. And I am most certainly the wrong man for friendship. But what if I could give you something that would help you have fresh surroundings, something that even a man of your standing could not get?" Will could see that the man was listening. "What would you say if I could obtain a legitimate United States passport for you?"

Harry laughed. "Since when does the U.S. Immigration Service hand out passports to men who are supposed to be war criminals?"

"They don't and won't. But I'm fairly sure that I can get the U.S. president to personally authorize one."

The man moved closer to Will. "The president would absolve me of my sins?"

Will chuckled softly. "Even presidents can't absolve sins." He followed Harry's gaze toward the now peaceful but once blood-drenched city below them. "But they can change the course of events. You don't need to be here anymore, Harry. You don't need to be trapped with your past. That passport would give you a new beginning if you wish for one." He turned to look Harry in the eye. "I saw that you were capable of redemption. But I gave you a severe warning in case you strayed from that journey. You heeded my warning. And as a result I am willing to give you a new life."

Harry reached out and shook Will's hand with a strong grip. And Will pretended not to notice that the aging man's eyes had begun to water.

Rather than sit in one of the other chairs, Lana had positioned herself on the sofa next to him. She was dressed in jeans and a loose V-neck sweater. Her feet were bare, and Will could see that she had decided not to wear a bra. Her hair was loose and glossy, and she had applied makeup, but not too much. She held a vodka tonic, and he could smell her Guerlain perfume.

She looked nervous. "I have packed my things."

"I forgot to mention that you'll need to leave everything. Bring only your passport tomorrow."

"Then you will just need to take me shopping when I get home." She smiled, but her words sounded forced.

"I thought you'd say that." He smiled and nodded. "I've never taken a woman shopping before." He watched Lana for a while before saying, "Are you sure you still want to go through with this?"

Her expression turned sharp. "Of course." She took a gulp of her drink. She looked away for a moment before regarding Will with an expression that was no longer hostile but instead confused. "It's just . . . the closer I get to him, the more the memories of him become real again, the stronger the hate I have for him becomes." When she next lifted the glass to her lips, her hand was shaking. "I don't want hate to consume me again. I do want to have what you said about me in Paris—to have other things to live for."

Will nodded. "When this is over, you'll have everything to live for."

Lana set down her drink down and stared at it. She turned to Will. "Make me lose the hate. Make me have those other things."

She placed her hand on the back of Will's head, pulled him to her, and kissed him fully on the lips. She smoothed her fingers against his face and whispered, "Let's not wait until this is over." She kissed him again, with increased passion.

Will desperately wanted their embrace to last forever, desperately wanted to lift her up and carry her to the bed, desperately wanted to make love to her and afterward lie next to her and hold her in his arms. Lana's embrace felt so good, so loving, so passionate, so tender, and yet so forceful. It felt right, and at this moment Will knew that with Lana he could face his fears, could love without being terrified of loss or weakness or mere normality and take those first steps toward a different life.

But he also knew that they had to wait, that it would be very wrong to do anything now, that he had to stay strong and in control of himself and his emotions, that the dangers of the mission required all these things from him.

He placed his hand over Lana's fingers and gently drew away from her. He loathed himself for doing so, even though he knew it was the right thing to do.

Her expression turned from longing and loving to confused and cold. She muttered, "You don't want me."

Will frowned and shook his head. "That's not right, Lana, I—"

She stood quickly, and in doing so she banged against the coffee table, knocking over her glass and spilling its contents. She turned and looked down at Will. She shook her head slowly, and her eyes now seemed completely devoid of any of the emotion she'd shown a moment ago. "Then all I have left is hate."

THIRTY-FIVE

Sarajevo was awake, and people and cars were on its streets despite the blizzard that was now hitting the city with ever-increasing intensity.

Will and Laith were standing on Zelenih Beretki. They both carried pastries, tourist guides, and cameras. They wore jeans and winter jackets with the hoods up. They smiled and laughed and took in the views of the Old Town and hoped that they seemed like a couple of men who were passing time while their wives shopped. Under their jackets they had skin-colored Motorola communication cords that emerged at the collars to earpieces and microphones. Within their pockets each of them had silenced SIG Sauer pistols and two spare clips of ammunition.

While gazing around and occasionally pointing at something or nodding, Laith spoke to Will. "Ben's in an SUV on Mula Mustafe Bašeskije, Julian's taken up a sniper position inside a building on Sarači, and Roger's on Ferhadija itself." It would be Roger who would be watching the position of Lana's handbag. From their own position, Will and Laith could not see the Black Swan café. "All seven of the Iranians are around her, and all are on foot."

Will did not look at his watch, but he knew that it was nearly ten o'clock. He took another bite of his pastry even though he was not hungry. "What shape are they in?"

"Too close to each other for good surveillance. They're just focused on protection now." Laith's head moved slightly, and Will knew that he would be scanning their surroundings. It had become a busy place. All around them, vehicles and shoppers and workers were battling their way through the weather. "Let's hope it's just protection. You know the last time seven assassins were sent to this city?"

"I do not."

"In 1914. They killed an archduke just upriver from here and sparked a world war." Laith pretended to examine his tourist guide.

"Thank you for reassuring me." Will tried to grin again.

Roger's voice came on the air. "Vehicle's just pulled up. Two men. One gets out. He's middle-aged. It could be him." He went quiet again before quickly relaying further updates. "Vehicle drives off. The other man enters the Swan. It means he's likely to be mobile after the meet."

Ben's voice. "Understood."

Will kept his breathing as regular as he could. He ignored his surroundings; for the moment that was Laith's job. His mind focused purely on the microphone in his right ear and any sounds coming from it, which would determine success or failure.

Roger's voice. "She stands. Hands are shaken. Hands are held. She kisses him on a cheek. They sit." Silence. "Vision blocked. Waitress." Silence.

Will counted seconds. He stopped counting. He could not count.

"They talk." Roger's voice was calm and authoritative. "He hands her an envelope. He stands. She remains seated. He makes cell-phone call. He speaks on phone. End of call. Glance at his watch. More talk."

Will scuffed his boots in the snow impatiently. All he wanted to hear was that Lana had set her handbag on to the table. All he wanted to know was that she was leaving the place safe and alone.

Ben's voice: "Same vehicle as before passes me. Heading south. Turning left onto Mula."

"Got it." Roger's voice was quick. "It's now on Ferhadija. It stops outside the Swan."

"Her handbag?" Will's voice was urgent.

"I'm waiting." Roger's voice remained calm. "Hands are shaken again. Man turns. He walks away from her."

Will glanced at Laith and could tell that the man was poised to run to the café as soon as the command was uttered.

"Lana removes her bag from her shoulder. She holds it away from her. She places it on the floor."

Lana was standing smoking in her hotel room and appeared to be on her second or third vodka and tonic. She looked at him and shook her head. "It was not him."

"Are you absolutely sure?" Will had a hard time not shouting the question.

Lana huffed and waved her glass at him. "You know I am the one person who can positively identify Megiddo. The man I saw today was too short. He spoke differently. He had different features. It was most certainly not him." She lowered her glass and slumped into an armchair. "Megiddo is playing with me."

Will stood silently examining Lana. She wore an expression he thought could be disappointment. His own emotions were numb with disbelief that he had not cornered Megiddo today.

"Did the man you saw give you his name?" he said at last.

Lana fluttered a hand. "He introduced himself as Mr. Nozari."

Will nodded once. The man had to be Gulistan Nozari. Which just confirmed what Ben had concluded when he had followed the man and his vehicle back to the Human Benevolence Foundation building, where Nozari was registered.

"He gave me that." Lying on the coffee table between them was a plain white business-size envelope. It was fat and had been opened.

Lana nodded at it, and Will picked it up. Inside were dollars and a folded letter.

Dear Miss Beseisu,

You are reading this letter because you told the man you met today that he was not me. It means you genuinely want to see me. This in turn means that your motives are probably not driven by monetary requirements. Otherwise you might have said nothing to the man and hoped that he would give you something for your efforts.

But you will also understand that I have needed to be very cautious. Your first letter to me came after years of absence from each other, and you have already advised me that for most of that time you have lived in Europe. A man in my position would naturally be suspicious, and as a result I have been forced to take precautions. One such precaution was getting you to meet somebody else first. You may think of the man you met today as my deputy. He is not, but think of him that way.

I still do not know what your intentions are toward me, so you will understand that I will continue to be careful. But since nothing untoward happened today, then you are probably alone and I will therefore finally meet you in person. You have my word on that now.

I have instructed my deputy to give you some money, which should be included with this letter. It is $15,000 and is to help with your expenses.

I have business to attend to in the United States of America. That is where we shall meet. You must fly to Boston tomorrow and stay at the Boston Park Plaza Hotel. On the day after, you must leave the hotel at noon and walk directly east until you reach the InterContinental Boston hotel. You must then walk alongside the harbor through downtown and the North End. I will meet you on that walk at a place of my choosing.

Yours,
Megiddo

Lana leaned forward, her head in her hands. "I promised my mother that I would be returning to Paris to care for her in the next day or two."

"You should not have done that."

She looked up quickly. "Why not? What reason did I have to think that you would fail?"

Will felt anger surge through his body. He breathed slowly and said as calmly as he could, "We both desperately wanted the man you met today to be Megiddo."

Lana shook her head, and Will could see that she, too, felt anger. "But he's always one step ahead."

"He is just being cautious."

"Cautious?" She laughed. "As far as he's concerned, you have information that could stop his plan to commit an atrocity. You'd think he'd have no time for caution."

"I think he has no time for impatience." Will sighed. "But you're right. I failed to anticipate that Megiddo would be able to hold his nerve to this extent." He went to her and crouched down, taking her hands in his. "I need you to go to America. I'm sure it will all end there. And you know, you really know, that I will take steps to make sure your mother is comfortable in your absence."

"We don't need your help now." She spat the words.

Will knew that whatever he said would be wrong or misinterpreted. He spoke anyway. "I *do* want your help. I want you to help me become a different man. But I want that to happen in the right way. I want that to happen"—he looked around before returning his gaze to Lana—"when nothing else matters."

Lana yanked her hands from his. "For a man like you, there will always be other things that matter. There'll always be other bad men for you to catch, other dangers for you to fight."

"Maybe, but you won't be involved in any of those. You are, however, very involved in what's happening right now. Let's not confuse things."

"'Things'?" Lana shook her head, and a tear rolled down her cheek.

Will drew a deep breath. "I want you to find peace, Lana. And even though I did not want you involved in this mission, maybe you were right to do this. Maybe you need to do this to put your hatred to bed, to find peace."

"And what about you? If you capture Megiddo, will that give *you* peace?"

For the briefest moment, Will wanted to tell her everything. He wanted to tell her about his father. He wanted to tell her why Megiddo was so important to him. He wanted to tell her why trapping and punishing the man could well give him some strange kind of meaning and tranquillity. Instead he said, "Maybe."

They were quiet for a long time. Lana's anger seemed to recede.

She sighed. "I try to imagine what Megiddo is like now."

"Do you think he is dedicated to the Iranian regime?"

Lana shook her head. "He never gave much away. I know only a bit more about him than I know about you. Which is nothing. But no, he has no allegiance to the current regime. He once told me that his father had served under the shah but secretly, toward the end of that era, was helping the revolutionaries plot the shah's overthrow. He told me that his father had been extremely brave but also foolhardy to do what he did. He told me that his father's secret work was discovered by people close to the shah and that he was killed." She narrowed her eyes. "When that happened, the young Megiddo was working with the revolutionaries, but even though his father had helped them, they still did not fully trust Megiddo because of his father's previous work for the shah. So in the early days his masters would give Megiddo tests just to see how committed he was to their new regime. His first task was to capture and slaughter an American. When he told me what he did to the man, I was revolted."

Will's stomach muscles tightened with a surge of anger and adrenaline.

"They kept giving him more and more new tasks, and Megiddo would complete them with such exceptional brutality that he came to the attention of the senior revolutionaries and was rapidly promoted though the new regime's ranks." She smiled. "But Megiddo was using them and had no real allegiance to the revolutionaries. He thought they were ideological fools. He needed them, though, because they gave him the power to do what he enjoyed."

Will shook his head. "The power to be an unbridled psychopath."

Lana frowned. "I saw no signs of that when I knew him in Bosnia. He was certainly ruthless and cunning and exceptionally clever, and he obviously had the blood of many men on his hands. But I did not see a deranged murderer."

Lana stood and looked at Will. "I don't think I'd hate him as much as I do if he were simply a madman." She bent and kissed Will briefly on the lips. "I'm sorry for my harsh words. Maybe you are right. Maybe now is not the time. Maybe the 'things' that are weighing so heavily on our minds do need to be fully resolved before we can have the peace to know each other properly. Maybe I do need to let my hate for him run its true course so that I can be a better woman. A woman for you."

Will sat alone in Lana's hotel room. She'd been gone for fifteen minutes, and he had just been informed by Laith that the Iranians were with her and that he was free to leave. He tried to think of many other things, but what Lana had told him of Megiddo's past kept repeating itself in his mind. He stood, walked to the door, and heard his cell phone ring. He recognized the number and answered immediately.

"Harry."

"Charles. Sorry to bother you." Harry's voice sounded uncharacteristically weak. "I was calling to see whether my equipment was up to the job."

Will paused for a moment. "It was not fully used."

There was a long silence at the other end before Harry spoke again. "I see."

Will frowned. "Is something wrong?"

Another long silence, and then Harry said, "Did you mean what you told me? The passport?"

"I meant it." Patrick had been furious at the request, but Will had garnered the CIA man's confirmation that the passport could be issued, provided that Harry's information led to the capture of Megiddo and prevention of his attack.

Harry made a sound like a sigh.

Will repeated, "Is anything wrong, Harry?"

"We need to meet. There's some new information I have which I must share with you."

"Where and when?"

"First thing tomorrow morning at my house. It will be safe there. I can SMS you the address."

"Sure. But can't you tell me about this new information now?"

"Not on the phone. Only in person. But I can say that what I now know will turn everything upside down."

THIRTY-SIX

Will drove north and then east alongside Sarajevo's Miljacka River. He had previously memorized the route and now mentally crossed off road and street names as he traveled.

Bulevar Meše Selimovića, Zmaja od Bosne, Obala Kulina Bana, north on Sagardžije, Vrbanjuša, Kulenovića, Skenderaj, east on Sedrenik, north on to Paššino Brdo, then exactly three point four kilometers up that hill route.

Harry had forewarned Will that his house was isolated and deliberately difficult to find, because it was set back in a wooded area away from the quiet road. But Will measured the distance up the hill, and at the correct point he found only one track leading off his road. It was a track that was clearly used by vehicles and was nearly hidden by overhanging trees. Will did not enter the snow-covered track but instead went on driving up the hill for another four hundred meters, until he came to found a place that could have once been a sniper post but was now a natural observation spot for hikers. A spot where one could stop and eat sandwiches and rest up. He exited his car and checked his watch. He was eighty-eight minutes early for his arranged meeting with Harry.

Will looked around. From this vantage a proficient sniper would have been able to strike the northeast tip of Sarajevo. He would also have a very clear sight of the city's road leading to this place. Will didn't have a sniper rifle, but he did have a small set of 10×25 bird-watching binoculars. He examined the road and could see no vehicles or persons. He walked back along the hill road and to within two hundred meters of the track leading to Harry's house. He stepped off the road and into the woods, where he walked parallel to the track. When he came to within one hundred meters of the house, he sat down. He stayed in this position for twenty minutes before moving to study the house from a different angle, where he again waited for the same duration. He repeated this process twice more, so that by the end of his eighty-minute watch he had observed the full perimeter of the property.

The S-Class Mercedes and Jeep Grand Cherokee were parked in an open garage toward the front of Harry's house. The house's windows had external wooden shutters, and all were open. Will could see no movement inside. He listened but could hear no human sounds.

He walked out of the wooded area and onto Harry's driveway. Then he put his gloves on and walked directly up to the front door to ring the bell. There was no answer, so he rang again. Again nothing. He pulled out his phone and tried to call Harry. The phone rang eight times before being directed to Harry's voice mail. Will replaced his phone and slowly walked around the house. He peered into ground-floor windows and knocked on a rear door. He continued to be met by silence.

He tried to open the rear door, but it was locked. He looked around the back garden and spotted a small hut. The door to the tiny building was unlocked, and within it he found what he was looking for. He returned to the rear door of the house and swung the mallet at the area around the door handle. The door crashed open instantly, and he stepped into the house. He walked through the spacious kitchen before him and into a hallway. To his left was a big, open living and dining area. There were three separate sofa-and-chair groupings, plus a heavy wooden dining table surrounded by eight seats. A sixty-inch flat-screen television was wall-mounted near one of the sofa areas, and a Bang & Olufsen stereo system was positioned adjacent to another. Gilt-and-marble coffee tables were scattered throughout, on top of huge woven silk rugs in red and gold. There were large paintings that looked to be originals and old. It was early-morning daylight outside, but had the room's lights been turned on, the room would have been illuminated by the glow from crystal chandeliers. Harry clearly liked luxury.

Will moved quickly through the rest of the house. The place had six bedrooms, eight bathrooms, two other lounge areas, and three studies. It was very big for one person, but Will imagined that Harry was the type of man who would like to throw parties for glamorous women. Will paid particular attention to the upstairs study and found lots of documentation and paperwork. But he decided it would take him hours to go through the stuff. He looked in the more obvious areas but could find nothing of immediate interest.

He returned downstairs. Everywhere seemed immaculate, and he could smell alcohol-based polish.

He walked back into the main living area and looked at the bodies he had earlier stepped over. Harry's four bodyguards had all been shot in the head and torso. They must have been dispatched with extreme swiftness, for none of them showed signs of having had time to arm themselves.

Will placed his hand on his throat pressel switch to speak to Roger. "Four bodies, but no sign of Harry."

"Understood." Roger spoke quietly, and Will knew that he would be hidden somewhere halfway along the three-kilometer hill route.

Will checked the pockets of the dead men but found nothing of interest. He heard Roger's voice again in his earpiece.

"I can see a four-seater sedan driving up Pašino Brdo. Three Iranians are inside. One of them is Nozari, and the other two are from the team. They're driving slowly and they're two point eight kilometers from your position. They'll be passing me in two minutes and with you in five. Let me know if you want me to stop them."

Will frowned. He had no doubt that the men who had killed Harry's bodyguards were the same people who had killed Kljujic, and he knew that Nozari had been directly or indirectly involved in both acts. But it made no sense to him that they were driving back to Harry's house at such a casual pace. If they'd been stupid and left something in the house to compromise themselves, they would be driving with haste. Likewise, if Will had been spotted by them going to the house—and he thought that impossible—they would be after him with speed and in greater numbers. But they were driving as if they were unafraid of time or consequences.

Suddenly the realization of what was happening hit him. He cursed silently and pulled out his SIG Sauer handgun, at the same time his free hand flew to his throat pressel switch. "They're coming to collect the assassin. He's still here."

"There could be more than one."

"There's only one empty seat in that car." Will swung his gun around. He could feel his heart race, and he kept moving. "But whoever's here is good enough to take out four men in the blink of an eye."

"Then I'd better be on my way."

Will held his gun in two hands and walked quickly but lightly across the room and into the downstairs hallway. Opposite him was one of the two smaller studies, and he reentered the room, walked around its perimeter, and then returned to the hallway. He stopped to listen but could hear nothing. The upper floor of the house contained the most rooms, closets, and other areas where a man could hide, and Will decided that unless the assassin had left the house already, he must be in one of those places. He ascended the stairs until he was back on that upper floor. Beams of white daylight traversed the expansive corridor area before him and came from open doorways and the external windows beyond them. He narrowed his eyes to try to focus through the strobelike effect they created, and he started moving through the floor, checking each room to his left and right. The smell of the polish was even stronger here, and he didn't remember noticing its pungency when he'd been up here a few minutes earlier. He exited the final room on the right side of the corridor and moved to the master bedroom at the end of the floor. It was the last room to be checked. He crouched low and to one side of the double-door entrance. He slowly turned the handle and pushed the door inward while remaining in position and out of sight of anyone inside the room. Within a split second, he poked his head into the room and out again. In that time he had seen no one in there, although he knew from his earlier search that there were at least nine places inside it large enough to conceal a man. He counted ten seconds while listening before moving steadily into the room with his gun held in front of him. He examined all nine places and then kicked at the bed in frustration. He was now sure that the killer must have left before he'd entered the house. He looked around the room one more time and sighed.

A loud thud came from behind him, and he instantly spun around to face the direction of the noise. It had come from the end of the long corridor, and through the fragmenting splinters of daylight he saw an open attic hatch and a man standing beneath it with his back to Will. The man turned toward him. Even though he was approximately thirty meters away from Will and partially disguised by the distorting effect of inconsistent light and darkness, he could see that the man was tall and middle-aged. He could also see that the man's arm was outstretched. Will raised his gun to shoot, but a tiny flash of another kind of light descended quickly from the man's hand toward the floor. Too late Will realized that the tiny glow belonged to a cigarette-lighter and too late he understood that the pungent alcohol smell belonged not to polish but to a fire accelerant. The lighter hit the floor, and blue flames instantly engulfed the corridor and sped along it toward the master bedroom. Will flinched slightly as the fire dazzled his vision. When he looked up again, he was surprised to see that the man was still standing in the same position. It then registered that the man was pointing a handgun in his direction. Will saw the gun's muzzle flash, sensed the tiniest moment of absolute pain in his head, and then felt and knew nothing.

THIRTY-SEVEN

I need you to live."

Will saw his body move away from floor. He saw black swirls, he saw yellow and red, and he smelled roasting flesh. Something sharp repeatedly banged against his chest and produced pain. But the pain on the side of his head was much worse. He felt things were moving, and he felt out of control. He closed and opened his eyes, and each time he did, he saw different images. He heard breathing and felt something wrapped tight and unforgiving around his back. Movement increased and became as rapid as the breathing he heard. He saw things and then no longer saw or heard anything.

"You're not safe yet." The voice sounded different.

Will's head whipped back, and he saw white light. It slumped forward, and he saw snow and feet and legs quite close to him. Again something angular banged against his chest, and the images before him jarred in time with each small impact. He felt that he was moving fast. He felt helpless. His eyes closed even though he

did not wish them to do so. His brain began to fall into some kind
of strange sleep.

Will opened his eyes and saw sky. Underneath him everything felt
cold. He focused on his hands and pushed with them without knowing what the action would do to his body. It forced him up into a
seated position and into a place that at first he did not understand. He
was seated in thick snow and on a steep hillside. He shook his head
quickly to try to focus his mind.

"Don't do that."

Will stopped. He looked toward the voice, which seemed real.
He saw Roger, but the man was not looking at him and was instead
crouched on one knee while looking back up the hill. He held a rifle
and was peering through its scope. Will shook his head again.

"You'll lose consciousness if you do that. And I'm not going to
haul you back onto my shoulder for another thousand-meter run if
you ignore me." Roger pulled away from the scope and looked toward
Will. "We must go."

Will touched a hand to his head and felt a long groove along the
right-hand side of his hairline. He knew that the injury must have
come from the assassin's bullet. He coughed and recalled the thick
smoke within the house. His vision blurred, and he blinked several
times to try to regain control of his sight. He breathed in deeply and
felt pain in his lungs. He slowed his breathing and tried to calm his
body and mind. He spoke. "How the hell did you get me out of that
house?"

Roger came toward him. "I didn't. But the man who torched the
place and then shot you most certainly did."

THIRTY-EIGHT

He should not travel that distance. He's been shot in the head."
Will heard the words from behind closed eyes. He opened them and saw Julian and Ben. The two men were standing over him. He looked around and recognized his surroundings as the superior suite he had stayed in before, in Sarajevo's Radon Plaza Hotel.

Ben looked at Will and said, "I bet it feels like someone's struck your head full force with an iron bar."

Will raised his hand to the side of his head and felt padding. "Shit. What time is it, and where's Roger?"

Ben spoke as he applied a damp swab to Will's face. "We got you here two hours ago. Roger and Laith are now on a plane, seated a few seats behind Lana. They'll be landing in Boston in eight hours."

Will pushed himself away from Ben and sat upright on the bed. He swung his legs off the bed and stood. He instantly felt giddy, and in his peripheral vision he saw the two CIA men come to his side to hold him. He closed his eyes, breathed, then opened them again. "Let go of me."

The two men held their grip for a while and then did as he asked.

"What time is the next flight to Boston?"

Ben frowned. "There's a Lufthansa flight via Munich at twelve fifty-five P.M., but that's in three hours' time and there's no way you can be fit for that flight."

"I've got to be. Lana's meeting is at lunchtime tomorrow. I have to be on that flight."

Ben took a step closer to Will. "There's no way . . ."

Will held a hand up. "Remove my bandages. Disguise the wound as much as you can. Make sure that I'm clean and that this stench of smoke and blood is off me. Get me into decent clothes, and get me on that plane."

Will was returning to the United States of America. Four weeks ago he had left the country in a severely wounded state, and he was now going back there in a similar condition. He reclined his first-class seat back a little and looked across the aisle toward his traveling companions. Ben looked to be sleeping, but Julian was awake, and he immediately got out of his seat and came to Will's side.

"Do you want some more painkillers?"

Will shook his head. "No. They'll stop me from thinking straight."

"You need to rest."

"I need to work through this."

Julian returned to his seat, and Will closed his eyes. He saw the assassin standing perfectly still amid the beams of light, saw him set the house ablaze, saw the man shoot him with a precision that ensured taht the bullet glanced along one side of his head rather than penetrated his brain. He wondered why the man had then lifted him onto a shoulder to carry him through the smoke and fire and out into the garden. He wondered why the man had told him he needed Will to stay alive. He wondered why the man had left him on that ground and whether he'd done so for fear of his own capture or death. He wondered why Harry had disappeared shortly after telling him that everything was now upside down.

Will opened his eyes. There was one thing he did not wonder about. He knew that the assassin had to be Megiddo.

THIRTY-NINE

It occurred to Will that the men before him were probably two of the most powerful individuals in the Western intelligence community. It also occurred to him how very alike they looked. But more important than their physical similarities was the near alignment of both thinking and action that Will now believed more than two decades of covert collaboration had produced between Patrick and Alistair. They looked at him now.

"You must never tell anyone about your actions against the French."

"Because even we would not be able to protect you from the repercussions if that event were ever disclosed."

"All that matters is your operation to seize Megiddo."

"If you're still up to the task of capturing him."

"But are you?"

Will patted a hand against freshly applied bandages. His wound had been examined and treated by the same small, bespectacled American man who had cared for him in New York. The man had told him he would need to keep the bandaging on for at least a week, and even then he would need to have minor reconstructive surgery to hide all traces of the bullet wound. Will had told him that he would be removing the bandages in the morning.

He looked around the minimalist room. It belonged to a CIA safe house in a residential area of Boston's West End. He looked back at the two senior men. "Lana will meet him tomorrow at noon, and I'll be there to watch it happen."

Patrick and Alistair did not look at each other and instead kept their attention on Will. "Even though you're now on U.S. soil, you do know that we still can't give you extra intelligence resources to cover that meeting? And even though we probably could get help from the local and federal police and the military, that cannot be an option yet."

"I know." Will had already concluded that police involvement would not work. If things went wrong, their primary objective would be to save lives. And military involvement, even special ops, was too risky, because any individuals deployed from that quarter wouldn't have time to learn the nuances of the mission and therefore couldn't be trusted to make correct decisions without direct instructions. He had to continue to rely solely on Roger, Laith, Ben, and Julian.

"So, aside from wishing to check on my mental and physical well-being, why are you both here?"

Alistair smiled.

Patrick did not. He took a step toward Will. "We have new NSA Hubble intelligence."

Will held up a palm. "It will be manufactured by Megiddo and therefore should be ignored."

"This cannot be ignored, because it is genuine." Alistair was no longer smiling. "It is not intelligence about the location or timing of the attack but rather intelligence pertaining to the movement of men. And it can be and has been verified by independent sources. We know that twenty-five men are traveling to the United States from Iran during the next forty-eight hours. We know that all of them are members of the Islamic Revolutionary Guard Corps, and we have positively identified four of them as IRGC Qods Force men. We must therefore assume they are all Qods Force personnel."

"They must be coming to Megiddo." Will looked at Alistair and then Patrick. "That will give him a team of thirty-two people in this country, and it must mean that his attack is going to take place here rather than in the U.K."

"Precisely."

Will frowned. "How do you know that the intelligence isn't false or misleading?"

"Because it is derived from multiple entry- and exit-port database systems as well as aircraft rosters. Even Megiddo cannot manipulate that amount or type of data."

Will thought for a moment and then asked, "Do we know anything about the men?"

Alistair answered. "Of the four that we know are definitely Qods Force, three of them have been linked to terror acts in the Middle East and South Asia. They are bombers."

"Then the rest must be their chaperones." Will drummed his fingers. "The men must remain untouched. I need Megiddo to feel confident that he has most of his tools in place to proceed with his mission. If we snatch his men, he'll be so hampered that he'll probably go to ground for who knows how long, and certainly the imperative for him to capture and interrogate me would instantly recede. He'd retreat, restrategize, regroup, and then hit his target when he felt safe to do so."

Patrick exhaled slowly. "An NSA report like this is automatically sent to the Central Intelligence Agency, the Federal Bureau of Investigation, and the Department of Homeland Security."

The anger in Will was immediate. He jumped up and kicked his chair away from him. "How could you let this happen, Patrick? The Iranians will be grabbed, and then everything will be lost."

Alistair shouted, "William, shut your mouth!"

Will had never before heard the man raise his voice.

Alistair came very close to him, cupped a hand around the back of Will's neck, and quickly pulled his head within inches of his own. His next words were quiet and strong. "Don't presume anything."

Will pulled away from him and looked at Patrick. His heart was now pounding with emotion. "I told you to have confidence in my abilities."

Patrick remained silent. He sat, crossed his legs and placed the tips of his fingers together. Then he looked at Will. "The NSA report was shown to me two days ago while it was still in draft form. I read it and came to a conclusion. I got into a car and drove to Baltimore to see the director of the NSA. Because of who I am, the man gave me an audience, coffee, and some nice cookies. I gave him an ultimatum: destroy this report, or I would destroy the whole Hubble project on the basis that one percent of it was absolute rubbish."

Will frowned and from Alistair to Patrick to Alistair again.

His Controller nodded once at Will and spoke quietly. "Patrick has prevented the Iranians from being touched. He has prevented the operation from faltering. He has done something that *you* do not have the power to do." He narrowed his eyes. "We both have confidence in your abilities, William. But we do not wish to see our dead friend's son be torn apart by others if he fails."

He exchanged a brief glance with Patrick and then continued. "Patrick and I are untouchable. You are not. If there is any doubt in your mind"—his voice sounded forceful—"*any doubt* that you may succeed given the greater odds you now face, then you must be honest with us. If we wish it to happen, the NSA report can be recycled through CIA channels and the twenty-five men can still be arrested upon arrival here. We still have time to thwart Megiddo's plan temporarily." His voice softened again. "If you have absolute conviction that you will succeed, then the men must be untouched by others. But if you do have any doubt, we can arrange matters so that you can still walk away from this operation with dignity. The alternative to both is beyond our control."

Will narrowed his eyes and shook his head. "If you touch those men, Megiddo will disappear. Leave them alone, and leave me alone."

"What happened to you, Nicholas?" Lana's eyes watered as she looked at his head.

Will had decided not to wait until the morning to remove his bandages but instead had taken the padding off and cleaned himself up as much as possible before meeting his agent in this Plaza Hotel room. "I made a mistake."

She came to him and placed an arm around his back. She pressed against his body, raising her other hand close to the gunshot wound. Will could feel her breasts and her warmth, and he could smell lotions on her skin.

Lana touched the wound. She moved her fingers and touched his lips. She looked at them, then at his eyes. She pulled him even tighter against her beautiful body and shook her head slowly. "Piece by piece you are being broken."

Will was alone in his own hotel room. It would be hours before the sun rose and many more before Lana needed to make her walk, but Will had no thoughts of sleep. He stripped and cleaned his P228 handgun, he paced the room, he studied his maps of Boston Harbor again, he poured and drank tea, he showered, he packed and unpacked and repacked ammunition clips, he checked his communications equipment, he exercised, he showered again, and he sat.

And then he wondered what mattered to him the most: getting his revenge on Megiddo or keeping Lana safe. He decided both mattered in equal measure. Both mattered to him more than anything else in his life right now.

FORTY

I t's started. She's on her way." Roger's voice was clear and measured. Will pulled his windbreaker's hood up over his earpiece so that his head was covered, and he began to jog slowly down Boston's Boylston Street. The road had been partially cleared of snow, but to his left he could see that Boston Common, populated with daytime strollers and frolicking families, was still carpeted with the stuff. He crossed the street and slowed to a walk until he was at the southeast tip of the Common. He checked his watch and listened.

"She's moving up Charles Street toward Boylston. Will, get off that street and move up Tremont. Everyone else, maintain your positions."

Will followed Roger's instruction and came to a stop when he was three hundred meters along Tremont Street. A northerly wind coursed along the route and brought with it new and heavy snow. People were moving around him, and some, it seemed, had decided to get off the streets and out of the park to take shelter in shops and cafés. He rubbed his bare hands together and waited for Roger to speak again.

The man did so within a few seconds. "I'm behind her on Boylston, and so are three of her watchers."

Will knew that right now only Roger could see Lana and the Iranians who were following her. Ben would be waiting in a vehicle to the south on Washington Street, Laith would be on foot to the east on Essex Street, and Julian would be standing over the dead in the Common's Central Burying Ground. Will scrutinized the people around him, but nobody here looked out of place.

"She's moving south down Tremont Street. Hold."

Will waited thirty seconds until he heard Roger's voice again.

"She's gone left on to Lagrange Street. I'm going to stay back for a while. Laith, move to the end of Essex Street and then move to a stop on South Street so that you're ahead of her. Julian, take over Laith's current position on Essex and move as quickly as you can. Everyone else, hold."

Will looked back down the street. In the distance he saw a man sprint across the road and knew that the man was Julian.

"Okay, she's moving ahead onto Beach Street and Chinatown. Ben, get your vehicle onto Hudson Street." Roger's audible breathing suggested he was walking quickly or running. "I'm moving closer to her now."

Laith spoke. "Two men are waiting near me. They're definitely part of the team."

Five members of the Iranian surveillance team had now been spotted.

Roger spoke. "Will, time for you to move east. Your destination is Milton Place. Try to be there in three minutes."

Will immediately sprinted. He headed off Tremont Street and past the Ritz-Carlton Hotel before moving onto Essex Street. He dodged pedestrians and cars, trying not to lose traction on the ice- and snow-covered pavement. He knew that passersby were watching him and no doubt wondering what he was doing, but he didn't care. All he did care about was meeting Roger's exacting deadline. He ran up Lincoln Street and Devonshire Street before turning right onto Milton Place and stopping. He checked his watch, panting. He had completed the thousand-meter run in just over two and a half minutes. He depressed his pressel switch and gasped, "I'm here."

Roger replied, "Excellent. Laith, move up to the InterContinental. Ben, get your vehicle onto Matthews Street. Our lady's now going north." There was silence for a while before the CIA team leader spoke again. "Yes, the other two men have joined my three. Julian, get down on to the Harbor Walk. Will, go to the Langham Hotel on Franklin Street."

Will sucked in a lungful of air and ran again. He moved up Federal Street before turning right toward his destination. As he neared the Langham, he heard Laith's voice say, "I've got another one at the InterContinental."

Six members of the Iranian surveillance team were now accounted for.

Will brushed snow from his shoulders and waited several minutes. He watched people coming and going from the Langham, watched them moving along Franklin Street carrying bags and with their heads low to shield themselves from the driving snowfall, and saw cars moving tentatively forward with headlights switched on to guide their path through the blizzard. He watched all those things, but he did so while mentally picturing the surroundings of the InterContinental Hotel.

"Laith, a vehicle's just passed me and our lady." Roger spoke quickly. "It's a Dodge Durango SUV and is moving toward your position."

"Seen." Laith picked up the commentary. "One man in the vehicle. His vehicle slows. It stops by the hotel. The other man moves up to it and waits."

The driver had to be the seventh man of the surveillance team.

Roger spoke. "You should have sight of our lady."

Laith replied. "I do. Hold." The radio went silent for a few moments. "My man on foot is walking away from the vehicle. The driver remains inside the vehicle. The engine is on."

"Yeah, I've got him." Roger's voice sounded tense. "He's coming straight toward us. My five are moving closer to her. So is the man. He stops before her. Everyone stops. I can see him talking to her. He places a hand on her elbow. He walks with her toward the vehicle." There was a split-second sound of nothing before Roger said loudly, "They're going to put her in the car. Ben, pick Will up now."

Will felt his heart start to race. He reached for his pressel switch and was about to tell Roger to stop the Iranians. He thought, he cursed, he knew it was probable that Lana was simply being taken to another predetermined location in Boston, and he knew that if he did anything now to stop her, he would not only destroy the mission but also endanger Lana. He withdrew his hand from the radio mike. He looked up and down his street, and as he did so, he heard Laith again.

"She gets into the vehicle. So does the man, and so do two of the five walkers."

Will saw Ben's Range Rover Sport driving toward him at speed and in the wrong direction on the one-way street. The car skidded a little as it came to a stop, and he jumped into the vehicle. Ben said nothing and drove on.

Will depressed his pressel switch to speak to Roger. "We're mobile."

"You're in luck. They're moving toward you along Pearl Street."

Ben braked, and their four-wheel-drive vehicle shuddered to a halt. Will looked at Ben and saw that the man was staring ahead grimly. He also saw Ben's hand reach down next to him toward the vehicle's handbrake and a sawed-off Remington 870 shotgun.

Roger sounded nearly breathless. "You should be able to see them at the Pearl Street and Franklin Street intersection any moment . . ."

Ben looked in his rearview mirror.

" . . . now."

Ben forced their vehicle backward at speed and swung it around to face the intersection. He moved the car quickly forward, and they reached the intersection in seconds. They turned right onto Pearl Street, driving in the wrong direction on the one-way street for about one hundred meters before Will could see the large Dodge Durango. Ben had the windshield wipers at maximum power to try to aid his vision through the snowfall, but the weather was becoming so bad that the car ahead of them appeared and disappeared with each movement of the wipers.

Ben muttered, "We've got to get closer to them."

They watched the vehicle turn right onto Milk Street, and for a moment they didn't see it at all. Ben made the turn so that they were on the same street. Will frowned. The Dodge was stationary and had its hazard lights flashing.

"Fuck. I've got to keep driving." Ben kept the vehicle moving forward, and Will knew that he was doing so because to stop would look suspicious.

They drove steadily toward the Dodge, and Will didn't dare look at it as they cruised past the target vehicle. As they reached the next intersection, Ben turned right onto Oliver Street and stopped their car. "Get out and get close to their vehicle on foot. Something's wrong."

Will walked steadily back up Oliver Street until he was at its junction with Milk. There were sufficient pedestrians and other vehicles on the route for him not to seem out of place, and he scanned left and right before crossing. That brief look had allowed him to see inside the target vehicle. His heart began pounding as he reached the other side of the road, but he kept his pace normal, and instead of walking toward the Dodge he continued up Oliver Street until he felt sure that he couldn't be seen by anyone in the vehicle. He spoke to Roger. "There're only two people in the target vehicle, and our lady's not one of them."

"Damn. Laith, move up Pearl Street. Ben, get onto Federal Street and wait there. Julian, move up the Harbor Walk until you're parallel with Oliver Street. Will, you're the only man to the north, so cover what ground you can there in case she's gone in that direction."

Will thrust his hands into his pockets, where he could feel his

handgun. He walked quickly but could not run now for fear of trip-
ping over Lana and her two Iranian custodians. He moved west along
Kilby Street, Hawes Street, then Congress Street before turning east
along Exchange, then Water Street, then turning south on Broad
Street and then west again, so that he was back where he'd started. On
this route he had seen two buses, eighteen moving cars, sixty-three
pedestrians, and one Boston PD vehicle, but he had not seen what he
was looking for. Snow fell around him, and he cursed the weather and
everything else. He spoke to Roger. "Nothing."

"Understood. Ben, anything?"

"Nothing."

"Then we must assume she's traveling back toward the harbor.
Laith, stay still on Pearl Street. Julian, don't move. I'm going to Bat-
terymarch Street. Will, I need you in Christopher Columbus Park to
the northeast, and get there fast."

Will moved now with no care for accidentally betraying his presence to the Iranian team. He ran back up Kilby Street and along State
Street and Atlantic Street until he was at the small harbor-adjacent
park. He bent forward and placed his hands on his knees while inhal-
ing rapidly. Then he stood upright and looked around. Children were
throwing snowballs. Adults stood nearby watching them. But there
was nothing else. He kicked at snow.

"Possible sighting." The voice belonged to Laith.

Will froze and quickly pressed a hand against his hood and the
earpiece beneath it. He waited and counted in his head. He ignored
the freezing air that came from the harbor waters to hit his face. He
ignored all things that were not relevant. He listened and waited for
Laith to speak again.

"One woman and two men. They're walking toward my position,
but on the other side of the street." Laith's voice was quiet, and Will
strained to hear him over the wind and the city noises. "I can't yet
confirm it's them."

Will took two involuntary and pointless steps forward while

continuing to hold his hand against his head. Nobody else spoke. They would all be waiting for Laith to speak again.

"Getting closer. Give me ten seconds." Laith's voice was even quieter.

Will counted the seconds. He imagined that his whole team would be doing the same.

"It's them. It's definitely our lady."

Will inhaled deeply.

Roger's voice was instant and urgent. "Laith, let them pass and then follow. Julian, get alongside Seaport Boulevard. Ben, get your vehicle onto Atlantic Avenue and hold wherever you can. They might go mobile again."

"Where do you want me?" Will pictured the layout of the area they were in.

"Stay where you are."

"I should be closer to her." Will could feel the tension in his own voice.

"Stay where you are."

Will was about to speak again when he heard Laith's voice. "They're going straight toward the harbor."

Will felt useless. He looked along the Harbor Walk before him, but he knew that Lana and her escorts would be at least nine hundred meters away from him.

Julian spoke. "I see them. They're coming right at me."

"Okay, Julian. Laith, hold back and let Julian pick up the slack." Roger's voice sounded calm again. "I'm holding position to their northwest in case they double back."

Will walked back and forth to get his circulation moving.

Julian spoke again. "They're breaking left along the Harbor Walk."

Will stopped moving. Lana was walking toward his position along the harbor.

"I'm ahead of them." Julian sounded relaxed. "Suggest you put two others in so that we have a three-man perimeter around them."

"Agreed," replied Roger. "Laith, get in behind. I'll move in closer to cover their west."

Will smiled for the first time on this day. Lana and her shepherds were now trapped between Julian, Roger, Laith, and the waters of Boston Harbor. He listened to commentary from Laith and Julian.

"She's on Rowes Wharf."

"She passes the Boston Harbor Hotel."

"Three members of the team have just overtaken me. They're joining our lady and the other two."

He heard Roger's voice. "I've got one man heading toward them along East India Row."

He heard Ben speak. "I'm in position on Atlantic, but it's difficult to remain static here. Hold." Will heard engine noises behind Ben's voice. "The Dodge Durango has just passed me. But it's going slow."

"A mobile extraction is still probable." Roger's voice was no longer calm.

"She's just broken right onto the Central Wharf." Laith's voice was also tense. "Julian, you should have her."

Julian's voice responded immediately. "Of course. Our lady and team are sixty meters behind me. They'll be passing the aquarium now."

Will stamped his feet against the cold. Children were still playing around him, and their noises were interspersed with the whistles of the harbor's winter wind. He looked out at the water and saw that despite the blizzard and the cold and the rocky sea, the place was alive with vessels carrying cargo and tourists and workers. He rubbed ice from his face and turned back to look at the Harbor Walk. Its zigzag path and intervening buildings prevented Will from having a clear sight of it, but he knew that Lana was now only two hundred meters away from him and less than a hundred meters from Long Wharf. He stared at the pier and saw Julian walking slowly toward him. He heard Roger speak.

"I see her stop. I see one of the team speaking to her. I see that man pointing. I see four other team members move in close around her."

Laith spoke. "I'm at stop one hundred meters behind them. What's happening?"

"Not sure." Roger's voice sounded as uncertain as his words. "Everyone hold position."

Will watched Julian stop. He saw him reach into a pocket and knew that he would be caressing a weapon.

"There's some discussion taking place." Laith's voice was strained. "One of them tries to put his hand on our lady's arm. She shrugs it off. She waves arms in the air. The man tries to touch her again. Two other men move close to her. Something is wrong."

Will frowned. He pictured the maps of Boston that he'd studied the previous night. He pictured the road routes out of the city. He pictured the alleys and side streets that could be used to move people quickly away on foot. He remembered the timetables and the layout of the city's subway system. He remembered the same for its public bus company. He pulled back his jacket hood so that frozen air could course over his head. He looked at the tourist families playing around him, and he looked back out at the harbor. He felt his stomach churn as he realized what was happening, and he reached for his pressel switch. He spoke very quickly. "The ferry. They're keeping her on Long Wharf because that's where the ferry terminal is. Either Megiddo's coming in on the next ferry or they're taking her out on it."

"Which is it to be, Will?" Roger's voice sounded as annoyed as Will's thoughts felt.

Ben spoke. "The ferry goes from Long Wharf to Charlestown Navy Yard in the north. It's a ten-minute crossing, but if you want me at Charlestown, you'd better tell me now, because this weather is killing the roads."

"Which is it to be, Will?" Roger's voice was now loud.

Before Will could answer, Laith spoke. "I can see the ferry coming in. It will berth in two minutes."

"Will?"

The icy air was now causing the bullet wound on Will's head to throb. He ran fingers through his hair and stared out at the harbor. He saw the ferry and could tell that it was slowing to come alongside the jetty. He desperately tried to think and define the correct course of action. If Megiddo was on that boat, Lana would signal that it was him by taking off her fur hat. If that happened, Will needed every available resource around Megiddo on Long Wharf. And if he sent Ben ahead to Charlestown now, he'd be taking a huge risk, as he'd be diverting the team's only mobile resource. But if he held back from deploying Ben to Charlestown and Lana did subsequently get on the boat, he would have lost invaluable time. There was no correct course of action.

Will spoke to everyone. "We wait to see if he's on the ferry."

"That's cutting it fine, Will." This was Ben. "If he's not on the ferry and she gets taken on board, I can't guarantee I can make the route to Charlestown before it reaches there."

"Will's given us his decision, so we stay here." Roger's voice was firm. Will wondered, though, whether Roger agreed with him.

The ferry moved alongside the pier. It bobbed up and down a little with the swell of water before ropes secured it fast against the jetty structure. People came off the boat. Will scoured Long Wharf, but from his position in the park a large jetty building prevented him from seeing Lana or the Iranians. He watched more passengers disgorge from the vessel, and then he saw no more people.

"Our lady's being ushered toward the ferry." Roger's tone sounded neutral. "He's not here. All six of them are taking her on the boat."

Will stomped on the ground in anger. He spoke to Ben with no attempt to hide the urgency or frustration in his voice. "Come and get me, Ben. The rest of you follow her onto the boat."

Roger spoke. "Will, if we put the whole team on there, chances are we'll be spotted by the Iranians. The vessel's too small. Do you want to take that risk?"

Will could not take that risk. If the Iranians discovered that Lana was being followed by others, everything would be lost, because Megiddo would suspect that she'd set him up.

"Julian, get on the boat. Everyone else, get onto Atlantic Avenue for collection by Ben."

Will sprinted out of the park and stopped on the adjacent road. He turned and looked back at Long Wharf just in time to see the ferry leaving. He checked his watch. He glanced back along the road.

"I've got Laith." Ben spoke loudly over the noise of his vehicle.

Will checked his watch again. The ferry now had nine minutes to reach its destination. Cars were moving very slowly along the road before him. Some had their hazard lights on, and in the distance to his right Will could see multiple rear taillights, meaning that traffic was grinding to a halt somewhere along the route they needed to take.

"Roger's with me. We're on our way to you, Will."

The ferry would be reaching Charlestown in eight minutes.

"Okay, we see you."

Will squinted through the blizzard, looking to his left. Multiple headlights were moving along the road, and he looked at them all to try to ascertain which ones belonged to Ben's vehicle. He saw a car drive diagonally across the roadway and at a much faster speed than the others around it. The car's headlights flashed twice, and as it came to within twenty meters of him, a rear door opened. The car slowed and moved alongside him but did not stop. Will ran alongside it and jumped through the open door. The vehicle immediately lurched forward at speed, and Will could feel its tires struggling to maintain their grip on the road. He pushed himself back into the seat. Roger was next to him, and Laith sat next to Ben in the front. Nobody spoke at first.

They had six and a half minutes to reach their destination.

Will looked at Roger. "I made the wrong decision."

Roger removed a handgun from his jacket. "It could have been the right decision if he was on that boat."

Will peered ahead. Laith was talking quietly to Ben.

"Stay on Atlantic Avenue. Switch lanes in fifty. Commercial Street joins us from the left. We're now on Commercial Street. Massachusetts 1A joins us from left. Progress through crossroads, traffic ahead slowing. Change lanes. Change back again. Take the gap between the two vehicles ahead."

Will placed his left hand on the back of Ben's seat so that it exposed his watch. They now had a maximum of four minutes to reach their destination.

"Traffic slowing. We'll have to take every gap we can. Move left, vehicle on your right. Accelerate. Now decelerate, move ahead, road goes forty-five left. Charlestown Bridge is in one hundred forty meters. Take the next gap at speed. Slow now. And accelerate."

With his right hand, Will removed his handgun. He heard Julian's voice. "Clock's ticking. I can see our jetty at the Charlestown Navy Yard."

Ben said nothing as he drove. He was clearly totally focused on his task and on the words coming from Laith.

"We move onto the bridge. Traffic looks lighter for one hundred. Make up ground now."

The car sped forward, and Will wondered how Ben was managing to stop it from careening off its route.

They now had two and a half minutes.

"Take the inside of the bus. Move right. Heavier traffic, try to make that gap—correction, too narrow. Go left and progress."

"What do you want me to do, Will?" Julian's words were hushed.

Will leaned forward to speak to the men in the front of their vehicle. "Are we going to get there in time?"

The men ignored him, and Laith carried on coaching Ben. Will sighed, because he knew they could not give him an answer. All they could do was focus on covering ground as quickly as possible.

"We're slowing up." Julian could barely be heard. "We're nearly there. Do you want me to stop them from getting off the vessel?"

Will punched the seat before him.

Julian spoke again. "It's decision time again, Will. Do you want me to intervene?"

Will looked ahead. They were nearing the end of the bridge and would soon be turning right into Charlestown.

"Our ferry will be there in thirty seconds. Do you want me to intervene?"

Will glanced at Roger while hearing Laith continue his instructions.

"Going ninety degrees right now onto Chelsea Street. Six hundred fifty meters to destination. Multiple traffic ahead. Shit."

Their car slowed quickly and then stopped behind a wall of stationary vehicles.

Ben looked over his shoulder at Roger. "No way through."

Roger instantly opened his car door and shouted, "Laith and Will, with me on foot! Ben, do what you can to meet us there in the vehicle!"

Will opened his door, shoved his weapon into a pocket, and ran. As he did so, Julian spoke again.

"We've stopped. If you want me to do anything, now's the time to say so."

Will's hand flew to his pressel switch. "Nothing. You're outnumbered, and she might get killed in the cross fire. Do nothing."

He moved with Roger and Laith between vehicles and over thick plowed snow. Cars were sounding their horns, presumably to try to get traffic moving, and some drivers had exited their vehicles and were looking ahead down Chelsea Street. Will dodged between cars and people and ran as fast as he could around the barriers ahead of him. Over the noise of the cars and his own rapid breathing, he heard more of Julian's words.

"They're walking off the ferry. They're walking down the pier. I see their vehicle waiting for them."

Will shouted, "Just watch them! No intervention!" He tried to run faster. He stumbled over a pile of snow, fell to the ground, and landed on the shoulder bullet wound he'd received on Medvednica Mountain. He winced in pain, felt a hand grab his jacket, and was hauled back onto his feet. He looked at Laith and continued running. He saw the navy yard to his right. With Roger and Laith, he moved off Chelsea Street and ran across open ground and a parking lot toward his destination. He pulled out his handgun. He sprinted. He heard Julian speak again.

"I see them get into their SUV. I see the vehicle drive away from my position. I see the vehicle drive away from your position. You're too late. They're gone."

FORTY-ONE

Megiddo's held his nerve—now it's our turn to do the same." Will spoke the words loudly while leaning over a map of Massachusetts. He was in the CIA safe house in Boston's West End. Patrick and Roger were with him. Will jabbed at the map and looked up at Patrick. "There's nothing else that can be done right now."

"There's nothing that can be done to undo your mistake." Patrick pointed a finger at Will before thrusting his arms in the air. "She should never have been taken away by them. Megiddo could torture her."

"I'm aware of that," Will snapped, running fingers distractedly through his hair. He felt sick with frustration and failure and an all-encompassing fear for Lana's safety.

"Then you'll also be aware that if she's tortured, she'll reveal our hand and everything will be finished."

"Is that all you care about?" Will shouted. "What about Lana? Her life? Don't you care about that?

"I care about the thousands of lives we might lose if she tells them what we're doing. She knew the risks in working with us."

"How could she? How could a woman like her know the real risks in the work we do?"

Patrick paced forward. "There is no excuse for losing her to them."

Will banged a fist down on to the table before him. "I'm not the first person in this room to lose someone."

Patrick shook his head quickly. "Don't throw that at me. You're deeply mistaken if you think that losing Lana to Megiddo is comparable to Alistair and me not capturing him in the first place."

"It's convenient for you to think that way now."

"Oh, for Christ's sake." Patrick's arms flew up in the air again. He spun around to face Will. "It's not comparable."

Will felt the anger increase within him. "Why not?"

Patrick spoke in an exasperated tone. "The comparison is flawed because you've done something that we could not do. We never had the young Megiddo in our sights. But you've managed to bring the older Megiddo, a man who is now the most wanted mastermind on this planet, to within a cat's whisker of capture." Once again he pointed at Will. "I'm angry with you because you've achieved far more than I or Alistair could manage to do and yet may have thrown it all away at the last moment. I'm angry because you are no longer in total control of events. I'm angry because we are now vulnerable to Megiddo's view of Lana."

"We're not vulnerable." Roger said the words quietly and calmly while staring out a window. "Megiddo will not torture Lana."

He had gotten everyone's undivided attention.

Patrick spoke up eventually, and his tone was tentative. "How can you be so sure?"

Roger shrugged. "All that matters to Megiddo is the successful completion of his mission. He could be suspicious of Lana, but he'll be equally mindful that she could be telling him the truth. If he tortures her, he'll lose her cooperation. His priority now is to get Will, and he's totally reliant on Lana to make that happen." Roger turned and nodded at Will. "It's Will he wants to torture."

Patrick did not move. "I hope you're right."

"I know Roger's right." Will rose to his full height and moved away from the map. He looked at Patrick. "Lana will call me to arrange a meeting. She knows it's what I want, and I know it's what Megiddo wants. We have to hold our nerve."

Patrick sighed. "We don't have time to hold our nerve. The other twenty-five men have now entered the country."

It was night now, and Will was alone. He stared at his cell phone. He desperately needed to hear it ring.

He wrapped his arms around his body. He wanted to believe his own words. He wanted to hold his nerve. But he felt helpless and hopeless.

He felt three bullets in his stomach, and he smelled New York grass. He saw Lana open the door of her tiny Parisian home and frown at him. He saw Ewan shake his head and fall down dead onto Bosnian snow. He saw a man who could have been Will or Megiddo holding a knife to Harry's throat. He stood close but not close enough to a young Lana as she curled into a ball in a Balkan forest while surrounded by rapists, and he saw her look of fear and defiance. He looked over his father as the man he did not know stood on a lonely road near Bandar-e 'Abbâs. He watched an old man no longer wish to be haunted by his past. And he witnessed a bomb rip through unknown lives somewhere in the United States.

Everything now seemed pointless, unreal, or inevitable.

He stood and walked across his hotel room and back again and did not know what to do. He heard noises. He looked at his phone. He stopped breathing. He stopped thinking.

Lana was calling him.

FORTY-TWO

Will stepped out of his hotel shower and regarded his reflection in the bathroom's full-length mirror. He saw scars, welts, bruising, puncture wounds, and burns. He stood for a moment and then reached for a towel. Then he turned and walked through to the bedroom. He looked at the clothes he had laid out over the bed, and for the third time this evening he checked every pocket and fold of every item. Once he was satisfied that there was nothing compromising within them, he dressed in an Ede & Ravenscroft white French-cuff shirt, silver cuff links, a Chester Barrie navy tie, a bespoke Huntsman blue suit, and a pair of Crockett & Jones black shoes. He examined himself again in a different mirror. With the exception of the darkened bullet groove on the side of his head, he was satisfied that he looked respectable.

He pulled on an overcoat and gloves and walked over to a side table where his wallet, cell phone, and passport waited. He removed cash from the wallet and stuffed it into a pocket, leaving everything else untouched. He glanced at a bedside clock, waited for a few moments, and then left the room.

He walked through the lobby of the five-star Mandarin Oriental hotel before exiting the place to face Washington, D.C. A doorman came to him and asked if he would like a limousine. Will rejected the offer and answered that despite the heavy snowfall over the city, he preferred to walk to his destination. The man politely told Will that he was crazy and then left him alone. Will pulled up his overcoat collar and walked.

He knew that Roger, Laith, Ben, and Julian would be close to him, but he didn't bother looking for them. He knew that they would be talking to one another, but he had no communications equipment to hear them. He knew that they would be sufficiently armed to compensate for the fact that he carried no weapons.

He walked though the barely populated Seaton Park, past the park's Smithsonian Institution and National Gallery of Art before heading north on Seventh Street N.W. He arrived at his destination.

He looked at the luxury Hotel Monaco and smiled. To anyone else the elegant, marbled, tastefully illuminated place would no doubt appear welcoming and inviting. But Will knew that the hotel held men who would try to kill him. He stood still for a moment and then walked though the building's entrance. He approached the concierge, gave his name, and said that he was a guest of Miss Lana Beseisu.

Will rode up four floors until he reached the area containing the hotel's Majestic Suites. He paused by the room he needed to enter. He breathed deeply and closed his eyes for a moment. After he opened them, he pressed the bell.

Lana stood before him. She looked stunning and showed no signs of being hurt. But her eyes were wet, and her expression clearly showed that she was under strain. She stared down at the floor and muttered, "Nicholas. Thank you for coming on such short notice."

Will wanted to step forward and hold her. But he knew he could not. He wanted to ask if she was okay. But he knew that the question had to remain unspoken.

Lana turned and walked back into the suite, which Will knew would contain two bedrooms and be of sufficient size to accommodate up to twenty guests. He followed her along the interior corridor and past a bathroom and a series of closets. He heard a noise behind him.

The blow struck him on the side of his neck and sent him straight down to the floor. Pain shot along his back and arms before settling on the wounds he'd received during the preceding few weeks. He shut his eyes and groaned loudly. He felt someone bind his wrists in plastic handcuffs. He felt arms lift him partially to his feet and walk him quickly forward. He opened his eyes and saw men and the weeping Lana. He heard voices, one of which was shouting, but not at him. He watched as if from outside himself as he was pushed onto a dining chair set in the middle of the lounge area. He looked around quickly and saw four men. One of them walked up to him and punched him on the side of the face. The impact caused both his body and the chair to fall backward. Men moved him upright and then proceeded to wind a rope around his torso so that he was tied tightly to the chair. They checked his pockets and other places but found only the cash he was carrying. They moved away from him. The man who was shouting was looking at Lana. He walked up to her and ushered her into an adjacent bedroom. When he returned, he pulled out a hunting knife and approached Will. He turned and grabbed another dining chair, which he positioned in front of Will before sitting down to face him.

The man looked to be in his midfifties. His black hair was meticulously creamed and styled in place, he was clean-shaven, and he wore an expensive-looking jacket and slacks. He smelled of tobacco and Chanel men's cologne.

The man's face had no expression. Will calculated that he spent one minute just looking at his captive. When the man spoke, his voice sounded polished and barely accented. "You can live if you deal with this situation in an intelligent way."

Will looked at the knife, then back at its wielder. "What is this situation?"

The man smiled a little. "I would have thought a member of MI6 would be able to make a very rapid assessment of what has happened here."

Will exhaled loudly. "Well, it's obvious that I've been betrayed."

"Why do you think that has happened?"

Will looked around. The other three men were looking at him but remained mute. Will recognized two of them as members of the Iranian surveillance team. They had silenced pistols resting on their laps. Will looked back at the man who was clearly their superior. "Go to hell."

The man moved his knife into his other hand. "Misplaced defiance has no purpose here." He leaned forward and stroked the tip of the knife along Will's face. "I understand that you are looking for a man."

Will smiled. "Are you going to help me with my task?"

The man pressed the knife harder so that it cut a path into Will's face. He moved back to watch a thin thread of blood bloom. "Do you think I am the man you seek?"

"I don't know."

"Correct. You do not know." The man nodded at one of the other men, then turned to look at Will again. "I am led to believe that you have information of value to us. I want that information."

"I will speak only to the man I seek. If you are he, then you'd better tell me so before I lose interest."

Will saw one of the men walk slowly around the room and out of his sight. Within moments he felt a cord around his throat. It was then pulled tight so that he could not breathe. Will stared at the seated man before him. He silently counted seconds in his head. At one minute of no breath, he began to feel weak. At two minutes his vision blurred. After three minutes he knew that his body desperately needed oxygen.

The cord slackened, and Will gasped for air while rocking back and forth on the chair. He shook his head and looked at the man before him. Then he smiled. "That was interesting."

The man waved a hand dismissively. "You may find it so, but I have no interest in brutality." He withdrew a cigarette from a jacket pocket, carefully lit it, and inhaled smoke. "But I do have an interest in doing my job to the best of my abilities." He watched Will for a while before saying, "It is important for us both to now discuss the information you have."

"What information?"

The man nodded at the underling who was clearly still behind Will. The cord was tightened again. Will counted up to four minutes before he saw his legs lash out violently and felt the cord go slack.

"I thought we had lost you then, but it appears you are strong." The man's cigarette had burned close to its butt, and he stubbed it out. "Now let's talk, and this time please do not be obtuse." He lit another cigarette.

"What do I get in return?" Will's voice was strained and weak. He coughed several times.

The man smiled. "What would you *like* in return?"

Will frowned and hoped that he appeared to be considering the question. Instead he was calculating time. He exhaled. "I'd like to walk out of here."

"I'm sure you would." The man studied his own manicured fingers. "But that is going to happen only if you talk to me first. And even then you won't be leaving this place"—he looked around—"until this event has served its purpose."

"That's hardly enticement to talk."

The man sighed and nodded. The cord dug deep into Will's lacerated throat, and at first the pain from the cut was more severe than the discomfort of the strangulation. Will began counting again. He knew that it would be longer this time, and he also knew that he could not under any circumstances lose consciousness and thus lose track of time. He counted to four minutes and felt his mind grow giddy. He counted to five minutes and felt his whole body shuddering and his legs again convulsing as if in a fit. The man behind him was very strong. Will counted to almost six minutes before he thought he could count no more and that his head might explode. The cord went slack.

Will fell forward and onto the floor. He felt his heart pumping too fast, and he wondered if it would seize and stop. He tried to slow his attempts at breathing, but his oxygen-starved body's instincts were too strong and made him gasp involuntarily. The act was excruciating. Men sat him upright and forced his head back so that his airway was fully open. A minute passed while he desperately tried to regain control of his body. As soon as his breathing finally slowed, he felt someone push his head aggressively forward. He looked at the man before him.

"I'm doing my job." The man sucked on his cigarette. "But your job now has no purpose. Only your life should matter to you now."

Will shook his head.

The man nodded at his strangler.

"No, no." Will said the words weakly. His head throbbed in agony, and the movement of blood within it was deafening to his ears. "No more."

"I will decide if there is any more, not you. But what you say next may inform my decision one way or the other."

Will wheezed for a moment. He knew that, give or take twenty seconds, he'd been in this room for nineteen minutes. He knew that the next minute was crucial. He also knew that he could not allow the men to strangle him again for fear of straying over that time. "There is no information. It was a lie."

The man narrowed his eyes and then smiled. "Subterfuge won't work on me."

Will shook his head quickly. His own eyes were wide. "I lied to Lana. I've never had information about the specifics of Megiddo's plan. I just wanted her to believe that I did. I just wanted her to lead me to him." He stopped shaking his head. Sweat poured down his face. "Are you Megiddo? I need to know."

The man before him tossed the hunting knife from one hand to his other. "You need to know?"

"You're going to kill me anyway. I need to know." Will's head slumped forward as he said the words. But the moment it did, a hand grabbed his hair and pulled at it so that he was again looking at the man.

"You need to know?"

Will coughed again. "I lied to her to get close to Megiddo. Please do me the honor of telling me that I succeeded, before you kill me."

The man stilled his hands and his knife. He looked around the room, at his men, and then back at Will. "It seems that this truly has been a waste of time. And I will not dishonor myself by closing your life with a lie, even though your lie has caused you to be here. I am not the man you seek. I am not Megiddo. I am his servant." He chuckled. "You are about to die, but I cannot lie to you and say that you have come close to your quarry."

The disappointment hit Will with more ferocity than the assaults that had just taken place against him. He had wanted to be here; he had wanted to be tortured to the extent that he appeared vulnerable and fearful for his life; he had wanted the man before him to be convinced that there was nothing lost in declaring his identity to Will. But he had most certainly not wanted to hear that the man wasn't Megiddo. He breathed deeply and then exhaled. He knew that he had been here for nearly twenty minutes now.

Will shook his head slowly. "You must know of his exact plans?"

The man barked a short laugh. He took a step forward and put the blade of the hunting knife against Will's forehead. "I'm going to spend the next two hours working on you. I will find out for sure if MI6 really has no information about what my master is doing here. You will tell me the truth simply to stop the pain. And when that happens, I will allow you to die."

Will nodded again and smiled. "Pain and death don't scare me." He now made no attempt to hide the strength in his voice. "But they might scare you. Your time is now up."

The man frowned.

"I gave myself twenty minutes to find out if you were Megiddo. Just twenty minutes"—Will smiled wider—"before I lost interest in this situation."

He heard a silenced pistol shot and felt the strangler's arms instantly release their grip on him. The man before Will looked quickly to his left and stepped back. Movement was rapid, and in an instant Will saw Roger run before him and shoot one of the guards in the head, saw Laith and Ben crouch by the room's entrance and shoot another man, saw the middle-aged Iranian step forward and thrust his hunting knife toward Will's body, saw a bullet exit the man's forehead and watched the man fall to one side before his knife could touch Will. And last of all he saw Lana standing at the rear of the room with tears streaming down her face, holding one of the dead Iranians' pistols.

Laith moved up to Will and cut him free from his cords. Will pushed himself up and had to steady himself as his vision momentarily blurred again. He drew deep breath and reached up to touch his ravaged throat.

Roger crouched down beside the middle-aged Iranian. "He's Gulistan Nozari. The deputy."

Will walked across the room to Lana. She dropped the gun and fell into his arms. He held her for a moment and smoothed a hand over her face.

She looked up at him. "Did I do the right thing?" She began to shake and cry.

Will pulled her closer and spoke softly. "You probably saved my life."

She shook her head. "You nearly died in here because I was forced into their vehicle in Boston. I did not know what to do."

Will held her tighter. "You succeeded in everything I asked you to do, but I placed you in an intolerable situation by losing you in Boston. I made a mistake, and I failed."

Lana shook her head vigorously. "You did not fail, Nicholas. I met him." She rubbed her eyes. "I met Megiddo before I was brought here by his deputy. You might not be able to catch Megiddo, but you can still stop his men from carrying out his mission. Because I know what he plans to do."

FORTY-THREE

The Camp David meeting?" Patrick folded his arms and exhaled.
"We were stupid." Will looked at the seven police vehicles and
three ambulances that stood stationary around them. Their flashing
lights caught the heavy nighttime snowfall. Some uniformed men and
women were moving in and out of the Hotel Monaco, while others
were clearly tasked with preventing the small crowd of onlookers from
trespassing on the scene. Will looked toward one of the ambulances
and saw Lana standing at its rear. She had a blanket wrapped around
her and was drinking something out of a plastic cup. He looked back
at Patrick. "We assumed that Megiddo was going after high numbers.
Not a small number of VIPs."

Patrick nodded slowly. "The president of the United States, the
British prime minister, the president of Egypt, the president of the
United Arab Emirates, a senior Saudi royal, and the president of
Syria. All premiers who stand in the way of Iran's ambitions within
the Middle East." He raised his palms in a gesture of incomprehen-
sion. "Exactly why the Camp David meeting had to be made public in
advance is beyond me."

Will watched his own breath turn to steam in the icy air and said, "A public relations exercise."

Patrick made a noise that sounded like a grunt. "Well, that exercise gave Megiddo his target." He turned to look Will full in the face. "It's a shame Lana could not find out how his men intended to penetrate the security surrounding the summit."

Will shook his head. "One of the bombers assumed she was part of Megiddo's team. The man let slip details of the target to her. But Megiddo walked in on the conversation and told the man to shut up. During the two days she spent with Megiddo, she never saw that man again." Will smiled. "I guess Megiddo punished him for his indiscretion."

"Where was she taken?"

"They rented a house on the outskirts of New York. But it's empty now. Megiddo and his men left before his deputy took her here."

Patrick nodded. "The summit was to take place in three days' time, but it will now be canceled. That fact won't be made public. And if Megiddo's men are stupid enough to carry out their strike against Camp David, then they'll meet a resistance they did not expect." Even though Patrick's expression was partially disguised by shadows and flashing lights, Will could see that he wore a look of deep regret. Patrick sighed and said, "You may think otherwise, but you have succeeded. You've identified the location of the attack."

Will dug his hands into his coat pockets, looked at Patrick, and shook his head. "Preventing Megiddo's mission from succeeding only ever had meaning to me if I had the man himself." He smiled but felt hollow and angry. "He's beaten me."

He walked to Lana. Looking exhausted, she nodded at him and pulled her blanket tighter around her body. "I killed a man. I don't know if I'll ever be able to get over that." she told Will.

He sighed. "I of all people can't tell you how to feel about taking another life. But I can tell you that the man you shot was a bad man who was very much involved in this terror plot."

Lana nodded slowly, and Will could see that her cheeks were glistening with tears. He looked around. Patrick was talking to a uniformed police captain. Roger and his men had long since disappeared into the shadows. All emergency services personnel were busy at their tasks. Nobody seemed to be looking at them.

Will placed his arms around Lana's waist. He pulled her close to him and held her still. He kissed her tears and her mouth. He leaned close to her ear and whispered, "I'm sorry that I never got Megiddo. I'm sorry that I couldn't finally relieve you of your burden."

Lana nuzzled her head against his shoulder. Her silky hair swept over Will's chest and face. She held him tight. "What will happen now?"

"You must go home, Lana. Go home to Paris and take care of your mother." He smiled, and the action caused him to feel the strangulation wounds on his throat. "You'll be safe there. I'll arrange for some men to watch over your house."

A siren from one of the adjacent police vehicles briefly sounded. Will looked up and saw ambulance and police personnel emerge from the Hotel Monaco carrying bodies on stretchers. Snow fell upon the dead, upon Will and Lana and everything. He turned her away a little so that she could not see the cadavers.

"What about you?" Lana asked.

"I need to stay on here for a few days to tie up matters."

She moved away from him. "I see."

Will pulled her back close. "Then I'll travel to Paris."

Lana smiled and embraced him fully. "My mother's in the hospital right now, undergoing further tests. She's apparently making excellent progress, and the money you gave her has enabled her to afford accelerated treatment. I'm not needed at home for at least five days. Why don't I book myself into a nice hotel somewhere in Washington and wait for you?" She squeezed him. "I would make sure the room is comfortable for two people."

Will thought for a long moment. He thought about his life, the time when he'd had hope and innocence and joy, the moment when all that changed, the years he'd spent developing armor to shield himself from mental and physical injury and the knowledge that behind that shield there was still a man who wanted peace. He thought about his only true fear: his fear of doing anything that could lower his shield, to take steps toward happiness and love. He gazed at Lana. He saw that she still had hatred, but he also saw her love and her desire for happiness. He saw what he now understood to be bravery.

He pulled her close to him again and decided that this was finally the time, that this was the moment for him to make his own brave decision, a decision that would be his bravest of all.

He looked around. Snow was still falling, but now it looked gentle and serene.

He looked at Lana, nodded, smiled, and said, "I will see you there."

Will called Roger. "There's no role for us in repelling the assault on Camp David. Laith is discreetly keeping an eye on Lana and will make sure she's safe in this city. Ben and Julian are stood down. But there's one last thing I need to do, and you're welcome to join me if you care to."

FORTY-FOUR

Y ou have the lock-pick set?" Will slowed his vehicle and brought it to a stop on Messenger Lane, in the Sands Point suburb east of New York City.

"Of course." Roger took out his handgun, checked its workings again, and placed it back in his jacket pocket.

"Okay." Will looked at the clock on the dashboard. It was nearly 5:00 A.M. and still dark. He wanted to reach the place and complete his task before sunrise. "Then let's go."

The two men silently exited their vehicle and walked briskly along the residential street before splitting up. Will began jogging until he reached the end of the block. He stopped, checked his watch, and waited, looking around. All the houses near him were in darkness. He checked his watch again and when satisfied that he'd been there for one minute, he walked past six houses before turning off the street and sprinting down an alley. Roger was waiting for him at the end of the route.

"I've opened the back door. It's quiet." Roger nodded toward the house to their right.

"There's no movement around the front of the house," Will responded. "Now's as good a time as any."

Both men took out their handguns and small flashlights and walked into the house's rear garden.

Will carefully turned the handle of the back door, partially opening it, and waited, listening. He could hear nothing. He crouched low and pushed the door fully open. When he entered the house, Roger followed him.

He immediately knew that everything was wrong. The kitchen around them looked lived in, had children's drawings stuck to walls, had a small cage for a pet on the floor, had a breakfast table set for four people. He walked through to a small lounge and saw cartoon DVDs scattered in one corner of the room, a newspaper folded open to its crossword page, two empty coffee mugs, and two cans of Coke. He moved upstairs. A bathroom with door open was at the top of the stairs, and to both sides of it were two rooms with closed doors. The whole house was just too small and contained things that should not have been here.

Will nodded at Roger and silently turned the handle of the first door. He eased the door open and stepped into the room. A double bed was positioned in the center, a man and woman asleep within it. Will walked up to the bed, pointing his gun at the adults. He stood over them, observing them for a moment, before turning and exiting the room. He opened the door to the other room and walked in. It was a children's room and had bunk beds on one side of the room. Everywhere else was messy with toys, comics, and other child paraphernalia. He walked to the lower bed. A boy lay sleeping there, his blond hair covering his pillow. He looked at the upper bed and used the muzzle of his gun to slightly lift the head of the duvet. Another boy lay sleeping underneath. He moved the duvet so that it was no longer resting over the child's head and so that the child could breathe more easily.

Will looked at Roger, shaking his head. He walked quickly out of the room, down the stairs, and out of the house. He walked until he and Roger were standing by their vehicle.

He looked back down the street toward the house. "I came here knowing that the place Megiddo used to house his men and imprison Lana for a few days would almost certainly have been cleaned and polished to remove all traces of them. I came here anyway with the tiniest of hopes that Megiddo might have slipped up and left us a clue to track him down." He looked at Roger. "But I did not come here expecting to find a small family house that has clearly never been rented out to a large group of extremely dangerous men. And I most certainly"—he felt the anger and emotional confusion within him—"did not come here with the expectation that Lana had lied to me about this address."

Roger drew his lips into a thin line. "What does it mean?"

Will shook his head. He wondered whether Lana had also lied to him about her mother's treatment in Paris. He even briefly wondered whether she'd lied to him about her desire for him to come join her at her hotel. He exhaled slowly. He knew that she had not lied to him about those things. She had too much respect and love for her mother to leave her in a potentially vulnerable situation, and she had only ever told him the truth about her emotions and feelings toward him. And she had also always been honest with him that her hatred for Megiddo would continue while the man remained unpunished. He surveyed their surroundings before returning his attention to Roger. "It means Lana has done something utterly stupid. It means that she deliberately withheld the details of the real address she was taken to. There's only one reason she would do that. She wants to go after him alone. She wants to take her own revenge against him."

He looked up at the empty sky. "But if she tries to do so, Megiddo will kill her."

FORTY-FIVE

Ten minutes later Roger was speeding across Long Island with Will seated next to him.

Will pulled out his cell phone. He called Laith and listened to what the CIA man had to say.

"I was just about to call you. She left her Washington hotel three hours ago. I've followed her in a car to New York. I thought she was going into midtown, but ten minutes ago she turned north and is heading away from New York City. I've no idea where she's going. Do you want me to stop her?"

Will thought for a moment. He cursed Lana's desire for revenge. But he also knew that as reckless and foolhardy as her actions were, she was now offering them some hope. He said, "No. I think she's heading for our man. Do nothing yet, but it's imperative that you stay close to her and keep her safe."

He called Ben, and it was obvious that he had woken the man. "You and Julian need to get on the road right now. Head north. Bring whatever weapons and equipment you can lay your hands on. We'll need enough for a major assault. Laith is mobile and following Lana in a northerly direction out of New York. I'll link communications among us all so that we can coordinate our routes."

Then he called Patrick. "Stay by your phone and reject all calls unless they're from me or one of my team." He gave a quick update, then said, "This is our last opportunity to catch him. And I'm taking that opportunity."

He reached down into the vehicle's cup holder, grabbed Roger's cell phone and hands-free device, and punched in the numbers to set the handset on conference call with all members of the CIA team. He fitted an earpiece over Roger's ear. The man nodded and drove faster.

Fifteen minutes later Roger muttered to Will, "Ben and Julian are in a vehicle. Laith's giving them directions, but they're going to have to drive like a bat out of hell given that they're still in Washington."

"Get their license-plate number."

Roger did so and relayed the information to Will.

Will called Patrick and gave him the details of Ben and Julian's vehicle as well as details of his own vehicle. "I've no idea how you are going to do so, but make sure every cop in this part of your country knows that their career or life will be over if they try to stop our cars for traffic violations."

Within forty minutes they were traveling on the New York State Thruway. Will watched their surroundings change from city to sub-urbia to wooded land. He tried to relax, but his mind and body were tense and alive again. The failure he'd felt during the last twelve hours had been replaced with a reinvigorated sense of purpose, focus, and strength. But the anger he'd felt at Lana's stupidity remained within him—as did his overwhelming concern for her safety.

He gave up trying to relax and instead tried to think clearly, to muster all his mental strength in order to piece together the preceding events and make sense of them. He thought about what had happened in Boston, what had happened in the hotel room in Washington, D.C., the failure he'd felt despite establishing that Camp David was

Megiddo's target, and he thought about what was happening now. More than anything, he thought about what was happening now. Thoughts, questions, and suppositions raced chaotically through his mind, and he discarded most of them. Some he did not. He wondered why one of Megiddo's men would have been so careless to mention the Camp David assault to Lana. He wondered why Megiddo and his men were still in New York State, given that Megiddo must know that his assault on Camp David would now be easily repelled. He frowned as more thoughts seemed to come together, thoughts that stood out from the others, thoughts that then rammed his body to attention and forced him to grab his cell phone, punch numbers rapidly into it, and wait impatiently while he listened to it ring on the other end.

Patrick answered.

Will spoke quickly and urgently. "Camp David's not the target. I repeat, not the target."

"What?!"

"Not the target. It doesn't make sense. Megiddo's probably spent years planning this operation. He would have thought through every angle. He never would have allowed one of his men to leak details about his target to Lana."

"Then why the hell did Lana tell us he was striking Camp David?"

Will breathed rapidly. "She told us the truth. She told us exactly what Megiddo wanted us to hear in case she and I were rescued from the Hotel Monaco torture room."

"Oh, damn!" Patrick's own breathing sounded swift and heavy. "He got one of his men to deliberately feed her a lie so she'd pass it on to us."

"Exactly." Will could feel his heart pounding in his own ears. "What could be worse than an attack on the premiers at Camp David?"

"I don't know."

"It has to be a target in New York State, because he and his men are still here."

"I agree, but I don't know." Patrick sounded exasperated. "I can contact the critical agencies, however, and place the whole eastern sea-board on high alert."

Will shook his head vigorously. "Absolutely not. Megiddo will go to ground. We have a last chance to catch this monster and finally stop him."

Patrick said nothing for a moment. When he spoke, his voice was quiet. "All right, Will. But I'm placing all my trust in you. I've got no other option."

Will ended the call.

Roger glanced at him. "Why don't we just stop her and force her to tell us where she's going?"

Will shook his head. "Megiddo's men are almost certainly watching her. If we move in, they'll alert him."

"Then call her. Tell her not to slow down, but ask her for details over the phone."

Will shook his head. "No."

"Why the hell not?"

"Because while I'm damn sure I know what's happening, I'm also damn sure I've underestimated Megiddo in the past. He could be monitoring her phone. He could be doing any number of things, and at this precise stage I am not one step ahead of him. I'm several steps behind. For the moment we have to just follow Lana until we can be certain where she's going. At *that* stage we'll move in and stop her."

Roger nodded. "Lana's car and Laith's car are ninety minutes ahead of us, but we're closing in on them."

"What about Ben and Julian?"

Roger smiled. "By the sound of things, Ben's driving their vehicle beyond all legal limits." He pressed a button on the phone to turn on its speakerphone, and Julian's commentary instantly shouted out over the noise of their vehicle's engine.

"Clear of Harrisburg, on to the seventy-eight. No vehicles ahead, traveling at one-thirty MPH, increasing speed."

Roger turned the phone back to normal and spoke. "Laith, update please." He listened, nodded, then relayed the information to Will. "Lana's in upstate New York now, driving at normal speeds."

Will rubbed a hand over his face and said, "If she's heading back to the house she was taken to by Megiddo's men, why is he still there? Megiddo must know that she set his men up after we killed them in the Hotel Monaco."

Roger held his index finger in the air, and it was clear that he was listening to his phone. He nodded and quickly glanced at Will. "Lana's stopped her vehicle, has gotten out, and is checking a map."

Will nodded his understanding. "She's not been to the place before." He looked out the car window. The scenery around them had become rugged and hilly. "So how the hell does she know where they are?"

Roger glanced at Will with a look of impatience. "She found something when she was in the house with them, something that gave her a clue where they were going." He changed gears as they sped around a bend in the road, and the car screeched forward at an even greater speed. "She wants her revenge. She was never going to let them disappear from sight." He paused, listening to his phone. "But wherever she's going, she's on the move again."

They passed Lake George and Schroon Lake before moving northwest on Route 73. Hills were now being replaced with snow-covered mountains.

Roger spoke while continuing to scrutinize the route ahead. "Ben's made up incredible ground. Their vehicle's now only sixty kilometers behind us." He frowned, clearly listening to his phone, and said nothing for a minute before saying, "Okay, I'll get instructions from Will." He slowed the vehicle and looked at Will. "Laith's just reported that Lana's stopped and exited her car in a wooded area near the town of Saranac Lake. She's walking away from her vehicle. And she's holding a handgun."

"Damn it." Will punched the dashboard.

"Do you want Laith to stop her?"

Will just banged his fist repeatedly against the dashboard.

"Will, do you want her stopped?" Roger's voice was tense and firm.

Will exhaled and stopped punching. "Stop her. Get her out of there!" He ran fingers through his hair.

Roger nodded and relayed the instruction over his telephone. Will watched the CIA man. He saw his eyes quickly narrow, and he saw that he was listening intently to his cell phone's earpiece.

"What's happening?"

Roger held a hand up again, wearing a look of total concentration. He spoke to the phone. "Absolutely not. You're outgunned, and you'll panic them into retreating and disappearing. Get as close to the building as you can, and get me an accurate layout of the place. But for God's sake stay out of sight." His voice became louder. "Ben, Julian—where are you?" He exhaled loudly. "Thirty isn't good enough. We need you here in ten minutes maximum." He looked at Will. "Megiddo's men have her."

"What happened?" Will shouted the words.

"Laith ran after her, got close to her, and saw that she was approaching a lakeside lodge. As she approached the place, men surrounded her, disarmed her, and dragged her into the building. Laith had to duck out of sight. But when the men's backs were turned, he wanted to go straight in and fight them on his own. You heard my response." Roger removed his earpiece, switched the phone into speaker mode, and pulled out his handgun.

Julian's voice was instant and urgent. "Hard right in twenty. Accelerate. Sweeping left. East right, hairpin bend. Oncoming vehicle. Straight road. Accelerate now."

Will's heart pumped fast, and adrenaline coursed through his body. He punched the dashboard again and swore. When he looked out the window now, he could see road signs telling him that they were only four miles from Saranac Lake. He looked at Roger and spoke with urgency. "Do you know anything about this area?"

Roger shrugged. "I've never been here before, but I know it's got three lakes and is surrounded by forest and the Adirondack Mountains. Lana's been taken to a lodge on one of the lakes. I'm betting it will be a isolated and as good a place as any to have our gunfight."

Will clenched his fists again. "We save her, and if he's there, we capture Megiddo alive. But everyone else dies."

Roger nodded. "Damn right."

Roger slowed their vehicle and then stopped by a deserted woodland picnic area. He looked at Will and said, "We're one mile from the target. I'm not going to drive any farther." He picked up his phone and advised his men of his location.

Will called Patrick and gave him a full update.

Both men got out of the car, and Will withdrew his weapon. He looked at his watch and muttered, "Come on, come on."

He heard tires screeching and the high-pitched whine of engine noise. It grew louder, and soon he saw Ben's car hurtling toward him along a narrow track at what must have been ninety miles per hour. The vehicle swerved sideways, skidded, and then came to a stop. Julian and Ben instantly jumped out and walked to the rear of their vehicle. Both men's faces were covered in sweat, and their hair looked sodden. They were opening the trunk as Will and Roger ran up to them.

"I've done some fast trips in my time," Julian said with a smile, opening one of two duffel bags inside the trunk, "but the one we've just made takes the prize."

Ben and Julian started withdrawing weapons and other equipment from the bags and laying them out in the trunk. Will saw Colt M4A1 assault rifles with attached scopes and flashlights, Heckler & Koch MP5-N submachine guns, MK23 pistols with KAC sound suppressors, a Barrett M82A1 fifty-caliber sniper rifle, combat knives, and waterproof tactical communications systems. Roger moved closer to his men and started checking the weaponry. Like Will, the CIA men were all dressed as if they were about to embark on a mountain hike.

Will breathed in deeply.

He saw memories and images: A young boy waving good-bye to his father. Megiddo carefully attaching a saline drip to his father's body. The boy sitting on his father's lap as the man read a story to him. Megiddo cutting off his father's feet. His father smiling as the boy ran toward him. A man who no longer looked like his father being dumped into the sea. The boy now angry, scared, and alone. The boy changing into a man who had no fear, who embraced isolation, anger, and death and nothing else. He saw the man he now was—a man who had decided to change all that and be with Lana, a man who was now in severe danger of losing that woman, of losing peace, happiness, everything.

Roger came to his side. The man lowered his gaze for a moment before looking at Will. "There's no turning back now. There's going to be a lot of killing."

Will stared at him. "That's what we do."

"It is." Roger glanced at the vehicle and his men before looking back at Will. He took his arm, pulled him a few paces away from Ben and Julian, and spoke very quietly. "Patrick told me that Megiddo killed your father."

Will nodded. "And no doubt Patrick gave you a secret instruction to stop me from killing him if we capture him?"

Roger shrugged. "He did. But I'm not going to."

Will said nothing.

"If you let Megiddo live," Roger said, "you'll have to spend the rest of your life knowing that you could have avenged your father but chose not to. If you kill him, you may have to spend the rest of your life knowing that your vengeance allowed thousands of people in this country to die. I don't have to live with the consequences of either decision, but you do." He looked at Will. "What you do now must be your decision and your decision alone, and I'm not going to get in the way of that."

Will nodded slowly. "There is a third option. I'll get his secret and then I'll kill him."

Jogging, Laith emerged from the trees but then slowed to a walk. He approached Will and Roger.

"I counted eight of them around the place," he spoke quickly. "There are almost certainly more of them inside."

"What guns are they carrying?" Roger asked.

"Three of them have shotguns, and the rest are holding automatic machine guns. Plus they're all carrying sidearms."

"What about Lana?" Roger beckoned to Julian and Ben, and the two men walked over to join them.

Laith shook his head. "No sign of her since they took her in there."

Will and Roger looked at each other. Will looked back at Laith and said, "Tell us about the place."

Laith crouched down in front of the four men and pulled out a knife. "Lower Saranac Lake looks like this." He began carving lines in the snow. "It's got about twenty tiny islands, and most of them are in the middle here. The lodge is on the east side of the lake, on the lake's edge."

"Are there other lodges, properties, or sites near the place?" Roger was carefully studying Laith's growing makeshift map.

"None." The ex–Delta operative didn't look up as he continued his task. "Unlike the other Saranac Lakes, this one's state-owned, and there's restricted property development around it. Our boys have obviously chosen it because they know they won't be disturbed there."

"What's the layout of the building?" Julian wanted to know.

"It's rectangular in shape, it's got a boathouse to the north here, and a pier goes straight out from the porch onto the water here. The lodge is on two floors and by my calculations has twelve rooms in total. Entrances to the building are here, here, here, and here. There's one road into and out of the place." Remaining in his crouch, Laith took a couple of steps back. "The area to the south is clear of trees for twenty-five meters, but we're fortunate because there's not much open ground around the north and northeast of the building."

Ben asked, "Where are the men?"

"They're rotating around the building, but at all times there are men to the north, east, and south." Laith jabbed his knife into the snow to show the positions. "And they always have two men on the pier to protect the lodge from the lakeside."

Will looked at Roger. "What do you think?"

Roger stared at the map and said nothing for a moment. He then nodded and said, "I don't think it's worth waiting for nightfall, because I doubt they'll cut back their numbers then. In any case, time is not on our side. I think we go for it now."

"I agree." Will looked at the other men, and they all nodded. He looked back at Roger. "You're in charge of the assault. Where do you want us?"

Roger drew a deep breath and said, "Ben and I will approach the building from the northeast. We'll take out the men there, and I'll then enter the building through the north door and Ben will take this entrance on the east. Will and Julian are going to approach the building from the south. You'll have to get wet to avoid the open ground. Julian can get into the building through the south door. Will, you keep going until you get to the pier." Roger looked up. "Laith, you'll be our sniper. I need you on this island , but to get to it you're going to need to swim six hundred meters with the fifty-caliber rifle on your back. And judging by the weather, you may have to break though ice along the way." He smiled with a look of mischief. "That's a job for a SEAL, not a Delta man, but I need to be in the lodge to issue commands. Do you think you can make the swim?"

Laith returned his smile. "Do you think you'll be able to shoot straight on dry land?"

"I'm sure we'll both do just fine." Roger looked down at the map again, and his face grew serious. "The first kills will have to be synchronized, and Laith will instruct us when that's to happen. Once we're in the house, we go through it room by room." He swept a hand over the snow. "And none of the targets must be allowed to escape the property." Roger stood up. "When it's over, we'll bring our vehicles to the lodge for extraction of any prisoners."

Ben asked, "Where are we driving to afterward?"

Roger shrugged. "Patrick's working on that right now." He looked at each man. "Any other questions?"

They all shook their heads.

It was now midafternoon, and the air was clean and still. Will nodded at the men. "There's nothing left to be said. Let's go."

They all walked back to Ben's vehicle and began arming themselves. Will donned communications equipment, gathered up a knife and pistol, which he secreted in his jacket pockets, and strapped a Colt M4A1 assault rifle to his chest. He saw Roger, Ben, and Julian choose their own weapons and watched as Laith checked the workings of the powerful sniper rifle. Will placed his cell phone into a waterproof pouch and tucked the parcel into an inner jacket pocket. The vehicles were locked, their keys were hidden under front tires, and they all walked out of the picnic area into the forest that stretched before them.

They were approaching their destination from the south, and though he could not yet see it, Will knew that the lake would be to his left. They walked slowly and in single file with five meters of space between men. Laith led the way, and occasionally he would signal silently for them to stop while he crouched and examined the route ahead of him through his rifle's telescopic sight. They continued like this for thirty minutes before Laith stopped again, turned to face them all, pointed at his own chest and then at another direction. He left them, and Will knew that the man was heading to the lake to brave the freezing swim across to his sniper position on the island. They stayed still for nearly forty minutes before they heard Laith's voice in their earpieces.

"I'm in position."

They moved with Julian now leading the way. The area around them was quite flat but dense with trees. They walked carefully and silently. Within ten minutes Julian stopped and pointed at Ben. Julian walked in a crouch position back toward Will and stayed beside him. The two men watched Ben and Roger move onward and out of their sight. They waited for fifteen minutes before Will heard Roger speak.

"We're in position."

Will looked at Julian. The man nodded at him and moved off toward their left. Will followed, staying low. Within minutes they were at the lake's edge.

Julian moved up close to Will and cupped a hand around Will's ear. He whispered, "The house should be two hundred meters along the shore."

They followed the shoreline for approximately eighty meters, and then Julian stopped, turned a little, and walked slowly into the water until he was standing waist-deep in the lake. He unstrapped his Colt assault rifle and lowered himself so that only his head was visible. Will moved into the water as well and immediately felt how cold it was. He focused his mind, controlled his breathing, and followed Julian.

He saw the lodge. He saw one man standing by the southeast corner of the building and two men standing on the pier over the lake. He watched Julian's head submerge and knew that the man was now going to swim underwater to his position. Will looked ahead and estimated that he would need to swim a hundred meters underwater to get beneath the pier without being seen. He inhaled several times, relaxed his body, and sank down. He swam out to deeper water before turning back to face the direction of the pier. Swimming onward, he ignored the cold and the ever-increasing pain from lack of oxygen. He counted his strokes in order to gauge the distance traveled, and within three minutes he knew that he must be close to the pier. He gradually moved up in the water and saw the dark shape of the jetty before him. He swam until he was underneath it and then slowly allowed himself to rise until his head was out of the water. He sucked in air silently and moved toward one side of the pier, turning to look away from the lodge and out to the lake. Ahead of him and more than half a kilometer away was the largest of the many lake islands. Laith was on that island, and Will waited to hear him speak.

"I see you, Will." Laith's voice was very quiet. "Move back and along that side of the pier until I tell you to stop."

Will moved several meters back.

"Stop."

He stopped.

Julian spoke. "I'm in position."

And Roger spoke. "Everything is set. Laith, you control the green light."

Will waited for nearly thirty seconds before he heard Laith speak again.

"Okay, there's movement behind some of the windows on my side of the lodge, so we're going to have to time this right. Will, you're two meters below one of the men on the pier. I'll take the other man, but everyone wait for my command."

Will pulled out his combat knife and carefully placed his free hand on one of the pier struts and one of his feet on a lower strut. He stayed in that position for nearly two minutes. A light snowfall began to descend over him.

"On my command . . ." Laith paused. "Go!"

Will pulled and thrust upward until he was fully out of the water and jumping vertically though air. Within a split second, he saw a man standing with his back to him and had grabbed that man's head, placed his knife against his throat, and cut deep into him as they both fell toward the lake. Before hitting the water and submerging, Will heard the crack of Laith's rifle, and he knew that the other guard on the pier was dead. Will held his captive firmly in his grip and ignored the man's thrashing legs as they both sank down toward the lake bed and as Will continued to saw through his throat.

Will let the dead man drift away from him and hauled himself back onto the pier. He sprinted toward the lodge, unstrapping his assault rifle. He spotted a man emerging from the lake-facing lodge door and saw that he was carrying a shotgun. One of Laith's fifty-caliber bullets removed the man's head from his body. Gunfire could now be heard in every direction, and as he reached the house, he heard Roger speak in a loud but controlled tone.

"We're in."

Will paused to one side of the door, glanced in, and entered the lodge. The noise within the place was deafening, and his ears instantly began to ring. He saw a woman run into the corridor he was in, turn, and then point a handgun at him. Will shot her across her chest and face. A man looked out of a room on the right-hand side of the corridor and, after seeing Will, just as quickly disappeared back into the room. He pointed a gun from inside the room and fired it blindly toward Will's position. Will saw the man's body fall into the corridor. Julian emerged from the room, glanced at Will, and kept walking.

Will moved along the corridor, ignoring the sounds of rapid machine-gun fire from the rooms around him. He saw stairs and climbed them slowly. A man appeared at the top of the stairwell and threw something before jumping backward. Will sprinted up the stairs shouting, "Grenade!"

As he reached the grenade thrower, he kicked the man in the stomach and pumped a burst of bullets into him, sending him falling backward. Will glanced over his shoulder, saw Julian at the bottom of the stairs, saw him quickly look first at Will and then at the grenade, and then saw him hurl his body over the explosive. His body blew apart into tiny pieces of flesh. Will knew that the man had sacrificed himself to protect him. He raised his M4A1 high and walked forward, scanning doorways to his left and right. He heard gunfire from one of the rooms and saw a man emerge from it in a crouch. Will swung his weapon toward the man but then realized that the man was Ben. He took a deep breath and moved on.

Laith spoke. "I can see two men in top-floor room three east."

Will and Ben moved together until they reached the door to that room. They stood on either side of the door, and and then Ben turned, kicked it in, and stepped inside. Will followed him, heard the sound of Ben's gun, and then saw a man to his right. Will shot the man, spun around, and walked out of the room.

Ben came alongside him and pointed at the last room along the corridor. "Every room up here's been checked apart from that one."

Will heard Laith's sniper rifle crack before the CIA man said, "No more hostiles in my vision."

He heard Roger shout over thunderous noise, "There are plenty of damned hostiles where I am!"

He looked at Ben.

Ben nodded, smiled, and kicked in the final door.

It happened in a fraction of a second. The door swung two or three inches before Will saw the wire. Before he shouted, "Trap!" Before he and Ben were lifted off their feet by the force of the explosion. Before Will landed on his back several meters away from the entrance. Before pieces of Ben's destroyed torso fell around and over him. Before his vision and hearing ceased working.

Will lay breathing heavily. He pressed his fingers into the wooden floor around him. He tried to feel things. He tried to move his legs. He tried to think. But he had no sense of time, no sense of location, and little sense of self.

He lay there and tried to muster any thoughts. Only one came to him: *If you keep lying here, you will fail and die.*

He shook his head and pressed his fingertips even harder into the floor. He focused on his hands and his arms. He focused only on the need for them to push him up from the floor.

A distant sound came to his ears. At first it seemed like gentle whistling, but the noise grew louder until it became the roar of the continuing battle in the house. He shook his head again, yelled out, and thrust with his hands and arms. He sat upright. Thought, sight, and hearing all came back to him with an immediacy that made him reel. He looked around and saw pieces of flesh everywhere.

He looked at the blown-apart doorway. He hauled himself to his feet, felt that he was going to collapse, but staggered forward a few paces until he seemed steady. He picked up his assault rifle, checked to see that it was undamaged, and walked close to the room. He crouched by the side of the door, gripping his gun. He decided that if there was anyone in the room, he would kill that person without any consideration for the consequences.

He moved quickly into the room with his weapon held high. The place had chairs, a bed, a television, and an open window. But no person, living or dead.

Laith's strained voice broke into his thoughts. "Eleven—no, twelve hostiles coming to the house through the woods from the north." There was silence for a few seconds before he added, "I can take some of them."

The distinct sound of Laith's Barrett M82A1 fifty-caliber weapon could be heard all around the place.

Roger shouted, "Ground floor clear! It's a fucking mess!"

Laith said in a more controlled and quiet voice, "One down. Two down. Now three down." He shouted, "I see snipers! Two of them!"

Roger entered the room. He was covered in sweat and black soot. He walked quickly up to Will and grabbed him by the arm. "What happened?"

Will sucked in air. "Ben and Julian are dead. Both of them stood in the way of explosive blasts that were meant for me." He looked at the open window and then at Roger. "Megiddo must have escaped through there."

Roger nodded quickly and spoke into his communication microphone. "Laith, just two of us left in here. We're going after our man, but you need to take out those snipers."

Two high-velocity rifle shots could be heard almost simultaneously. They did not sound like Laith's weapon.

Roger turned sharply in their direction. He shouted, "Laith? Laith?" He kicked at a nearby chair, sending it crashing to the other side of the room.

"They must have killed him. It's just us now, Roger." Will looked at the window again. "I'm going after Megiddo. But there must be at least nine hostiles still coming our way. Do you think you can keep some of them off my back?"

Roger nodded and ran out of the room.

Will sprinted and jumped through the open window. He fell eight meters before hitting the ground and rolling over snow. He crouched, looking left and right through his rifle's sight.

He heard Roger's voice. "I'm out of the house and one hundred meters to the north. I count seven men coming toward me, but I can't see the two snipers."

"Can you see anything else? Lana? Vehicles? Movement on the lake?"

"There's nothing else."

Shit. Will looked away from Roger's hidden position to the north of the lodge and turned to face the south. He looked out at the lake to his right and at the island where Laith now lay silent. He looked ahead again. Everywhere before him was forest, and its trees were laden with snow. Six kilometers in the distance, one of the Adirondack mountains looked down at him and everything around him.

"There's no way to be sure," he said to Roger, "but I've got to assume he's heading south, away from the firefight."

"Maybe he was never here."

Will thought about the room's booby trap. He pictured Ben's body being torn apart by its violent force. "No. That room was important. He was here."

"Then look for high ground. That's where he'll go. He'll wait there until his men have killed us all."

Will narrowed his eyes and focused on the mountain in the distance. He heard Roger's MP5-N submachine gun suddenly emit short, controlled bursts. He knew that Roger was now occupied and that he was on his own. He tightened his grip on his assault rifle and ran.

He dodged between and around trees, the entire time alternating his gaze between what lay ahead and to his sides and on the ground, desperately scanning for footprints in the snow or freshly broken foliage—any signs of Megiddo's route. He sprinted until the lake was no longer by his side. He sprinted until he was at least one kilometer from the lodge.

Roger shouted, "Two confirmed kills, but the bastards are flanking me! I'm dead if I hold my position!"

Will immediately stopped. "Get out of there, Roger."

"Not until you have your man in your sights."

Will kicked the ground in frustration. He looked ahead at the elevating ground. He looked back in the direction of the lodge and Roger's dire position. He cursed and pointed his gun at the sky. He fired all the bullets that remained in his magazine. The noise from his gun echoed and bounced around the lake valley.

"If that was you"—Roger was almost screaming over the sound of his own machine gun—"then you definitely got their attention! The four men on my right flank are leaving me alone! You've given me a chance! But those four hostiles are coming for you!"

Will placed a new clip into his rifle and sprinted onward. Fresh snow started to fall in gentle flurries, and he fervently hoped that it was not going to become heavier and destroy any chances he had of finding tracks. He ran for another two kilometers, and all the time he could hear gunfire coming from the area around the lodge.

When the gunfire stopped, so did Will, momentarily. He jabbed a finger against his earpiece and waited. He sighed with relief as he heard Roger's voice.

"All hostiles by the lodge are dead. You've still got four on your tail, though, and there's no sign of the snipers. But I'm coming for you."

"I'm about two point five kilometers away from you. Head toward the mountain."

Fresh wind blew into Will's face. He looked at the sky and its darkening clouds and shook his head. He wondered if the assault on the house had been in vain. He wondered if the bravery and sacrifice of Julian, Ben, and Laith would ultimately be meaningless. He wondered if Roger would be able to stay alive. And he wondered if today would be the day his own life came to a pointless end.

He forced his legs into action and pumped them harder to accelerate over the thick snow and rising ground. His breathing came loud, and his lungs ached from the icy air. He ran faster until he'd covered another two kilometers, still constantly scanning his surroundings.

Then he saw them.

They were two distant dots at first, but when he looked through his rifle's scope, he saw a man and a woman running up the lower slopes of the mountain. He adjusted the scope to intensify and magnify the image. He saw that the woman was Lana. The man had his back to him and was pulling Lana's arm.

Will clasped his fingers to his throat mike and shouted, "I have a visual! One man and Lana! At the base of the mountain!"

The noise of a rifle shot boomed through the valley behind him. Will called, "Roger?"

A few seconds later, Roger spoke. His voice sounded weak. "Hold on, Will . . . busy."

More gunfire could be heard, and it sounded like it was coming from Roger's weapon.

Then Roger spoke again. "One sniper confirmed dead. But he shot me first."

"How bad?"

"Not critical. But it tore out a chunk of my calf muscle. Short of dragging myself along the ground, I'm immobile."

"I'm coming to get you."

"No, you're not, Will." The man's voice was raspy but firm. "You're going to get them."

Will stomped the ground in frustration. "All right. Stay where you are. Stay in radio communication. Shoot anything that comes near you."

He quickly glanced through his scope again and estimated that his quarry was approximately fifteen hundred meters ahead of him. He inhaled deeply and ran forward. After ten minutes he knew he was now at the base of the mountain. He saw footprints and felt an immediate sense of hope.

"Can you see me from your position,?" he asked Roger.

Roger's words were strained. "No. The trees are too dense. But"—he paused—"I'm using the dead sniper's rifle scope to look around the area between us both. I'm getting brief glimpses of the men on your trail, but they're so brief that I'm not getting any chance for clear shots. The men are about one kilometer behind you. I still can't see the other sniper, though."

"Understood."

A loud crack sounded by Will's ear, and he was instantly thrown sideways. He put a hand to his head and felt blood and shards of wood. Looking at the tree next to him, he saw that a high-velocity bullet had hit it and sent splinters straight into his face. He pulled himself into a crouch and glanced behind him. He knew that the bullet had come from the sniper. He was now within deadly range of that man's weapon.

"Roger, the sniper's onto me."

Roger coughed. "The one I killed was wearing an arctic camouflage suit. That's why I didn't spot him until it was too late. You've got to take your man out, or he'll easily kill you before you get halfway up the mountain."

Will looked in the direction of Lana and her captor, then back in the direction of the valley, and knew that Roger was right. He quickly examined the bullet mark on the tree again and decided that the man must have made the shot from the east. He decided that the shooter was on his own and away from his colleagues to the south. He had to be close to make a meaningful shot through the wooded area around them. Will calculated that his assailant had no reason to deviate from his easterly position, given that the very last thing he would expect was for his target to turn back and try to hunt him down. Will strapped his carbine to his chest, pulled out his combat knife, and commenced his hunt.

He jogged downhill, and despite zigzagging to make his route unpredictable, he knew he was still an easy target for the sniper. He wanted it that way. His only plan was to expose the sniper by encouraging him to shoot at him, since he didn't have time for a more sophisticated and patient tactic. But he knew that the chances of his being shot were great, and he knew that if the high-velocity bullet hit him anywhere in the upper thigh or above the waist, he would most likely die from the wound. He resisted the urge to sprint and instead kept his pace steady.

He reached a small clearing, stopped, and looked around. He listened but heard nothing. Snowflakes caressed his face. He moved ahead into denser forest and then caught the very slightest of movements in his peripheral vision. He turned to face the direction of the movement but saw nothing, and he wondered if his eyes were deceiving him. He moved again just as a very loud crack sounded close by, followed by a rush of air close to his head. He saw a flash of light and realized that it belonged to a rifle scope. Behind the scope was a man whose white combat clothing made him barely visible against the backdrop of snow. The man was pointing his rifle at him. The man was only forty meters away.

Will dived sideways just as another shot was fired. He immediately got up and sprinted at the sniper while the man was frantically trying to chamber another round into his weapon. The man slammed the bolt action of his rifle forward as Will came to within a few meters of him. He raised his weapon, but Will hurled himself forward and crashed into the sniper. Legs and arms lashed out violently at Will's head and body, and he was pushed back a little with the force. Smashing the butt of his rifle into Will's head, the sniper tried to break away. Will shook his head in pain and knew that the man needed a few meters of distance from him in order to shoot. He did not hesitate. He pulled himself to his feet, kept his head low, gripped his knife tightly, and charged at the man. When he reached him, he raised his upper body, grabbed the back of the man's neck, and punched the knife into his stomach. Despite the thick padding of the arctic camouflage, the knife easily sliced through clothing and flesh until its blade was fully inside the man's body. Will held him like that for a moment and then wrenched the knife upward so that the sniper's entire stomach was ripped open. He pulled out his knife and watched the sniper's pure white suit become saturated with his blood. He let the man fall backward, unstrapped his assault rifle, and shot him twice in the head.

Will breathed heavily and spoke into his throat mike. "The second sniper's dead."

Roger's reply was instant. "You've got no time to stand still. I can see that the four-man team has fanned out, meaning they've lost your position. But they're close to you."

"Are you sure that you can't pick any of them off with your rifle?"

Roger said nothing for a moment. Then: "I've tied the rifle to a tree to try to enable a steady shot. And I've tied myself to the same tree."

Will closed his eyes, sighed, and spoke softly. "How much blood have you lost, Roger?"

"Enough to make my arms and legs shake and make shooting near-impossible. Not enough to stop talking to you." He coughed. "A little blood loss doesn't bother me. I'll do what I can. Just focus on what you have to do."

Will opened his eyes, rubbed a bruise on the side of his head, and winced in pain from the touch. He gulped in air and ran back toward the mountain and Lana and the man who was dragging her up its slopes. Snow still fell serenely, at odds with what was happening here. Will ran faster than he thought he was capable of until he reached the point where he'd last seen his quarry. He looked through his small rifle scope but saw nothing ahead, so he urgently scoured the ground for the footprints he'd seen earlier. He found them, now under a powdering of fresh snow, and sprinted onward. His feet trampled over the route that Lana and the man had taken.

The ground rose sharply, causing Will to slow. He looked left and right, trying to find any evidence of a mountain track to aid his ascent, but everything around him was wild and inhospitable.

Five or six bullets hit snow-covered ground in rapid succession to his left. They were wide of their mark, and Will knew that they'd come from an automatic weapon. But he also knew that he'd been momentarily spotted by at least one of the hostiles behind him. He looked down at the footprints and saw that they followed an almost straight route up the mountain. Will thought for a moment. He made a decision and ran to the right of the tracks as fast as the severity of the grade would allow him to. After traveling for three hundred meters, he stopped, breathing heavily. He turned, sat down on the snowy slope, calmed his breathing, and scoured the area below him through his rifle scope. Everywhere was beautiful, with the Saranac Lakes in the distance, the hills around them, a carpet of pure white snow covering all ground and trees. Will ignored the beauty of his surroundings and focused on finding the man who had shot at him so that he could kill him.

He spoke to Roger and gave the CIA man his approximate location. "One of the hostiles is close to me. Can you see anything?"

Roger took a moment to respond, and Will knew that he would be searching for signs of life through the powerful lens of his sniper rifle. His words came quick and quiet. "I saw something, just briefly, to your southwest and approaching the base of the mountain."

Will swung his rifle in that direction, moving it so that it was looking between trees, at ground, at streams.

"Movement again." Roger's words were barely audible. "Same location. He must be about nine hundred meters from your position."

Will breathed deeply. Then he saw the man and stopped breathing. The man was walking quickly and carried his rifle in one hand. His head and upper body were bent down. He was clearly moving to another position to try to shoot Will. And he was clearly oblivious to the fact that Will could now see him.

Will relaxed his body, moved the crosshairs of his scope slightly in front of the moving man's head, and waited for the right moment. The distance between himself and the hostile was at least twice the effective range of the Colt M4A1, and Will knew that he would have only one chance of hitting the man. If he missed, the man would sprint for cover and vanish. His quarry appeared and disappeared through trees and was heading toward a large outcropping of mountain rock. Will decided that he had to shoot the man before he reached it. He breathed in fully, then partially breathed out before holding his breath. He waited. He shot.

The man slumped to the ground. Will's bullet had struck him in the center of his head.

Will stood and turned back to face the steep incline of the mountain. "He's down."

"Good, but the others will know where you are now." Roger's voice sounded very weak. "It's now or never. Save Lana. Get Megiddo."

Will exhaled. "Roger, you and your men have gone beyond what I asked of you. You don't need to stay where you are. I'm sure your injury is worse than you told me. Crawl back to the lodge. There are probably medical supplies in there."

"There's one bullet in my gun, and I'm not going anywhere until I have the chance to use it."

Will nodded and ran farther up the mountain, occasionally stumbling as his feet hit snow-hidden rocks and branches. Its summit grew closer until he knew that he was only a few hundred meters from the mountain top. The wind became stronger and brought with it ice-cold air.

He narrowed his eyes and tried to look at everything before and around him. He heard Lana's words.

One day you'll be here for me.

He squinted through the rifle scope; he moved his gun left and right; he ran; he walked; he crawled; he did everything he could to remain a hunter rather than a corpse.

He ran again and stopped suddenly. He crouched, raising his weapon. He could see them. The man still had his back to Will and was dragging Lana with him. Will focused the crosshairs of his scope on the man's back. At this range the shot would be easy.

He thought about his father. He thought about the savagery inflicted on him by the man he now had in his crosshairs. He thought how easy it would be to quickly incapacitate the man with one shot and then to kill him in a slower, more satisfying way.

He held his breath.

He thought about the thousands of lives that could be lost if the shot killed Megiddo and his secret. He thought about Lana and how she would suffer at Megiddo's hand if Will's shot did *not* kill him instantly.

He lowered his rifle.

Roger's voice sounded quietly in his earpiece. "The three hostiles are now together and seven hundred meters from the summit."

"Roger, I'm very close to my quarry, but I need time." Will took one step forward. "Try to make a shot. Try to draw the three men away from me."

Roger sighed. "They're nearly three kilometers away from my position. But I'll try."

Will looked through his scope again, but Lana and her captor were gone from sight. He cursed. He moved farther up the mountain.

He knew that the sound of the high-velocity shot had come from a distance, but its noise still echoed around the valley and over the contours of adjacent mountains. Will instantly dropped low, spinning around. He listened for nearly ten seconds before he heard Roger's voice.

The CIA man's words sounded labored. "I got him in the head. He's dead."

Roger had just killed one of the three Iranian men following Will.

The distance of the shot, the adjustments required to compensate for elevation and weather, and the fact that Roger was injured made the shot remarkable.

Roger spoke again. "Damn it. The other two went to ground for a moment, but now they've continued pursuing you. I'm sorry, Will. I thought they'd turn and come back to kill me. Either way, that was my last bullet."

Will cursed. "Okay. Keep trying to track their movements. Stay in radio communication. That's all that matters now."

Another rifle shot rang out from the distance. Will frowned. "I thought you were out of bullets."

"That wasn't me, but one of the two Iranian hostiles following you is down."

There was another rifle shot.

"I've shot the two men coming after you." The voice belonged to Laith. "The snipers put me on my ass for a while. But I'm back in it now." He coughed. "I'm off the island and positioned by the lakeside."

Will nodded. "I'm glad you're back in the land of the living. Get to Roger and help him.

Will sprinted up the mountainside for nearly a hundred meters before seeing something that looked out of place. He dived to the ground, brought his rifle up high, and raised himself to a crouch.

Lana was before him.

She was on her knees, her head was slumped. Ropes had been lashed around her throat, upper body, and legs, fixing her to a tree. Her hands were tied across her chest to form the shape of a cross.

He looked all around her and through the large flakes of snow that still fell slowly. They were on the summit, and with the exception of the tree that held Lana, the mountaintop was bare of life. He looked at her, his heart pounding as thoughts raced through his mind. He knew she could be bait for a trap. She could be a means to delay him, allowing Megiddo time to escape down the other side of the mountain.

Megiddo must have been aware that Will was following him up the mountain. There were still two armed and dangerous men behind him who were coming to kill him. Whatever was happening, he could not leave her like this.

Will walked carefully forward, scanning to the left and right of Lana with his gun. He reached her, squatted, and lifted her head. Her eyes were closed. She was unconscious.

He looked at the hands crossed over her chest. Drawing out his knife, he began cutting carefully through the cords that bound them. He pulled his knife upwards, slicing through the last of her wrist cords. The movement forced her hands toward him. He looked down and for the tiniest moment frowned.

Lana's unbound arms involuntarily released two hidden grenades. The devices fell toward the ground, and in that fraction of a second Will cursed his own stupidity. Megiddo had tied her up in such a way as to kill both her and Will the moment her cords were cut.

The immense noise and light momentarily destroyed everything. There was no thought, no pain, no sight, nothing.

He opened his eyes. Or maybe they were open already. He thought he saw white. He sensed that he was suspended in nothing but white. He did not know if he saw or sensed anything real. But white was all around him.

Seconds, minutes, or hours passed. He had no way of knowing anything about time.

Then the white gradually drifted away and left other things in its place. Will's eyes thought they saw sky, flecks of snow and land. His face was cold. He started hearing things. He started seeing things. He started thinking.

He knew he was lying on snow. He knew that the ringing in his ears was from the explosion. He knew he could not move his legs and arms. He used all his strength to turn his head to look at Lana. Her own head was still slumped, but he could tell that she was breathing heavily. He felt overwhelming relief. They both should have been dead. And then he realized what had happened. The explosives had been stun grenades. Megiddo had wanted to keep him alive.

He turned away from Lana. The movement was excruciating, and he could still do nothing more than just lie on the ground.

Then Will saw him. Even though his vision kept blurring and fragmenting, he saw him.

The man seemed distant at first. He walked quite slowly. Snow fell around him, but it did not seem to touch him. He carried a gun. He was looking at Will. He was coming toward him.

The man was tall. His gun was a rifle, and it was held in one hand with its barrel resting on his shoulder. The man looked calm. He came right up to Will. He looked at him. He said, "You deserve a better death than one by explosives or being shot like a dog on the ground. And I have now decided that there are things you need to know before I give you that more honorable death. But now is not the time."

Then he slammed the butt of his rifle onto Will's skull.

FORTY-SIX

"Come on, come on." The man's voice was hard, and his hand felt icy as it moved roughly over Will's face. "I know you can hear me, so start thinking and start moving."

The large hand moved roughly over Will's face and felt even colder.

For a moment Will thought he could not move or do anything. His head throbbed. His face tingled in pain from the man's hand. He felt anger at the man and decided that whoever the man was, Will was going to make him stop. He sucked in air, and the action caused an icy slush to enter his mouth. He shook his head to try to break away from the man's hand. The man kept smothering his face. Will felt overwhelming anger. With all his strength, he grabbed the man's wrist and yanked it away.

Laith was above him. He looked serious and concerned. His face was bloody, and he had half an ear missing. He nodded and said, "About time."

Will sat upright and felt his face. It was covered with snow. He brushed the snow away and looked around. He was still on the mountain summit, wind and snow swirling around him. He looked at Laith and knew that the ex–Delta operative had been rubbing snow into his face to try to bring him around. "How long have I been unconscious?"

Laith checked his watch. "The last time you and I spoke was over sixty minutes ago. I'd say you've been out for twenty to thirty minutes."

Will cursed. He placed fingers against the area on his head where the rifle butt had struck. He winced in pain but could feel only bruising. He held out his hand, and Laith grabbed it to pull him to his feet. He wobbled, steadied himself, and stared out over the southern valley below him. He muttered, "Why the hell didn't he kill me?" He looked at Laith. "Where's Roger?"

"I strapped up his leg and took him back to our vehicles. He's got a limp, but he'll live.

Will checked his pockets. His handgun, knife, and tactical communications system were gone, but he was relieved to find that his hidden cell phone was still in place. He pulled out the phone and called Roger. "Can you drive?"

Roger told him that he could.

Will nodded and turned around to face the lakes, the lodge, and Roger's location. "All right. Megiddo's still got Lana, and they must be heading back north toward you, since there's nothing but endless wilderness to the south. All the time they're on foot, Lana will slow him down, so he'll be desperate to find a vehicle or other means of transport to get out of here quickly." He thought for a moment. "After we attacked the lodge, Megiddo's reinforcements came through the woods from the north. Tell me about the road network around the lakes."

Roger told him that there was only one road that ran along the eastern side of the lake, the road they came in on, the road that Megiddo's men would have had to use to approach and leave the lodge.

Will nodded. "Okay, Megiddo's vehicles must be somewhere close to that road, northwest of your position and beyond the lodge." He checked his watch. "He's got a head start on us of probably thirty minutes, but I doubt he's reached the vehicles yet. Drive in that direction now, and we'll head to you on foot."

Will scoured the ground around him. He saw his Colt M4A1 assault rifle, walked to it, picked it up, briefly examined the gun, swore, and tossed it away. The bolt had been removed. He looked at Laith. "What weapons do you have?"

"Only one handgun. I had to leave the fifty-caliber behind to reach Roger and you quickly."

"Goddamn it." Will looked in the direction of the lodge, then at Laith. "We need to move very fast."

"You sure you can do this?"

Will's head throbbed with increased pain. "I have to."

The two men sprinted down the mountainside. They kept a gap of thirty meters between them to minimize the chances of them both being shot, but even so, Will knew that they were running too fast and too blindly to spot Megiddo before he could easily shoot one of them. Will desperately hoped that Megiddo's only priority now was escape.

They ran past the bodies of men they'd shot. They ran until they reached the base of the mountain and the slope leveled. They ran faster and changed direction slightly so that they were heading toward the road. They ran over ground covered with snow and trees, ground that had earlier been pretty and innocent but would soon be remembered by others as the location where a bloody battle had taken place.

Laith stopped suddenly and crouched. Will did the same, sucking in air after the excruciatingly fast run. Laith looked around him, looked at Will, and pointed ahead. He was silently telling Will that they were now very close to the road.

Will nodded, calmed his breathing, pulled out his phone, and called Roger. He cupped his other hand over his mouth and the phone to reduce sound and spoke as quietly as he could. "We're very close. What can you see?"

"Nothing. Not even any signs of recent tire tracks."

Will briefly closed his eyes in frustration. "Could he have gotten past you in a vehicle without your seeing him?"

"Impossible. But it's possible he got to a vehicle and headed southwest away from me on the road."

"What do you think?"

"I can't be sure. But I've been driving up and down this road, and I *can* be sure I've seen no evidence of recent vehicle movement."

"Shit. All right, well, I can't be sure either, but I think we've got to assume he's still on foot and heading north to the village of Saranac Lake."

"I agree. I'll meet you on the road."

Will ran low to Laith, patted him on the shoulder, and moved forward with Laith close beside him. Trees began to thin, and Will spotted glimpses of the road. Laith turned, held up a hand to tell Will to halt before moving forward in a crouch position while twitching his handgun left and right. As Laith came to within a few meters of the edge of the road, he stopped altogether, lay down on his front, gathered snow up around him, and waited.

From his spot forty meters behind Laith, Will also waited. He looked around and felt totally exposed. He imagined Megiddo emerging from somewhere in the dense forest behind him, walking up to him unseen, and cutting his throat with the knife he'd removed from Will. He heard a distant noise and glanced quickly toward the road and Laith's hidden position close to it. The noise grew louder, and Will knew it belonged to a vehicle. He watched Laith, but the man remained motionless.

Will scoured the area between the gaps in the trees in front of him. He saw nothing at first but then spotted movement to his far right. The movement was large and dark, and it flashed between the trees. It was the vehicle. Most likely it was Roger, but it could also belong to Megiddo or to heavily armed police. He looked back at Laith and knew that he would be thinking the same.

The vehicle moved slowly from right to left. Will ignored it, looked at Laith, and saw that he was continuing to stay very still. But as the vehicle got closer, Laith gradually started to raise himself out of his self-made shallow snow hole. The vehicle was almost right in front of him. Laith immediately stood, held his gun high, and took five steps forward. The vehicle stopped dead. Laith held his gun trained at its driver.

Will sighed with relief as he saw that the driver was Roger.

Will glanced quickly around again before sprinting to Laith. They entered the vehicle, Laith getting into the front and Will into the back.

"How far is it to the village?" Will asked Roger.

Roger turned to look at him. The man's face was etched with pain. "Six kilometers. Keep your eyes peeled on the way, because if Megiddo and his captive aren't there yet, they could be on foot, paralleling this road."

Roger punched the accelerator, and the car immediately reversed. He spun the car around so that it was facing the direction of Saranac Lake and drove forward at a medium speed. Laith fully lowered his passenger window and said nothing as he held his gun in two hands and examined the passing roadside. Will looked at the vehicle's trunk and was relieved to see the bags containing some of the unused weapons that Ben and Julian had brought for the assault. He reached to them and took a silenced Heckler & Koch MK23 pistol and three spare magazines. He rolled down his own window so that he could cover their right flank.

Snow fell fast, and Will could hear that Roger had put windshield wipers on full power to help him see through the blizzard. But Will didn't dare look away from the tree line by his side. He slitted his lids to try to focus; he moved his eyes to try to prevent becoming disorientated by the rapid white dots of ice and snow; he scoured the gaps between the trees and the darkness of the forest beyond. He called to Roger without looking away from his task, "How much time do we have before sunset?"

Roger answered loudly over the sound of the engine, the wipers, and the wind, "With this weather probably no more than twenty or thirty minutes."

Will cursed and muttered to no one in particular, "We don't have enough time to try to find them here."

"I agree." This came from Laith.

Will looked straight at Roger. "Put your foot to the floor and get us to the village as fast as you can. I don't think Megiddo and Lana are there yet, so we'll overtake them now and wait for them to arrive."

Their car lurched forward, fishtailing wildly on the icy road before Roger expertly manhandled the vehicle to get it speeding ahead. Will and Laith rolled up their windows and sat back in their seats. "Try to clean the blood off your face," Will told Laith. "We're heading to a place populated with civilians, and we don't want to stand out. You look like shit."

Laith smiled. "You should talk."

Roger leaned forward, opened the car's glove compartment, rummaged inside, and then tossed back a small parcel. Will caught the package and smiled as he saw it was a packet of baby wet wipes. He withdrew some of the disposable cleaners, gave the packet to Laith, and started cleaning his own face, neck, and hands. His smile faded as he began shivering. He looked down at himself and realized where the new coldness was coming from: his clothes had been saturated in the lake swim and later frozen solid in his pursuit to the mountaintop; they were now defrosting due to the heat inside the vehicle. He knew that Laith must be suffering in the same way. Roger had his own severe injuries to deal with. Will decided that the best he could do for now was to ignore the cold, the pain from his wounds, and the fatigue.

But he could not ignore the thoughts that hurtled around his earlier question to Patrick:

What could be worse than an attack on the premiers at Camp David?

Nor could he ignore another question he had for himself:

When will Megiddo decide that he's safe enough to no longer need Lana as a hostage?

He thought about calling Patrick. He thought about telling him that his trust in Will had been misplaced. He thought about telling him that all hope of success was rapidly fading.

He thought about what Patrick would almost certainly say: "Megiddo's men are all dead, so it's a manhunt now. I'm going to blow this open and get local and federal police involved. Whatever happens, he's going to kill Lana, so all that matters now is capturing him."

Will looked at Laith and Roger. He wondered whether he should lie to them or withhold his thoughts. He remembered Roger's words during their first encounter in the safe house in Zurich:

I know that none of us—my forefathers, their brothers, or me—has fought for our organization or our country. We've all fought for the man by our side.

He decided that he could never lie to the men who were sitting with him in this car. He had never worked with such professional operatives as the two CIA men here with him or the two heroic dead colleagues they were leaving behind.

He spoke. "Roger. Laith. I'm still convinced we need to do this our way and without others. I think that if other men are brought in, Lana will be killed. I think that if Megiddo feels that capture is inevitable, he may have emergency protocols in place to carry out his attack anyway. I think we still have to allow him to believe he has a chance to escape and conduct his assault." He paused. "But I could be wrong. I could be very wrong, and I'm certain my handler in MI6 would think that and I'm certain your master in the CIA would draw that conclusion." He looked at them both. "Patrick would not want us to go it alone at this stage, and if either or both of you agree with him, then I need to tell him what's happening right now."

Laith regarded him with a look of steel. "Fuck that."

"Yeah, fuck that." Roger gunned the car harder, and it sped faster toward the now-visible but still distant village of Saranac Lake.

Almost at that same instant, bullets rang out from ahead of them and tore through the vehicle's engine, through the windshield, and through Roger.

The car swerved left, and Will lunged forward, wrapped one arm around Roger and his seat, and grabbed the steering wheel with the other.

Laith shouted, "Keep us on the road!" He punched an elbow through the glass in his window several times, gripped the headrest in front of him, and leaned out the window with his gun. "I'll deal with the shooter!"

Will yanked the wheel left and right and left to try to compensate for the movement of the out-of-control vehicle, but they were going too fast and had no grip on the icy road. He shouted, "Too late! Brace for impact!"

The car spun 360 degrees, lifted into the air, rotated, crashed onto its side, and slid along the road before shuddering to a halt. Will breathed hard for a moment. He tentatively moved his arms and legs and knew he was uninjured. When he heard a banging noise, he looked over and saw Laith kicking at his passenger door. He heard the CIA man curse and felt him clamber over to haul himself through the window. Will was still holding Roger. He could hear the injured driver wheezing, but otherwise he was motionless and quiet.

Laith was now outside the vehicle, and Will could see that he was holding his handgun in front of him, looking for the man who had destroyed their car with an assault rifle, looking for the man who was definitely Megiddo. Will knew that Laith was an easy target for Megiddo if the man was still close to them. And he knew that if he himself stayed in the vehicle a moment longer, he could die.

He gently eased Roger's head against the bare road that had smashed through the man's side window and pulled himself though the sky-facing window that Laith had punched a hole through. He jumped down onto the asphalt and pulled out his gun. He looked up and down the road, at the roadsides, and into the forest, but he could see nothing. He glanced at the sky. Darkness was rapidly descending.

Laith had moved ten paces ahead of the vehicle and was crouched down in the middle of the road, pointing his gun directly ahead and in the direction where the bullets had come from. He remained very still, and Will knew that he had positioned himself so that he presented a human barrier against any bullets intended for Will.

Will climbed back onto the vehicle and tried to open the front passenger door. It seemed jammed, but after four attempts he managed to yank the door open. He looked into the car and at Roger. The injured man's eyes were screwed shut, telling Will that he was in severe pain but also, more important, that he was conscious. "Roger, can you speak?"

The man wheezed but said nothing.

"Roger, I want to get you out of there. But if I move you and you have a broken neck or back, I'm likely to kill you. Do you understand?"

Snow fell hard over Will, through the window, and onto Roger. At first there was no response. Then Will could see the man move his hands and his feet slightly. He could see that Roger was trying to determine if he had any broken bones.

Finally he spoke. "Bullet in my left arm." His voice sounded weak and thready. "At least one bullet in my shoulder . . . think I can be moved, though."

Will wasted no time, lunging headfirst so that his upper body was facing downward in the vehicle, thrusting his hands under Roger's armpits and hauling him up. Roger screamed, but Will kept pulling, focusing all his strength on slowly dragging up the large CIA man's deadweight. Will's biceps and back muscles tightened in agony, and as he moved Roger inch by inch, he wondered whether his body was strong enough to do this. His breathing increased rapidly. He squeezed his eyes shut. He focused on nothing else but lifting his colleague upward little by little. He spread his legs wide against the vehicle's exterior to give himself extra leverage and stability. For a moment he had to stop pulling and just stood there panting with the strain of the effort. Then he sucked in a lungful of air, held his breath, banged his legs hard against the car, and heaved with every muscle he had. He pulled until his whole body was racked with pain. He pulled until he felt Roger's head brush against his chin. He held still momentarily, knowing that he would have to adjust his grip and in doing so support the injured man's entire weight with one hand. He exhaled and inhaled again, braced his right arm, released his left hand's grip, and immediately felt his right bicep tighten to the point where he thought it would burst. He quickly thrust his left arm around Roger's chest and breathed again. He yanked with both arms and guided the man through the window. Then he slowly moved onto his feet and used his leg muscles to aid him in pulling the man the rest of the way out of the car.

He called to Laith, "You'd be dead by now if the shooter's still here. I need your help."

Laith came to the vehicle and helped Will to gently lower Roger down to the road and onto his back. Will stood on top of the car for a moment, breathing heavily and trying to relax his muscles after their supreme effort. Eventually he jumped down and crouched next to Roger. Laith joined him.

Will saw three bullet holes in Roger. "I'm not going to leave him here. He'll die."

Laith nodded. "Damn right. But what are we going to do?"

Will looked up the road in the direction of Saranac Lake. It was nearly night, and the distant village was illuminated with artificial light. "Megiddo's got his own burden in Lana," he told Laith. He looked at Roger. "Now we have our own burden. But nothing changes."

Laith nodded. "I'd say we're about two kilometers away from the village. Switch over every five hundred meters?"

Will agreed. "Roger, you know this is going to hurt a lot, but you also know how this works."

"Do it," the CIA team leader muttered between clenched teeth.

Will grabbed one of the man's arms, swept his other arm under Roger's back, lifted him to a seated position before hauling him onto his shoulder. He stood looking at Laith. "You take point. Let's go."

Laith jogged ahead with his handgun at waist level, pointing directly at the route they were taking. Will ran a few meters behind and tried to keep his feet flat on the snow- and ice-covered ground in order not to bounce and cause Roger any further discomfort beyond what he was already suffering. They ran down the middle of the road toward Saranac. They ran using only moonlight and the faraway glow of the village to guide them. They ran knowing that a man with an assault rifle or a machine gun could cut them in half before they could do anything about it.

Will silently counted every step, and he knew that Laith would be doing the same. He kept his grip tight on Roger and focused on moving. Just as Roger would have done when he carried Will on his shoulder to get him away from Harry's house. Just as the man they were now hunting would have done when he carried Will on his shoulder out of the inferno within Lace's residence.

Will counted to five hundred and shouted, "Switch!"

He placed Roger carefully on the ground, pulled out his handgun, and moved ahead of Laith.

He heard Laith moving Roger to hoist him up onto his own shoulder. He heard Laith say, "I'm ready! Go!"

They ran on. Will held his gun ahead of him, his elbows crooked and squeezed together. The forest on both sides of them was now in total darkness, and he made no effort to search for hidden dangers within its blackness. He just looked down the road ahead, looked for oncoming cars, looked for anything that could be a man with a rifle pointed at them.

After a few minutes, they switched over again, and Will ran with his head low and with the deadweight of Roger on his shoulder. He heard him wheeze, occasionally rasp in pain, but he heard no complaints from him.

Soon Laith called "Switch!" and he took possession of Roger. They were now only one kilometer from Saranac Lake.

Snow fell fast through the night air and caked on Will's face as he took point and ran forward with his handgun. He felt light-headed, exhausted, but single-minded. He cared about nothing other than keeping Roger alive, finding Megiddo, rescuing Lana, punching Megiddo to the ground, pointing his gun at the man, finding out what could be worse than attacking Camp David, and then shooting him in the head. He ran over thicker snow, and his legs felt weak—but he kept running. His feet sometimes slipped and stumbled—but he kept running.

They changed over one last time, and Roger's weight on Will's shoulder felt almost unbearable. But Saranac was now very close and easily visible. Will focused on Laith's back and ran behind him, concentrating on every footfall and ensuring that he just kept up. Every second seemed to last a minute, every lungful of air seemed to be a lungful of ice, every footfall seemed to be a naked step onto a bed of nails.

It seemed an eternity before Laith finally slowed, ran off the road into the edge of the forest, and stopped. Will stood looking at his back for a while before allowing his legs to buckle and send him down to his knees. He gasped for air as he rested Roger on the ground. He rubbed his hand over the man's face to brush away ice and snow. He asked, "Are you still alive?" and saw Roger give the tiniest of nods. He arched his back to try to ease the searing muscular pain. Laith came over and crouched down next to Will. Both men looked through the trees at the village of Saranac Lake. They were right beside it but remained hidden in the forest's darkness. They saw a few cars, a few distant pedestrians, and a few buildings and streetlamps, and they heard a few noises of normal human existence.

Laith placed two fingers against Roger's throat artery and stayed still for a while. He nodded. "He's not in shock. This freezing weather has probably helped keep him alive and stable. The cold will have slowed the body right down." He looked at Will. "But it will also ultimately kill him. He'll be dead in less than two hours unless we can get him some medical care."

A hand gripped Laith's fingers. The hand belonged to Roger, who spoke with a strained but firm voice. "I'll die when I want to, not when you say I will." He coughed and smiled a little. "Remember, I'm a Navy SEAL. Among other things, we're used to cold and pain." He looked serious. "Leave me here. You go into town and find him. Then and only then come back for me."

Will shook his head. "We'll take you with us and find medical help. We can leave you there."

"I have gunshot wounds," Roger reminded him. "They'll call the police to have you arrested. You'll have to run, and then you'll have no chance of finding Megiddo."

Will looked at Laith's expression of uncertainty. Will's own thoughts were uncertain, too.

Roger released his grip on Laith, grabbed Will's jacket, and pulled Will's face close to his own. "Leave me here. The priority is getting Megiddo."

Will shook his head once more. "For all your strength, you *will* die, and I can't let that happen." Then an idea came to him. "Whatever happens, your role in this mission is now over. If we get you medical help, you'll be properly cared for, although the police will be notified and you'll be held in custody while they work out what the hell happened to you. But that doesn't matter, because in due course you'll be sprung from custody by Patrick." He looked at Laith. "How many cops do you think they have in Saranac Lake?"

Laith shrugged. "I can't be sure, but I'd say three or four at most, and they probably only have two on duty at any one time, outside of emergencies."

Will nodded. "I'm going to call the Saranac Lake Police Department.

I'm going to say that I saw a vehicle on its side on this road about a mile outside the village. Then I'll hang up." He looked at Roger. "That should draw most if not all of Saranac's tiny police contingent out of the village. We'll use that time to get you *into* the village, find medical help, leave you there, and go for Megiddo." He glanced at Laith. "We should have twenty or thirty minutes to scour the town before the cops return to hear about the man with gunshot wounds who's been dumped at the hospital." He looked back at Roger. "Say nothing to the doctors or the cops." He smiled. "It shouldn't be hard to do, but act like you're dying."

Roger nodded slowly, held him close for a while before saying quietly, "It's been a pleasure working with you, Will."

Will squeezed his hand. "I'm sure this won't be the last time we work together. I certainly hope not."

He patted Roger's pockets, found the man's cell phone, and smiled as he said, "It doesn't matter now if they trace a call from this phone." He opened the phone, called 911, said that he wished to be redirected to the Saranac Lake Police Department, spoke for a few seconds before saying that he had very bad phone reception and then hung up midsentence. He closed the phone, pulled out the SIM card, snapped it into pieces, and threw the pieces and the handset into the forest. Then he walked closer to the tree line adjacent to the village and waited. In two minutes he heard a police siren. In three minutes he saw a police four-wheel-drive cruise steadily past him along the road where they had crashed.

He walked quickly to Laith and said, "I'll carry him. You do the talking." He looked down at Roger, nodded at the man, and said, "One last journey to make, my friend."

Laith and Will secreted their handguns. Will lifted Roger onto his shoulder. The three men left the darkness of the forest and entered the village of Saranac Lake.

FORTY-SEVEN

There weren't many people on the streets, but those who were brave enough to be out in the driving snowfall and the dark looked at the odd trio as they moved carefully through the village. Will examined them all and didn't care that they were staring at Laith, at him, and at the man he was carrying, but he wondered how much they would care if they knew that the men they were staring at were armed and extremely dangerous. He walked with Laith along a road called Olive Street. It took them into to what looked like the center of the village, and it was clear to him that the whole place was a popular tourist destination, because the few people they did see were dressed in winter sports attire. Will knew that Laith would be ignoring them, that he would be looking for someone who looked like a local resident.

Will checked his watch and cursed. Time was running out.

Laith stopped, waived a hand by his waist to signal Will to wait, then walked quickly ahead to a man and woman on the other side of the street. He spoke to the couple for a few seconds, pointed in the direction of Will and the man he was carrying, shook his head, pointed in another direction, and nodded at the couple before leaving them. Will expected Laith to come straight over to him, but instead he stood in the street and looked up and down its length. A car approached him, and Laith walked out into the middle of the street, waving his hands. The car stopped, Laith spoke to the driver, then stepped back as the car sped away. He then repeated the action with another oncoming car containing a solitary male driver. Laith pointed at Will and Roger, gave the driver something from his pocket, and jogged back to Will. "Not good. The nearest hospital is the Adirondack Medical Center, two kilometers away on Route eighty-six to the north. But for fifty dollars I managed to persuade the man in the car to take us there. I told him there's been a hunting accident."

Will moved quickly to the car. Laith opened the rear door and helped him get Roger into the passenger seat. Will sat next to Roger and held the injured man against him with both arms. Laith jumped into the front passenger seat and began telling the driver all about the hunting accident as he drove along. The driver looked like a clerk or a shopkeeper, and most of what Laith said to him seemed repetitive and unnecessary, but Will knew that Laith was simply minimizing the opportunity for the driver to speak to Will—or to speak at all.

Within a few minutes, they pulled up at the medical center. Laith turned to the driver. "You heading back into the village?"

The driver responded, "For sure."

Laith nodded. "I'll give you another fifty dollars if you wait for us and take us back there after we check our friend into this place."

The driver seemed to hesitate. "How long would I have to wait?"

Laith smiled. "Hardly any time at all."

The man looked unsure but nodded.

Laith jumped out of the car and helped Will get Roger out. Instead of putting him onto his shoulder, Will lifted Roger into his arms. While Laith stayed by the car, Will walked alone, carrying his precious burden into the small reception area. A solitary woman was sitting behind a counter, but otherwise the area was empty. The woman looked at them and instantly slammed a hand down onto a buzzer. She had clearly called for immediate medical assistance. Will set Roger down on the floor, looked at him, and fought back an overwhelming urge to stay. Roger shook his head and gave the tiniest of smiles. Will nodded at him, smiled, turned, and jogged out of the hospital, ignoring the calls of the woman behind them. Laith slapped the roof of the car just as Will approached the vehicle. Both men got back in, and Laith told the driver they'd been instructed by the hospital to report the incident to the local police in the village.

Within minutes they were back in the heart of the village and on foot. Will checked his watch again. He looked at the police building in front of them and said, "I need you to find out about transportation links out of here. Find out where Megiddo and Lana may now be waiting. But we can't be seen right here."

They darted into the darkness and emerged into Woodruff Street, adjacent to a wide, sweeping river. Laith looked up and down the street before walking briskly up to a group of three men. He spoke to them and returned to Will. "Megiddo's out of luck. There are three public transportation services in the village—the Franklin County Public Transportation bus service, the Greyhound coach service, and the Adirondack Scenic Railway—but they're all closed right now. The buses will be running in the morning, and the railway is closed for the winter season. There's also an airport, but it's seven miles away."

"Taxis?"

Laith shook his head. "There are a couple of local private firms, but they've shut up shop while the weather's this bad."

"It's us who are out of luck," Will said urgently. "If any of the village transportation services were open, we could hope to pin Megiddo down at one of their locations. Instead"—he looked around—"he could be anywhere here."

"Maybe he'll wait until morning and get a bus then."

"I doubt that. He's got Lana with him and won't want to hang about and risk her screaming for help. And if they wait out the night back in the forest, they'll freeze to death."

"Maybe he'll do what we did—pay someone to drive them out of here. Maybe he'll head to the airport."

"Maybe, maybe." Will kicked the snow-covered ground in frustration. "Maybe." He looked around again and grew calm as a thought came to him. "Maybe he doesn't *know* what to do yet." He looked at Roger. "Just like us. Maybe he's still on the streets trying to work out what to do."

Laith nodded. "Neither of us knows the layout of this village." He looked at the river. "But I'd say this river runs northeast. I'd say that the best we can do is split up. You cover ground on the east of the river. I'll cross it and cover the west."

Will agreed and said, "If you see him, don't engage the man, because he'll use Lana as a shield. Just stay out of sight and call me."

Laith sprinted up the street and broke left along another street to cross the river. Will looked around, pulled out his gun from the small of his back, and stashed it in a lower front jacket pocket where he could reach it quickly. He jogged forward before running at a full sprint. He ran left onto Main Street and left again onto River Street, where the icy river beside him immediately widened. His boots crunched on thick snow as he moved over road and pavement and dodged parked vehicles, slow-moving pedestrians, and dim streetlamps. The wind dropped, and snow now fell fast and vertical. As he raced forward, he looked at every man, every woman, every house entrance, every shop façade, and every vehicle interior. He looked at everything but saw nothing that made him want to pull out his gun and shoot.

He moved away from the broad river and headed up Shepard Avenue, crossed onto Clinton Avenue and Franklin Avenue, moved northeast along Helen Street, and north along Pine Street until he was back at the river and not far from where he had started his search. He cursed aloud.

A siren sounded very close by, and Will immediately ran off the road and dived behind an empty car. He lay on snow and heard the siren come closer. He watched a police vehicle speed past him, and he stayed still until it was out of sight. He was certain that it was heading to the Adirondack Medical Center and that doctors had called the police after taking charge of their strange new patient. He was also certain that the police would return quickly to the village to search for the man who had delivered Roger to the hospital and then disappeared.

His cell phone vibrated silently in his trouser pocket. He withdrew it and saw that the caller was Laith. He answered.

Laith's voice was barely audible. "Can't be sure, but I can see two people who could be them. They're about one hundred meters from my position on Prospect Avenue. If it is them, then Megiddo's discarded his rifle. But the man I'm looking at is holding the woman very close to him, and that could mean he's got a handgun trained on her."

Will spoke quickly and with no effort to hide the urgency or tension in his voice. "Stay on them, but for God's sake keep your distance. I'm coming to you. Guide me in."

"Okay. Prospect Avenue is about four hundred meters northwest of the river. As soon as you hit either William Street or Leona Street, slow down or you'll run into them."

Will kept his phone in his hand, sprinted across a road over the river, and headed west. He ran along Bloomingdale Avenue and could see shops closing for the evening and restaurants and diners opening. He ran into a quieter street and immediately recognized it as Olive, the route they'd used to enter the village. He slowed, looked around, and decided he needed to head north to find Laith's approximate location. He jogged up William, and all around him was now quiet and deserted. He slowed to a walk, called Laith, gave his location, and listened to his colleague's quiet instructions.

"Turn left onto Neil Street. Take the second turn on your right, onto Fairview Avenue. You'll then see me about hundred meters ahead of you. But go slowly. If they move, I may need you to change direction quickly and flank them from the east."

Will placed his spare hand into his pocket and gripped his MK23 pistol. He walked slowly, resisting every urge to get to Laith as rapidly as he could. He moved onto Neil Street and could see that houses were evenly spaced to his left and right and that most of them had inside lights on. He imagined that the families within were now settling down to dinner. On the other side of the street, a group of four men and one woman walked quickly in the opposite direction. They had their heads low and scarves and hats wrapped around them to shield them from the weather. Will kept his own head down low, too, until they were behind him. The street was now deserted.

He passed the first turn on the right and kept walking ahead, pulling out his handgun and keeping it flush against his stomach. He breathed evenly and saw his breath turn to steam in the icy air. He made himself slow his pace even further in case he received an instruction from Laith to reverse direction and sprint up one of the routes he'd left behind. He gripped his gun tighter, glancing around.

He drew close to corner where he needed to turn in order to see Laith. He knew that the couple being observed by the CIA man was still in situ, or else Laith would have urgently told him otherwise. He looked back down the route he'd just taken before looking ahead again. He flicked off the safety catch on his Heckler & Koch and decided to make the turn. He walked carefully forward, went right onto Fairview Avenue, and stopped.

He could see Laith. But he appeared to be sitting on the ground, leaning against a low retaining wall beneath the dim yellow glow of a streetlamp. Will frowned and began jogging toward him. After twenty meters he began to sprint, holding his gun directly in front of him.

He reached Laith, swung his weapon toward Prospect Avenue, swung it in the opposite direction, could see no one, and crouched opposite his colleague. Laith was smiling, looked calm, held his phone in one hand against the ground, and held his other hand against his stomach. The snow around him was red. The ex–Delta man looked down before looking up at Will. He pulled his hand away from his stomach. His jacket had been ripped through with something sharp. His stomach had been slashed open.

"Oh, my God. What happened Laith?"

Laith shrugged. "The couple walked toward me." He enunciated each word as if he had to force it out of his mouth. "I didn't want to call you, since that could have looked suspicious. So I moved and casually walked toward them. As we passed each other, the man pushed the woman to the ground and rushed toward me. I dropped low to take out his legs, but he must have anticipated that, and he dived over me, grabbed my throat from behind, and stabbed me."

Will looked up Prospect Avenue. "Which way did they go?"

Laith nodded toward Fairview Avenue behind him, the street Will had just sprinted up. "You must have seen them."

Will frowned before widening his eyes in absolute frustration at his stupidity. "Oh, fuck." Will recalled the group of five hatted and scarved people on the opposite side of the road on Neil Street. He recalled the man and woman at the back of the group. "I walked right by them. They attached themselves to three random walkers. Megiddo might even have had a gun trained on them."

Laith breathed deeply. "My wound is bad. My liver is punctured. I'll be dead without urgent treatment."

Will nodded. "And that's exactly what you're going to get."

Laith exhaled slowly. "I know, but I don't need your help to get it. I need you to get after that bastard and finish this."

A distant siren wailed. It sounded different from the one Will had heard from the passing police car.

Laith smiled again and raised his phone a little. "I knew that when you found me like this, you would never leave me until I had medical help. So I took the decision out of your hands and called them myself to let you get on with the mission. That siren belongs to the ambulance coming to get me. I said I was mugged. When the police arrive at the hospital, they won't believe that story considering everything that's happened here tonight. But what the fuck can they do to me?"

He smiled wider. "If I'm still alive when I reach the hospital, maybe I'll get a bed next to Roger. I hope not, though. The man snores like a buzz saw."

Will tried to smile but felt utter desperation. "Keep applying pressure on your wound. Stay conscious."

Laith responded in a firm, stronger voice. "I know exactly what to do, Will Cochrane."

Will nodded. "I know you do." The noise of the siren was drawing nearer. "Have you got anything compromising on you?"

Laith shook his head. "No ID, only cash. But you better get rid of my phone, gun, and clips."

Will took them, glanced over his shoulder, then back at Laith. "Thank you for everything, Laith."

"There's no need for thanks. If I'm still alive and and my liver's up to it, just buy me a beer when this is over."

Will was about to go, but Laith grabbed his hand, holding him firm with incredible strength. "After he ripped open my stomach, the man crouched before me. He said he knew that Nicholas Cree was close by. He told me that I needed to stay alive long enough to tell you that I'd been gutted by a man called Megiddo, the man you seek." He winced in pain and coughed. "He wants to meet you alone in one day's time in New York City. If you don't meet him, many innocents will die." He spat a clot of blood away from him onto the snow and cursed. "If he has the slightest suspicion that the meeting is being watched or that you have others with you, Lana will die." He sucked in air between gritted teeth and was clearly in severe pain. "You must be in a private location, or the meeting will not take place. You've got to send Lana a message saying where you will be." His breathing became shallow, but he gripped Will even harder. "He said that you must make the most of the next twenty-three hours, because on the twenty-fourth hour he will come to you, talk to you, and kill you."

Will checked his watch. It was just after 6:00 P.M. He shook his head. "What the hell is he doing? He's risking his own operation.

What's his game?" He felt a rush of adrenaline. "Whatever is going on, the attack must be taking place in New York City."

Laith nodded, released his grip, placed his hand over the other hand that was pressing against his wound. "There's something else you should know." He spat more blood. "I've beaten or killed every man who's ever pissed me off. No one's ever been stronger than me, faster than me, or better trained. But"—he coughed again and winced—"Megiddo was different. Will, listen to me. The man was so fucking fast, so damned deadly."

The siren was very close now. Will nodded, stood, looked at Laith, turned, and ran after the man who had killed or severely injured the best special-operative team he'd ever worked with.

He ran back down Fairview Avenue and moved onto Neil Street. He kept his gun held forward and didn't care if he was spotted holding a weapon. He scoured the area before him and around him for the group he'd seen earlier. Two hundred meters ahead of him, he saw an ambulance speed across the road and up William Street before it disappeared from view. He kept running until he reached the intersection, looked left and right and ahead, cursed as he saw nothing, wondered which of the three routes Megiddo would have taken, and decided that the man would have headed south along Leona Street and away from the area where Laith had been stabbed. He moved quickly down the street until he was at the junction with Olive. He looked right and saw nothing. He looked left and saw them.

The group of five was approximately 150 meters away from him. Will raised his weapon, breathing fast, and pointed it at the man at the rear of the group, walking next to the woman. He focused his eyes through the snowfall. He knew that he could make the shot and send a bullet into the man's brain. But he also knew that in doing so he would kill all remaining hope of stopping Megiddo's assault, that his bullet might cause Megiddo's hand to squeeze tight around a handgun pointing at Lana and send a bullet into her, that Will's high-velocity projectile might pass though Megiddo's skull and enter any of the three innocent men in front of him. He cursed and lowered his weapon slightly, taking several steps forward. He saw the man and woman break away from the group and start walking to the other side of the road. He quickly raised his weapon again. He heard noise. He saw flashes on the ground around him.

He heard a man shout, "Stop! Police!"

Will exhaled slowly but did not move.

He heard a different man shout, "Drop the weapon! Raise your hands and kick your weapon away from you!"

Will did not move.

"Do it or we *will* shoot you!"

Will knew that there were at least two police officers behind him. He sighed, moved his arms outward, paused for a moment before dropping his Heckler & Koch MK23 to the ground. He turned quickly to face the police. Two male officers were before him, standing apart from each other at a distance of about thirty feet. They had handguns pointed straight at him. Behind them was their stationary police vehicle. Its doors were open, and police lights flashed silently on its roof.

"Stand still. Nobody told you to turn around." This came from the officer to his right. The other officer took two sideward paces, and Will knew that the man was creating a greater angle between him and his colleague so as to minimize the chance for Will to assault the men and escape.

Will silently cursed. A moment ago he had been very close to Megiddo. But now the man would be rushing away with Lana and no doubt searching for a populated place to hide among other civilians. He cursed that the men before him were doing their job but were also unwittingly allowing the most dangerous man on the planet to escape in their village. He looked at the faces of the police officers. He could see no fear in their eyes, no hesitation and no uncertainty. They looked professional and competent. But he knew that he would be quicker; he knew he could pull Laith's handgun from his pocket and put bullets into their brains before they could even blink. He sighed as he looked at them. He knew there was no way he could shoot dead two American police officers.

"Keep your arms out. Get on your knees."

Will did what he was told.

"Now lie flat, facedown and hands together behind your back."

Will moved his body into the position but kept his face forward. He could see the cop to his left take more sideways steps until he was out of sight, moving behind to handcuff Will. He looked at the other police officer. The man was motionless and kept his gun pointed at Will's head.

"I said facedown."

Will pushed his face into snow and waited. He felt a knee punch into the small of his back. He still waited. He felt strong fingers wrap around one of his hands, and he knew that the cuffs were about to be placed on him. He moved fast.

He grabbed the police officer's wrist, spun rapidly on the ground, twisted the man's arm with the movement, forced him to spin with him until he was momentarily by Will's side, heard shouting from the other officer, knew that the other officer would not shoot for fear of hitting his colleague, grabbed the prone officer's throat, wrenched his head up and in front of him, moved onto his knees, pulled the man with him, moved into a crouch position, lunged forward with the man toward the other officer, and pushed his captive directly into his colleague. The two officers flew though the air before crashing to the ground. Will sprinted at them, kicked the gun out of one of the men's hand, stomped on his solar plexus to render him temporarily immobile, moved to the other man as he was trying to get to his feet, jabbed an elbow down into the man's collarbone, and simultaneously swept a leg around his ankles to force him back down to the ground. He picked up their guns and threw them down the street. Both officers were moaning in pain, but Will knew they would recover in minutes. He looked at them both, sighed, and said, "I'm sorry."

Then he turned and sprinted away. He ran knowing that he could not spend a moment longer in this place. He ran knowing that he now stood no chance of finding Megiddo or Lana in the village. He ran knowing that his only hope to finish everything would be for Megiddo to come to him in New York.

He ran knowing that in just under twenty-four hours' time he had to be face-to-face with Megiddo and that his quarry would be there to kill him.

FORTY-EIGHT

Will headed north through forest but not too far from Route 86, where he had earlier seen signs for the Adirondack Regional Airport. Wind was blowing hard and sent snow and ice fast into his face. He moved, sometimes blindly, through the pitch-dark forest, using only the occasional road light on his right to maintain his bearings. He felt very cold, but he also felt angry and determined to keep moving.

He walked for six kilometers, only occasionally stopping to crouch down when a vehicle passed on the road. He reached an area where he could see the road fork, adjusted his position, and continued his journey in a westerly direction, keeping the new road thirty meters to his right.

He thought about calling Patrick and telling the man everything that had happened on this day. He thought about telling Patrick where he was so that the man could send help to get him to New York immediately. He thought about Roger and Laith, and his next thought echoed the words they had earlier used:

Fuck that.

The night grew even blacker, and the temperature plummeted further. His clothes felt heavy now, and he knew that was because they were frozen.

He saw the lights of the airport ahead.

He jogged forward so that he was very close to the road. He looked up and down the route before walking quickly across it and into more forest. He kept moving forward until he was close to the airport perimeter. He breathed deeply, even though every lungful of icy air felt excruciating. He crouched down, lowered himself onto his knees, and fell forward onto his stomach and chest. He pulled himself a few feet along the ground until he was satisfied that he could see the complex properly.

The airport had only one building, and it was small and clearly both the arrivals and departures area. But it was in total darkness. Beside it he could see glimpses of snow-covered single-engine planes on tarmac and three runways beyond them. He'd come here hoping to find a busy airport, active twenty-four hours, and maybe even a direct flight to New York City. The place before him was anything but that, though, and it was clearly shut for the night. He would have to wait in the freezing night until the airport opened in the morning.

He heard cars, looked quickly to his right, and saw two of them move slowly along the narrow entrance road to the airport. He tried to focus his eyes through the snowfall and saw that one of the cars was a white SUV and the vehicle behind it was a police vehicle. He stayed still and watched them pull up close to the solitary building.

The cars stopped. A man exited the SUV, and two police officers got out of their vehicle. Will could not see the officers' faces clearly, but he could tell from their builds that they were not the men who had pointed guns at him on Olive Street. He knew that more police officers would have been drafted into the area to look for the man who had disarmed the two policemen. But he wondered what was happening in front of him right now.

The civilian walked up to the reception building, paused by the door, seemed to be looking for something, and opened the door. He entered but stopped inside within a few feet of the doorway and looked at one of the adjacent walls. He raised his arm and spent a few seconds standing where he was before walking out of the building and nodding at the two police officers. They walked into the building with the civilian, and the three men momentarily disappeared from view.

Will knew that the civilian was the key holder to the airport and that the man had punched numbers into a wall-mounted alarm unit to disable the security system. But he did not know why he or the police were here. He waited and rubbed his hands to try to aid his circulation.

Lights came on in the building until the whole interior was illuminated. Will looked at the windows and saw glimpses of the men moving through the place before stopping in one room. The policemen seemed to be doing nothing other than standing by the civilian; the civilian was making telephone calls from different phones. He looked focused and picked up phones as quickly as he put them down. The men were in the room for maybe ten or fifteen minutes before lights were turned off and they appeared at the main doorway. The civilian tapped buttons on the alarm pad, locked the door, and headed quickly to his vehicle. The police officers joined him, shook his hand, and walked to theirs.

Will now knew exactly what had been happening. The police had called the head of the airport, brought him to the place, and protected him while he made calls to other airports telling them that the Adirondack Regional Airport would be closed until further notice while authorities conducted a manhunt for the individual who had assaulted two police officers and was most certainly associated with two men who were currently in supervised medical care suffering from gunshot and knife wounds.

He felt a surge of frustration. He rubbed ice from his face, watched the police officers enter their vehicle, saw one of them talk on their radio, watched them drive off with lights flashing. He imagined that with their task done, they would now be heading off to continue their role in trying to find him.

The civilian paused by his car door, tried to light a cigarette, failed, opened the door, and sat for a moment in the driver's seat. Will saw a glow behind the man's cupped hands, followed by smoke from his cigarette. Will stood, pulled out Laith's handgun, and ran toward the seated man. He slowed and held his gun in two hands. Falling snow swirled around him.

The man glanced up, his eyes widened, and he looked very scared. "Are you the man they want?"

Will pointed his gun at the man's head and took measured steps forward. "Maybe. Are you armed?"

The man shook his head. "Do I look like the type of person to carry a gun?"

"No, you don't."

The man briefly looked over his shoulder before looking at Will. He was breathing fast. "I imagine that you came here to get on a flight out of Saranac Lake. But there won't be any flights now while the local police think you're still at large within their jurisdiction."

Will nodded. "I need your car, your cell phone, and the keys to this building."

The man appeared to be on the verge of panic. "If you take those things, I'll have to try to walk back to the village with no means of letting anyone know where I am."

"That's the idea."

The man looked up at the sky. "I'm overweight and unfit, and in this weather I'm not sure I'd make it. I'll probably freeze to death." He looked at Will in total panic. "Is . . . is that what you want?"

Of course the man was right. He was middle-aged, at least forty pounds overweight, and looked as though he'd dressed in a hurry and with no intention of spending more time than he needed away from his home or his heated SUV. Will kept his gun trained on the man. "Throw me your cell phone."

The man reached into a breast pocket, pulled out his cell, and tossed it onto the ground by Will's feet. Will slammed the heel of a boot onto the phone, smashing it into pieces. "Stand up and walk two paces away from your vehicle."

The man hesitated for a moment before standing. "Please don't do this." One of his legs was shaking. "Please. I'll die."

Will kept his gun pointed at the man and slowly walked around the vehicle until he was by the front passenger door. "You will if you stand there. Get back into the car. You're going to drive me out of here."

Will entered the vehicle and gripped his gun over his lap and pointing at the driver's seat. The man entered, exhaled loudly, looked at Will, and turned the key in the ignition. He drove the car forward.

They moved out of the airport complex toward Route 186. When they reached the end of the airport road, the man stopped the vehicle and asked, "Where are we going?"

"Anywhere away from Saranac Lake." Will looked at the driver. "But I do need to head south."

The man looked to his left along Route 186. "Then we'll have to drive through the village."

Will quickly placed his gun against the man's temple and said nothing.

The man glanced sideways but did not move his head. He looked terrified and spoke rapidly. "We can take a different route. We can go right instead, go southwest on one eighty-six and thirty so that we're traveling on the west side of Upper Saranac Lake."

Will held the gun still for a moment before lowering the weapon. "All right."

The man swung the SUV right so that it was on 186. Will frowned in thought. "What did the police officers say to you?"

"You saw them with me?"

Will nodded.

The man breathed in deeply as he drove. "They said that they were looking for an extremely dangerous man. They said that they were guarding another two very dangerous men at the Adirondack Medical Center. They said they were getting early reports that something very big had happened near one of the lakes."

Not good. Will had hoped that darkness and the severe weather would delay the police from finding out what had happened at Lower Saranac Lake until the morning. "How many cops will have been drafted into this area to look for me?"

The man wiped his brow. "How would I know? I'm not in law enforcement."

Will shouted, "No, but you run an airport, which will have very close links to the emergency services! You'll have some idea!"

The man's eyes widened, and he nodded quickly. "We had an incident a year back. The pilot of one of our planes radioed ahead that a passenger was acting suspiciously, that there were concerns he was a terrorist. We told the pilot to keep his course toward our airport. We also told the police, and within forty-five minutes they had thirty-five men and twenty vehicles encircling the airport. Most of them had been called in from the neighboring towns."

Will glanced at the speedometer and asked, "Is this route well used?"

The man shook his head. "Most traffic will go via Saranac Lake. I doubt we'll see many vehicles on this road at this time of night."

"Then drive faster."

The man accelerated. The car was now quite warm, and Will could feel his clothes defrosting.

The man asked in a strained voice, "What should I say if we're stopped by the police?"

"If we're stopped by the police, you won't have to say anything, because by that time it will be too late for words."

The man darted a look at him. "Who are you?"

"You wouldn't believe me if I told you."

"Well, I can tell that you're not from around here."

Will pressed his gun hard into the man's flabby belly. "Just drive."

There were no road lights on the route. Windshield wipers were straining to try to combat the snowfall, and the car's headlights were their only guide on the lonely road. Soon they were traveling beside a very large lake, which Will saw from road signs was Upper Saranac.

Will looked at the man. "Have you got a map of the state?"

The man nodded toward the dashboard. "My GPS is the best route finder."

"That's no good to me. I just need a map."

"There should be one in the glove compartment."

Will opened the compartment and found the map. He studied it for a while and made a decision. "You're going to drive me to Albany."

The man shook his head. "In this weather that could take up to three hours."

"You'd better drive quickly, then." Will rubbed his face and felt his muscles and skin tingle as coldness within them was replaced with warmth. "What time are you expected home?"

The man shrugged. "In my line of work, I'm often called out at odd times and I often have to stay out for chunks of time." He smiled a little. "I run an airport. Many things go wrong." He glanced at Will. "I'm not going to lie to you and say that my wife will call the police unless I'm back soon."

Will studied the man. He knew that someone would have to be smart to do the job he did, that he would be rapidly assessing Will and his situation just as Will was now assessing him, that the man had just told him the truth because he'd decided that Will would have spotted a lie, and that the man had decided to cooperate with him in full so that he could stay alive and return home safely. But he wondered if the man now suspected that Will was not a criminal, that something unusual was happening in this part of the country.

Will said quietly, "I have no intention of hurting you. Just get me to Albany, leave me there, and go home."

The man chuckled, although he still sounded nervous. "You know I'll call the cops once you're gone."

Will nodded. "Of course you will."

They drove for an hour and saw no other vehicles on the road. They drove for another hour and during that time saw only three vehicles pass them from the opposite direction, but all of them looked normal. Forest and mountains and occasional strips of water straddled their route. Everywhere looked uninhabited.

Will checked his watch. It was now 3:00 A.M. He asked, "How long before we reach Albany?"

"We've made good time. I'd say another twenty to thirty minutes." The man glanced quickly at his rearview mirror and frowned before returning his eyes to the road ahead.

Will instantly looked at the mirror on his side and saw headlights behind them. They were approximately four hundred meters away, but they seemed to be moving fast. He gripped his gun and ordered the man next to him, "Keep going the way you are unless I tell you otherwise."

The lights were drawing closer. Will desperately tried to establish what kind of car the lights belonged to, but the glare and the driving snowfall made his task impossible. The vehicle was now about three hundred meters behind them. Will checked the speedometer. They were currently traveling much faster than the road's speed limit, moving at nearly 150 kilometers per hour. The car behind them was clearly traveling faster.

Will gripped his handgun and said, "Pull over quickly and stop."

The driver's hands tightened on the steering wheel, and he did as Will instructed.

"Turn the engine off and give me the keys." He looked at the man and smiled. "I'm going to get out of the car and wouldn't want you driving off without me."

The man turned off the ignition and handed the keys to Will. Will exited the SUV and walked to the rear. He faced the oncoming vehicle.

He kept his gun hidden in one hand behind his back. He waited.

The vehicle was about two hundred meters away but was still hidden behind its headlights. Will watched it come closer, watched it dip its headlights, moved his gun a little, now clearly saw that the vehicle had the markings of a police car.

Will stood still. The vehicle was now about five hundred feet away. He kept still and waited. It moved toward him until it was three hundred feet away. Will decided that now was the moment for him to act. He dropped into a crouch, swept his gun in front of him, shot the front near-side tire, saw it skid and swerve to the left, shot the front far-side tire, watched the vehicle slump forward a little and swerve back toward the center of the road, sent three shots into the car's engine block, and watched it shudder to a halt. He turned, walked back to the SUV, entered the vehicle, handed the keys to the driver, and said, "Let's go."

The man started the engine, fully depressed the accelerator, and shook his head as the vehicle lunged forward along the road. "What the hell did you just do?"

Will responded calmly, "The occupants of the car behind us were police officers. Things would have been very bad if I'd allowed them to get too close to us. So I just saved their lives." He glanced behind him and saw men exiting the police car, but he knew that they were too far away now for the men to shoot them. But he also knew they would radio for help. "Drive very fast now."

Within ten minutes the lights of the city of Albany were before them. Will looked at the driver. "Are you familiar with this city?"

The driver nodded. "I come here about once a month."

"Good. Use any route you can find to get me into the city, but get off this road as soon as you can."

Within minutes the man took a right turn so that they were on a different road. Within another few minutes, the man had changed roads twice more. Buildings were now around them. The city was now around them.

"Now drive at normal city speed limits." Will pulled the bullet clip out of his gun, checked its contents, and replaced the clip into the MK23. He looked at the man. "Your journey's nearly at an end."

The man glanced down at the gun before looking at Will. He had an expression of pure terror.

Will shook his head. "In a moment you are going to stop your car, watch me get out of it, and walk away. You will then drive home."

The man's fear seemed to recede. "The police told me that you disarmed but didn't kill their colleagues in the village. And I just saw you stop a police vehicle but not harm its occupants. Are you sure I wouldn't believe you if you told me who you are?"

Will slid his gun into his jacket pocket. He pointed ahead. "Stop over there."

The man slowed the vehicle and stopped it on a deserted side street.

Will sighed and looked at the man. "I brought you here at gunpoint, but nevertheless I'm grateful for your help." He drew a deep breath and smiled. "You would not believe me if I told you who I am. But you might believe one thing. In less than twenty-four hours' time, I'm certain all the media channels will be filled with news of an event that will shock the world." His smile faded. "If I fail in my task, that event will be terrible." He steeled his expression. "But if I succeed, the media will tell how a terrible event was averted. Either way, you can watch that news and know that you were part of that story, that for a few hours you helped the man who tried to save hundreds, maybe thousands of lives."

The man looked back at him, narrowed his eyes, and gave the briefest of smiles. "Even though I come here every month, I always get lost in this city. It'll probably take me at least an hour to find a public phone to call the police. By that time, if you keep off the streets for the remaining few hours of darkness, you should be nearly impossible to find in this place."

Will returned the smile and said, "Drive safely." He got out of the vehicle, walked, and then jogged away.

●　●　●　●

He emerged from the shadows of an alley as early-morning sunshine hit the city of Albany. The sidewalks and roads of the metropolis were caked in frozen snow, and the temperature was still well below zero, but the sunlight made the place look picturesque. Will tried to remember when he'd last seen a sky filled with anything other than snow, clouds, or darkness.

He checked his watch and saw that it was nearly 8:00 A.M. He felt his cell phone vibrate in his pocket and pulled it out. Patrick was calling him. He cursed but knew that the CIA man would have spent a sleepless night wondering what was happening, would have broken operational protocol to call him because he was under immense pressure by the president of the United States and the prime minister of Great Britain to give them an update and was one of the few remaining allies Will had. He wondered what to do. He decided, took a deep breath, answered the phone, and spoke before the man on the other end could say anything.

"I am alive, Ben and Julian are dead, Roger and Laith are severely injured and are being kept in the Adirondack Medical Center. You need to get them out of there so that they can be taken to an Agency facility. I am in pursuit of our target, but anything else I say at this moment may compromise this mission."

He closed his phone and turned it off before Patrick could respond.

He looked around him. People and cars were moving on streets and roads, and Will joined them. He decided that he needed to buy new clothes and a few other things to make him look normal. He decided that a flight out of Albany's airport would be too risky. He decided that he would make the final leg of his journey to New York City by train.

Will entered the train's bathroom compartment, shut the door behind him, and locked it. He grabbed a handrail to steady himself as the Amtrak train moved forward toward Manhattan. He placed two shopping bags on the floor and pulled out all the items within

one of them, setting them on a shelf. The contents of both shopping bags had cost him over fifteen hundred dollars and had been
sold to him by Albany shopkeepers who had looked at him as if
he were a homeless man who had wandered into their shops from a
local shelter. He filled the sink full of water, removed his watch, and
stripped naked. He soaked his face and applied gel to his stubble. He
shaved carefully, then rinsed his face. He filled the bowl with fresh
water and used a large towel to soak his entire body. He thrust his
head into the sink water and shampooed his hair, then ran the tap
and rinsed. He brushed his teeth. He used a hand brush to clean his
fingers and under his nails. He dried his head and body with a hand
towel before taking lotions from the shelf and applying them to his
body and face. He squirted men's Chanel Platinum Égoïste eau de
toilette onto his throat, neck, and wrists. He brushed his short hair
and looked at his reflection in the bathroom's small mirror. His face
bore deep lines of fatigue, and his body looked battered, bruised,
and broken. But he now looked and smelled very clean and despite
appearances to the contrary still felt strong and focused. He pulled
out brand-new clothes from one of the other bags and dressed in
underwear, a crisp white French-cuff shirt, a black Hugo Boss suit,
and matching brogues. He looked at the pile of soiled clothes on
the floor and rummaged in their pockets. He pulled out the silenced
Heckler & Koch MK23 handgun, the three spare clips of bullets, a
waterproof plastic envelope containing approximately two thousand
dollars, and his cell phone. He secreted them all into his new suit,
gathered up the soiled clothes, and placed them in one of the empty
bags. He swept the toiletries from the shelf into the other bag, studied himself again in the mirror, decided that he looked good, and
walked out of the compartment carrying the two bags. He dropped
the bags into an empty part of the train car he was now walking
through. He continued forward so that he was heading to the very
front of the train. When he reached the lead car, he chose a vacant
seat, and looked around at the other passengers. They were reading

or talking to one another or looking out the window or sleeping. He checked his watch, and knew that the train would arrive at New York City's Penn Station in fifty minutes.

He wondered if he should sleep. He decided that sleep was the very last thing he needed, given that he might be dead in seven hours' time.

FORTY-NINE

Will stood on a side street just off Broadway in Washington Heights, Manhattan, and decided that the small hotel before him looked perfect. There were backpackers, badly dressed tourists, and dubious-looking women attached to dubious-looking men constantly coming and going from the place. It looked cheap, and its occupants looked cheap. In Will's experience, cheap hotels were anonymous and often the best places to go to disappear from unwanted intrusion or to conduct covert meetings. He stepped across the street and entered the building.

A man stood behind a small reception desk and looked bored as he fiddled with room keys and papers. He glanced up at Will and continued to look bored as Will asked for a room for one night and said that he would be paying with cash. The man took two hundred dollars from Will and asked him for ID. Will told him that he'd lost his ID but was willing to pay him an extra fifty dollars just to get the room. The man hesitated, took the additional money, and gave him a key. He told him that there might or might not be hot water in the room's

bathroom, and that the room's door lock was sometimes a bit temper-
amental. He announced that Will was not allowed visitors in his room
after 7:00 P.M. but that in truth nobody here would give a damn how
many guests he had in his room during the night or when he had them.

Will took the key and walked up narrow creaking stairs to the
hotel's second floor, squeezing past a short-skirted woman with gen-
erously applied makeup as she tottered down the stairway in high
heels. He reached the top of the stairs and saw that his room was
immediately to his right. He fiddled with the door lock until he felt
the bolt snap open and entered the room. It was larger than he expected and had a lounge area, which led to a double bed on the far side of
the room. But the room smelled musty, and aside from the bed it had
only one armchair, a couple of lamps and side tables, a minifridge,
and an old-looking TV. He looked out of the room's window, saw the
daylight of New York, and heard the city's noise.

He pulled out his cell phone and typed a message, which he sent to
Lana's number, knowing that it would not be read by her but instead
would be seen by Megiddo. He told the man where he could find
Nicholas Cree. Will replaced the phone in the inner pocket of his suit
jacket and rubbed his face.

He wondered if tonight a huge hole would be carved into the city
of New York. Then he wondered if that would happen shortly after he
was murdered in this hotel.

FIFTY

The day was darkening.

Lights were being switched on in the city, and its buildings sent shards of white light bouncing off their windows and into Will's hotel room. Will kept his room lights switched off and went to look outside. He stood still and thought of everything that had happened to bring him to this place and everything that could still happen. He looked around the city, peering at the cracks between the buildings, and saw activity everywhere. He wondered if Lana was alive somewhere in the city. He wondered if instead her throat had been cut by Megiddo and her body had been dumped somewhere near Saranac Lake. He decided that he had to believe she was still alive, that Megiddo had to keep her alive, and that she would do everything she could to stay alive.

He heard laughing and shouting and arguing and swearing from other rooms and corridors in the shabby hotel. Doors opened and banged shut, and footsteps ran fast over wooden floorboards and stairs. He looked down at the street and saw a group of six men and women noisily exit the hotel. They seemed drunk, and Will imagined that they were going out to make themselves drunker. He was glad. Their departure meant the hotel was quiet for the moment.

He moved away from the window and wondered whether he should turn on one of the corner lamps. He decided to leave the room in darkness, save for what was visible from the lights that came from outside. He walked to the armchair and picked up his suit jacket.

Then he heard a creak on the stairway.

He put his jacket on and moved to one of the side tables. He picked up his cell phone, turned it off, and placed it within an inner jacket pocket.

The stairs creaked again.

He picked up his wad of cash and carefully secreted it within another pocket. He moved to his bed and looked at his Heckler & Koch MK23 and the three spare magazines that were laid in the center of the bed. He placed the magazines in his trouser pockets.

The stairs creaked again, and this time the noise was closer.

He looked at the gun and wondered if he would ever have a life without guns, and how it would feel to have such a life. He picked up the gun and checked its workings. He tested the weight of it in his hand. One day it might feel good to live a life without weapons. But not today.

The creaking on the stairs was now accompanied by audible, deliberate, and slow footfalls.

Will turned from his bed and looked at the room. Outside, it was now total night. Thin streaks of white city light slashed diagonally through the window and across his room and illuminated dust particles in the air. It reminded Will of the way Harry's corridor had looked moments before Will had been shot in the head.

The footsteps were very close now. They clearly belonged to one person.

Will breathed in deeply and suddenly felt very calm. He felt as if everything outside this room was artificial; all that mattered was this room. He exhaled slowly, shut his eyes, and smiled. When he opened his eyes again, his smile was gone.

The footsteps stopped outside his door.

Will gripped his gun and raised it to eye level, pointing at the door. He waited, knowing that it was now 6:00 P.M., that now was the most important moment in his life, that it was the most important moment in many lives.

He held his gun steady and knew that directly outside his door was a deadly mastermind called Megiddo.

FIFTY-ONE

The doorknob groaned as it turned slowly.

Will stood very still five meters away from the entrance. He kept his gun held high, pointing at the door. Outside his room he heard traffic, voices on the streets, distant sirens, and the overall hum of a nighttime city that was alive and energetic. Inside his room everything was different. It was quiet, and the night and the light made everything either black or white.

Thin diagonal blades of white light traversed the unlit room through the window blinds, flickered, and seemed to be cutting the room into slices. Will looked through those blades and moved one foot forward so that he was poised to shoot. The knob groaned louder, and the door moved open an inch. Yellow light from the hotel corridor was framed by the partially opened door. An icy breeze that had clearly traveled up the stairway from the streets below entered the room. Despite his having spent weeks in freezing temperatures, the air seemed colder than anything he had felt before.

The white light flickered and moved to different parts of the room.

Will remained motionless, carefully controlled his breathing, and waited.

A final gust of the dreadfully cold air hit him in the face as the door swung open wide, showing the silhouette of a man before slamming shut and sending the doorway into total darkness.

Will knew that the man was now in the room.

For the briefest of moments, the city became utterly silent, the outside world seeming to pause and hold its breath.

Will said calmly, "Show yourself."

Nothing happened. The white lights darted around the room but kept away from the door.

"Show yourself."

Will heard a foot tread on the room's floorboards. He heard something breathing. Something moving very slowly.

The white light flickered wildly but still did not go near the door. There was another step. And another.

The man appeared in the frenzied light.

Will's heart pumped fast, but his mind felt focused. He pointed his gun at the man's face, at a man who was as tall as he was, had slicked-back black hair, a smooth face, and black eyes, at the man he had seen looking down at him from the mountain outside Saranac Lake but who was now holding a handgun pointed straight at Will's head.

The light settled and seemed resigned to providing snapshot images of the man. It showed a man wearing a tailored dark suit and an open-collared white shirt, a man who looked slender but very powerful, a man who was dressed like Will but was many years older, a man who looked totally in control of himself and all around him.

The man took another step forward and stopped. He looked straight at Will's eyes. His gun hand was absolutely steady. His face showed no expression, no emotion.

"You know who I am?" he said.

The man's voice was deep, polished, and barely accented.

Will did not move. "I do."

The man nodded. "But you do not know why I am here."

"No, but I do know that while you are here, you will try to kill me."

"And I know that you will try to stop me from doing that and try to stop me from doing anything ever again."

The two men were three meters away from each other. They were both very still. Their guns were at exactly the same level.

Will ran a finger over the trigger.

The man breathed in slowly through his nose before speaking again. "At every step of my journey to this room, I have felt your presence. You have exceeded my expectations. You have proved to be the most worthy opponent." He angled his head. "You have intrigued me, gained my admiration, and shown me that you never stop." His smile vanished, and he looked very intense. "At first you inconvenienced me. Later you slowed me down. Finally you took nearly everything away from me." He breathed deeply. "But I never fail. I am not a man like other men." His eyes widened and looked filled with death. "I am Megiddo."

Time stood still.

Will kept his gun pointed at Megiddo's forehead. He knew that if he lost any focus, the man could kill him. "Do you know what I want?"

Megiddo smiled, but his expression was very cold. "You want my secret and my life." He shook his head slightly. "I am willing to give you one of those things." His smile vanished. "But I will not give you both."

"We will see."

"We will indeed."

Will took one step toward Megiddo. "I, too, never fail. I, too, am not like other men."

Megiddo took one step toward Will. "I can see that, Will Cochrane."

Will felt his stomach tighten. He gripped his gun tighter.

Megiddo bared white teeth. Light flickered over his face.

Will breathed slowly and spoke with a commanding voice. "Very few people know my real name. How are you one of them?"

Megiddo shook his head. "You will have some of my secrets, but not all of them."

Will kept his eyes fixed on Megiddo. He would not blink. He dared not blink.

"What is your mission?" Megiddo asked.

"I should ask you the same question."

"You will in a moment."

Will narrowed his eyes. "My mission is to stop you from killing others."

Megiddo snapped, "What else?"

Will raised his own voice. "That is the mission, and that is what I will do."

"What you want to do is determined by many factors, and not just because you fear that others will be killed by my hand."

For the briefest of moments, Will wondered whether he should end this now and send a bullet into Megiddo's skull.

Megiddo stared at him. "Lower your weapon, Mr. Cochrane. I will do the same. Our intentions toward each other are in danger of killing words that need to be spoken."

Will remained still.

So did Megiddo. "I could have killed you in Sarajevo. I could have killed you on the mountain. I could have killed you on the street in the village of Saranac Lake. But I chose not to for a reason. Instead I chose to come here to talk to you. Only after that is done will I pull my trigger. So let us lower our weapons together and not fear each other for a few important moments."

Will stared at Megiddo and wondered if the other man was trying to trick him. He decided that he was not. "Together."

Megiddo nodded.

They kept their guns still for a moment, each staring at the other's weapon. Then they simultaneously made the tiniest of movements until the handguns were moving down at the same pace and were by their sides.

But they kept their guns firm in their grips. Will knew that when the guns were raised again, one of them would be dead. He recalled Laith's words.

The man was so fucking fast, so damned deadly.

Megiddo nodded. "Why else is your mission so important to you?"

Light moved again and exposed different aspects of Megiddo's face. It showed a handsome man with features that suggested immense intelligence but also deadly intent, knowledge, coldness, experience, death, and some other things that Will could not yet define. It was a face of contradictions and hidden depths.

Will exhaled slowly. "Saving lives is what matters to me."

"For a man like you, I am sure it is all you have to explain your existence."

"A man like me does not need to explain his existence to a man like you."

Megiddo shook his head. "True. But you are also a man who is now driven by vengeance . . . a vengeance that must be fulfilled, a vengeance that requires my death."

Will felt his heart miss a beat. "Then you will know why I demand vengeance."

"I do."

Anger raged through his body. "Why did you kill my father?"

Megiddo looked at Will's gun before looking at his face. "One of the two reasons I am here is to answer that question. But before I do so, I should ask you whether you have ever killed fathers. I'm sure you have. I know you have."

Will shook his head and muttered through clenched teeth, "If they were bad men, yes. But I've never savaged a man in the way you savaged my father."

Megiddo smiled.

Will fought every urge in his body to kill the man before him.

Both men stood still.

Will breathed deeply. "Why is *your* mission important to you? Why do you wish to commit a massacre?"

Megiddo smiled. "The massacre is not important to me. It will merely be the result of what is important to me." His eyes darted toward the window and New York City before looking quickly back at Will. "I hold the rank of general in the IRGC Qods Force. I have been the strategist behind every major Iranian terrorist attack during the last few years. Those attacks have been deemed by others within Iran to be an important means to further the country's ambitions in the Middle East and beyond." His eyes narrowed. "But more important than the ambitions of others, the attacks have increased my power and influence within my country. This massacre will cement my power. It is going to be my masterpiece."

Will thought for a moment. "But a masterpiece needs a master artist who is seen and recognized by others. Aside from a tiny number of Iranian leaders, nobody will know that you are the mastermind behind your attack."

For a mere instant, Megiddo's face filled with anger.

Will made ready to sweep his gun upward.

But then Megiddo's anger receded. "You are right. And that is the other reason I am here. I have chosen to make you my audience, to tell you what I am going to do." He flashed a brief smile. "It matters not to me, because you are too late to stop me, and in any case I am going to kill you."

Will kept still.

Megiddo took a small step toward Will. "There is a children's concert at the Metropolitan Opera House in this city. There will be four thousand attendees and performers, and most of them, naturally, will be children. The concert is sponsored by a wealthy Middle Eastern foundation and is intended to promote peace, learning, and intercultural compassion within the Gulf and Levant regions. The concert will start at eight this evening. My bombs will destroy the child performers and everyone else in the building at nine P.M."

Will felt his stomach tighten. "That is an indiscriminate atrocity."

Megiddo chuckled softly. "Not indiscriminate." His face hardened. "Certain women, Mr. Cochrane, are the real targets. There are to be guests of honor at the event. The wives of the Emirati, Syrian, Saudi, Egyptian, American, and British premiers attending Camp David. And the wife of the Iranian president." Megiddo smiled. "Her husband is not allowed into this country, but she has been invited as a gesture of goodwill."

"The premiers' wives?" Will felt incredulous.

Megiddo had no expression. "I will destroy the place in the same way I would have destroyed the German government"—he shrugged nonchalantly—"had that not merely been a ruse intended to throw you off my scent. A ruse you uncovered."

Will silently cursed as he remembered the devices that the German GSG 9 assault squad had found in the attic of the house in Berlin's Onlauer Street, bombs that contained combined thermite cutting agents and explosives so that they could propel fire through any material, including concrete and steel, and destroy everything around them.

Megiddo looked at him intently. "I managed to get employment passes for the opera house so that my bombers could pose as cleaners within the building. They planted their tiny numerous bombs over the course of several days. The building will have been swept today by antiterrorist police with their equipment and sniffer dogs, but they will not have found the bombs. They are too well hidden, away from scent, sight, or special detectors."

Will shook his head. "You plan to burn everyone in the Metropolitan Opera House to death? Why?"

"No doubt you find it utterly abhorrent that I am prepared to kill four thousand people, most of them children, as well as the wives of the premiers. But that is not my endgame, my masterpiece. No, my masterpiece will be of a far more epic scale."

Will waited.

"The collective attendance of the premiers' wives is unprecedented and has been organized amid grave concerns from their husbands that should anything happen to the women, the results could be catastrophic. But the American security services have given the Arab leaders an assurance that nothing will happen to their wives in this country." Megiddo chuckled. "It was a very cavalier and foolish assurance."

Will felt a sudden sickness as a realization struck him. "The Arab and Persian populations of the premiers' countries would blame the West for any attack on the women."

"They would indeed." He nodded. "I live in a part of the world that is deeply conspiratorial. The fact that the First Lady and the wife of the British premier were killed in an assault would not matter to most people from my world. They would see that as simply a devious means to cover the West's hand in the attack."

"But you're also going to kill the wife of the Iranian president. How can you allow that to happen?"

Megiddo leaned forward. "She needs to be sacrificed. No fingers must be pointed at Iran. The president of my country knows nothing about the attack. I have ensured that." He was enjoying himself. "The concerns expressed to the United States by the Arab premiers were simple and blunt: Should anything happen to their wives, then the populations of their country would blame the United States. The Arab premiers and their administrations would try to calm their countrymen and tell them that the United States was not behind the attack, but their people would not believe them, would think they were weak and puppets of the West. And they would rise up fueled by anger and hatred toward them and the United States."

"There would be revolutions, regime changes, armies mobilized." Will shook his head. "Chaos and war."

"Not total chaos," Megiddo corrected him. "Iran would remain strong and would be the only nation whose leadership blamed the West for the attack. But the Arab nations would tear themselves apart before transforming themselves into new regimes that were steadfast allies of my country. Iran's former Arab enemies will unite with us against the United States and its supporters. They will engage in total war against the West. It will be genocide, and hundreds of thousands, maybe millions, will be killed in the battles that will follow."

Will gritted his teeth but spoke calmly. "Nuclear weapons would be deployed to stop this from happening."

Megiddo shook his head. "Only Israel will deploy nuclear weapons. The former Soviet Union and Asian and European countries will strengthen their borders, and fight terrible battles there. But as long as the Middle East is contained by those countries, they will not risk deploying their nuclear weapons in case we have the capability to do the same. And America will not deploy nuclear weapons for fear of our striking back at its European NATO allies. But Israel will certainly send missiles into Syria and Egypt, missiles that will kill thousands of people. That will result in the destruction of Israel. It will be defeated by the sheer weight of Arab and Persian armies as they sweep through the country. The other battles will then stop, and although many will have lost their lives, the loss will have been worth it for the result—the result that will be an all-powerful Middle East. A superpower whose leadership resides in the Iranian capital of Tehran."

"And no doubt you will part of that leadership," Will concluded.

Megiddo smiled. "My intention is to be at the very pinnacle of that leadership, to be president of a superpower."

Will gripped his gun hard. "Where is Lana? Is she alive?"

"For now she is alive. But she will soon die with the children and the premiers' wives. She is tied up in the basement of the Metropolitan Opera House." He watched for Will's reaction. "I want her to burn alive. I want her to scream in agony as flames destroy her pretty face.

I want her to suffer for thinking that she could deliver a man like me to a man like you."

Will felt as if he'd been punched in the stomach. He swallowed fast to fight back an overwhelming need to be sick. He breathed slowly to try to calm his body and mind. He knew that he had to remain in control. He knew that everything relied on his staying in charge of his emotions. "You said that the other reason for your being here was to tell me why you murdered my father."

"Murdered?" Megiddo frowned. "I did not murder him. I executed him."

"Whatever words you use, my father was killed by your hand."

Megiddo nodded. "He was. I killed him because he killed *my* father."

"What do you mean?"

Megiddo shrugged. "Your father was part of a small CIA contingent, based in Tehran, during the lead-up to the Iranian revolution in 1979. The CIA supported the shah and had no desire to see the revolutionaries succeed in overthrowing him. They worked closely with the shah's inner circle to protect him and to feed intelligence to the shah's regime to help him try to thwart his opponents. In the course of their work, the CIA men discovered that there was a high-ranking traitor within the shah's inner circle. That traitor was my father. The CIA men exposed my father, and he was brutally killed by the shah's SAVAK intelligence organization." Megiddo's eyes took on a faraway look. "When I found out what had happened, I constructed a plan to seek my revenge on the CIA men who had caused the death of my father. I posed as a revolutionary defector, approached the American embassy, discovered that there were only two CIA men still operating in Tehran, discovered that one of them was the more senior of the two, decided that it had to be that man who had uncovered my father's secret work, told them that I wanted to get out of Iran while I still could and that in return would tell them everything about the revolutionaries' intentions for a newly built Iran.

"The two American men and an MI6 officer took me in a car toward Bandar-e 'Abbâs," he continued. "I thought that's where they would go, and in any case I had ensured that roadblocks were set up on Iran's main roads to its borders and coastline. The younger CIA man and the MI6 man escaped, but your father was captured by soldiers from the Bandar-e 'Abbâs roadblock. He was kept in captivity for years, and I later visited him in Evin Prison and spoke to him." He smiled. "Despite what I did to him, he never admitted that his information had caused the death of my father. He was a very brave man and would not say anything about his work." And then the smile was once again gone. "But that bravery was not enough to stop me from hating him and ending his life." He nodded at Will and spoke quietly. "He did, however, inadvertently betray one important piece of information about himself. He called out the name of his son at the end. He called your name as I tore out his stomach."

Will gritted his teeth.

Megiddo's eyes seemed even blacker. "The shah's SAVAK did not just brutally kill my father. They also killed my mother, my sisters, and my brothers." He nodded slowly. "You can therefore imagine my delight when I discovered that the MI6 man pursuing me over the last few weeks was none other than the son of the CIA man whose information had caused the death of my entire family."

Will fought to control his breathing. "There was no way he could have known that his information would have resulted in the death of your family."

Anger flashed across Megiddo's face. "He was an intelligence officer working alongside a brutal, corrupt, and desperate regime. He would have known *exactly* what actions could have been taken based upon his information about my father."

Will shouted, "He was doing his job! Working alongside one abhorrent regime and witnessing the rise of an even worse one. He would not have enjoyed the decisions he had to make. But he was there to make decisions and was no doubt under orders to do any-thing he could to slow down the shah's collapse until the Arab neigh-bors of Iran could complete their preparations to protect themselves from the new Iranian regime."

Megiddo spat, "Justify your father's actions in any way you see fit. It makes no difference to me, because he still caused the slaughter of my family."

Will flexed his muscles and felt the weight of the gun. He frowned as he recalled Patrick telling him that his father had entered Iran for the first time three weeks before his capture. He asked quietly, "When was your father killed?"

Megiddo's eyes glared at him. "Two months before we captured your father."

Anger raged through Will. He imagined plunging a knife into Megiddo's stomach. He imagined doing to the man what the man had done to his father; imagined taking him apart piece by piece. He shouted, "My father was not in Iran when your father's secret work was exposed to the shah! He was not the CIA officer whose intelligence caused your father to be killed. He arrived in Iran only twenty-one days before you captured him. You murdered him for no reason!"

Megiddo frowned and stood very still. "You are lying to me in a futile attempt to justify your father's actions."

Will lowered his voice. "If I were, I would also be lying to myself."

Megiddo considered this. Then he asked quietly, "Do you know the identity of the other CIA man who took me in the car to Bandar-e 'Abbâs?"

Will nodded. "I do, and you'll never learn his name."

Megiddo smiled, but the look was very bitter. He seemed to think for a long time. "Well, that matters not now. Even though it would have been perfect if I could have taken revenge against my father's murderer by killing his family, just as he killed mine." He seemed to be tasting his own anger. "It would have been perfect." He breathed deeply, and the anger seemed to go. "But it appears that my presence here has been pointless."

Will frowned. "You may not be facing the son of your father's killer. But you came here for another reason as well. You came here to make me the audience for your masterpiece."

Megiddo looked hesitant. "Yes . . . yes, that as well." He looked away for a brief moment and shook his head. "Everything changed for me when I lost my father."

"As it did for me."

The two men locked gazes.

Then Megiddo's expression steeled, and he spoke in a deep, harsh voice. "And so here we both are, men who excel at things because we have nothing in our lives to give us peace, men who are very alike."

Will steeled his own gaze. "You wish to kill millions of people and cause mayhem and the destruction of borders to gain power and control over the Middle East. We are not alike. You are a monster. And I am here to kill you."

"And I you."

The room was silent and dark.

Will knew that no more words would be spoken. He knew that now was the time to finally settle matters with Megiddo. He studied Megiddo's eyes and saw how cold they looked, he heard the man's breathing slow down, he felt his presence and his strength. He knew that the man was watching him just as closely, looking for any indication that Will would raise his gun just as Will was looking for such signs from him. Will used his breath to steady his body and prepare to move his gun with absolute speed and accuracy. He decided to take three more breaths of air before holding his breath to shoot. He desperately wanted to see any signal from Megiddo that would tell him the man was going to move first—a flicker of his eyes, a change of expression, an adjustment of his stance, anything. But Megiddo was motionless. Will breathed. He saw Megiddo do the same. Will took another lungful of air. So did Megiddo. Will took his third breath. Megiddo stopped breathing.

Will knew that was the sign. Megiddo was about to raise his gun and shoot him.

For one second nothing happened.

In the next second everything began and ended.

Megiddo moved his gun with lightning speed. Will moved his arm upward, pulled his trigger, and dropped his body slightly lower. He heard his gunshot and Megiddo's gunshot simultaneously. He felt a rush of air over his head. He saw Megiddo's mouth open slightly and knew that Megiddo had missed his target.

He watched his bullet strike Megiddo in the center of his head.

FIFTY-TWO

Will ran south down Broadway. He ran past groups of pedestrians, he ran between moving cars, he ran as snow began falling gently from the sky, he ran in a nighttime that was brightly illuminated by the city's lights.

He checked his watch and cursed the crowds and traffic. He cursed everything that was slowing his attempt to get to the Metropolitan Opera House. What was the fastest way south? He knew a subway could work, but he could also be waiting on a platform—and he had no stomach for that. He knew his only hope was finding a cab.

As he ran, he wondered what he should do. He knew that under other circumstances the correct thing for him to do would be to call Patrick and instruct the man to get the FBI Critical Incident Response Group to take over what was now a federal police matter. It would secure the area around the opera house, and it would have drills and procedures to evacuate the building while simultaneously searching for terrorists and bombs. But Will was unsure if that was the right thing to do, because he was sure something was wrong. Something had been said by Megiddo that did not sound right. He knew what it was.

I will make you my audience.

He sprinted across an intersection blocked with traffic, still keeping his eye out for a south-bound cab. And he desperately tried to think. He knew that Megiddo was not the type of man who needed an audience. He knew that the man had told him about his plan for another reason. But he could not grasp what that reason was. He wondered whether Megiddo had simply fed him another lie and had bombs planted at a different location. He concluded that made no sense at this stage, as Megiddo would have forced Lana to confess everything, including the fact that Will did not really have information that could thwart his plot. He wondered if Megiddo had *wanted* his plot foiled and maybe even had a desire to stop the death of the children and wives and, ultimately, millions of others. But he recalled the look of death in Megiddo's eyes and knew that the man had no intention of stopping his attack.

He cursed, then saw a cab turning onto Broadway half a block ahead and knew he had to catch it. Another sprint later, he caught it as it slowed down at a stop light. He jumped in and told the driver "Lincoln Center. As fast as you can."

He kept thinking, trying to outthink Megiddo, reminding himself that the man was a mastermind, telling himself that the man did everything for a reason, would have left nothing to chance, and would have thought through every possible potential outcome.

Megiddo told me about his plan because he knew that if I killed him, I would take action to stop the bombs from detonating at 9:00 P.M. He wanted me to be in the opera house or, if not, close to it when bombs went off. He wanted me to suffer, because he thought I was the son of his father's killer. But I am not. And that was why he finally concluded that his presence in the hotel room was pointless.

He knew he was right. And he also knew that even though Megiddo was dead, he was still outsmarting him.

Why was Megiddo so confident that he would succeed no matter what I did?

He closed his eyes for a moment as the answer banged into his brain.

Megiddo has a bomber in the building. That man took Lana into the building earlier in the day and is watching over her. That man is there to detonate the bombs ahead of 9:00 P.M. if I or the FBI tries to evacuate the building. The man is prepared to die by his own hand.

He opened his eyes, saw the city racing past him, and he felt hopeless.

Traffic and sidewalk crowds were growing as they got closer. He checked his watch and saw that it was just after 7:30 P.M. The concert would begin in less than thirty minutes. Bombs would destroy the place in less than ninety minutes.

The cab slowed as traffic became heavier. Will looked around. He could see glimpses of trees beyond two blocks to the east. They belonged to Central Park. He would never think of that place and not think of Soroush. Every place in New York now reminded him of Soroush.

He forced the recollection out of his mind to focus on what was happening here.

By the time the cab got to Sixty-Ninth Street, it was bumper to bumper traffic, so he threw some cash at the driver and got out to run the rest of the way. He dodged pedestrians for several more blocks, then stopped to get his bearings, bent over, and sucked in a lungful of air. When he stood up, a bus pulled away from the curb and revealed the massive glass-fronted Alice Tully Hall and the Juilliard School right in front of him, only one more block to the south. He knew The Metropolitan Opera House would be just beyond, slightly to the west.

When he made it to Lincoln Center Plaza, crowds of people were outside the front of the Met, and it was clear that they were there for the concert. Most were children, and they were being marshaled into groups by supervising adults wearing different-colored fluorescent jackets bearing the names of various schools or clubs. Everyone was dressed in coats and other warm clothes as protection from the cold and snow, and some held umbrellas. Gradually the crowds were organized into long, snaking lines that curled across the open plaza and around the brightly illuminated fountains. The supervisors moved back and forth, barking instructions at the children, and they were no doubt anxious to get their wards out of the cold and into the building as quickly as possible. Will slowed to a walk and moved among the crowds. He felt his hidden Heckler & Koch MK23 brush against his hip bone as he did so.

He stopped and knew that he needed to make a decision, even if it was the wrong one. He decided the FBI could not be involved because its arrival here would be too visible, that he had to enter the building covertly and alone, hope that he was not seen by the bomber, and finish this one way or the other.

He moved close to the building's entrances and saw members of the opera house's staff standing by them. He turned and looked back at the crowds. He saw five lines of children and their supervisors, and he saw a sixth line that contained only adults. He looked away from the lines that led to the house's entrances and examined adults who were not part of any lines. Many were clearly parents of the children standing in the lines, waving and calling to their sons and daughters. A small number were media types and were taking photographs or using video cameras or holding microphones. Some seemed to be passing tourists or New Yorkers who were taking in the evening spectacle. Some *looked* like parents or media types or passing tourists or random New Yorkers, but Will's trained eye could see that they were none of those things. He saw one of them, then another, then counted six of them before deciding that there were nine of them spaced out in the plaza area before the building. They were not wearing their trademark and recognizable black suits and lapel pins but instead were dressed like anyone else in this weather. They were Secret Service and were clearly here because of all the VIPs. And they were clearly positioned among the crowds to search for bad people or people like Will.

Will looked around in frustration. He was in danger of appearing out of place and therefore being identified by one of the Secret Service men or women. They would have no hesitation in trying to put him on the ground with guns pointed at him for simply looking as though he shouldn't be there. They were trained to be some of the quickest and deadliest shooters in the world, although he knew he would be quicker and deadlier than all of them put together. But if a confrontation ensued, the bomber might be warned that something was happening.

He walked casually away from the plaza so that he was looking down one side of the opera house. Police were gathered there, and they stood alongside barricades that stopped pedestrians from getting too close to the building. Will swore under his breath, although he had expected all but the main entrances to be sealed off and protected. He moved to the other side of the building and saw more barricades and more police and also more Secret Service men and women. He stood for a while watching them. He stood as one limousine, two unmarked cars, and four police vehicles pulled up to the side of the building. He saw doors open and men exit and stand by their stationary vehicles as a group of four indistinguishable women walked quickly from the limousine into the opera house. He watched the cavalcade move off quickly. Within an additional ten minutes, three more cavalcades came and went after offloading three more women. Will walked back to the front of the house, knowing that the premiers' wives were now in the building.

The lines were moving forward, and Will estimated that at least half of the crowd was now inside. He checked his watch again and saw that the concert was due to start in minutes. He heard the staff members by the entrances call to their crowds to keep moving forward, saw the children's supervisors liaise with them while holding clusters of tickets and sheets of paper, and watched uniformed police officers walking slowly through the crowds.

He knew that he was running out of time and options. He felt his handgun press hard against his body, and he decided he had to get rid of the weapon. He looked around, saw a garbage can, walked to it, and quickly dropped the gun and spare bullet clips inside. He walked slowly back to the center of the plaza and looked at the line containing only adults. There were approximately three hundred people in the line. Most of them were couples and therefore of no use to him, as he knew that they were most likely parents of either child performers or spectators and therefore would never give up their space in the line. But a handful of them were solitary adults, and Will looked up and down the line at them. He wasted no time in moving toward the line.

He approached a man who looked to be in his midthirties. "Do you have a ticket?"

The man frowned at Will and no doubt briefly wondered whether he was an official before deciding he was not. "Of course. Why?"

Will shrugged and nodded toward the opera house. "My daughter's playing in there tonight." He shook his head. "I only found out two days ago. My ex-wife didn't feel like telling me. I would do anything to see her perform, but I know the event's sold out. Would you sell me your ticket?"

The man looked sympathetic. "Tough break. But I'm here with *The New York Times* to write a review of the concert, so unless that's something you could do in my absence, I'm going to have to decline your request."

Will nodded, thanked the man anyway, and moved farther up the line. He spotted a woman and gave her the same story. The woman told him to get lost.

He walked up to a man who looked to be in his sixties and was clearly suffering from the cold, with his arms wrapped around his torso. Will said, "Cold night."

The man said, "Damn right."

Will said, "My daughter's playing in there tonight. I'm sure she'd love to see me in the audience. Could I buy your ticket?"

The man said, "My granddaughter's playing in there tonight. That's why I've spent forty minutes out here freezing my ass off, and I'm not about to move an inch away from this line."

Will felt frustration coursing through him as he again looked up and down the line. He spotted a solitary adult toward the front and walked over to him. The man was very young, maybe only twenty, and was dressed like a student. Will said, "I'll give you a thousand dollars for your ticket."

The man looked at him in surprise. "A thousand dollars?"

Will nodded.

The man frowned, looked unsure, then repeated, "A thousand dollars?"

Will spoke in a stern voice. "In ten seconds you can walk away from this line with that cash in your pocket. But if you don't want it, I'm sure someone else here does."

The young man shook his head quickly and thrust his hand into his coat pocket. "Here." He showed Will his ticket.

Will put his hand into his suit pocket, pulled out the plastic envelope that he knew contained just over two thousand dollars, looked at it, and said, "It's a bit more than I told you. Take it and go."

They exchanged the ticket and the cash, and Will joined the line. The young man walked quickly away.

Will was approximately ten meters from the opera house's entrance. He pulled up the collar of his suit jacket and stamped his feet on the ground while hugging his chest to try to make him look cold to any observers. Officials kept calling, telling people to move forward. Nearly all the children were in the building now, and the plaza area was no longer crowded. Will casually looked around the place. The nine Secret Service men and women had all moved position but were still on the plaza. He looked toward the entrance and saw glimpses of the inside of the building. He saw people in his line move through a metal detector and felt huge relief that he had disposed of his weapon.

As people entered the building, Will shuffled forward until he was five meters from the entrance. He turned a little to look back up the line. His eyes narrowed as he saw the woman whom he had earlier approached take two steps away from the line and talk to a police officer. She was about forty meters from Will, looked up and down the line, shrugged her shoulders, and stepped back into the line. The police officer spoke on his radio. Will immediately fixed his eyes on one of the plainclothes Secret Service men. The man was very still for a moment before walking quickly toward one of his colleagues. Will's heart beat faster. He knew that the woman had reported his approach to her as suspicious and that all security officials in the vicinity of the opera house would now be aware of that approach. He turned to face the entrance and shuffled forward a couple of yards.

There were three people in front of him now. Will pulled out his ticket and breathed carefully to calm himself. The ticket attendant by the door looked stressed and grabbed tickets with one hand while waving people through the doorway with the other. Will took a step forward as the three people in front of him became two. He glanced over his shoulder and saw a police officer walking slowly along the line, examining every man and women standing behind Will. He looked away from the line and saw that four of the Secret Service people had moved closer to the line. He willed the line to move more quickly. The two people in front of him became one, and Will stamped his feet to make himself look colder. The man in front of him handed his ticket to the attendant and walked in.

Will took a deep breath and smiled as he handed his ticket to the official. He exhaled slowly as he stepped into the opera house.

He moved through the metal detector, stopped, calmly looked at the officials who were monitoring the detector, saw them nod at him, and then walked on. He moved quickly, knowing that other attendees who were not yet seated were doing the same. He glanced at his ticket, saw that he was supposed to be seated on one of the balcony aisles and that he would need to walk up the sweeping red-carpeted stairway to reach his place. But he had no intention of going there and instead walked onward at ground level, scouring doors to his left and right. People were all around him, and some seemed to know where they were going and some not. He moved forward and wished that he'd had time to study the layout of the huge building he was in. But he was grateful that he was not the only one who didn't not know the layout, and for a while he hid among the ranks of the lost.

He moved along a corridor until he was away from other people and door entrances to the auditorium. He moved on until he was alone. He reached a door that said NO ADMITTANCE, STAFF ONLY. He looked back down the corridor. Nobody was looking at him. He swiveled back to face the door, turned the handle, opened it, and walked through. Narrow stairs were immediately ahead of him. He walked quickly down them until he knew he was in a part of the building that was below stage level. A slender corridor was before him, with other corridors leading away from it to its left and right. Everywhere was dimly illuminated. A corridor on his right was lined with lockers that he imagined were used by performers, as was another corridor on his left. He kept walking.

He stopped suddenly as a huge sound came from above him. His heart pounded. He realized the sound was the start of the concert. He could now clearly hear instruments and singing. His heartbeat slowed, and he kept going. The music quieted.

There were more corridors to his left and right. Some had signs and arrows directing him to rehearsal rooms, management offices, changing rooms. Will imagined that before the concert this whole subterranean floor would have been bustling with performers getting ready, officials fretting about schedules and timings, backstage well-wishers, and crews that would move curtains and stage pulleys and manhandle props on and off the stage. But right now the labyrinth of rooms around him seemed empty.

Rapid footsteps suddenly told him that the place was *not* empty. He looked around quickly, trying to ascertain where the steps were coming from. He decided they were behind him but heading in his direction. He jogged forward and darted left into yet another corridor. He stopped, swiveled, crouched, and wished he still had his gun. The footsteps grew louder, and he realized they belonged to more than one person. Police officers? Secret Service? As the footsteps drew nearer, he bunched his right hand into a fist and waited, briefly wondering what he would do if armed officials found him here. He decided he would have no choice other than to inflict rapid, absolute, but nonlethal pain on them and render them unconscious.

The footsteps were nearly directly in front of him now, and Will clenched his fist tighter, braced his body to move fast, and focused solely on the corridor ahead and the other corridor traversing it. The footsteps slowed. Will got ready.

A woman and a girl appeared at the end of the corridor. Will exhaled slowly and unclenched his fist. The woman had her arms around the girl and seemed to be consoling her. The girl was wearing a black dress and a white blouse and was crying. She carried a flute.

They stopped, and the woman told her, "It's called stage fright. I used to get it when I was your age. Let's find you a warm drink and see if you feel like going back out there afterward."

They walked away from Will's position, and soon they were gone. He stood upright and looked around. He decided that he was in the wrong place. He decided that the bomber would be hidden someplace where he could not be accidentally found by innocents. He moved on, and the noise of the concert grew louder as he went.

He tried to imagine the layout of a building like this and what it would need to support it and keep it running. He decided that the Metropolitan Opera House would need power generators and air-conditioning and heating units and thick pillars to support its stage and overall structure. He could see that most of those things were not on this floor. He knew that there had to be another floor beneath him and that it would be the perfect place for the bomber to wait while holding Lana captive.

He rubbed his face and desperately tried not to think about Lana, her condition now, and whether she was even still alive. He tried not to think of anything that would hinder his focus and concentration to stop the most terrible event.

Lights flashed to his right, and Will instinctively pushed himself against a wall. The lights were close and moved over floor and ceiling. He knew that they were flashlights, that in a place like this flashlights were unusual and would be carried only by officials who were looking for something. He decided that the officials had to be looking for him and were probably armed. He turned and ran away from them along the corridor he was in. He moved into an area of shadows and looked back down the corridor he'd just covered. He saw two men dressed in windbreakers, jeans, and hiking boots. They were carrying handguns. He couldn't see their faces clearly, but they were dressed like the Secret Service men he'd spotted outside the opera house. They hadn't seen him, but he knew that if he stayed where he was, he would be found.

He moved deeper into the shadows, turned into another corridor, jogged silently along it, past empty rooms and other corridors, and stopped. The lights were some distance behind him but had now separated. Will looked at the ceiling above him. Judging by the sounds coming from it, he knew he had to be directly under the stage. He ran along another corridor and estimated that he was close to one of the building's exterior walls. He looked at every opening and every doorway near him, desperately searching for a route that would take him down to the opera house's basement.

He ran to the end of the corridor and stopped. A door was before him that had a sign saying MAINTENANCE ONLY. He was about to move to the door when light struck the floor only a few feet in front of him. He silently moved backward and sidestepped into a corridor on his right. He stood still and watched the floor near him. He could still see the flashlight, and it was getting very close. The music above him grew, and Will cursed the noise as it obliterated any chance of his hearing the movement of the men on this floor. He breathed in deeply and tensed his muscles to lunge forward if the man closest to him turned into his corridor. The flashlight moved left and right over the floor and walls. It came closer. Will stayed still.

He saw the gun before he saw the man. It moved slowly across his vision and was almost within arm's reach. The gun stopped for a moment and then moved forward. The man stepped into view and walked carefully along the corridor. Will pushed himself flush against a wall, even though he knew he would be seen if the man looked hard left in his direction. But the man kept walking and soon disappeared from view.

Will waited for thirty seconds before stepping carefully forward to the edge of the corridor containing the Secret Service man. He lowered himself down so that he was not at eye level and quickly poked his head out into the corridor before pulling it back. The Secret Service man was gone. Will slowly moved out and ran low toward the door for maintenance men.

He carefully shut the door behind him and saw stairs heading down. He took them, and with every step the sounds from the concert above him grew quieter. He reached the subbasement and now more than ever wished he were armed. He looked around him and knew that this was a perfect place to hide Lana. And he knew that it was also a perfect place for Megiddo's bomber to wait and detonate his bombs ahead of schedule if anything happened.

The area around him had large, square metal vents jutting out of its roof and traveling at head height through space before reentering the roof at different points. Big generators were positioned nearby, humming in a low drone. He saw thick steel pillars that reached from floor to ceiling and assumed they supported the opera house's stage and everything on it. He saw wall-mounted fixtures and occasional ceiling fixtures, but the light here was even dimmer than that on the floor above. He looked back up the staircase and wondered if the Secret Service men would soon open the door and search this basement. He looked around the vast area before him and wondered if there were other routes into this place. He decided that there had to be other entrances, that the Secret Service men could use any of those routes to find him here, and that they would know every inch of the place.

He checked his watch. It was now 8:20 P.M.

He walked forward, occasionally ducking his head to avoid the vents, and scoured the area to his left and right and ahead of him. But the place was a tangled mess of big machinery, narrow spaces, and dark recesses, and he could barely see beyond a few yards ahead of him. The hum of the generators was everywhere, and the concert could hardly be heard.

He walked faster and moved into an area that contained instrument panels, with switches and levers and warnings about voltage. He brushed a hand over one of the panels and saw that it was covered with fine dust and had therefore clearly not been touched for a few days. He moved on through an area containing dozens of thin pipes at floor level. He stepped over them into an area that was clear of anything at floor level, and as he did so, he heard a clunk of metal behind him. He spun around and saw that the metallic sound had come from one of the pipes. Whatever was coursing through it was causing it to vibrate and bang against an adjacent pipe. He turned to move forward.

Then he felt a hard object against the back of his head.

He stood frozen. He heard feet scuffing the floor. The object pressed harder against his head. He knew it had to be the muzzle of a gun and that the gun could belong to Megiddo's bomber, but he also knew that it more likely belonged to one of the two Secret Service men who were searching for a man who had been desperate to enter the opera house. He wondered whether to spin around, grab the muzzle, simultaneously grab the hand holding the gun, and twist both so that he was in possession of the weapon. He could do the movement in under four-fifths of a second. But if the gun belonged to a Secret

Service man, his colleague could be with him, and that man would shoot Will before he could complete the movement. He turned slowly.

Lana was before him. She was holding the gun.

Will frowned, looked to her left and right to see if some hidden person was pointing a gun at her to make her do what she was doing, saw nothing, and looked back at her. He felt totally confused. He felt as if nothing made sense.

"What are you doing?" Will said the words slowly, and they did not seem like his own.

Lana stared at him. Her expression was cold. She looked unharmed and strong. She looked in command of herself.

"What are you doing? What's going on?"

Lana shook her head slowly. "If you are here, then he is dead."

Will's heart pounded. Confusion overwhelmed him. "What is going on?" He could smell Lana's perfume, feel her presence, and see her beauty. But he could also see that she had death in her eyes and that she wanted to kill him.

"You have been such a fool, Will Cochrane."

She used my real name.

She smiled. "Such a fool."

"Megiddo told you my real name?"

"I always knew your real name."

Will felt an immediate sense of nausea and anger. "You've been working with Megiddo all along?"

She no longer smiled. "Ever since I met him all those years ago. From the beginning to the end."

Will shook his head in disbelief.

Lana waved the muzzle of the gun a little before steadying it toward Will's head. "You've been tricked by us all. Tricked by Megiddo, me, and . . . all of us."

Will narrowed his eyes as a realization struck him. "All of you, including the man who introduced your name to me."

Lana nodded. "Harry as well." She widened her eyes. "I have

always loved Megiddo, and he has always loved me. I had to be here to complete his masterpiece because you killed all his other soldiers." She smiled. "I came here to trigger the bombs if someone like you tried to stop our attack from happening."

Will's mind raced with questions and confusion. There was so much he didn't understand about what was happening, but he also knew he had no time to find answers to these questions. "How can you detonate the bombs?"

Lana patted a breast pocket. "I have a number programmed into my cell phone. If I call that number, the bombs receive my signal and detonate ahead of their preprogrammed time of nine P.M."

Will checked his watch. It was 8:45 P.M.

He desperately tried to think. "You will have another number in your phone. A number that if called will stop the bombs from going off at nine P.M. A number that was to be called only in the event that the concert was postponed to another day or called off."

Lana narrowed her eyes. "That number will never be called, because I have everything I need in the concert hall—the premiers' wives and the thousands of children."

Will shook his head. "Surely you don't want this atrocity to happen? Surely you don't want their deaths?"

Lana smiled. "They will die, you will die, and I will be with Megiddo again. I will be happy when the bombs destroy everything around us."

Will felt sick. The woman before him was a woman he did not know. Lana meant what she said. If she had any heart, it was a heart that cared for nothing other than Megiddo. He decided that his only hope now depended upon her believing a lie. He shook his head. "Lana, it is you who's been the fool. Megiddo never loved you."

She glared at him. "You know nothing about the love we had for each other."

Will shook his head again. "I came here expecting to find you tied up and a bomber holding a gun to your head."

Lana sniggered. "That is what Megiddo wanted you to expect."

Will nodded. "He did. Even when he was on his knees and I had a gun pointed at his head, even when he knew he was about to die, he knew that there was nothing I could do to stop his attack." Will frowned. "So why would he describe the bomber in the opera house as a naïve and gullible pawn whose death would be as trivial as the deaths of the children? Why would he say that when he had no need to say such a thing to me?"

Lana frowned. "You're lying."

Will shook his head. "I'm not, but the comment he made was unnecessary. If Megiddo loved you, he would just have kept his mouth shut about his views of the bomber. Or maybe he would have used a more positive description. But he had absolutely no need to be disparaging about the bomber unless"—he nodded sadly—"unless he wanted me to truly know the magnitude of his strategy. He wanted me to know how he had manipulated every single person around him. Every person, including the man *or* woman who was going to detonate his bombs."

Lana shook her head, but doubt clearly showed on her face. "He . . . he loved me. He always loved me."

Will checked his watch. It was 8:52 P.M. His heart was hammering, but he kept his voice calm. "Think about it, Lana. He lived his life solely to outwit others."

"You know nothing about him!" Lana spat. "He loved his work, but he also loved me."

Will spoke forcefully. "He has always used you, and he is using you now. That is why he described you as a naïve and gullible pawn. And I agree with his description, because that's precisely what you are!"

The generators near them seemed to hum louder. Pipes rattled and hissed. Vents groaned. The music from the concert above them sounded distant but was still audible.

A tear ran down one of Lana's cheeks. "I love him."

"But he has never loved you."

Her gun moved slightly.

Will watched her. "Lana, *I* loved you. But *he* had no love for anything other than his work."

Lana looked away for a moment. When she looked back at Will, she had tears rolling down both cheeks. She spoke with a weak and trembling voice. "Then I have indeed been the fool."

Will smiled with a look of sympathy, even though he felt anything but sympathy for the woman in front of him. "We have *both* been fools. And victims."

She took a step back and leaned against a vent. She was breathing rapidly, and Will wondered if she was starting to hyperventilate. She shook her head, cursing. She lowered her gun and held it by her side. She looked around the basement and up at the ceiling. She shook her head some more and banged the butt of her handgun against the vent. She looked at Will. "What . . . what should I do?"

Will took a step toward her. "You must do something to show Megiddo that you are no longer a fool. You must do something to show him that you are no longer his pawn. You must do the one thing that will hurt him the most. You must call the number to disarm the bombs."

Lana shook her head, and tears now streamed down her face.

"Lana, if you die here, you will never be with him. You will have died for nothing. Everyone here will have died for nothing."

Lana again banged her gun on the vent and muttered, "Oh, dear God." She looked at Will. "He told me he loved me. He showed me he loved me."

"He did that so you would be here."

Lana looked up at the ceiling and screamed, "A fucking pawn?"

She lowered her head and began breathing slower. She closed her eyes. She rubbed the back of her gun-carrying hand against her face. She looked at Will.

"Call the number." Will looked at the time. It was 8:57 P.M.

She reached into her breast pocket and pulled out her cell phone.

She looked at it. For a long time. She frowned. Then she looked at Will before looking back at the cell phone.

It was now 8:59 P.M.

"We have no time, Lana!" Will's heart was racing.

She breathed in slowly. She pressed numbers into the phone. She held it to her ear. She waited a moment, then nodded. She dropped her arm to her side, still clutching the phone. She began weeping and shaking.

"Are the bombs disarmed?"

Lana wrapped her arms around her body and shook violently with emotion.

Will shouted, "Lana, are they disarmed?"

Lana inhaled slowly, and her body steadied. "They are. They're safe."

Will checked his watch. It was 9:00 P.M. He looked around, waited, counted seconds, could barely hear the concert, but life was clearly continuing in the building. He sighed and looked at Lana.

Her gun was pointing at him. She rubbed tears away from her face and breathed loudly. She shrugged. "So it's over now."

"Put the gun down, Lana."

She shook her head.

"Put the gun down, Lana."

Lana huffed. "You'll put me in a prison cell for the rest of my life."

"Lana, put the gun down! You've disarmed the bombs. That will go in your favor."

Lana shook her head again.

"Put the gun down." The voice was not Will's.

He spun around and faced a man who was pointing his gun at Lana and Will. One of the men whom Will had seen on the floor above. A Secret Service agent. He was alone.

The man looked at Will. "We've been looking for you."

Will nodded. Now that the bombs were disarmed, he decided that his work was done. He decided that he had to tell the Secret Service what was happening here.

The man looked at Lana and fixed his gun on her.

Will said, "I am a British intelligence officer."

The Secret Service man glanced at Will.

A shot rang out, and a bullet struck the Secret Service man in the center of his head. Will closed his eyes. He turned slowly to look at Lana. Her gun was pointing at the now prone and dead agent. She moved the gun so that it was pointing at Will's head.

Lana smiled. "My next bullet's for you."

Will shook his head. "Why did you kill him? Why are you still holding a gun?"

"Because I have fucking nothing now. Because it seems I've always had nothing."

Will sighed and briefly felt pity for her. "You could have had so much more. I hoped that you and I could have been together."

"I know you did." She laughed humorlessly. "I might have been a pawn in Megiddo's game, but you were certainly a pawn in mine. I wanted you to love me. I needed your emotions for me to cloud any possibility that you might suspect my true role in Megiddo's plan. I had to try to get you to expose your soul to me so that I could watch you suffer when you realized that your emotions had been totally duped."

Will shook his head. He felt a coldness descend over his mind. He felt momentarily numb. "I see."

Lana watched him without emotion. "We often see the truth only at the very end of things. We both now know our truths, but only one of us is going to walk out of this place."

"I know." In a movement that was too quick to be seen and stopped, Will stepped forward, grabbed the barrel of Lana's gun, used his other hand to twist her hand, and took possession of the gun, now pointing it at *her* head.

Will held the gun close to her. He no longer felt numb, and instead his heart filled with anger, regret, and sorrow. "I lied to you. Megiddo never described you as a pawn in his game. I think he really did love you."

Lana's mouth dropped open in a look of total surprise. Which swiftly turned to anger. "You tricked me!"

"I stopped you from making a dreadful mistake."

Lana's eyes darted left and right, and she seemed to be making some kind of calculation. She looked at Will. "I have to be with Megiddo again."

"No, Lana."

She raised her hand and brought her cell phone close to her chest.

"Lana, do not do that."

She smiled and moved her other hand toward the phone's number pad.

"Lana, stop now."

She moved a single finger close to the cell phone. Her smile faded. "In a different life, it would have been wonderful to get to know you."

Will's heart pumped fast. "Don't touch that phone! Don't trigger the bombs!"

Her finger moved until it was an inch from the phone. She smiled again. "Good-bye, Will Cochrane."

Her finger descended to the number pad.

In that tiniest moment, Will knew that it was too late to say anything else, that action was all that mattered now, but as he watched her finger move and squeezed his own finger back rapidly on the handgun's trigger, he felt nothing but overwhelming sorrow. He heard the sound of his gun, felt the weapon recoil, saw his bullet strike Lana in the side of the head and rip open her beautiful face. He watched her move away from him, her knees buckle, her body start to fall, and her hand release the cell phone. He saw the death of Lana Beseisu.

He dashed forward and caught the phone before it fell to the floor alongside her. He looked at the display screen and sighed with relief as he saw that his trigger finger had been quicker than hers. No number had been depressed.

He looked at Lana's dead body and felt giddy and sick. He had thought this woman would change everything for him. But now he stared at her, knowing that she'd been prepared to help Megiddo slaughter millions of people for no other reason than her love for the monster.

He looked around and imagined the floors above him in the opera house, the boxes where the premiers' wives were sitting during the performance, the other boxes and the ground-level seats containing the audience of children and the orchestra area holding excited child performers. He pictured bombs and fire raining down from the ceiling and tearing through all of that, causing the total war that would have resulted from the abhorrent act were he not standing over the dead body of Lana Beseisu. He shook his head in disbelief.

He looked at Lana one last time. There was so much he wanted to know about her, so much that did not make sense. But he knew that things could have been different. He knelt beside her and smoothed a hand against her bloody face. He ran fingers through her hair and whispered, "If I'd been there at the beginning, you would not be here now."

He closed his eyes and saw the young Lana walking desperately through frozen Bosnian woods, her clothes torn and offering no protection against the bitter winter, her legs staggering, her eyes wide with fear, her body weak and in shock after being raped, her mind focused only on reaching the besieged city of Sarajevo and being with the man called Megiddo. He imagined her falling to the ground, crawling through thick snow, pulling herself to her feet again, staggering forward, falling again, crawling again, but continuing to use all her remaining strength to find the man she believed was her savior. He watched every movement she made and every exertion take her inch by inch closer to a man who would corrupt her life so that it would end with a bullet in her brain.

He wished he'd been there as she dragged her mind and her

desecrated body through the terrible war-torn forests. He would have gone to her, taken her hand, and walked her away from Sarajevo and the deadly man it contained. He would have spoken soft but commanding words to her. *Come with me. I am taking you to a better life.*

FIFTY-THREE

Will looked at the clear blue sky above him, at the snow-covered Swiss Alps around him, at the empty mountain valley far below his feet. His cell phone rang, and he saw that the caller was Alistair. He answered, listened to what the Controller had to say, shut his phone, and turned to look at the ski chalet beside him. He pulled out his handgun, strode quickly through the snow, opened the door to the building, and walked through one room before entering another.

Harry was there, seated behind a desk, smoking a cigarette. Two British Special Forces men flanked him. They had brought Harry to this place after tracking him to the city of Lausanne.

Will moved up to the desk, kicked a spare chair to one side, pointed his gun at Harry's head, and said, "Talk."

Harry lifted his face so that he was looking at Will. He looked exhausted but not terrified. Instead he had the look of a man who had moved beyond fear to a state of resigned calm, a calm driven by the knowledge that his execution was now inevitable. He scratched the stubble on his chin, extinguished his cigarette, and lit another one. He took a sip of water, cleared his throat, frowned.

Will slammed his boot against the desk, causing it to bang against Harry's chest and sending a glass of water to the other side of the room. "I know you've been working with Megiddo all along. Talk."

Harry winced in pain, placed his cigarette in an ashtray, put both of his hands flat down on the desk, and spoke in a strained but measured tone.

"When Megiddo realised that the NSA had discovered he was planning a massive strike against the West, he decided to adopt a dual strategy to hide the details of his attack. First, he manipulated the NSA breach to send misinformation about the location of the attack and to stretch Western intelligence resources. Second, he decided to lure out a Western intelligence officer with the endgame of getting that officer to believe that he had discovered the location of the attack. He deployed me and Lana for that second complex task." He looked away briefly before fixing his eyes on Will. "Your Head of Sarajevo Station introduced me to you, I decided that your gravitas made you perfect for the role, and I killed Ewan so that I had a direct link to you."

Harry looked at one of the Special Forces men. "May I have another glass of water?"

"No, you may not!" Will shouted the words. "Keep talking."

Harry breathed in deeply. "We had to make everything look credible—the letters via the Iranian embassy in Croatia, the Iranian surveillance team following Lana—making Megiddo appear cautious. And all the time Megiddo manipulated the NSA communications breach, including trying to get you to think the real target was Berlin. But you uncovered that ruse, so he decided to focus solely on the second strand of his strategy. He used one of his men—the man you knew as his deputy, Gulistan Nozari—to act as if he were Megiddo. He got me to alert you to the HBF offices, he had the man Dzevat Kljujic killed to add weight to the notion that Megiddo was operating

out of those offices, and he ensured that the deputy's name was listed
in those offices for discovery by you when you inevitably searched the
place." Harry frowned. "He was sure that you would be convinced
that his deputy was Megiddo, so he was therefore very surprised when
you did not follow or seize Gulistan Nozari. He realized that you
had not automatically assumed that Nozari was Megiddo. He realized
that Lana could therefore not pretend that the man was Megiddo or
you would have become suspicious of her. She had to tell you that the
man she met in Sarajevo was not the man you sought."

Will nodded. "If I was so important to Megiddo, why did he allow
his men to attack me in Zagreb and Vienna?"

Harry shrugged. "You forced him to do so by deliberately reveal-
ing your identity in your letters and by ensuring that you were seen
with Lana in the Diana Bar of the Westin Hotel. His men had to go
after you aggressively, but Megiddo hoped that your men would rescue you immediately after your capture. As it happened, you killed
most of Megiddo's men and were not captured yourself, so you solved
that problem for him."

Will moved closer to Harry. "After you disappeared, were you
aware of what subsequently happened?"

Harry shook his head, picked up his cigarette, and inhaled smoke.
"How could I?"

Will nodded. "It's clear to me now that Megiddo changed his strategy after realizing that his ploy of using his deputy could not work.
Instead he ordered his men to seize Lana in Boston, knowing that I
would go after her and rescue her and hoping that I would believe
her when she told me she'd spent time with Megiddo and learned
the location of the attack." He narrowed his eyes. "Megiddo nearly
succeeded."

Harry sighed. "Our objective was always to get you to think that
Camp David was the target, when in fact the Metropolitan Opera
House was always the real target."

Will moved his gun closer to Harry. "How did Megiddo get

employment passes for the opera house? How did his men plant their bombs without fear that they would later be detected?"

Harry blew out smoke. "That was down to me. I established that before the concert the Metropolitan Opera House was to undergo some major renovations, particularly to the stage, the floors, and the auditorium and balcony seats. Because of the amount of mess caused by the renovations, I knew that the place would need extra cleaners during the week preceding the concert. I set up a company, approached the management office, said my company specialized in professional cleaning work, said I had a team of five people I could subcontract to the building, and said that they were very reliable and cheap, and could do aerial cleaning work if required. The management office snapped up my offer because they were desperate to get the place looking good for the event but were still short-staffed. Megiddo chose four of his men and one woman to bring in thirty bombs over the course of five days. The bombs were small—each of them is about the size of a thin paperback book, and the bombers could easily conceal them on their persons as they came and went from the building during the course of those days." He massaged his temples. "The cleaning work required a thorough cleaning of not only the ground level but also the vast ceiling area. Most of the bombs were to be secreted in ceiling alcoves, much too high to be seen and detected, and in any case they were all caked in wax to minimize scent."

"All the bombs were found and safely removed by the FBI." Will frowned. "How did the bombers pass security checks to work there?"

Harry extinguished his cigarette with a shaking hand. "Megiddo identified a woman in the Western intelligence community who was senior, who had the ability to wipe clean the records of the bombers minutes before they entered this country—and who had financial problems."

Will looked sharply at Harry. "Who is that person?"

"I don't know. Megiddo decided that the woman was very useful and that her identity had to be protected. But I do know that the individual was not told why she needed to wipe clean the records. Instead she removed any traces showing that the bombers were IRGC, took Megiddo's money, and kept her mouth shut."

"Even though that woman did not know why the individuals' records had to be erased, she's still a traitor. She'll be found and punished."

Harry sighed.

Will gripped his gun. "How did Lana get into the opera house?"

"It was never the plan for her to be there." Harry shrugged. "The easiest thing for her to do would have been to take the identity of the female bomber in my cleaning crew."

Will nodded. "Megiddo came to me at the end. Why?"

Harry shook his head. "He was diagnosed with cancer. The assault on the opera house and the wars that would follow were to be his final work, his greatest masterpiece. He realized that he would not be alive long enough to fulfill his ambitions to lead the Arab and Persian nations." He met Will's eyes. "As soon as he found out who you were, it was always his intention to come to you when he felt that nothing could stop the bombs from going off. He wanted you to know about his father before he killed you. But he also knew that you might kill him, so his plan was to tell you about the opera house, knowing that you would go there and die. He had nothing to lose and everything to gain by coming to you." He exhaled slowly and raised the palms of his hands. "That's all I know."

Will moved his finger over his gun's trigger.

Harry looked at him and smiled. "You were not what I expected. You made me see things differently. That's why I decided to tell you everything about Megiddo's plan when I was due to meet you at my house." His smile faded. "But Megiddo discovered my treachery and came to my house to kill me. I escaped only because you arrived and he had to hide himself." Harry carefully withdrew another cigarette from the pack on the desk, lit it, and examined the burning tip before looking at Will. He smiled again, but this time the look held sorrow.

"I worked for Megiddo because he told me that if I did not do so, he would release my name and location to various Bosnian Serb men who would take pleasure in tearing me apart for what my men did in that Serbian village during the war. I worked for Megiddo because I was a coward who wanted to protect my own neck, even if that meant the deaths of millions." He sighed. "I couldn't do it in the end." He brought the cigarette to his mouth, inhaled smoke, and nodded once. "But I deserve to die in this house, and I am glad it is you, not Megiddo, who is going to be my executioner."

Will glanced at the two Special Forces men. "Leave the room. I don't want you to witness what is about to happen."

The men walked out.

Will picked up a chair, positioned it directly opposite Harry, and sat down. He placed the muzzle of his gun against the agent's forehead and asked quietly. "Are you ready for this?"

Harry nodded. "I am."

"Is there anything you wish to say to me before I pull the trigger?"

Harry smiled. "Your men told me you killed Megiddo. I am glad that I am about to die knowing that you won and he lost."

Will nodded, stood, held the muzzle flush against Harry's forehead, readied his finger against the trigger, and braced his body so that it was still. He breathed deeply and relaxed his hand. "I am not going to kill you, Harry. You're too useful to me."

He lowered his gun.

Harry frowned.

Will looked toward the windows of the mountain chalet. He looked at the Alps beyond them. He looked over the Swiss mountains to the east. He smiled, turned, and looked at Lace. When he stopped smiling, he spoke with steel in his voice. "I have a new mission, Harry. You are a man of means. You have particular, rare talents and connections. You can help me."

Spartan raised his gun again and pointed it at the agent. "People are either my allies or my enemies. Which one are you?"